"Even when we mortals don't understand, God's plan is unfolding around us. *Summer's Winter* is an incredible mystery that teaches us to believe in that divine plan for our lives. The twists and turns in *Summer's Winter* kept me reading into the night...I couldn't wait to reach the end! Robin Johns Grant's *Summer's Winter* is a heartwarming read in which good and evil collide. I loved it!"

—Nancy Grace, HLN host and author of
The Eleventh Victim and *Death on the D-List*

"Part murder mystery, part Hollywood dream-world and part thought-provoking Southern lit, *Summer's Winter* takes the reader on a romantic ride, filled with movie-star moments that plummet into hair-raising hairpin twists and turns. Jeanine and Jamie's relationship crackles with sparring, spirituality and suspense, leading to an ending worthy of your favorite Hollywood finale."

—Elizabeth Musser, author of
The Swan House and *The Sweetest Thing*

SUMMER'S WINTER

SUMMER'S WINTER

ROBIN JOHNS GRANT

STORY MERCHANT BOOKS
BEVERLY HILLS
2013

http://www.robinjohnsgrant.com

http://www.facebook.com/robinjohnsgrantauthor

Story Merchant Books
9601 Wilshire Boulevard #1202
Beverly Hills CA 90210
http://www.storymerchant.com/books.html

PROLOGUE

In those days, a pecan orchard guarded the grounds of the Calvary Christian School. Teachers and parents were unsentimental about the graceful old trees. To them they were just a source of revenue, and not a very large one, at that. Their children, however, loved playing in the shadowy grove at recess and after school, shaded from the brutal Georgia heat in spring and summer, kicking through the brittle leaves that littered the ground in fall.

Even for the children, however, this particular day in late October was different. The trees' branches were bare and harsh, the trees strangely transformed from the gentle green protectors of spring. Gnarled and gray, they stood watch like silent sentinels as six-year-old Billy Holland began to scream.

As his screaming dissolved into hysterical sobs, the other first graders stopped their playing, gathered around him and stared in shock. Teachers poured into the orchard, but the first to reach the boy was Mrs. Frances Xavier—huffing and puffing for breath, not just from her sprint across the grounds but also out of fear. She had visions of blood and broken arms. And lawyers.

Pushing the other children aside, she collapsed to her knees in front of the boy. "What's wrong, Billy? For goodness' sake, what's the matter!" Her sharp eyes checked for damage. He was still standing, apparently hadn't fallen out of a tree or broken any limbs. No blood visible. Bee sting, perhaps? Yellow jackets were relentless in Georgia in the fall of the year.

Billy was still blubbering and incoherent, and now that Mrs. Xavier could see that any physical damage was either slight or nonexistent, she started to lose patience. "Now, Billy, I want you to calm down right now and tell me what happened."

Billy's eyes widened. Mrs. Xavier was the boy's own first grade teacher, and her students knew she brooked no foolishness. He mumbled something in reply. But what he said was murmured so softly—no, be truthful. What he said was so bizarre that she demanded, "What did you say?"

He took a deep breath and then spoke clearly. "I said she grabbed me. And I don't want her to. She's a witch!"

"What! Who is?"

"Her."

He pointed at one of the little girls in the crowd of children. But after he pointed, the others drew away and left the girl standing alone, as though a magic circle had been drawn around her. All eyes shifted from Billy to the girl.

Mrs. Xavier glanced at her, and then turned back to the sniveling boy. "I don't know what's gotten into you, Billy. You know Jeanine. That's Preacher DeValery's daughter. She sits behind you in class every day."

She shouldn't have pointed that out. Billy's lip started to shake as he geared up for a new round of sobbing. Exasperated, Mrs. Xavier turned to Jeanine, a smart and quiet little girl. Her chief vice seemed to be a penchant for daydreaming in class. But she must have done something to make Billy this hysterical. "Now Jeanine, you tell me this instant—"

She stopped short, the words trapped in her throat.

Something about little Jeanine DeValery did seem different today. Not her appearance, precisely. She had that same disheveled look that she always developed within an hour of arriving at school. No matter how hard her mother tried to tie the wavy mass of dark hair into a neat braid, it snaked and curled its way out little by little throughout the day as though each strand had a life of its own. The little girl looked pale and serious, but that was not unusual, either—although her dreamy eyes had come into sharp focus and were meeting Mrs. Xavier's with unusual confidence and power.

Power. That was it. There was no visible reason for it, but somehow this little girl was radiating such an unnamable force that Mrs. Xavier felt if she touched Jeanine DeValery right now, she too would dissolve into hysterics.

Of course, there was no reason to touch Jeanine. Right now, her duty was to Billy Holland. Feeling somehow ridiculous but at the same time relieved, she turned her back on Jeanine DeValery and reached for the little boy's hand. "Come on, Billy. We'll talk about this inside."

And I'll have a little talk with Lee DeValery later, she promised herself.

*   *   *

"Come on, Jeanine, play with us!"

"No, I don't feel like it. Leave me alone."

The little girl sat in the swing, fingers gripping the chain, and stared at the back door of the school building. Daddy was in there right now. Mrs. Xavier had called him.

"But we don't know what to play without you."

Jeanine looked at the cluster of five or six boys and girls gathered around her. "I'm usually not here this late. What do you usually do?"

They looked at each other, shrugged. "I don't know. Mess around. Wait for our mammas. But it's more fun with you."

Jeanine sighed and pushed a few strands of hair out of her eyes. "You're not gonna start screaming, are you? I'm in enough trouble already."

"No! Course not."

She stood up, the canvas of the swing bumping the back of her legs. "Okay, so listen. I'm the wicked witch. Those trees over there—" she gestured wildly with her arms—"used to be kids just like you, but the witch got them and turned them into those twisted old skeleton trees, and they have to stay there forever and ever—"

She led them deeper and deeper into the complex story and soon had them running and screaming (happily this time) through the pecan grove. Really, they were playing a glorified game of tag, but Jeanine had infused it with magic. They were deep in an enchanted wood, and shivery, skin-tingling surprises lurked behind every tree. It was wonderful.

Jeanine suddenly looked up and saw Daddy standing at the edge of the orchard, hands shoved down in his pockets, watching her. She stopped short, and without her, the others one by one wound down, as well.

When he saw they had stopped, Daddy motioned for her to come. For a moment she stood paralyzed, but then his face broke into its usual smile of welcome, so she ran toward him.

He grabbed her hand and bent down to smack a big old kiss right on top of her head. She looked up at him as they strolled toward the car. "You're not mad at me, are you?"

"No, I'm not mad." He sighed and gazed into the distance. Jeanine looked in the same direction, searching with her eyes, but she didn't see a thing and started to fidget. She knew from Daddy's expression that he was about to start talking about something that wouldn't make a lick of sense.

Sure enough, he said dreamily, "It's a special time, Jeanine—to be as young as you. Everything is so real. Heaven is as tangible as the taste of a juicy peach on a hot day, as easy and close as stepping out the school door and into another world at recess. But evil, too—so real that at night your closet is filled with monsters and your head with dark dreams. Sometimes I wish I could make my congregation feel all that, too, but by our age we're so grounded in this world. Our heads are filled with scheduling meetings, stretching our paychecks, running the kids to soccer practice."

He looked down at Jeanine, and then laughed. "You don't have a clue what I'm talking about, do you?"

"Well...I didn't do anything wrong?"

"Umm...let's talk about it in the car, okay?"

Shadows played across the car hood as he pulled out into the road. It was getting dark.

"Mrs. Xavier was pretty upset. That little game of yours scared Billy Holland to death."

"Oh, Billy is just a scaredy-cat, that's all. And he has too much imagination."

"And you don't!"

"I know it's just pretend."

"I see. And do you think witches are what you should be pretending about?"

"What do you mean?"

"You know what I mean. Witches aren't fun. They aren't for play."

She nodded vigorously. "I know it. That's why I had the angels fighting her. And I always make sure they win—sooner or later."

"And why are you the one that always plays the witch?"

Jeanine shrugged. "Because none of them do it right."

She thought Daddy started to laugh, but then he made a kind of snorting sound and started to cough, instead.

"Well, honey, I'm sure you meant well, but people are funny the way they look at things sometimes. I don't think my congregation would like it if they heard about this."

"You mean I might get you in trouble?"

"You're a preacher's kid, Jeanine. People are always going to watch how you act."

She frowned. "People watch me?"

"That's right. You have to set an example for the other kids. And people will judge me by how I run my home, how my children behave."

She looked down at her shoes, clicking the heels of her tennis shoes together like Dorothy did with her slippers. The ground had been muddy under the leaves, and the toes that had been white this morning were a splotchy brown. Mamma would be mad and would fuss, but it was Daddy's soft voice that was making her stomach feel fluttery.

She felt him touch her arm.

"You okay?" he asked.

She looked into his eyes. "Yes sir. I would never do anything to get you in trouble, Daddy."

He laughed. She wasn't sure why. "That's my girl. Just remember that when you're older."

*   *   *

On the same day that Jeanine DeValery was causing trouble at the Calvary Christian School in Georgia, an eight-year-old boy named Jamie Newkirk was giving his uncle Richard a raging headache. Not that there was any connection between Jamie and Jeanine. They had never met, never heard of one another. In fact, Jamie lived on the other side of the Atlantic Ocean, and had no particular dreams of ever setting foot outside the U.K. There was no connection between them whatsoever.

Richard was already tense and tired as they entered his agent's office building, and Jamie's bouncing a football around the lift like a little hooligan didn't help matters. Just before the doors opened to their floor, Richard snapped, "Do stop that, *please!*"

Jamie snatched up the ball and said nothing, but the silence was deafening.

Richard sighed and pushed his hair back from his face, wishing he had managed a haircut before coming to see Cynthia. "Look, I'm sorry I made you miss your football match, but what was I to do?"

He had to lean forward to hear Jamie's sulky response. "You knew where I would be."

"I knew you would be at the game for the first hour or so, but then what? The way you wander off lately. Can you imagine how I felt coming home last night and not knowing where the devil you were for the next two hours! I almost rang the police."

"I was only riding the tube, watching people. I wasn't doing anything horrid."

"You could get yourself killed, do you understand that? This is London, not that little town in Warwickshire you're accustomed to."

Jamie spoke in the direction of the floor. "It isn't fair. You expect me to sit in that grotty old flat by myself all the time."

They were directly in front of Cynthia's office door, but Richard stopped and faced Jamie. "Do you think it's been easy for me, having my whole life turned upside down for you? I'm trying to make it work for both of us, but when I'm offered a decent acting job, I've got to take it. If I'm out at night for a few weeks—well, you could try giving me a spot of help, couldn't you?"

Again Jamie said nothing—and he said it quite eloquently.

Richard took a deep breath and gripped the doorknob. "Okay. Look, I just need to talk to Cynthia for a few minutes, and then you can go to my rehearsal with me. So you'll not be sitting home alone, after all."

"Oh, lovely."

Richard left Jamie sitting moodily in an outer office while he spoke with Cynthia about his so-called career. When she walked him to the door of her office fifteen minutes or so later, the sound of Jamie's blasted football thunking around was the first thing that hit their ears.

"Sorry." Richard rubbed his throbbing temples. "I had to bring him with me this evening. Long story."

She nodded. "It must be hard, Richard. It's bad enough having to drive a cab and wait tables and try to squeeze in your art, but when you become a parent overnight, too, well…"

Her brown eyes filled with sympathy, and for a moment Richard wondered why he had never asked her out. Then he took in the designer suit, the manicured nails. Oh, yeah. That was why.

Cynthia was stepping out into the front room, sticking out her hand to the brat. "You must be Jamie."

To the boy's credit, he turned his attention from the football and gave Cynthia a smile. A brilliant smile. She beamed back at him, and Richard felt himself relaxing. You couldn't help it, somehow. Jamie had a way of dazzling everyone in his path when he felt so inclined. His dark good looks didn't hurt, of course.

Cynthia was apparently under his spell already. "Oh, Richard, he's gorgeous!" She folded her arms and gave the boy an appraising look. "You are very handsome, do you know that? And such exotic looks—nothing at all like your Uncle Richard, are you?"

Richard winced. "Jamie looks like his mother. She's Spanish."

"Oh, really? Is that where she is now? Spain?"

"Who knows?" Richard tried to edge Jamie toward the door.

Cynthia's eyes were still fixed on the boy. "Richard, can he act?"

"He certainly can when he wants something," Richard said wryly. And then, the possible meaning of Cynthia's words occurred to him. "Why do you ask?"

"Well, I was just thinking—they need boys for the cast of *Twist*! Feagin's lads are continually outgrowing the parts. They've even got to replace the lead, the one who plays the Artful Dodger, soon. Andrew Stiles has five o'clock shadow and has got to go."

Richard was momentarily speechless. "*Twist*! You don't mean—a West End production, when he's never acted at all!"

"Yes I have," Jamie piped in. "At school."

Richard looked at him. "You played a tomato. Once."

Cynthia was shaking her head. "The *Twist*! cast is quite large. Some of the boys' parts don't have any lines at all. A few basic dance moves, looking alert and dressing up the stage. And who could resist this one? Look, Richard, I'll ring them right now if you like and see if we can send him over."

Richard felt stunned. He looked at Jamie. "Do you want to?"

Jamie shrugged. "Why not?"

When Cynthia popped back into her office, Jamie grinned up at him. "I'm gorgeous."

In spite of himself, Richard felt his face melting into a smile. "Yeah, well, she doesn't know you like I do, does she?"

A week later, Richard was watching Jamie in a matinee of *Twist!*, and the shock he had been feeling for days over this unexpected turn of events started to give way to something else, some vague and unpleasant emotion that was hard to identify. He glanced around at the other theater-goers, wondering if they, too, had a hard time tearing their eyes away from his nephew's face. Jamie had landed the role of one of the background characters, with a grand total of five lines. And yet, there was so much going on with his face, with his body, that you could swear some dramatic plot turn was going to come from him at any moment. He was far more interesting than the carefully-rehearsed Andrew Stiles emoting at center stage.

One of Jamie's lines came along—a throw-away line, designed to set up some gag of Andrew's. But Jamie popped it out in such a way that a little ripple of laughter started to move through the audience, and there was a light spattering of applause. Andrew hesitated before his next speech. Whether he was trying not to step on Jamie's laugh or was thrown by the audience's reaction to this little upstart in the cast was hard to say.

But Richard himself was no longer shocked. He felt queasy, shaky. For five years now, Richard had been in London trying to make himself into an actor. He had studied, auditioned, starved—the whole bit. He had been successful enough not to despair of his talent, but not successful enough to actually be able to support himself from it. At least not on a regular basis. But he hadn't minded. Even after Rob died this year and he had to buckle down and start driving a taxi to feed and clothe Jamie, he had refused to give up his dream of acting, because he was certain that he was growing and learning and that someday he could rise to the top. But in those five years, he had never given a performance like Jamie had just given on his first try and with five meager lines to work with.

As the audience rose to its feet to applaud at the final curtain, Richard knew with a sickly certainty that more had ended for him than tonight's performance.

*   *   *

Jamie was ten when he landed the role of The Artful Dodger in *Twist!*

Eleven when he won the Laurence Olivier Award for playing the Dodger, and eleven when casting started for the film version. Of course Jamie got an audition. But for the first time since Cynthia suggested he try out for *Twist!*, Jamie's career hit a brick wall. The actor who'd been playing the Dodger on Broadway landed the part. Jamie just shrugged his shoulders and said he was sure he liked the live theater audiences better, anyway. But Richard had been certain Jamie would get the job and chafed with frustration every day he escorted Jamie to the little theatre in Drury Lane, which had lost its glamour in his eyes and now looked small and shabby and dead-end.

Richard was not one to be thwarted. Through some of the other boys in the *Twist!* cast, Richard had heard of an intriguing little book called *Summer and the Sea*, by a first-time author named Hannah Raney. The book had started out small—small press, small first run, low expectations. But it was catching on, and Richard watched with interest as the boys passed the book from one to another and chattered about what might happen in the sequel to the young hero, Danny Summer—who was right around Jamie's age. Scared and exhilarated by what he was considering, Richard made a few tentative inquiries about the film rights and discovered, to his dismay, that the rights were available.

Then he discovered why. Hannah Raney, the author, was that rare bird who loved the world she had created more than money, and she ferociously guarded her literary offspring. She was making unreasonable demands, wanting many of the filmmaker's typical rights for herself. Among other things, she insisted that no movie sequels about Danny Summer and company could ever be made unless they were based on her books—she was planning a whole series. Her demands were ridiculous, and yet...

Richard had a feeling—about Jamie, and about Danny Summer. And maybe the old girl's stubbornness could be worked to his advantage. He gave her everything she wanted, and in return offered her a fee that should have been insultingly low. She accepted that same day. After that, the whole project snowballed, and a year later Richard found himself on a movie set not just as Jamie's guardian, but also as the producer and director.

*　*　*

Jeanine DeValery caught her first glimpse of Jamie Newkirk when she was ten years old. Her nine-year-old sister, Ginella, had friends over for her birthday. They were supposed to play outside, but a monsoon seemed to develop out of nowhere, so they played music at a roof-rattling level and danced and ran back and forth through the house. Jeanine curled up by herself in a window seat with a book and was oblivious to it all. But her poor frazzled mother apparently didn't do so well, because she suddenly pulled the book from Jeanine's hands and announced that she was taking them to a movie. All of them. The movie was *Summer and the Sea.*

In the theater, all the other kids fidgeted, giggled, nudged each other and whispered, but Jeanine scarcely breathed or moved. As Danny Summer laughed, schemed, faced imprisonment and even threats from supernatural forces—all for the sake of a band of street urchins that he had led in crime and was now attempting to lead to a new life in the American colonies— Jeanine felt every emotion as her own. She had always gotten caught up in movies and books, but nothing like this. Never anything like this feeling of complete oneness with a character.

She left the theater in a daze. In the DeValery home, God had always been a constant presence. He had revealed himself gently to her throughout her life, starting when she was barely out of the cradle, not in a blinding flash as he did to the apostle Paul on the Damascus Road. But on the day she first saw Jamie Newkirk, Jeanine felt as though she had had her Damascus Road experience. God had abruptly, shockingly intervened in her life, had blinded her with the gift of something bright and wonderful and just for her, and she could almost hear him speaking to her in an audible voice.

And he was telling her that somehow, someday, this wonderful boy was going to be a part of her life.

Eleven years later...

CHAPTER ONE

SOMETIMES JEANINE HAD HEARD HER FATHER PREACH ABOUT THE FOUR HUNDRED years of silence between the Testaments, when the people of Israel desperately waited to hear from God. Jeanine felt humbled at the very idea. So far, eleven years of silence had proved excruciating.

Since that amazing day in the theater when she had heard the voice of God, presidents had risen and fallen. The stock market had teetered, and there were wars and rumors of wars. Jeanine drifted through it all, barely noticing, growing taller, growing up. Listening. Waiting.

And then one day, everything changed.

Oddly enough, in the very hour that things were changing, Jeanine was standing in front of her mother's desk at the university, gazing sullenly down at the floor and thinking, "Here we go again."

Her mother sat behind the desk, frowning and staring at Jeanine as though trying to figure out some complicated Geometry problem. Daddy stood to one side, looking uncomfortable, bless his heart, as though he wished that Mamma hadn't called him in. Or had she called him? Just how much trouble was Jeanine in? She sighed and wondered how someone like herself, who didn't smoke, drink, or fool around, could cause so much parental anguish.

Mamma fiddled with a pencil. "I was entering grades for Dr. Calley this morning and came across yours."

"Oh." Jeanine cleared her throat. "Not good, I take it."

Mamma's head jerked up. "You're lucky I didn't have a heart attack."

Silence. Jeanine rather hoped that Daddy would jump in and save her, but he remained quiet. So Jeanine took a deep breath and prepared to defend herself. "You knew I missed that exam a few weeks ago. I've said I'm sorry. I tried to study and bring my grade back up. I don't know what else I can do."

"I thought you were going to try to make up the test," Daddy said.

Jeanine glanced at him, trying to read his face, but it was unusually blank. "Dr. Calley wouldn't let me. He said I..." She trailed off, not wanting to finish the sentence. Not wanting to start all that up again.

"He said you didn't have a good excuse," Mamma finished.

"That's right." Jeanine could hear the irritation in her own voice but hoped Mamma didn't notice. Fat chance. Jeanine took a deep breath and tried to calm herself. "Maybe if you talked to Dr. Calley—"

"I will do no such thing." Mamma's lips tightened into a thin, straight line. "I won't beg my employer for special privileges for my children. You screwed up, Jeanine."

Words were rushing through Jeanine's bloodstream, pounding in her head, tumbling over themselves in an effort to burst out. *I did not screw up I didn't I don't want to be like you and give up everything so I can be a secretary and answer phones and sit in a desk chair till my bottom goes numb and go home and cook and clean toilets and get up and do it again and never dream and never try and I tried and it was not screwing up—*

She clenched her teeth until her jaws ached but she managed to keep the words from spilling out. She knew her face was a blank mask, the one she had practiced in front of a mirror and that drove her mother crazy. When she was able to speak normally again, she said, "It doesn't matter, anyway."

Mamma's eyes narrowed. "What do you mean?"

"It was an Education class and..." She took a deep breath, and then spilled it. "I've decided I don't want to teach."

"What!"

"When did that happen?" Daddy had obviously been trying to let Mamma handle this, since the offense was happening on her turf. But this was apparently too much for him. At least he just looked interested, not furious like Mamma.

"It's been coming a long time." She felt a stray curl hanging down in her face. Absently, she pulled it to her lips, and then let it go as she remembered that this "nasty habit" annoyed her mother even on a good day. "I just can't teach teenagers. I didn't understand teenagers when I was one of them."

Mamma dropped her head into her hands and moaned. "Jeanine, you're supposed to start your student teaching right after the holidays. You're supposed to graduate in five months. And you're deciding this now?"

Mamma looked tired. Jeanine noticed it for the first time and felt a pang of guilt. Mamma seldom looked tired or dull like Jeanine. She looked bright and youthful, her plump cheeks smooth and rosy and not a speck of gray in her wavy brown hair. So maybe Jeanine really had messed up. And now Jeanine was remembering the reason her mother worked at this boring secretarial job every day, even though she probably could have done something more interesting. She worked here because the employees got free tuition for their children, and it was the only way Jeanine and Ginella could have afforded college.

"I'm sorry." This time she said it with feeling. "But it's okay, really. I've talked with Dr. Persons and it turns out I can just take English courses next semester and still finish up in time with a plain old English degree."

"And then what?"

Jeanine turned to her father, feeling a little betrayed that he'd been the one to ask such a mundane question. "I guess I'll pray for God to show me."

He pressed his lips together, and Jeanine knew he was trying not to laugh. "Touché."

Mamma let out a long sigh. "I can't tell you how thrilled I am to be having this discussion today of all days."

"What do you mean?"

"Tell her what I mean, Lee."

Daddy was stroking his chin, a nervous gesture that never failed to make her anxious, too.

"Is something going on?" she asked. "Other than my grades, I mean?"

They exchanged a look. Finally Daddy spoke. "So…I take it you haven't heard the news this morning."

"News?" Jeanine shook her head, confused. "You mean, like, family news or church news or—"

"Like CNN or Fox." Mamma looked even grimmer than when she'd been discussing Jeanine's grades. Surely Jeanine couldn't be in trouble for something that had made national news…could she?

"Obviously I haven't heard, because I don't have a clue what you're talking about," Jeanine said.

"Why don't we all sit down?" Daddy motioned her to the hot seat in front of Mamma's desk while he pulled up another chair, so they were both facing Jeanine. Scary.

"There hasn't been a terrorist attack or something, has there?" she asked.

"No, no, nothing like that." Hands on his knees, Daddy leaned toward her. "It's about Jamie Newkirk."

Jeanine's heart lunged in her chest, as it always did on hearing that name. But she had learned not to let it show in her voice. "Really? What?"

Daddy took a deep breath. "His girlfriend was found dead in his house this morning. You know, that blue-jeans model, Paula Klein?"

The words came out automatically, even as her brain processed the news. "She's not his girlfriend. They broke up months ago."

"Anyway, they're not sure how she died yet, but it must look like foul play. Jamie Newkirk was arrested."

"Arrested! For what?" She looked from Daddy to Mamma, then back again.

"Honestly, I'm not sure."

Jeanine shoved her suddenly shaking hands into her pockets, tried to compose her features and breathe normally. But this time the trick must not have worked, because both parents were staring at her—Daddy looking concerned and Mamma irritated.

"You okay?" Daddy said, inching his chair closer.

Mamma let out her breath in frustration. "This is ridiculous. We're acting as though we're telling you a family member died." She leaned across the desk and pointed with her pencil. "He's a movie star, Jeanine. You don't know him."

"I realize that, Mamma. Do you think I'm crazy?"

"Of course not," Daddy said.

"But you do crazy things sometimes," Mamma added.

Daddy looked shocked. "Marielle!"

"Oh come on, Lee. You know what I mean." Mamma picked up a folder on the desk and shook it. It must have been full of test papers—the infamous test that Jeanine had missed. "Did Jeanine miss an exam for an important reason? Or even an unimportant reason that made sense, like a real flesh-and-blood boy?"

Again Jeanine clenched her teeth, damming back a flood of hot words that would boil her mother alive if she let them spew out. When she felt she had enough control, she cracked her mouth just enough to say, "Jamie Newkirk is real."

"Not as far as you're concerned. And yet, you were willing to throw away your very real future to go chasing after him last month."

"I wasn't chasing him. I knew he wouldn't be there."

"Even worse. You skipped a test just to get near the boy's uncle!"

Jeanine jumped to her feet. "I've had enough of this."

Daddy laid his hand on her arm, and for him, she stopped. When he spoke, he was looking at Mamma. "Marielle, maybe we should cut her a little slack."

Jeanine wanted to laugh. We? Daddy wasn't the one giving her the hard time.

"It's not as though Jeanine ditches tests every day." He winked at her. "First time ever, that I can recall. You know how dependable she is. She's a straight A student and—"

"It's not the first time she's gone nuts over this stuff. Remember when that writer Hannah Raney died? And we couldn't find her for hours?"

"Well, yes, but—"

"That was connected to her Newkirk obsession or Danny Summer obsession or whatever it was, too. Come on, Lee, you're here in my office because you were worried how she would react when she heard a movie star had been arrested for murder. I ask you, is that normal?"

"Murder!" Jeanine stared at her father. "He was arrested for murder?"

Again the agitated chin stroking. "I'm not sure, Jeanine. You know how it is these days. They jump on the news with a story before they have all the facts—honey, come back!"

This time, not even Daddy's voice could stop her. Running into the hallway, she slammed the door and sliced the words off, neat and clean.

*   *   *

Jeanine sat in her ancient red Mustang under a winter-bare oak tree and devoured every morsel of news from the talk radio station. They were babbling about something unimportant. She waited as patiently as possible. There was a cycle to their programming: news and weather updates every fifteen minutes, interspersed with live call-in shows. She shouldn't have long to wait.

She had only felt this stunned one other time in her life—the day she heard that Hannah Raney had died in a fire at the home of Charlie Edenfield, one of the other *Summer* actors. On hearing the news that the author of the *Summer* books was dead, Jeanine had been stricken with a grief as acute as when her grandmother died. More than that, she had felt herself being swallowed up by an emptiness that was hard to describe, a suffocating panic at the idea that it was all suddenly over—the books, the movies, the online chats with other fans, the speculation, the dreaming…all of it. Danny Summer's quest had come to an end as abruptly as though he had been killed in that fire, and no one would ever know the answers to his secrets.

Her gaze drifted over to the backpack she had tossed into the passenger seat when she got into the car. The contents were spilling out, and she could glimpse pages of now-useless instructions about her practice teaching, as well as a portion of a glossy magazine.

She pulled out the magazine almost reverently and stared down at the face on the front. Jamie Newkirk, gracing the cover of *People* once again. Dark, Mediterranean good looks. Rugged features, softened by a bright smile and dark brown eyes that appeared warm and kind. Glowing, bronze skin and an athletic build. You could easily picture the guy pulling himself up the sheer face of a rock cliff by pure muscle and skill, but only for some noble purpose, like rescuing a nest of orphaned eaglets.

Jeanine was so deep in thought that she missed the first few words of the story when it finally did come on. Then the sound of the Name jolted her back to her surroundings, to the droning voice from the radio:

"…that Newkirk is at this point only charged with violation of the Controlled Substances Act. Sources with the Los Angeles County Sheriff's Department say that a small amount of heroin was found in the actor's house, as well as drug paraphernalia. Initial speculation is that Paula Klein's death was probably caused by a heroin overdose. However, there are reports of multiple contusions and bruises on the young model's body that could indicate a struggle. And there were, perhaps, signs of sexual assault, as well. It's too early to tell exactly what went on in Paula Klein's last hours, but the police want to know how she ended up dead in Jamie Newkirk's living room.

"Klein, the model best known for Nirvana jeans ads, had been Newkirk's live-in companion, but there were rumors of a break-up in October when

Klein went into a drug rehabilitation clinic and Newkirk left for a location shoot in England. However, Klein apparently left the clinic after only a couple of weeks and, as far as family and friends can say, disappeared and wasn't seen again until she was found in Newkirk's house this morning.

"This is the second tragic death for the Newkirks in a very short period of time," the announcer concluded. "The body of Teresa Dane, Jamie Newkirk's mother, was discovered by the actor at the same Malibu beach house less than two years ago. Illegal drugs figured into that case, too, when a coroner's investigation showed that Dane had been heavily using cocaine at the time of her death. Dane's death was ruled a suicide."

As the emotionless voice moved on to other stories, Jeanine was surprised to find herself shaking, not with fear or anxiety, but with anger. She threw open the door of the Mustang, grabbed her backpack and its spilling contents from the seat, and marched over to a nearby dumpster.

When she had heard the amazing news a few weeks ago that Jamie Newkirk's uncle would be coming to Middleboro to work on a movie, she had thought that something meaningful was finally beginning to happen in her life. She had actually viewed skipping that test and going to the movie's local casting call as an act of faith. She had prayed for something and waited patiently for an answer for over ten years, and here it was being dropped neatly into her lap.

And nothing had happened. She hadn't even been chosen as an extra with no lines. And now this Paula Klein business, this terrible development that had to make her wonder whether Jamie Newkirk was worthy of her dreams and prayers at all.

She first wadded each sheet of the practice teaching instructions into a tight, hard ball and threw the pages into the dumpster with all the other trash. *People* followed close behind it. She caught a brief glimpse of Jamie Newkirk's dazzling smile as it sailed over the top of the green dumpster. Feeling grimly proud of herself, she threw the empty pack into the car.

Of course, like an alcoholic falling off of the wagon, three hours later she was camped out in front of her television and drowning herself in CNN video of that same brilliant, promising smile.

CHAPTER TWO

After about six hours with the Los Angeles County Sheriff's Department, Jamie was on the verge of a panic attack. He remembered a story on one of those TV magazine shows about three young boys accused of killing the younger sister of one of them. After thirty-six hours of sleep deprivation and questioning, two of the three had broken down and confessed. When the true killer was later found, the boys said they had been so exhausted by the whole process that they were willing to say anything the police wanted to hear, just to make it stop. Jamie would never make it thirty-six hours before starting to babble.

And he had known right from the start what the police wanted to hear from him.

Lieutenant Regis began gently enough. "Things get a little rough last night, son?"

The question was repeated to him at regular intervals throughout the day, like a phrase in a litany. It was obvious what they thought. He and Paula had been partying in typical Hollywood fashion, rough kinky sex and heavy drugs, and as one of the detectives put it, "We know things get out of hand sometimes. It's better to be up front with us about it now."

Over and over he would wearily tell them, "I haven't been involved with Paula for months. I hadn't even seen her. I was in England shooting a picture until last night. I got home around midnight, and I heard a sound. So I went down the stairs to the living room and there she was, trying to get into my safe. I could tell she was in terrible shape. The drugs again, I mean. She knew the combination, but she couldn't get the door open. She was shaking and crying and slapping it—you know, frustrated—and trying to jerk it open. I walked up behind her and said her name, and it startled her really badly. I could tell right off what she needed. Her nose was running and she wasn't even bothering to clean herself up, and she was scratching at her arms until they were bleeding. Same as before we got her into rehab.

"I got fairly nasty about her being in my house, and I was especially upset that she was in that condition again. And then she started to beg me for help. She said there was no way she could get work and she had no money or anywhere to stay, so she came to me."

Lieutenant Regis's eyebrows rose, as they tended to do every time Jamie spoke. The man used them like hairy little lie detectors.

"What happened to rehab?" the detective asked. "Where had Paula been all these weeks?"

"I don't know." Jamie tried not to watch the climbing eyebrows. "She just said it didn't work. I didn't know what else to do at that point. I was exhausted, I—I told her she could stay the night and that we'd talk again in the morning. But this morning she was dead. And that's all I know."

They didn't believe him, of course. So the litany started over again. "We know what you did with her, son…" Until Jamie was ready to start screaming like a madman.

Fortunately, he had better representation than the boys on that magazine show. Richard showed up, along with a criminal attorney named Ira Schwartz that someone had recommended.

An aggressive knot of paparazzi turned Jamie's exit from the police station into an ugly scene, so as Richard and Ira drove him back toward Malibu, he tried to mentally prepare himself for something similar at his house. Still, he was in no way prepared for the cars and people crowding both sides of the road when they were still a half mile from his gates. Richard slowed the Mercedes to a crawl to avoid hitting vehicles jutting out into the roadway, fans holding up signs of support and peering into the car—and of course, the media and the camera-wielders. Even worse than all that, once Jamie's wrought-iron gates had closed behind them and he figured he had reached safety and solitude, he found his drive packed with cars, as well.

"What the devil is going on!" he demanded. Before Richard could answer, a thought struck him. "Are the police still here?"

"No, they finished ages ago," Richard said.

Jamie waved a hand at the vehicles as they got out of the Mercedes. "Who's all this, then?"

Richard shot him a look of disbelief. "What did you think? You'd just come home and forget about what's happened today?"

"I was hoping to, yes. At least for a few hours."

"Damage control can't wait," Ira said briskly.

Richard's mouth twisted in a grim smile. "Besides, so many of your loved ones want to show their support."

"Loved ones?" Jamie echoed, getting a bad feeling as he opened the door.

He was right to be worried. As they twisted down the staircase from the mezzanine, Jamie could see that the sunken living room was as packed with people as it had been during his mother's infamous parties. When he reached the bottom step and had a clear view of who was waiting to pounce on him, he froze.

On the left-hand side sat his publicist, Lindsey Morgan, her dark blue suit and bright red hair standing out sharply against the beige and white and ivory tones of the room. Her right leg, crossed over her left, bounced up and down with nervous energy, as though she were just itching to go into battle, just waiting for him to arrive so that the mayhem could begin. In front of her, a television set broadcast a charming video of himself being led from this house in handcuffs earlier in the day. And then, on the right-hand side were Lindsey's minions, mostly talking on cell phones or working feverishly at laptops.

None of that was the worst of it. The absolute worst were the two people who jumped to their feet and came rushing toward him, jabbering in concern and reaching their hands out to touch and console. His lady-killer stepfather, Elliott Dane, and of all people, loony Vette Jackson.

He slipped out of their clutches and took a step back toward the stairs. "What the—what are you doing here!"

Jamie was talking to both of them, but Elliott answered first. "We were concerned, of course."

The man's perfectly-bronzed forehead was crinkled with concern, his gray eyes grave. He ran a hand over his dark hair as though to smooth it, but of course there wasn't a hair out of place. Elliott and Richard were about the same age, but Jamie noted that Rick was beginning to look a bit saggy and middle-aged, and his clothes were perpetually wrinkled, whereas Elliott seemed to look more virile, more powerful, more perfect every year. Even at this time of night, he looked as fresh as though he'd just got dressed for the day.

A light touch from Vette reminded him of her presence. "You know how I feel about you, Jamie," she was gushing.

And indeed he did. He had been trying to avoid Vette Jackson for ages—ever since one ill-advised date with her a couple of years ago that he couldn't even explain to himself now. His mother had died and he hadn't met Paula yet and he was mad with grief. That was his only excuse. And Vette had seemed so exotic, with her heavy-metal band and crazy stage antics. Not to mention her wild red hair and willowy body, and the piercings in the most interesting places. Even now, he found his eye drawn to the glittering little diamond in her nose that reflected the green from her eyes. Her wide, scary eyes that were drinking him in. She was no longer willowy, though. She'd grown as painfully thin as Paula.

"Poor Jamie." She'd moved closer. "Poor, poor Jamie. All alone now."

"If only that were true," Jamie said wryly.

He retreated up another step, but she kept coming.

"I can't believe they dared arrest you. How could they possibly think you would ever hurt anyone?" Her huge green eyes were searching him, and he noticed they were abnormally dilated. "I knew it from the moment I met you. You and I are different. We're star children."

"Uh…you were a child star, too?" Jamie thought she had only become famous a couple of years ago, mainly by doing things so outrageous on the stage that she overcame the handicap of her scratchy voice.

She made a noise of frustration. "Not child stars. Star children. You know…different. Not of this reality. We were seeded here from the stars, you and I. No wonder they—people like the police, like that Paula girl—can't understand us."

As she finished up her declaration, she reached out a bony hand and closed it around his wrist, no doubt as a gesture of affection. But her long fingers felt so skeletal that a flash went through his mind of Paula, emaciated and wasted and probably lying on a slab awaiting autopsy. With an involuntary shudder, he jerked his hand away from her.

For a moment, she stared at him in disbelief, her eyes filling with tears. Then, with a choked sob, she pushed past him to run up the stairs—presum-

.o the door on the mezzanine level.

Before Jamie could say anything, Richard rounded on Elliott. "Really? .ou brought her here tonight? You were scheming about pitching your movie *tonight!*"

"Wha—what?" Jamie turned to Elliott. "Pitching a movie?"

"I have no idea what he's talking about," Elliott said placidly. He looked at Richard, appearing genuinely bewildered. "Jamie's my stepson. How could I not come here tonight?"

"And bring Vette Jackson along with you." Richard snorted and headed for the sideboard where his favorite whiskey was kept.

"Vette and I are doing business together. I happened to be with her when we heard the news."

"What movie?" Jamie repeated, trying to remain calm.

"I can't believe you haven't heard," Richard said, replacing the bottle and taking a sip from his glass. "Everyone else has. He's been trying to talk Vette into starring in a movie—a musical, which he would produce, of course. The rumor is she'll only do it if you're in it, too."

Something clicked in Jamie's mind, and suddenly everything was so clear, so sharp that the edges cut into his mind. The anger that filled him was so strong he couldn't shout or scream. He could barely breathe, but he managed to choke out a few words to Elliott. "Get out."

"But Jamie, this is ridiculous—"

Jamie addressed the room at large. "I will talk to Ira and Lindsey and Richard tonight. The rest of you...get out of my house."

Turning, he ran up the stairs the way Vette had gone, only he continued past the mezzanine, aiming for the sanctuary of his bedroom. When he was only halfway up that second flight, however, he heard Richard and Elliott coming up to the mezzanine—presumably, Richard was showing Elliott out—and for some reason he paused, squeezing against the wall so he was out of sight as they crossed to the front door .

"—assure you, I was only thinking of Jamie," Elliott was saying.

"Yeah, yeah."

"Really. I thought if anyone could take Jamie's mind off things it would be Vette. She's so—"

"Capable of making you loads of money." Richard's tone—cynical, but light—reflected his opinion of Elliott. Richard constantly said the man was "a lazy good-for-nothing who lives off women and children" but at the same time considered him a harmless joke, a buffoon.

Elliott heaved one of his dramatic sighs. "Well, Richard, I wasn't consciously thinking about a film deal, but I don't know—times are rough since you and I aren't working together."

Richard guffawed. "Working together? When did you do any work? That was the problem."

"Richard, seriously—"

"I am serious. Look, Elliott, I'm sorry you're having a bad time of it lately, but I only started Headwind Productions with you and Teresa because the two of you had already ruined your nephew's career and I didn't want you to do the same thing to mine."

"I'm sorry you feel that way, Richard," Elliott said, sounding perfectly good-natured about the whole thing. "But you can hardly compare Charlie and Jamie's chances. Charlie will never have the kind of talent Jamie has. I don't think even you could have made him a star."

"Maybe not, but—I'm sorry to say this, Elliott, but you and Teresa ruined any chance he did have. One day you'd have him doing a sitcom, and the next you would decide you could produce a movie for Charlie the way I did for Jamie. After you took up with Jamie's mother and the two of you started mucking about with his career, too, I couldn't just sit by and wait for you to ruin Jamie, could I? It was easier to do the work for you than to try to repair the damage."

Now Elliott sounded wistful. "Those were the days, Richard—when Teresa and I were still getting along, and it was like one big happy family. A *Summer* film every couple of years for the boys, and another good, quality picture in between."

"Yeah, well, those days are over. Hannah Raney's dead and *Summer's* over. And Teresa's dead and Jamie can fend for himself—in his career, at least. Frankly, when I first heard that Teresa was dead, all I could feel was a sort of relief."

"Richard!"

"I know, I know, I should be ashamed to admit it, but I felt I was finally free—that Jamie was finally free. I may think you're lazy, Elliott, but I loathed Teresa. Her showing back up in his life was such lousy timing. Jamie was only just starting to get over his father's death. He was having success with his career, just starting to enjoy his life again when she turned up and convinced him to go live with her. After that, he barely had an independent thought. I tried to stay in his life as best I could, but she managed to cut him off from me almost entirely, except when we were doing a picture together, of course. She'd tell him things, poison him against me. And then she was gone. Dead. And Jamie seemed to be turning around again. We sorted things out between us—I actually thought he was going to be all right."

"And then came Paula."

Richard heaved a sigh. "Yeah. Paula."

Elliott clucked, and Jamie could just picture him shaking his head sadly. "I only met her once, but it seems to me she was worse for him than Teresa ever was."

"Just as bad, anyway," Richard said. There was a moment of silence, as though both men were thinking. "I thought Jamie was going to have a breakdown last fall. He had no idea how to get Paula out of his life. So I helped him get Paula into rehab, found a picture shooting in England that he could start on straightaway. Best medicine in the world for him—a great role to lose himself in, staying in his own flat in London, visiting old friends. But here he is, only unemployed and back in California for one day, and look where we are."

Jamie didn't wait to hear any more. As silently as possible, he turned and continued up the winding staircase and into the master bedroom. Without turning on a light, he flopped down on the king-size bed and listened to the sound of the pounding surf—a sound that was hard to escape in this house. The shoreline in front was narrow—nonexistent at this moment, with the tide in. Stark black lava rocks lodged right up against the foot of the house, and spray would bounce off them and splatter the living room windows. The sound of the surf was always near, unrelenting and sometimes violent. His mother, who had designed it, had loved it. Jamie found it nerve-wracking, even in the best of times.

But at least the surf drowned out the sound of the voices jabbering downstairs. Voices of the vultures who would spend the next days or weeks helping him, supporting him, smiling on camera, lying for him. Because they needed him—or his money, at least.

He wondered where Paula was right now. Her body was in the morgue somewhere, he supposed, awaiting the autopsy. He wanted very desperately not to think about that. Anyway, that wasn't the real Paula anymore, was it? He stared up at a vast dark canopy of space through the skylight in the ceiling. It was a cloudy, starless night, with nothing to look at but empty blackness. Thinking about Paula's soul wasn't very comforting.

The first time he'd met her, she had been so pretty—curvy and voluptuous, nothing like the willowy model she became, certainly nothing like the skeletal heroin addict. What was the name of that movie he'd been screening at James Poynter's house the night he met her? *Blood and...something*—which was fitting, since there had been little to the picture but violence and bloodshed. It had been too soon after his mother's death for him to stomach it, so he'd wandered outside for some air and a smoke. A few minutes later, Paula appeared, plopping herself down on the steps next to him and, without introduction or preamble, saying, "I saw you leave the movie. All those freaky dream scenes and murders must be really hard on you. You lost your mother recently, didn't you?"

Jamie had felt a little electric current run through him as her eyes gazed into his with such deep concern. From that first remark, he had felt as though she'd been sent to him, exactly what he needed at exactly the right time. As they talked, the feeling only grew—that they already knew one another, that she sensed what he was feeling, what he was thinking. By the end of that evening, Jamie had been smitten, absolutely certain that their meeting was Fate.

When he'd found her this morning, lying there on his floor, he couldn't bring himself to ring the police right away. If she hadn't been so obviously dead, he would have steeled every nerve in his body and forced himself into some sort of heroic action—or so he comforted himself. But clearly, Paula had been beyond needing or taking anything from him. So before he dialed 911, he had punched a number on the speed dial.

The familiar voice answered on the second ring.

"She's dead," Jamie had announced.

He was answered by a long pause. "Dead...Paula?"

"Who else? I thought you were going to take care of her. I thought she was leaving with you."

"Turns out she didn't want to. What could I do?"

"Was she dead when you left?"

"Would I have just left her there if she were dead?"

"Yes…maybe…I don't know. What the devil happened last night? What did you do?"

"Jamie, come on! I don't know what happened to her, either. She was fine when I left. She'd gotten what she needed and seemed to be happy. But somehow after I left, she overdosed, that's all there is to it. It isn't my fault and it isn't your fault. But at the same time…well, there are things we don't need to talk about, not even to each other. Things that people wouldn't understand about this whole situation. Don't you agree?"

Jamie laughed shortly. "Oh, yes, you're right about that. I can't say that I understand any of this myself."

The sound of the bedroom door opening brought Jamie back to the present with a start. Someone hit the light switch and he blinked against the blinding glare as he sprang to a sitting position on the side of the bed. Richard, Ira, and Lindsey were pulling chairs and footstools over—or in Richard's case, plopping himself down on the bed.

"We have to talk," Richard said.

Lindsey leaned in toward him, right in his face. "We have got to have some damage control immediately. We need you on camera—innocent, grief-stricken, remorseful—shedding tears! You've got to tell your story and not let everyone else make it up for you. We need people to have the same kind of sympathy for you that they did when your mother died. They need to see that you loved Paula and would never hurt her."

Lindsey smoothed her hair back into place. "And then maybe we help you with a discreet leak here and there. Subtly, in the right way, we can show you were really the victim of this girl's lifestyle. I know a couple of friendly reporters who would just eat it up."

"This isn't what I want." Jamie struggled to keep his voice from shaking. "I don't want this."

"Jamie—" Lindsey started.

"I don't want you spreading stupid rumors about Paula or anything else. Let the police handle it. And I for one have no intention of going all over television talking about our relationship or her drug abuse or—or anything else. It's no one else's business."

Lindsey threw up her hands. "You've been in this business since you were eight years old, and you haven't figured things out yet?"

Jamie turned back to Ira. "What would happen if I pled guilty to the possession charge?"

Ira's eyes widened. "I hope you're not serious."

"Would you answer the question, please?"

"Well, normally, you would probably get ordered into some kind of drug program, probably pay a fine and maybe get a suspended sentence."

"No jail time?"

"Probably not, but then, there was a death associated with this, and who knows? But Jamie, you're not guilty."

Richard jabbed a finger at him. "You cannot do this! The studios, the producers, the companies that insure the pictures—they'll put up with almost any sort of crazy behavior and still hire you if they think you'll make money for them. But if your name is associated with a possible heroin addiction, they'll start to think of you as a bad risk. Anyway, why would you want to take the punishment for something you didn't do?"

"It's what I intend to do." Jamie stood up. "Feel free to put the best spin on this thing possible, as long as you don't expect me to go on camera and cry big crocodile tears. Good night."

He fell back down on the bed and turned his back on them, ignoring the few minutes of murmuring behind him. Then finally, he heard Richard say, "Jamie's had enough for tonight, all right? Let's give him a break."

He heard the flick of the light switch, a millisecond before darkness swallowed up the room again.

"Where are you, Paula?" he whispered.

No one answered, of course, and after a long moment staring up at the dark sky, he reached into the drawer of his nightstand, grasping for the bottle of pills that would make that darkness not press quite so hard against his chest, that would let him breathe and sleep for a while. But the bottle wasn't there. Someone had confiscated the bottle—the police or Richard or somebody. He flipped over onto his back and stared again at the infinite expanse of sky.

Where are you?

CHAPTER THREE

THE SOUND OF SHOUTS, SQUEALS, AND BUMPS JERKED JAMIE OUT OF A LIGHT, tenuous sleep. Pulling on his clothes as he ran down the stairs, he jerked open the front door to see a mob surging against the fence at the left side of the property. They were all either staring at or snapping pictures of something on the ground just outside the fence—something Jamie couldn't clearly see because of the overturned dustbin blocking his view.

He was debating whether to head for the fence and investigate or run back inside to ring the police when a couple of wrestling bodies rolled into view. One of them yelped as the other grabbed his hair and pulled his head back, and Jamie had a clear view of the familiar face.

"Charlie!" Heedless of cameras or screaming teen-aged girls in the crowd, Jamie hit the button to open the gate and ran outside. As he pushed his way through the throng, he heard gasps of surprise, heard cameras clicking, felt hands pulling at his shirt as girls yelled his name. He shook off an uncomfortable memory of one of his dad's stories, about Jesus in the throng of adoring people, and the sick woman desperately trying to grab the hem of his robe. The thought made him feel vaguely blasphemous—but then, he wasn't the one doing the grabbing.

By the time he pushed through to the fight, the situation had reversed, and Charlie Edenfield was sitting on the chest of a brute about twice his size and pummeling him. As Jamie grabbed his friend and pulled him up, the bloke on bottom wiggled out and jumped to his feet. Clapping one hand to his face, the man jabbed at Charlie with the other and said, "You're going to jail, pal. You attacked me."

Jamie had to tighten his grip as Charlie lunged and yelled, "Oh, yeah? Want to explain what you're doing with Jamie's property? What you've got stuffed in your pockets?"

Jamie became aware of the clicking cameras, the wide eyes, the delighted smiles all around them. "Not out here!" he hissed in Charlie's ear.

"Trash is no longer property," said the burly man. "It's fair game."

"Not when it's inside a fence, on a private estate." Charlie grabbed something off the ground and waved it—a long rod with a hook duct-taped on the end. "I saw him using this when I drove up. He had pulled the dumpster over to the fence with it, turned it over, and was pulling papers out through the bars." Charlie threw off Jamie's arm and sprang toward the man again, brandishing the rod-hook contraption like a weapon. "Give that stuff back."

Moving faster than Jamie would have believed for a bloke that size, the man suddenly pivoted and ran for it, throwing aside the bodies in the crowd and not slowing down until he reached a green Chevy parked on the roadway. In a flash, the car was tearing away from the scene and out of sight. As all heads turned in the direction of the car, Jamie dragged Charlie back toward the gate. "Your lip is bleeding," he said. "Come on inside."

"Please tell me," Charlie said as he turned on the faucet in Jamie's downstairs loo, "why you don't have security around here."

Jamie shrugged. "Rick sent a couple of goons over but I couldn't stand them. Ira's supposed to be finding someone else. You want the job? I think you'd make an excellent goon."

"Very funny."

Jamie leaned against the bathroom door and watched as Charlie washed the blood off his lip. "You okay?"

"Yeah, of course."

But as Charlie dried his face, Jamie could see the little lines of worry starting to crease his forehead. He knew his friend's pattern well: blind anger, lose control, explode, regain control, and then enter the "oh crap, what have I done" phase. The duration of the "oh crap" phase was generally in direct proportion to the enormity of the related explosion.

"So," Charlie said, looking at him as steadily as he could out of his swelling eye. "Are you going to call the police?"

"What's the point?"

"He took papers out of your trash. I know he still had stuff in his pockets when he ran."

Jamie shrugged. "There's nothing in my trash worth worrying about."

"You sure? You know how people can twist things."

"Trust me. I'm very cautious these days."

Jamie tried not to laugh at the look of relief that flooded Charlie's face. Yep, he was definitely in the "oh crap" phase.

Sure enough, as they headed out to the garage—they almost always tinkered with Jamie's old cars while they talked—Charlie said, "Maybe it's just as well. I would particularly like to stay out of trouble right about now."

"Why is that?"

Charlie came to a stop in the middle of the garage as Jamie picked up a rag and started polishing his latest baby, a really sweet '73 Porsche 911. He continued to stand there until Jamie said, "Well?"

"Well, because I...I've joined the Army."

"You've done what!" Jamie stared at this person who for all intents and purposes was his brother—or at least a sort of step-brother—and tried to convince himself he hadn't heard correctly. "Are you completely mental!"

Charlie sighed, running a hand through his mop of honey-colored hair. "I knew you'd say that. Things haven't been going too well lately. I need a change."

"So you go on a safari or go lie on a beach somewhere. You don't join the Army." The *Army*! The very thought of little Charlie in the military sent him shaking his head in disbelief again. Even now, as Jamie leaned against the Porsche and crossed his arms, not even standing up straight, he felt as though he were towering over the little five-foot-seven idiot.

Charlie barked out a laugh. "You seem to think I have money."

"How could you not have enough money—" A picture of Elliott flashed through Jamie's mind. "Oh."

"Yeah. Exactly." Charlie lifted his shoulders and let them fall, as though shrugging off money troubles. "It's okay. Joining the Army's not a whim. I've been thinking about it a long time. You're kind of on probation when you first join. They can chuck you out for almost anything, so it's just as well if I don't get accused of assault right about now."

Jamie looked down at the rag in his hands, folding it carefully as though it were a lace handkerchief before laying it down on the hood.

"Look, Jamie, it's not like I'm throwing my life away. I'm going to be training to be a medic, so maybe I can finally do something useful."

Jamie studied his friend's face. "You trying to do penance or something?"

Charlie jerked up his head, his eyes flashing. "What do you mean by that?"

Jamie put up his hands, placating. "Don't get excited. I just…we all have things to feel guilty for, don't we?" He picked up an oil can off the floor and threw it into a dustbin with more force than necessary. "God knows I do." Before Charlie could say anything else, Jamie asked, "When are you leaving?"

"I don't have to report for basic training for a few weeks. But I'm leaving tomorrow to go back to Virginia for a while."

"Well, isn't that lovely?" Jamie busied himself tidying up, picking up rags and tools so he didn't have to look at Charlie. "I thought you'd come over here to support me. And instead you're deserting me."

Charlie exhaled sharply, sounding frustrated. "I know this is hard for the great Jamie Newkirk to believe, but the whole universe doesn't revolve around you and your problems."

"My problems?" Jamie straightened up and faced him. "You make it sound like I have a scheduling conflict or something. My…friend…died in my house. Remember how you felt when Hannah died at yours? You still haven't got over it."

"Yeah, well, my whole life ended that night, didn't it?"

"No, of course it didn't."

"My career, anyway. At least you don't have to worry about that."

"Oh, don't I? That's not what Rick and the lawyers say."

Charlie snorted. "Oh, please. The 'greatest actor of his generation'? Nothing can kill your career!" As Jamie started to protest, Charlie put up his hand to stop him. "No, no, don't bother. Look… I am sorry about the timing of all this, but I signed up with the Army before all this with Paula happened."

"Okay," Jamie said. He took a deep breath, willing himself to calm down. "So…what do your Aunt Phoebe and Elliott think of this?"

"Aunt Phoebe's all right with it, I think. She's pretty realistic about my career options. She says I've been living off Newkirk charity too long as it is."

"Charity? What do you mean?"

"Oh, come on. I could always count on a couple of scenes in one of Headwind's movies with you, couldn't I?"

"That certainly wasn't charity. Your aunt shouldn't have said that."

"Yeah, well, she's never had any faith in me. She didn't even want me to go to the screen test for *Summer and the Shore.* Elliott took me. And Elliott gave up his real estate business so he could be my guardian on the set, so I could have my dream." Charlie shook his head. "Too bad Aunt Phoebe turned out to be right."

"Stop it, okay?" Jamie started tidying again. He was growing impatient with Charlie's whining and didn't want it to show.

"Whatever. Anyway, Elliott's not upset about me joining the Army, either." A cloud passed across Charlie's face. "He's been kind of distant lately. I had a hard time pinning him down long enough to tell him."

Without thinking, Jamie blurted out, "Well, naturally. You're not making money for him anymore."

"That's not true," Charlie said, in that tight, strangled voice that Jamie knew signaled trouble. "Elliott's been taking care of me since I was a year old, years before I got in the *Summer* movies and started making money."

"Your aunt took care of you before you started acting."

Charlie threw up his hands. "He was married to my aunt Phoebe, so yeah, she was there, but—"

"I've never understood why you always side with him against your aunt, your own flesh and blood." Jamie shook his head. "Even when Elliott left her for my mother."

"Maybe because I spent my whole childhood with them and I know them better than you do."

"I spent a big chunk of my childhood with Elliott. I know he tried to use me the same way he did you. He only married my mother to get control of my money. If it hadn't been for Richard, I'd be broke now, too."

Charlie's eyes flashed. "You're paranoid. Just because your mother never even visited you until you had money doesn't mean all parents are that greedy."

Jamie forced himself to take a breath. If he didn't back off, Charlie would explode again. "Okay, yeah, I've pretty much got over any illusions about my mother. But maybe it's time you open your eyes about Elliott, that's all I'm saying."

Charlie sighed, seeming to deflate. "I don't want to fight now. I'm leaving tomorrow."

"I don't want to fight either. It's just…you, of all people, know why this is so horrible—all of this—Paula dying and…" Jamie started losing steam, seeing the look of concern that was coming into Charlie's eyes. "You know…"

"Yeah," Charlie said softly. "I know. But you're gonna have to let it go, Jamie."

Jamie laughed drily. "Yeah, right. The way you let things go."

Charlie took a deep breath and opened his mouth as though about to speak, but snapped it shut again as the door into the garage banged and Richard appeared.

For a moment, the man stood looking at them, a questioning look on his face, as though he could sense the emotion in the room. Deciding to head him off, Jamie nodded toward Charlie and said, "Tell Rick your news."

The two of them started to talk, and he heard the surprise in Richard's voice as he responded to what Charlie was saying, but Jamie had trouble focusing on the actual words. After a moment, he didn't even try.

CHAPTER FOUR

THE RADIO BLARED IN THE BACKGROUND AS JAMIE LITERALLY SCRUBBED THE hood of the Porsche with the rubbing compound. He took a deep breath and forced himself to step back. He would never even use a power buffer on the delicate, aging paint of his cars; he had developed just the right touch to coax a finish back to life by hand. And now here he was, scrubbing the 911 with no more regard than he would give a dirty cement sidewalk.

What a lovely couple of weeks. He'd barely noticed Christmas come and go, what with Paula's funeral, and Charlie leaving, and then his court appearance. And now this latest humiliation—the phone call from Bill Vermeer a couple of hours ago. He couldn't get it out of his mind, and the poor Porsche was suffering for it.

When had it all started to go so horribly wrong? When had the acting stopped being his joy, his salvation? Long before Paula, he knew that. He thought about the questions as he took another go at the car.

For him, the whole acting business had been very much like Paula's drug addiction—the giddy euphoria of his first experience on the stage, followed by a season of pleasure. Then the imperceptible slide into total dependence, so that he needed the acting to function, like breathing—but got just about as much excitement out of the process.

Stopping in mid motion, he closed his eyes and allowed himself to relax, to think. The first day he remembered going at an acting job with a sense of drudgery had also been the day he met Charlie. As they arrived at the studio for screen tests for three or four kids being considered for the part of Newt Fairchild in the second *Summer* film, he and Rick had been in the middle of

42

a colossal row. Jamie hadn't wanted to do another film, period. After shooting *Summer and the Sea*, he had played the young Pip in *Great Expectations* for three months in a West End production and enjoyed it immensely. So the morning of the screen test, he had explained to Richard—quite reasonably, he thought at the time—that he wasn't going to do any more films after this one. He was going to be a stage actor. Rick had gone ballistic, yelled about money, called Jamie an ingrate.

Jamie had tried to smile and shrug it off during the auditions, particularly since the third kid they tested looked as though he were about to throw up and Jamie didn't want to push him over the edge. In *Summer and the Shore*, Danny's quest would take him to colonial America, so there would be several new characters, including the high-spirited ten-year-old Newt. The first couple of boys they tested were hyper and attacked their lines with so much gusto they made Jamie tired, but this third one seemed so washed-out and bland that Jamie couldn't imagine how he'd got this far in the audition process. To give Rick credit, he was patient with the kid, whose name just happened to be Charlie Edenfield, as he sputtered out his first lines.

But when Jamie read his response, Rick jumped all over him. "Jamie, the mechanical voice on our answering machine is more exciting than that. I realize you're in a snit, but I'll thank you to remember you're a professional."

"You leave him alone!"

All heads turned toward the source of the explosion—Charlie. He looked like a totally different boy now. His gold eyes were blazing, his cheeks were flushed, and his fists were opening and closing as though he would like nothing better than to punch Richard on the nose. For the first time, Jamie understood why Rick and the casting director had thought this boy could play Newt Fairchild. Jamie had a feeling this wasn't the first outburst Richard had seen from him, because the man's mouth was twitching as though he were about to laugh and he looked totally unsurprised.

Charlie wasn't finished. "You leave him alone, because he knows what he's doing. He knows Danny better than you do!"

"Charlie! Stop it this instant."

Heads swiveled again, this time toward the boy's guardian, whose handsome face was also flushed. Looking back over all these years, Jamie couldn't remember many times when Elliott Dane had looked so angry. The man was a jerk, but he usually had it under control—or hidden under a smooth smile.

But at that moment, he'd looked murderous. The red in Charlie's face started to subside as he bolted for the door, and Jamie had figured the boy really was about to be sick.

Elliott stood, his face dark and dangerous. "I deeply apologize," he said, the last word sounding almost like a hiss. "I'll go get him."

"No!" Jamie said, jumping between the man and the doorway. "I'll go." After all, Charlie had just stood up for him.

Jamie had found Charlie in the hall, sitting on the floor with his back against the wall and his knees drawn up to his chest. The boy's eyes widened when he lifted his head and saw who had come after him. Jamie recognized the look from fans he had been meeting over the past year. It was sheer adoration. He sighed and decided to nip this thing in the bud. "I'm not Danny, you know."

Charlie had snorted, the adoration extinguished. "I realize that. I'm not crazy."

"I know, I just—I appreciate you sticking up for me, but you don't have to." He grinned. "I'm used to Rick's tantrums." He thought of the violent-looking man back in the conference room who had yelled at Charlie. "How about you? Are you used to that, uh…kindly old gentleman you came with?"

Charlie laughed, flooding his face with light. "Yeah, Elliott's okay. He's taking two days away from his business just to bring me here—my Aunt Phoebe thought it was pointless. We're just both really nervous." He shook his head. "How do you do it?"

"Do what?"

"I've seen you on talk shows and stuff, and believe me, I know you're nothing like Danny. I was scared to go see that first movie, because I loved the book so much and I figured the movie would be all wrong. I could see it so clearly in my head, how it should be. Some of the movie wasn't so great, but you…you were Danny. How did you do it?"

Sliding his back down the wall, Jamie sat down next to Charlie and studied him. "Tell me. What do you like about the books?"

Jamie couldn't remember the details of the conversation after that point, but he did remember Charlie's animated face as he spoke, painting such a magical picture of Danny Summer's world that Jamie felt his own pulse quickening, his own excitement building, so that when Richard finally came out and dragged them back to the screen test, everything had changed.

Sparks flew, the air crackled with emotion, and when they finished the test, Jamie knew that Charlie would be getting the part. Even though Jamie had done a passable job on the first *Summer* film, it had been nothing but a lark to him. Charlie had made Jamie fall in love with Danny, too.

Jamie jumped, drawn back to the present by the sound of his name blaring from the chat show on the radio.

"…and of course, Jamie Newkirk appeared in court on that heroin possession charge yesterday. He was given a pretty light sentence. Complete a drug education course within the next six months, pay a fine, and do one hundred hours of community service. I'd like to know what you think about that. Is it too little, considering that Paula Klein ended up dead? Since he pleaded guilty, is he more or less saying that he bears some responsibility for her death, or just that he bought some drugs for a little party for two? Phone lines are open. Give me a call."

Jamie straightened up, tensing to hear what the first caller would say.

"The way Jamie Newkirk has acted through this thing is just abominable. Didn't he care about that girl at all? He's just gone about his business like nothing's happening, up there in that fabulous beach house of his without a care in the world, while that poor girl is dead. And he hasn't had one kind word to express about her, hasn't shed one tear!"

Jamie absently started to rub the hood, then realized he was bearing down again. The metal was showing through the tiniest bit where the paint was thinnest on the corner. He threw down the cloth and leaned back against the Porsche.

The next caller continued, "I don't think it's just that he's cold. I think Jamie Newkirk has a lot more to answer for than just this little drug charge, if you get my meaning."

"Well, the Medical Examiner did rule this was an accidental overdose. He said the other—the bruises and such—happened at least forty-eight hours before her death, and Jamie Newkirk was in England at the time."

The caller snorted, making a little explosion of static. "The coroner said there are signs on that girl's body that she'd been abused over a long period of time, maybe for months. Where's Jamie Newkirk's alibi for all that, I'd like to know."

That did it. Jamie jerked a key at random from a selection hanging on hooks. Jumping into the corresponding roadster, he started the engine and hit the buttons to open the garage door and front gate simultaneously. Without looking back, he threw the car in reverse and floored it as soon as he had an opening. He had a vague image of paparazzi bodies scattering, leaping out of the way, of flashes going off in the night as he shifted gears and headed away from them. He was chuckling at their startled white faces in the rear view until he saw that part of the crowd consisted of fan girls, and that one of them was helping the other up off the ground. He slowed for a moment, but when he saw her dusting herself off and laughing, he gunned the engine again, heading nowhere in particular, just away.

He had started the climb up into Topanga Canyon when the phone rang. He almost didn't answer it. Not for any safety considerations, because he frankly could have cared less if the car went sailing off a cliff right now. But since so few people had this number, and it was probably Richard, and Richard would drive him insane until he answered—

He punched the button. "Hello?"

Sure enough, there was Richard's voice, barking orders.

"You're not doing it, Jamie. Not now."

For a moment, Jamie was clueless. "Doing what?"

"I just found out that this community service nonsense involves you picking up trash next to a major highway. You're not doing it."

"Richard, if I don't do my community service, they'll put me in jail. Which, actually, I have plenty of time for." He took a deep breath. "Bill Vermeer called me a couple of hours ago."

There was a brief silence, as Richard took this in. "I assume it wasn't good news."

"You assume correctly. I'm out of *Conquest.*"

"He can't do that."

"Apparently he can. I hadn't signed anything yet."

"Verbal contracts have been known to hold up in court. I'm going to call our solicitor—or better still, Elliott."

"Elliott!"

"They're friends, aren't they? Elliott and Vermeer?"

"Well, that would make sense. Two of a kind."

"Look, Jamie, I know how you feel about Elliott, how he deserted your mother. But if he can be of some use—"

"No, Richard. I'm serious. Anyway, I've really lost the desire to work with

Bill Vermeer. He's a coward. I thought he was going to burst into tears when he explained how much he thought of me, but how his whole comeback as a serious director depended on this one picture, and how he had heard how undependable I was when we were shooting *Message to Marilyn*. Which I probably was, but it wasn't because I was doing drugs." He shrugged, even though Richard couldn't see it. "Something else will come along. It's no big deal."

It was a huge deal, and he was sure Richard knew that. Jamie had campaigned for this part in *Conquest* as he had seldom done for any role. It was going to be his best since Danny Summer. A Spanish explorer—confident and bold, brilliant and charming, but with a dark side to boot. It could have been the pinnacle of his career.

But even more important than that, what was he going to do with the next six months of his life now?

"All right, look," Richard said. "We'll deal with your career later. In the meantime, I will not allow you to subject yourself to the humiliation of that idiotic community service. Every lunatic with a camera will be staked out in that road waiting for you."

"It is supposed to be punishment, Richard," Jamie pointed out. "And anyway, I'm tired of being trapped in that mausoleum of a house."

"Why don't we talk to Ira and see if we could arrange for you to come to Georgia with me and do your community service work here?"

"You could do that?"

"I'm no legal expert, but I don't see why not. I'll find you a part in the picture, and we'll say you're needed out here. And you do need to go back to work, for your own sanity."

"Also you could keep an eye on me and tell me what to do on a daily basis."

"Of course. So, what do you think?"

Jamie felt the car slowing as he eased his foot off the accelerator and considered. It actually sounded wonderful…to do what he had just done to that crowd of paparazzi but on a larger scale. To just gun his engines and get away from all of it, from the pointing and shouting and noise. Away from his punishment.

He shook his head, trying to clear away the thought, and steeled himself. "No, Rick. I'm going to stay here and take my licks."

Rick threw another fit, of course, but Jamie kept his resolve until his uncle finally hung up on him. He hung onto it while he drove around aimlessly for the next hour, held firm as he turned around and headed back toward his big glass house and the inevitable knot of vultures waiting to pick his bones.

But the moment he approached his gates, his resolve started to slip. Not because of any obnoxious cameraman. But because one of the crowd of scantily-clad adolescent girls—what were they doing out this time of night, anyway? Where were their parents?—one of them was holding up a sign that read, "I love you, Jamie." And then the one next to her, even worse. In big bold letters, her sign proclaimed, "I would die for you."

Jamie jerked on the wheel so sharply as he turned into his drive that he scraped the side of the Porsche on the gate. He got inside the house and first pulled out a cigarette, which he lit with shaking hands. Then he dug out his phone and dialed Richard.

"I changed my mind," he said, barely finding the breath to spit it out. "I've got to get out of here."

CHAPTER FIVE

IRA AND RICHARD PULLED IT OFF, SOMEHOW, AND ON FRIDAY NIGHT JAMIE FOUND himself on a private, borrowed Gulfstream jet heading for Georgia—some town a hundred miles or so south of Atlanta, called Middleboro. He felt his stomach drop, his ears muffling, and knew they were starting their descent, but when he looked out the window, all was still dark. Not like flying into L.A., where the solid carpet of flickering lights came into view long before landing.

How had he got here? Just a few weeks ago he'd been home in England shooting a picture. The most comfortable place in the world, doing his favorite thing. Only it hadn't worked any more. Something was so wrong with his head that even the enchantment of a new role—a borrowed soul— couldn't help this time.

And then had come a night in early December when he hit rock bottom. At least it had felt like the bottom to him. But maybe it wasn't. He hated to think so, but maybe there were much worse times ahead. Maybe the pit was bottomless. He was only twenty-three. What did he know?

He knew that December night had been different. He'd coped with his father dying when he was eight years old because he was a mere baby who thought someone would always take care of him. He'd coped with things after that because he still had a flickering flame of belief that what his dad had told him was true, that a powerful and loving God would always be looking out for him.

But years of dealing with the Teresa situation and then with Paula had beaten him down, left him weak and vulnerable and almost completely in the dark. For the first time in his life he had been totally alone—no Richard,

49

no girlfriend, no family. The only thing he did have was a huge, mocking load of guilt buried in his brain, so ragged and painful that he would have done anything to escape from himself for a while. But he was even more afraid of the drugs and the booze after recent events, and his last, best escape, his acting, was like a sealed door that he couldn't even fathom—couldn't even remember touching or opening or seeing before.

On that December night, his spirit had felt like a bird trapped on the wrong side of a plate glass window, alternately beating its wings in frenzied panic and throwing itself against the glass, then falling into exhausted resignation. During one of the cycles of frenzy, he had found himself beating his head against the God-wall.

"If you're there, you're going to have to do something. I know what I've done, but—help me! I just can't do this anymore!"

Had he said it out loud, or was the scream just inside his head? He couldn't really remember, and apparently it didn't matter either way. But he'd expected it to matter. Even after so many years, he'd remembered sitting in his dad's church, and every now and again hearing a dramatic testimony from someone who'd reached just such a low point and made just such a cry. And without fail, God had supposedly delivered for them. Either their circumstances had immediately changed, or they were filled with peace and certainty as they waited for a change. Something.

As for him, nothing had happened. Morning came, at which time he dressed and went to the studio and did his job. Then one night, a couple of weeks later, Paula died in his living room.

Still, he was surviving, whether he wanted to or not. Perhaps that was the only answer, the only gift—sheer survival. Perhaps ninety-eight percent of tantrums for heavenly attention like the one he'd thrown were answered in just this way. People just didn't go into churches and talk about that.

The plane touched down with just the slightest bump, and Jamie looked dismally out the window. Middleboro, Georgia on a Friday night. Wonderful. Absolutely brilliant.

* * *

When Trev Holliday had invited her to this party, Jeanine's logical voice had insisted it was a bad idea, but the side of her brain in charge of fantasies and lies had won out. So here she was, handing over her coat to a total stranger and almost choking on second-hand smoke, as Trev and Ginella disappeared into the gloom of the apartment.

Jeanine had been admiring Trev from afar for a year, ever since he had sat in front of her in a Western Civ class last spring. In fact, she had spent that whole term trying to ignore the way the light flashed in his reddish-brown hair and focus on the professor's droning voice instead. Then she had seen him play the guitar. His band had been playing a school dance, and as some dull-voiced guy sang, Trev had been lost in the music, fingers dancing and face totally absorbed as he bent over the instrument. Ever since then, when Jeanine would see him strolling across campus, she toyed with the idea that he might be one real guy—as opposed to movie or book characters—worth getting to know.

So naturally, he was now dating Ginella.

Jeanine recognized a few faces in the packed room, including the other members of Shady Lane, Trev's band. They were already plucking at guitars or keyboard, warming up, so maybe at least there'd be entertainment soon, other than watching couples making out in dim corners. Trev started introducing her and Ginella around, and a few folks recognized Ginella and squealed a happy greeting. Jeanine recalled the faces of two or three of them as her classmates, but their eyes of course were totally blank as they nodded at her. As Trev pulled out his guitar and started to tune it, Jeanine marveled at the way Ginella settled in on the couch next to him, as though she had known these people all her life. The tiny living room of the duplex was crowded and stuffy. The only place Jeanine could find to sit was a spot on the floor at the back of the room.

Soon, however, she was so caught up in Trev's playing that she didn't really care where she was. The minute he touched the strings, the music really started, the weak notes from his companions overpowered as they attempted to keep up with him. Trev's normally relaxed and carefree features were sober as he bent over the instrument, fingers flying, weaving the notes of a Spanish-sounding instrumental in the air. Jeanine leaned back against the wall and closed her eyes, mentally basking in shimmery moonlight in a hacienda courtyard...

And then the song broke off, and she jumped, startled, as she heard Trev say, "So, Jeanine, how about singing something for us?" He looked around at the others. "You won't believe this girl's voice!"

This was why Trev had brought her to the party—to give her a chance to sing with Shady Lane. They were losing the dull-voiced lead singer and Trev actually wanted Jeanine to replace him. But Trev thought it was better to let his band members think they were discovering her.

So she forced herself to smile and say brightly, "Wow, thanks! Sure, I'd love to sing."

She sang two or three selections. And she was fine. Everyone listened, and they clapped when she was finished. And then their attention turned away again. She saw Trev giving her a puzzled look, but then he turned back to his music, and it was all over. The dream was already dead.

Jeanine faded to the back of the crowd again. Before long, she was listening to Ginella's mock argument with one of the band members as she swore that she could, indeed, play a fiddle—country, bluegrass, whatever you wanted. The blond keyboard player (Marty, who was one of the party hosts) went off to find his own fiddle and have her prove it. Before you could say, well, anything, Ginella had become the center of attention. She laughed along with everybody else at the first screechy sounds she managed, and then she launched into a mournfully beautiful Irish melody. Jeanine unfolded herself from the floor, stepped over a few other legs, and fled to the kitchen.

In the space intended for an eating table, she was surprised to see an antique upright piano. Judging from the canisters, bags of potato chips, and a couple of unwashed glasses on top of it, the piano was apparently having to earn its keep as a piece of kitchen furniture.

"Also as a recycling bin," Jeanine muttered to herself as she noted the stacks of newspapers under and on top of the bench.

She found a glass on the counter, rinsed what appeared to be dust out of it, and bravely fixed herself a Coke with ice. Then the piano pulled her toward it, the way pianos always did. As she shifted newspapers so she could sit down, a page caught her attention. There was a huge reproduction of Paula Klein's famous Nirvana jeans ad, and a headline boldly demanded, "Who was Paula Klein?"

Jeanine sighed. There was just no getting away from all this, was there? Of course, as bored as she was right now, maybe that was a good thing.

She had seen this photograph many times, on billboards, the sides of buses, in magazines. But that was a year or two ago when the girl had her fifteen minutes of fame. Even back then, Jeanine had spent way too much time studying the picture, since she knew that Paula Klein was living with Jamie Newkirk.

The model looked like a child. She wasn't wearing a shirt. Heck, she almost wasn't wearing the jeans. They were unzipped and seemed in danger of sliding down her almost non-existent hips at any moment. Her arms were crossed over her chest, and she was so emaciated that the faint outline of her ribs could be seen. Her eyes were huge and waif-like, and her short, red-gold hair was cut in fashionably mismatched and tousled lengths. What was it that had attracted Jamie Newkirk to this girl? What was it that had made this advertisement so popular?

Jeanine started to scan the article. "…born in the heartland of the country, in Wichita, Kansas. But her parents, Allison and Reuben Klein, were both free spirits eager to taste all that life could offer. So little Paula spent her formative years sampling a veritable smorgasbord of cultures: the cold of Alaska as Reuben worked on the pipeline; singing on the street corners of New York City to earn spare change. Always more concerned with the spiritual than the material, the Kleins spent two years in Mexico with a commune, growing vegetables and living off the land. 'Freedom and love,' Allison Klein says, 'those were the two most important things to us as a family. Those were the gifts that we wanted to give to Paula. Absolute freedom and absolute love.'"

Jeanine's eyes skipped through the story, past the stale speculation about Paula Klein's life after her failed attempt at rehabilitation and about the last few days of her life, in particular. She glanced at the sidebar on heroin use in the modeling profession. "Oh, everybody does it," confessed one model who wished to remain anonymous. "It ain't easy staying this thin, you know?"

But Allison Klein apparently thought her daughter's drug use had little to do with her career. "This is all his fault, no doubt about it. Jamie Newkirk bullied and coerced her into starting drugs. And who knows what happened to her there in his house, there at the end."

Jeanine jumped as a voice broke her concentration.

"So, what's the latest news from the Jamie Newkirk scandal?"

Jeanine glanced up and found Trev looking over her shoulder at the paper. "Oh, well, this paper is old, actually."

"Didn't he have to go to court or something?"

"Yeah. He got community service."

Trev guffawed. "So he got away with it, huh? Big surprise." He shook his head. "I'll bet he's laughing his head off. He got away with everything."

"That's not how he looked," Jeanine murmured, remembering the video on TV when the sentence had been handed down. He had almost looked...disappointed?

Trev tapped a finger on the newspaper photo of Paula Klein. "That was a real tragedy, though. Her dying that way, I mean. I loved that ad. I nearly ran my car off the road the first time I saw that billboard."

Jeanine couldn't help but smile as Trev started to rummage around at the kitchen counter.

"There must be a clean glass here somewhere," he grumbled.

"Yeah, well, good luck." She watched him rinsing a tumbler under running water. "What was so attractive about her?"

"Who? Oh, I don't know." He turned to grin at her. "It helped that she was nearly naked. But there was something about her that made you feel big and strong and protective, you know?"

"Not really."

He shrugged and pulled open the freezer. "Guess it's a guy thing."

"Yeah...Trev, would you do me a favor?"

"What's that?"

"I know this is a big inconvenience, but would you mind running me home?"

He paused with his hand in the ice bin and looked at her. "So soon?"

"Yeah, well, I'm not very good at parties and I have to say I'm a little uncomfortable tagging along on Ginella's date."

"But what about your audition?"

"I've already had it."

"No, you haven't." Trev leaned against the counter and studied her until she became uncomfortable. "When I saw you singing in church, you were so bright you were almost blinding. It was like you had all the windows and doors thrown open, and I could almost feel the power of God streaming out through you."

Jeanine laughed a little. "Did you expect to have that kind of thing happen singing country music in your living room?"

"It's not my living room," Trev pointed out. "But yes, I think God wants you to use the talent he gave you, wherever you are." Trev nodded his head toward the front of the apartment, where her sister could be heard belting out a rowdy song. "If you tell her I said this, I'll deny it, but you're far more talented than Ginella. But if you let her, she'll always be more successful than you. You know why?"

Jeanine tried not to snort. "Because she's blonde and gorgeous."

"So? You're brunette and gorgeous. But the difference is, she shows what's inside her. She draws people in." Again he tapped the newspaper. "Just like that girl did."

Jeanine looked at him doubtfully. "Oh, I don't know. I don't think a girl who had a secret drug habit could be all that open. I mean, no one even knows what she was doing the last few weeks of her life."

"Then maybe you could fake it like she did."

Jeanine turned back to the piano and absently reached for the keys, but the lid was closed. She ran her finger along it, marking her path in the dust. "I don't know. Maybe I'm just not cut out to be a performer. Maybe I should stick to writing."

"What do you write?"

"Bits of everything. Stories—I've got most of a novel manuscript finished. I have absolutely no focus. That's why I'll probably never amount to anything."

"You ever write any songs?"

"Yeah, a few."

"Let me hear one." He leaned next to her and started opening up the piano. "Don't let the potato chip crumbs fool you. Marty actually keeps this thing in tune. It sounds great."

She touched the keys gingerly, testing them. They had a lovely, sweet tone, with just the slightest vibration that gave the notes the sound of bells. "Oh, you're right. I love this sound. It's so nostalgic. It reminds me of something."

As she ran her fingers over the keys, she thought of just the right story she wanted to share. And out of the chaos of the purposeless notes she started to draw a beautiful, wistful sound. The world of her ballad took form as her hands stroked the old piano, as her strong voice sang.

The light that rose that bright spring morn
looked down upon a field forlorn,
red with clay and sun and blood,

poured out from hearts that beat no more—
the hearts of men who'd feel no more.

But there upon the field so stained
one heart still beat, one soul remained.
Rising, weeping, looking 'round,
he spoke a prayer, he spoke their names.
He sang a dirge in sweet refrains.

And then he left, his battle done.
His day was new, his war song sung.
Southward only then he marched,
toward the hope to which he clung.
To home and hearth and her he clung.

But years and miles between them lay,
and though he thought he knew the way,
lost he roamed through Southern land.
Hungry and desperate for many a day,
he wandered his homeland for many a day.

At last he saw, on hilly ground,
an olden hut with moss all 'round.
From within a voice sang low,
"What thou hast lost cannot be found,
this side of heav'n will not be found."

Toward the hut he ran until,
upon his cresting of the hill,
he stood alone—the hill was bare.
He cried once more, his dying will
to rest there on the dying hill.

She might as well have fallen down a hole, into another world of her own creation. She hardly glanced up until the end, and when she did, she was surprised to see that three or four others had drifted in from the living room.

All of them, including Trev, were standing motionless, eyes fixed on her. The minute she stopped playing, they exploded.

"That was incredible!"

"Wait—was he a ghost?"

"I didn't think he was a ghost, just that she was dead."

"No, no, didn't you hear 'his dying will'?"

"I think he's going to be wandering forever—"

Jeanine felt a discernible thrill go through her, like the piano keys still vibrating inside her. As the group begged her to tell them the secrets of the story, she felt both a oneness with these people and a pleasant power over them.

Marty suddenly laughed. "I wish our band could have this kind of effect on an audience. Maybe we need you to sing with us!"

Trev looked at her and smiled, triumphant.

* * *

It was nighttime when Jamie deplaned from the little jet and started looking for Richard. Wearing a Dodgers baseball cap, his glasses rather than his contact lenses, a two-day growth of beard, and a huge sloppy jacket, he thought even Rick would have a hard time recognizing him. Richard, however, was standing out on the tarmac waiting for him, and the minute he was within earshot said cheerily, "You look like a derelict. An American one, at that, judging by the hat."

Jamie grinned back at him. "And I've missed you, too."

He shifted uneasily as a woman came walking out of the darkness, then stood behind Richard and stared at him, a hesitant smile on her face. Who was she? Fan? Richard's assistant? Paparazzi?

Richard took the woman by the arm and pulled her forward. "Jamie," he said, "I'd like you to meet Ruth Christopher."

"Hello, Jamie," she said warmly. "We're so glad you came."

We? Jamie's happy plans for sharing some time alone with Richard started to fade. Still, he had one last hope. "Hello. Are you working on *Right Angle*?"

She laughed. "Indirectly."

"I met Ruth a few months ago when I came out here to scout locations with the director," Richard explained. "Ruth owns a lovely, creepy old warehouse that we're using." He slid his arm about Ruth's waist and looked at her affectionately. "She's been making it very difficult for me to concentrate on the picture. Very difficult, indeed."

Jamie had no idea what to say to this. There was a long pause, and finally he said, "Do you suppose we could be moving along? I feel a bit exposed—"

"Oh, of course, of course." Richard took his arm away from the woman, looking sheepish.

She grabbed Rick's hand as they led the way to the car. Jamie sighed, heaved his carry-on to his shoulder, and trailed along behind them.

CHAPTER SIX

JAMIE PULLED INTO THE PARKING LOT AND KILLED THE ENGINE OF THE INCONSPIC-UOUS little Ford he had rented. A sign at the front of the parking lot read, "Salem Hill Baptist Church. Robert Lee DeValery, Pastor." Terrific. He looked at his watch and saw that he was ten minutes early, so he lit a cigarette and rather desperately inhaled.

If he weren't so superstitious, he wouldn't be in this situation right now. He had looked over a list of organizations he could work with to fulfill his community service, and there had been listed the Jones-Holly Village, along with this man's name as the contact person. The thing was, Jamie had read the name wrong the first time, thinking it said "Robert L. De Valera." Since De Valera was his mother's maiden name and Robert was his father's first name, it had struck him as an omen. Only after he was signed on had he discovered his mistake.

But he had thought it would still be all right. Some sort of homeless shelter or something. It should still be a worthy cause. But then the man had rung him this morning and asked him to come in and talk, and Jamie had discovered he was going to a church. A Baptist church. To talk to a minister. Jamie pulled down the rear view mirror and studied his face rather critically, looking for any telltale signs of last night's debauchery. Of all days for this interview!

Yesterday had started out with a particularly ugly scene. Richard had coerced the director of *Right Angle*, Larry Levy, into finding a part for Jamie in the picture, a sort of moody, film noir suspense drama. Larry had agreed, but had cast Jamie as a menacing serial rapist who threatens the female lead in the opening scenes of the picture and is quickly dispatched by the movie's hero. Normally Jamie would have found this a rather intriguing role, even if it were small. He had spent the last decade playing adorable romantic leads or noble heroes, and he would love to do a part or two that dashed everyone's expectations of him and really stretched him as an actor.

But not now. He had no desire whatsoever to present himself to the public as a serial rapist at this particular point in his life. Jamie's fans sometimes had trouble separating truth and fiction, and considering all the tabloid hints and innuendos about his treatment of Paula lately—well, it was just too much.

Richard had agreed with Jamie. A quick telephone consultation with Lindsey revealed that she also felt this cameo role would be one more in a long series of Jamie Newkirk Bad Career Moves. So yesterday there had been a rather nasty meeting with Richard, himself, and Larry about some alternate casting for Jamie, and the director had thrown a temperamental snit about being "jerked around" for the sake of the personal lives of various Newkirks. Jamie had finally walked out and told them to forget the whole thing.

Unfortunately, on his way out he had run into a gorgeous blonde hair stylist named Debbie and a couple of crew members he knew. He had spent a few moments chatting with them in the car park, and somehow they had all ended up in Jamie's hotel suite with a large amount of tequila and a few joints that Debbie provided. Jamie had simply sipped respectably at a beer, watched the antics of his friends, and refused to even touch the harder stuff.

And then Charlie showed up. He was on his way to report for basic training in South Carolina and had decided to rent a car and drive from Virginia, since he wouldn't be allowed to have a vehicle again for a while. At first Jamie had been delighted to see him, but when Charlie hunkered down in a corner, brooding and exuding about as much personality as a rock, Jamie became irritated.

Sliding down next to Charlie, Jamie spoke into his ear, just loud enough to be heard over the loud techno music Debbie had chosen. "You must really be looking forward to this Army thing, huh?"

Charlie scowled at him. "I am, actually."

"I can tell. You look deliriously happy."

He looked away. "That's not what's on my mind."

"Really? Then what is?"

Turning back to him, Charlie's eyes appeared so troubled that Jamie rather wished he hadn't asked. Now it was Charlie leaning next to his ear, speaking only as loud as he had to. "Jamie, I never knew whether I should tell you this while Paula was alive, but now…it's been eating at me. I keep thinking, maybe you need to know."

"Know what?" Jamie took a deep breath, pushing past the sudden tightness in his chest.

"Well, one time last year—I think it was one of those times when you were trying to crack down on Paula and keep her away from the junk—she turned up at one of Alex Painter's parties, and she was really in bad shape. You know…in need. And eventually, well, she offered me a business proposition, if you get my drift."

"No, I'm afraid I don't," Jamie said coldly.

"Come on, Jamie. She offered to do all kinds of things for me—she needed money for drugs."

Jamie felt as though he were in an elevator that had just plummeted ten floors before catching with a sharp jerk. He tried to catch his breath so he could speak. "And did you take her up on the offer, Charlie?"

"No, of course not!" His eyes went wide. "You know I wouldn't do something like that! I just, well, I don't know that this was the only time she ever made somebody an offer like that. So I thought it was something you should be aware of…for your health, if nothing else."

After that, Jamie hadn't been in a party mood, but he had felt in desperate need of anesthesia. He'd drunk so much he couldn't clearly remember Charlie leaving. Plus, now he was hung over and his eyes were red and puffy and he looked like a walking billboard for The Wrong Path Chosen. It would be this morning that a Baptist minister would want to see him. Of course.

Well, time was up. Jamie climbed out of the Taurus and ground the cigarette butt into the pavement under his foot. He entered the church through a side door as he had been directed. A gray-haired woman with a pleasant smile offered him coffee, then ushered him into the pastor's study.

The youthful-looking man behind the desk stood up and extended his hand. "Hi, I'm Lee."

"I'm, uh, I'm Jamie," he heard himself stammering.

The minister laughed. "I know. Thanks for coming."

Jamie nodded, took the seat offered in front of the desk, and accepted his coffee from the assistant. He sipped awkwardly as the man pulled out some paperwork and flipped through it, obviously glancing up to study Jamie from time to time. Jamie had learned to give people a moment to look him over, so he turned his own attention to a quick perusal of the room.

It was just worn enough to be friendly, and Jamie always felt at home in a room lined with books. Of course, these were no doubt all religious books. There was a huge Bible on the corner of the Reverend's desk. More intriguing, on the opposite corner where you might expect a photo of the man's wife or family to be, a silver picture frame was turned face down. Jamie had to fight an intense desire to pick it up and see what he was hiding.

Forcing himself to move on, he turned his gaze to the wall behind the minister, then froze. Behind the Reverend's head was a painting, obviously of the Garden of Eden. A close-up of Eve studying the apple, to be exact. In the luscious green swirls that made up the leafy backdrop, only two things stood out: the full red apple hanging from a branch, so voluptuously curved and shaded that he felt shameful looking at it; and Eve's young, naked face, gazing up at the fruit with painful longing, but also with conflict and struggle in her eyes. A strange, twisting shadow fell across half her face, and after another moment's study, Jamie realized that the shadow was serpentine in shape.

"Wow!" he blurted out. "Amazing painting!"

For some reason, Lee DeValery frowned as he turned his head to glance at it. "Yes, I've always liked it," he murmured, rather unenthusiastically, Jamie thought.

The Reverend turned his attention back to his paperwork, but Jamie couldn't let it go. "Rather odd choice of art for a pastor's study, though. At least, it seems to me…you can just feel it. The hunger, the passion for what she knows she shouldn't have. You feel very bad for her. Like she never had a chance."

Abandoning the papers, the man sighed and leaned back in his chair. "Well, my sister-in-law painted it, so what can you do? I'm probably going to take it home and hang it there soon, though. A lot of the church members seem to be disturbed by it, too." He touched the stack of papers. "So, Jamie, finding your name on my volunteer list for this week was something of a shock."

Jamie nodded in sympathy. "I can just imagine."

Again there was a silent moment as the man rested his chin in his hands and gazed intently at Jamie, who resisted the urge to put on his sunglasses.

Finally the minister said, "I guess you're wondering why I asked you to come in here."

"A bit, yes."

"I just wanted to clarify a few things. For example, why are you doing this?"

"Oh, ah...I thought you knew. I have this community service sentence—"

"I know, I know." The man smiled good-naturedly. "I always know we're in for a great time when someone calls working for the Village a 'sentence.'"

"Sorry."

"No, no, I understand that you're not exactly a volunteer."

"I suppose not." He shifted uncomfortably in his chair. "But I was allowed some amount of choice as to how I fulfilled my...obligation. And I chose your organization." Blast. He had almost said "sentence" again.

The minister nodded. "Believe me, we're grateful for an extra pair of hands. But I couldn't help but wonder...are you expecting to get anything else out of this experience?"

Jamie shook his head a bit. "Do you mean, like, character or growth or understanding or—I'm sorry." He broke off as the pastor started to laugh.

"In the interest of better cross-cultural understanding," Reverend DeValery said with a smile, "why don't I just be a little more direct. When you show up to help us tomorrow, will you be alone? Or will you be trailing camera crews behind you, documenting your work for the needy so you can broadcast around the world what a great guy you are?"

"Oh no, no, of course not..." Jamie's voice trailed off. Actually, it would be just the sort of thing that Lindsey would want to do. "Wow, you really understand how this works, don't you?"

Reverend DeValery leaned across the desk. "I know how I want it to work. Would you like me to tell you?"

Jamie nodded weakly.

"Okay. I've been on the board of the Village for a little over a year now. It was started as a kind of regeneration center for women who are basically out on the streets. They get a place to stay, counseling, treatment for addictions, job advice or referrals for training, that sort of thing. I have taken on the responsibility of being a sort of volunteer coordinator of volunteers, recruiting individuals to get certain projects done, making sure that people stay motivated and their talents get used." He smiled a little. "And every now and then, of course, we have someone like yourself who is serving a 'sentence' with us.

"That last group hasn't worked out very well. They tend to be bored, offended by the idea of any menial task, and generally unpleasant and unproductive." He finished up jovially, "So you can imagine what I thought when I saw your name on my list."

Jamie nodded. "Rather as though you'd hit the mother lode, I should think."

The minister laughed out loud. "You could say that, yes."

Jamie took a deep breath. "Look, Reverend DeValery—"

"Lee."

"Oh…okay. Lee. The way my life is going right now, well, I'm not in a position to be particularly cocky. If you wanted me to scrub toilets tomorrow, I wouldn't consider it beneath me."

"It's funny you should say that," Lee said archly.

Jamie looked at him, and he started to laugh again. Well, at least the man had a sense of humor, even if it mainly seemed to be triggered by Jamie's continual bludgeoning embarrassment of himself.

"No, actually," the minister continued, "what we're doing this week is renovating the main shelter. We have some bungalows for women who are with us long-term or who have small children. But for those who just need somewhere to go at a crisis point in their lives, we have a shelter that meets more basic needs. And I do mean it's basic. A large area with very little privacy and even less personality. But we've had a generous donation of wallpaper, carpeting, that sort of thing, and we're going to try to make it a little more homey. Of course, we have no money to pay contractors, and we have very little time to do the work ourselves, because these women have nowhere else to go. That means we'll have to work quickly and efficiently, with no nonsense. So, are you interested?"

"I can handle the quickly and the no nonsense part," Jamie said meekly. "As for efficiently, well, I have very few useful skills, I'm afraid."

Lee smiled. "That's okay. We can work around that." Lee looked down at his desk for a moment and fidgeted with a pencil. "Jamie, there are people on our board whose job it is to raise money, just as it's my job to find volunteers and get some of these chores done. I imagine if they knew you were going to be working with us, they would be all too happy for some media coverage—get the Village's name in the spotlight. But that sort of thing just doesn't sit well with me. I believe if God is in a mission like this, then he'll provide the funds for it, although he might make you work a little bit yourself. These women are having a bad time in their lives, and I don't want to see them exploited. For that matter, I don't want us to exploit you at a bad time in your life, either. So...do you think we can be pretty discreet about this whole thing?"

Jamie was oddly touched. "I'd like nothing better, I can assure you. And I can promise you that no one from my camp will make a nuisance of themselves. Hopefully no one else knows I'm in this area of the country, although I can't guarantee how long that will last."

"That sounds genuine enough." Lee smiled. "Although I hear you're a great actor. So how would I know whether you're being sincere?"

Jamie shook his head. "No, actually I'm not that good if I have to write my own dialogue."

Lee stood up, so Jamie did, too. As they walked to the door, Lee told Jamie when and where to report on the following morning.

And then Lee paused with his hand on the doorknob. "Jamie, there is one more thing. A lot of the women at the Village are there because of drug addictions. I absolutely will not have one of my volunteers showing up with anything or on anything—"

"Oh no, no, of course not!" Jamie said. "Don't worry. I don't do drugs."

Lee looked at him. Then he folded his arms and drawled, "Son, have you forgotten why you're here today?"

Jamie could feel his face starting to burn. He tried desperately to think of something to say to recover his dignity, but then gave it all up and leaned heavily against the door frame. "Shall I tell you the truth about that?"

Lee's eyes were gentle. "I'd like that very much, yes."

"It was Paula's heroin they found in my house. I probably could have got out of it. My attorney said so, at least. But I didn't want to."

"And why is that?"

"Because every time Paula needed a fix—well, most of the time I'd buy it for her. I thought at the time it was because I couldn't stand to see her suffering, but I don't know. Maybe I didn't want to be uncomfortable, myself. Even the night she died...well. Anyway, I'm not innocent. And I think I rather hoped the court would give me some real punishment, a term in jail or something, and I could serve my time and pay my debt and it would be over." Jamie shrugged. "But this is what they gave me, so here I am."

CHAPTER SEVEN

JUST FOR SPITE, JAMIE PLANNED ON ARRIVING AT THE JONES-HOLLY VILLAGE A FULL hour early. So he went to bed righteously early and sober the night before, although he noted as he went to shave the next morning that the gesture hadn't accomplished much. He looked as tired and puffy as he had on the previous day.

Jamie stared at himself for a long time in the mirror after he was dressed, wishing that he had the *Right Angle* make-up and lighting people around and that they could somehow work their magic on him in real life. He uneasily evaluated his features, wondering if Richard was right to worry about his health. Rick badgered him constantly to take an HIV test, ever since finding out that Paula was an intravenous drug user. Wouldn't he be thrilled to know that she had also apparently dabbled in prostitution?

By the time he was starting his car, Jamie felt calm and resigned. Death had always been alive to him, a shadowy female figure never quite in full view but always close at hand. She was dark and shapely, but her features couldn't be clearly seen, and it was difficult to tell whether her face would be lovely or nightmarish. But he fully expected her to come for him while he was still young. Perhaps she had already slipped something lethal into his body, like one of those spy-movie seductresses slipping a drug into the hero's martini. His father's fatal illness had started when he was only twenty-eight; his grandfather had died at thirty-five. Why shouldn't it happen to Jamie, who was already twenty-three, himself?

After dawdling and fretting at the mirror, Jamie wasn't quite as early as he intended, but he still managed the satisfying experience of lounging on the front steps and waiting for Reverend DeValery. And whatever the man thought of Jamie's looks, he seemed friendly enough as he arrived and called out a greeting.

Soon five or six additional workers joined them, running the gamut of age and girth. Lee had apparently warned them all beforehand that Jamie was coming, because no one seemed particularly shocked to find him in their midst. Some of them had already been working here the previous day, and had erected a network of low walls dividing the large common area of the shelter into a series of semi-private cubicles.

"Each one of them will have at least one bed and a small dresser," Lee told Jamie. "And we hope to put up curtains at the entrances for more privacy."

One of the rotund volunteers in seriously paint-stained overalls took Jamie under his wing and showed him how to hang wallpaper. By lunchtime, the two of them had completed several of the cubicles, with no two of them having the same pattern or color scheme. Then someone brought in sandwiches and soft drinks, and Jamie sat on a patch of withered brown grass outside the shelter with Lee as they ate. Although it was January, the sky was bright blue and the temperature was in the high sixties. Having lived in Southern California for years, Jamie wasn't particularly impressed, except for the fact that the high on the previous day had been thirty-eight degrees.

"Is the weather always this unpredictable here?" Jamie asked, breaking the easy silence.

"The changeability of our weather is pretty much the only thing you can count on these days," Lee answered. After gulping down the last of his sandwich, he reached for a box of chocolate chip cookies. "Nice job this morning. You catch on pretty quickly."

Jamie laughed. "I've got to learn all sorts of things quickly when I'm playing a part. At least learn them well enough to look good in the shot."

"So in other words, you quickly learned how to look like you'd been hanging wallpaper all your life, but as for how well your work will be holding up in a month or so—"

"You could be in trouble, yes."

"Well, I don't think Ed Rawls would have let you get away with shoddy work in there. Don't worry."

Jamie thoughtfully sipped his Coke. "Your program here—for addictions. Does it work?"

"Actually, we don't have our own program on site. We mostly try to give the women a haven and help them find a way to get back on their feet. We refer them to other substance abuse programs in the area. And to answer your question about that, well, it depends on the person in the program. We give them a choice. What they do with it is up to them."

Jamie hesitated for a long moment, then blurted out, "Do you really believe that—that people can really make choices, change their lives?"

Lee looked surprised. "Of course. Don't you?"

"I'm…not sure." Jamie squeezed the empty Coke can, absently watching as it crumpled in the middle. "As for the people in my life, it's almost as though they're programmed. Maybe some of them are lucky enough to be programmed for stability or achievement. But a lot of them are absolute slaves to something inside them, and no matter what they do or what you do for them, they can't break free. It's like that painting in your office—there's some desire or obsession or… or something that's just too strong."

Lee nodded. "You've just put your finger on one of the central teachings of Christianity—that we are all in bondage, and that only the power of Jesus Christ can allow us to break free."

Jamie looked at him coldly. "Yes, I do understand Christianity, thank you. My dad was a lay minister for some of the little chapels in our area. You know, churches that were too small to have a proper pastor. He worked in a garage during the week, took care of me every day from the time I was born, and then on Sundays he would preach one place or another. But I can't see that his faith made him particularly free. First of all he developed some temporary obsession for my mother that nearly ruined him, and then he ended up a slave to cancer. No matter what he believed, he didn't have any choice about when or how he died, or about getting to stay around to look after me."

"How old were you when he passed away?" Lee asked gently.

"I was eight."

"I'm sorry, Jamie. But it sounds as though you had quite a relationship for those eight years."

"He was—he was an extraordinary man. I realize it more now than I did then."

Lee shook his head. "I won't insult you by trying to give you some clever little answers for why you lost him that way. There are a lot of things in this world I'll never be able to comprehend." After a thoughtful moment, he added, "But I will tell you this. From the sound of it, you certainly couldn't call your father a slave to anything. I mean, we all have our human frailties from time to time, but, as far as his illness, there's a difference between suffering and slavery. Even Jesus himself suffered horribly during his life on this earth. The Bible calls him 'a man of sorrows and acquainted with grief.' But he was the epitome of liberty and peace."

Jamie didn't answer.

Lee glanced at him, and then started to gather up sandwich wrappers and napkins. "Now my father, on the other hand, there's a different case. His entire life for at least thirty years has revolved around alcohol. I'm a minister that's supposedly got all the answers for everyone else, and my own father hasn't spoken to me in years, or me to him. I wouldn't have had a clue what a normal family was like if I hadn't spent most of my adolescence hanging out at Marielle's house."

"Marielle?"

"My wife."

"Oh, so you married your childhood sweetheart, did you?" Jamie said, relaxing and leaning against the tree again.

"Not exactly." Lee grinned. "Her brother Scott was my best friend. Marielle couldn't stand me. She thought I was a bad influence on Scott, which I was from time to time. That was before I found the Lord, of course."

"Of course."

At that moment, Ed Rawls started to hustle them all inside and back to work, so the conversation ended.

Jamie found himself working next to Lee on the second afternoon. As they hung wallpaper or hauled rubbish away, there was little time for conversation. But Jamie still found the time to be oddly companionable, and he managed to get in a simple question or two, such as, "Do you have children?"

"Uh…" Lee smoothed a section of rose-patterned paper until Jamie feared that one of the roses would be completely rubbed out. "I have two daughters," he finally answered.

"How old are they?"

"Twenty and twenty-one."

"Oh, really?" Jamie smiled broadly at Lee. "Have you got pictures?"

"Absolutely not," Lee said glibly. "We've never taken a single picture of them, as a matter of fact. Don't believe in it, myself."

Jamie continued to tease him. "You realize that a cover-up like this could only mean one thing. They're gorgeous."

"Well, hopefully you'll never know." Lee laughed, as though joking.

But the remark stung, and the words hung there between them the rest of the afternoon.

They walked out to the car park together when work was finished, nodded to one another and murmured good-bye, and started to their vehicles. Lee's was nearer, but as Jamie started to pull away, the man still didn't have his car started. After a moment's hesitation, Jamie pulled up next to him. "Are you having trouble?"

"Yes, to put it mildly," Lee called back.

Lee popped the hood latch, and they both climbed out of their cars and studied the engine. Jamie leaned over and poked around a bit, then declared, "Fan belt's broken."

Lee looked at him in surprise. "I thought you said you had no useful skills."

Jamie shrugged. "I spent my childhood in a garage. I still like pottering with classic cars." He paused for a moment. "I actually could repair this pretty easily for you. If we had a new belt, of course."

Lee laughed. "Now there would be a story to tell. Jamie Newkirk worked on my car. But I can probably manage it myself. My wife can run me to a parts store sometime this evening."

"Do you need a ride home?"

Lee closed the hood and seemed to spend an eternity brushing an invisible speck of dirt from the car's shiny surface. Then, finally, he spoke. "Sure. That would be great, thank you."

They both got into Jamie's rented Taurus, and without any further conversation, started off for Lee's house.

CHAPTER EIGHT

They rode most of the way in silence, except for Lee's occasional directions to "turn right" or "take the left fork." He directed them out of the city, with its quaint skyline of steeples and spires overlooking the Ocmulgee River, and onto the freeway. They eventually turned off into a rural area largely inhabited by pine trees and dense banks of thick leafy vines. Jamie was burning with curiosity about Lee DeValery, and dying to ask a hundred questions about his life, but the man sat so rigid, staring straight ahead, that Jamie didn't bother.

As they rounded a wooded curve, Lee pointed to the right. "The driveway kind of pops up all of a sudden. There it is."

The drive led to two houses. The one on the right was a two-story white frame structure; the one on the left was a little stone cottage peeping out from under trees like something out of a fairy tale. Lee directed Jamie to the larger house.

As Jamie drove to it, he asked, "Who lives in the other place?"

"No one right now. Marielle's mother and sister used to live there. Actually, with all the college expenses we have for our daughters, we're probably going to be renting it out soon."

Jamie stopped the car, and Lee reached for the door handle. "Thanks for the ride, Jamie."

"No trouble at all," Jamie said.

And then there was an awkward moment, as Lee paused and looked at him. This was obviously the time for him to invite Jamie in, but the man hes-

itated, opened his mouth, started to say something, stopped, and closed his
mouth again. Finally he said limply, "Well, thanks again. I know you're working at the Village again this week, but it'll probably be next week before I'm
there again."

"Right," Jamie said.

Jamie watched as Lee disappeared into the white haven, and sat for a
long moment after. Then he cranked up the car and moved on.

At first, Jamie wasn't certain where he was going. Then he found himself
driving out to the *Right Angle* shoot, which just happened to be at Ruth's
warehouse today. He timed his arrival well. They had just finished one scene,
and crew members were dragging cables about and moving lights and props
for the next. Richard was standing at the door of the big, gloomy building in
heated discussion with Larry Levy, but Larry threw up his hands and stalked
away just before Jamie reached them. He found himself alone with his uncle
as he lounged against the doorway and watched the activity.

"So." Richard tapped a pen against his lip in between words. "Have you
chipped away at your debt to society?"

"Eight more hours today." Jamie watched the pen bounce against Rick's
mouth—a sure sign of nerves. "Larry giving you a hard time?"

Richard rolled his eyes and shook his head. "Look, we'll be finished here
in an hour or so, unless Larry throws another fit and demands twenty or
thirty takes. Then I've got to see the rushes. But after that, do you want to get
something to eat?"

Jamie was surprised. Since his arrival in Georgia, he had only been able
to snatch moments here and there with his uncle, who was always either
working or with his new love interest. An entire dinner with Richard was a
mind-boggling prospect.

But then, of course, Richard added, "With Ruth and me, I mean."

Of course. Jamie shrugged. "All right, why not?"

Jamie ended up not only watching the rushes from that day's shooting
with Richard and Larry, but also chiming in with a few opinions. When
Richard agreed with Jamie that one scene was weak because it rushed the
actress's reaction to her colleague's death, Levy literally ground his teeth.
Jamie heard the sound from several seats away.

Still laughing about it, Jamie walked with Richard to his car. Rick drove
them to the downtown restaurant, where they were slipped in like secret

agents to a dark, private booth in the back. They ordered drinks as they waited for Ruth to finish up some paperwork and join them.

As they chatted companionably for the first time in months, Jamie found himself complaining to Richard, "Lee DeValery acts as though I have some sort of nasty, contagious disease. It's all right if he's around me for charity, but I can't possibly be allowed to get near enough to contaminate his family."

"And why on earth would you want to?" Richard demanded irritably. "That's all I need right now, for you to go falling into a nest of fundamentalists."

"What!"

"I'm serious, Jamie. You're too impressionable for your own good, and I don't like your being under this man's influence day after day. Especially being forced into it by the authorities. I thought they had separation of church and state here."

"This has nothing to do with Lee's church," Jamie said. "He's on the board of directors of that shelter, just like the bankers and attorneys that are on the board."

"Fine." Richard heaved a deep, dramatic sigh. "Don't worry about it. Carolyn John used a marvelous deprogrammer when her daughter got involved with that UFO cult. I'll give her a call and get his name, just in case."

Jamie was not amused. "What is the matter with you tonight? You know very well that my father believed the same things as Lee DeValery."

"Yes, and a fat lot of good it did him, didn't it?" Richard snorted.

Jamie didn't allow himself to be pulled down that familiar path. He buttered a slice of the warm, dark bread and asked as he chewed, "What do you suppose is keeping Ruth?"

"I don't know."

Now Richard was tapping his lip with a butter knife. Jamie swallowed his bread and watched the familiar gesture with concern.

Laying down the butter knife, Richard leaned in close to Jamie and lowered his voice. "I'm glad she's late, because I wanted a chance to talk to you first. There's been a rather unexpected development with Ruth."

Jamie smiled. "Don't tell me. She's pregnant."

Richard looked at him. Jamie felt as though someone had punched him. "No! It can't be. At your age!"

"And just what is that supposed to mean?" Richard demanded.

"I mean, how could you have let something like this happen? And—come on! How old is Ruth, anyway?"

"She's all of thirty-five," Richard said through clenched teeth. "Not exactly ancient."

"But I—I don't understand this. You've only just met her!"

"I met her last September, when I was scouting locations. And then she spent a few days with me in California, while you were in England."

"So that's why you didn't come to England the whole time I was there," Jamie said. "I thought it was the picture."

"A little of both." Richard smiled ruefully. "Ruth was the reason I was in such a big hurry when I picked you up at the airport the night that Paula died—too big a hurry to come in the house with you."

Jamie smiled faintly. "I knew something was up. You barely wanted to talk to me. Normally, after I've been away, you bark questions and orders at me for hours."

"Yes, well, Ruth was waiting back at my house. She was supposed to have left the day before, but I convinced her to stay another day."

Jamie tried to think of the right thing to say. "So…how do you feel about the baby?"

"I don't know." Richard sighed. "Ruth considers it a miracle and is over-joyed. She wasn't supposed to be able to have children. But, well…I won't lie to you, Jamie. The idea of starting over with a child—it's terrifying." He smiled a little. "I'll never forget that night when your mother called from the hospital in London and told Rob that you had been born. The two of us went and fetched you back to Warwick, and we were both scared out of our wits. You were so tiny and so helpless, and we had absolutely no idea what we were doing.

"Somehow that first night Rob managed to bathe you without drowning you, and then he put you to bed. And then he waited. You see, everyone had warned him that new babies wake up and cry constantly, and that he shouldn't expect to get any sleep for months. I woke up hours later, and it occurred to me that I hadn't heard any fuss, so I went in to see about Rob. He had twisted himself into an armchair next to your cot and was asleep in that miserable position. He could scarcely move when he woke up. You, on the other hand, apparently were quite comfortable and sleeping like a—well, like a baby.

"I woke Rob and asked him why he wasn't in his bed, and he said you had only cried once during the night. He had expected you to make so much noise that he kept thinking something must have happened to you, and he had to check on you every few minutes. All in all you were a very well-behaved baby. But I don't think Rob got a good night's sleep for at least two years, anyway."

Jamie took a sip of water, and then set the glass down carefully. For some reason his hand was shaky. "So what are you going to do now?"

Richard looked down at the butter knife, ran his finger along its edge. "That's what I really wanted to tell you. Ruth and I...we're getting married."

Jamie fell back in his seat. "You're joking!"

"I love Ruth, Jamie, and I don't want to lose her. Anyway, I'm forty-three years old, and well, work just isn't enough anymore."

When Jamie was able to find his voice again, he said tartly, "Good thing for Ruth you feel so strongly about her. I mean, we know how you treated my mother when she was pregnant. And theoretically, her pregnancy had nothing to do with you."

Richard took a deep breath. "Jamie, I'm sorry Teresa ever told you that story—about what I did when she was expecting you. I would think your own mother would have wanted to spare your feelings, but I suppose she was more interested in making me look bad. But Jamie, I've tried to explain. I don't know what else to do. I thought we were past all this—"

"We are, we are," Jamie cut in. "Your wonderful news is just hitting a little too close to home, that's all. Look, Ruth's coming."

Jamie tried not to spoil the evening, which he now realized had been planned so they could celebrate Richard and Ruth's engagement. Ruth refused to take even a couple of sips of champagne, so he toasted them with Perrier water and ordered one of every dessert for Ruth to sample.

Richard shook his head as Ruth wolfed down a slab of cheesecake, but Jamie noted the glow in his eyes as he watched her. "This baby's the size of a pea," Rick teased her. "Not a good excuse yet."

"So, when are you actually planning to get shackled together?" Jamie asked.

"As soon as we finish shooting here," Richard said.

Jamie looked at him in surprise. "That's only a couple of weeks, isn't it?"

"That's right." Ruth was beaming. "We're planning on a week from

Saturday. And then we're going on a honeymoon to Hawaii."

Jamie stammered, "But—but, Rick, what about all the things that you still have to do for *Right Angle*? All the post production back in L.A.?"

Richard shrugged. "Sal is going to have to handle it this time."

"Sal! I mean, I realize that he's your partner and all, but has he got enough experience for you to leave him in control?"

"He's just going to have to figure it out." Richard took Ruth's hand. "We're going to be a family soon. And I want the two of us to have as much time alone together as we can before the baby comes." He turned back to Jamie. "I am sorry that *Conquest* fell through. Bill Vermeer is a slimy git. But I do wish you had something to occupy you right now. No chance at all of going sailing or hiking or something with Charlie, I don't suppose?"

Jamie grunted. "I don't think they give you time off from boot camp for a holiday."

Richard shook his head, looking amazed. "I just still can't believe that little idiot joined the Army."

"Yeah, well, Charlie's got his own issues, doesn't he?"

"Obviously." Richard stroked his chin and appeared to be thinking. "Maybe you should go back to England for a while. Just for a visit. Change of scene."

"Change of scene? I just left there. Anyway, Eric's too busy with medical school for me to hang about and distract him. I know, because he told me that constantly over the past three months."

"What about Warwick?"

"Well…Rose asked if her daughter and grandson could stay there a while. Her daughter's getting a divorce. So the house is rather full."

Richard's mouth turned down in disapproval. "So, let's see. You can't stay in your flat in London because you might disturb the caretaker—"

"Richard, Eric is my friend—"

"And there's no room for you in your house in Warwick because the housekeeper's family is staying there."

"She's not just the housekeeper, Richard." Quickly changing the subject, he said to Ruth, "You're not leaving yourself much time to plan a wedding, are you?"

"It's going to be a simple ceremony at my house. Just a few friends and family."

Jamie briefly pictured himself alone in a horde of Ruth's family. He asked hesitantly, "Do you have a minister lined up?"

"No, not really."

"How about Lee DeValery?"

"Absolutely not," Richard said firmly.

Jamie looked at him. "And why not? Are you saying that someone you choose out of a telephone book will be better than someone I suggest?"

"We won't be choosing someone out of a phone book," Richard snapped. "I'm sure that Ruth's family knows a suitable minister."

"Suitable?" Jamie repeated. "Meaning what? One who isn't actually religious?"

"Actually," Ruth said, "I know Reverend DeValery."

They both looked at her in amazement.

"I've met him, anyway—several years ago. I do some work with the animal shelter, and one of his daughters was helping with a pet adoption day at the mall. Lee DeValery came to pick up his daughter."

Jamie leaned forward in his seat. "So you know one of his daughters?"

"I don't really know her, although I think she's worked with us on two or three projects."

"What does she look like?"

"What does that matter?" Richard wanted to know.

Ruth furrowed her brow and thought. "It's funny, I can't really remember what she looks like. Except that she had long, dark hair, almost down to her waist. But frankly I have a clearer picture of Reverend DeValery." Ruth chuckled. "The one thing I do remember about this girl was that, at the end of the adoption day, we had two animals left that no one wanted. One was a huge dog, a Great Dane, I believe. And then there was a sickly-looking pregnant cat. We started to load them up to go back to the shelter, but she told us to stop and said she would take them home with her. Well, she was young, and we knew she still lived with her parents, so we didn't really figure that was going to work out. But when Reverend DeValery came, she had him wrapped around her finger in no time, and off they went, this gargantuan dog pulling Lee DeValery through the mall and the girl clutching this terrified-looking cat that probably presented them with five or six more within a couple of weeks. It was a riot!"

"What did you think of Lee?" Jamie asked her.

As she pushed away her third dessert plate, Ruth said, "I didn't meet him long enough to think much of anything, except I'm always impressed by an animal lover. Of course, you can't live in this town long without hearing things about Lee DeValery."

"Oh really?" Richard said archly. "What kinds of things?"

"He's involved in all sorts of causes. That women's shelter that Jamie's been working with, and other kinds of work with the homeless. Projects for the community food bank." Her eyes crinkled mischievously as she glanced over at Richard. "And a few that were more controversial. Organizing pickets of convenience stores that were displaying pornographic magazines in the open, where children could see. And he came out pretty strongly against some movie—you know, that one about the life of Christ that got everybody so worked up because it was supposedly so distorted."

Richard slapped the table and nodded at Jamie, as though to say, "There, you see!"

"All right, fine, forget it." Jamie sighed. "Your wedding is none of my business, anyway."

He turned his attention back to his food, but he could tell from his peripheral vision that they were looking at one another. When he heard Richard sigh deeply, he knew that Ruth had won the silent battle.

"Of course it's your business," Richard said. "Why don't you ask Reverend DeValery if he would do the honors for us?"

CHAPTER NINE

LEE DEVALERY WAS ALREADY STANDING AT THE FRONT OF RUTH'S LIVING ROOM, ready to start the ceremony, when Jamie dashed in and took his place next to Richard. Trying to ignore Richard's scowl, plus the excited twitterings from the other wedding guests at his appearance, he smoothed his hair and tie as best he could. He still felt disheveled, though. How he could have screwed up and overslept on Richard's wedding day was beyond him, unless it was some sort of Freudian thing, and subconsciously he'd wanted to give the whole thing a miss.

The radiant bride came in, and everyone's attention turned to her. Richard's frown was magically replaced by a goofy grin. If Ruth could continue to have that kind of effect on him, this wedding thing might not be so bad after all, Jamie thought.

The rest of the wedding went off without a hitch, and soon a glowing Ruth and a relieved-looking Richard had been pronounced man and wife. Jamie turned to speak to Lee but found himself carried away by a sea of Ruth's excited relatives. By the time he finished murmuring hellos, smiling and nodding and even signing a couple of autographs to earn his escape, he saw Lee and a plump, pretty woman that must be his wife edging toward the doorway. Breaking through the crowd, he made his way across the room and flagged them down.

"You're not going, are you?"

"Well, my job is pretty much done."

"You can't leave me alone with all these people!" Jamie smiled at the woman while saying to Lee, "Is this your wife?"

She stuck her hand out. "Hello, Jamie. I'm Marielle."

"Hello," he said, awkwardly shaking her hand. Then he grinned at Lee. "Not bad for an old preacher."

They all laughed, and they chatted for another moment. But when Lee again tried to say goodbye, Jamie said, "Look, Richard and Ruth will be going soon. Stay until then, all right?"

Lee looked at Marielle, and she gave a little nod. They spent a few more minutes in small talk, with Jamie telling Marielle stories of his unskilled exploits in carpentry under Lee's tutelage in the past weeks.

As Jamie tried to think of another story, Lee asked, "What are you going to do now?"

Jamie shook his head slightly. "What do you mean?"

"I mean, you've fulfilled your community service. Richard has finished his movie and is leaving town. So what are you doing next?"

"Oh, I'm going back to L.A., I suppose."

"Tonight?"

"No, tomorrow, probably."

"Are you starting work on another movie?" Marielle asked.

"No, I, ah—I don't have my next project lined up yet, I'm afraid," he said vaguely.

Just about then, Richard and Ruth reappeared after changing for their honeymoon. Richard was wearing a blazer and slacks, and Ruth had changed into a tailored winter white pantsuit. She stood on the stairs and threw the bouquet, which was fought over by two of her laughing nieces. Everyone followed them outside and threw birdseed as they made their way to a waiting limousine. And then Richard and Ruth were gone.

For a long moment, Jamie stood watching the empty space.

Lee cleared his throat. "Are you okay?"

"Of course. Why do you ask?"

"You look kind of like a deer caught in the headlights."

Jamie fiddled with his tie, trying to straighten it but making it worse. "I'm fine. It's just been a crazy day. Crazy week. Crazy year so far, actually."

He glanced up and saw that not only Lee, but also Marielle were studying him with looks of deep concern. She asked him, "You're not going to be alone now, are you?"

"Oh, well, it's just for tonight."

Another silence fell, and Jamie saw them exchanging looks, communicating silently—probably over whether or not they should ask him to dinner or something. He had to work hard to squelch a desire to tell them not to worry about it, that he had no desire to come anywhere near their perfect home or family or to contaminate them in any way.

Lee said gruffly, "Jamie, we appreciate your good work at the Village, and I—"

Larry Levy and his entourage walked past, drowning out the rest of Lee's words as they made very loud plans for sampling Atlanta's night life that evening. Levy made eye contact with Jamie, then deliberately looked away without speaking. It was such an obvious snub that Lee raised a questioning eyebrow at Jamie.

He gave a little shrug. "Artistic differences."

To Jamie's surprise, Lee blurted out, "Why don't you come home with us tonight? Have dinner with us?"

Marielle's eyes widened—probably with shock.

Jamie wanted to smile coldly and turn them down, but instead he heard himself stammering, "Oh, well, I—I should hate to impose at the last minute…"

"Oh, nonsense," Lee said, sounding more confident now. "It's no imposition, is it, honey?" He shot a look at his wife.

To Jamie's surprise, she smiled warmly. "Of course it's no imposition. That is, if you don't mind taking your chances on the food. I hadn't planned anything fancy—"

"Oh no, please, don't worry about that," Jamie assured her. He considered another moment, trying to hold onto his cold, righteous attitude. But it was no use. He took a deep breath. "All right, if you're certain. I'd like that very much."

"Great!" said Lee.

"That's wonderful," said Marielle—and Jamie tried to convince himself she didn't look a bit stressed under her smile.

They separated to go to their respective cars, then Marielle turned back to Jamie. "I'm sorry, but it just occurred to me…do you eat meat?"

He grinned. "Yes, I do. I just feel horribly immoral and guilty afterwards."

Marielle still looked uncertain. Lee leaned toward her and said, "That means yes. He eats meat." He then took his stunned-looking wife by the hand and led her back to their old Pontiac.

* * *

As Jeanine started up the back porch steps, she stopped for about the twentieth time just since leaving the car and tugged at her thigh-high stockings, which were slipping again. As soon as she got into the house she was going to yank the blasted things off, wad them up into a ball, and hurl them into the nearest trash can. It had been that kind of day.

Stockings in place for the moment, she continued up the steps, this time cursing the high heels that were making the balls of her feet ache. Jerking open the door into the kitchen, she sniffed the air in disbelief. "Oh, no. Please tell me I don't smell barbecued chicken." She addressed the remark to Mamma, who was standing in front of the stove, but barely glanced at the woman as she continued to grumble. "I swear, I cannot believe this stupid career fair. Do you want to hear about the only company that was interested in me? A poultry processing plant, can you believe that? The job's in their P.R. department." She kicked off her shoes for emphasis.

Mamma cleared her throat. "Jeanine, please, I need to tell you that—"

"I know, I know what you're going to say. It would be a perfectly honorable profession, and I've got to start somewhere, and what am I going to do with no experience, etc., etc. But I do have my limits."

"Jeanine, listen—"

"Working for a place that spends each day slaughtering small animals is definitely my limit." Propping her foot on a kitchen chair, she bent down over her knee, shoved her skirt as high up on her leg as it would go, and started to strip off one of the cursed stockings.

At that precise moment, the door from the hall swung open, and Jeanine glanced up, expecting to see either Daddy or Ginella. Then she froze, still bent over her leg, with one stocking pulled down to her ankle.

One figure standing in the doorway, eyes wide and hands clapped over her mouth, was indeed Ginella. The other figure, looking just as shocked, was…a hallucination.

Only explanation it could possibly be. Just as her mother had always warned her, she had pushed her mind too far, fantasized too much, and it had gotten stuck or something. Because her mind right this moment was showing her a crystal clear image of Jamie Newkirk standing in the doorway to her kitchen, inches away from her sister.

Ginella removed the hand from her mouth and giggled. Then, sounding strangled with laughter, she said, "Jamie was looking for somewhere to smoke, so I was taking him to the back porch."

Jamie? Oh, great, now she was having auditory hallucinations, too.

Ginella and whoever the other figure was—assuming there actually was someone else there, and Jeanine's brain wasn't completely making up a second person—started to edge past her toward the outside door. As they did, she jerked up into a standing position, trying to look as dignified as possible with one stocking pooling around her ankle.

The moment they were gone, Jeanine turned to face her mother, who was staring at her, a questioning look in her eyes. "Jeanine, honey," she said, "you do know who that was, don't you?"

Jeanine considered for a moment, not wanting to commit herself right away to an answer that might land her in a mental hospital. "I don't know," she finally said cagily. "Who do you think it was?"

For some odd reason, Mamma started to laugh.

CHAPTER TEN

Somehow, in spite of her wobbly knees and the sort of light-headed, druggy feel of her head, Jeanine managed to get herself upstairs and change clothes. Mamma had urged her to "put your blasted stockings and shoes back on and try to make good use of your looks for a change." But she just couldn't sit around her house dressed in a suit and high heels. It would be too phony, and she needed to inject a little normalcy into this otherwise bizarre evening. Besides, she had an overwhelming desire to cover up her legs.

She put on a pair of dark jeans and a white cotton shirt, an outfit that usually made her feel fairly attractive but still left her feeling like herself. She freshened her make-up and hair. Then she stood at the door of her bedroom for a few minutes with the doorknob in her hand, trying to make herself go back downstairs.

She had never been so terrified in her life. She had prayed for this very happening for half her lifetime, had prayed with a pure and absolute and unshakeable faith—and with a little kernel of realism that said it would never actually happen.

But it had. And it was bad enough to try to figure out what to do about Jamie Newkirk. The shocking thought that she might have the full and undivided attention of the God of the universe, expectant and waiting for her to do something brilliant with this marvelous gift—well, that was almost overwhelming.

When Jeanine got back downstairs, Mamma was in the kitchen alone. She glanced over at Jeanine. "You okay?"

"Yeah," Jeanine said shortly. "Don't I look it?"

"You look very nice, actually."

Jeanine raised an eyebrow. "Wow. Rare praise indeed." A sudden suspicion hit her. "Where's Ginella?"

Mamma turned to stir a pot on the stove. "Um…she said it was rude for us to just leave him alone like that. So she went outside with Jamie."

"'With *Jamie*'?" Jeanine repeated, noting how casually her mother referred to him. Then her sluggish brain managed to process the sense of what her mother had just said, that Ginella was outside cozying up to their guest, and she felt the butterflies in her stomach growing even more agitated.

Mamma studied her again. "Are you sure you're all right?"

"Of course. I'm just waiting to wake up and find Auntie Em and the farm hands standing over me."

Mamma smiled distractedly at her. "Okay, fine. So how about helping me cook?"

Ginella and the Visitor didn't come back inside until they were called to the dinner table. And of course, Ginella walked in at his side and slid into the seat next to him—which appeared to be fine with their guest of honor, who laughed and joked with her as they took their places. They appeared to have bonded already, Jeanine thought grimly. Surprise, surprise.

In a way, it was even harder on the rare occasions when Jamie Newkirk wasn't ignoring Jeanine, when he would glance over at her and flash a rather awkward smile at her. It was like suddenly having the full power of the bright noon-day sun turned on her naked body, exposing all its splotches and flaws for the world to see. The image of him was too bright for direct study. She had to fragment him, examine the graceful movement of his hands or the way his eyes crinkled when he smiled, then quickly look away before his outline was seared too deeply into her brain.

He was the most physically attractive person she had ever seen—even though he seemed to have a tendency to hunch or slouch in his chair that diminished him, somehow. The hair that she had considered black was actually the deep brown of pure coffee, much like her own. His dressy attire from earlier in the afternoon hadn't survived much longer than Jeanine's interview suit. His coat and tie had been discarded, the top button or two of his white shirt were undone, and he had rolled up the sleeves. Her mind traced a trail up the bare forearms, underneath his shirt, and she thought of the muscular, naked chest she had seen in films. She felt her face turning red…

"…Don't you think so, Jeanine?" she suddenly heard her mother's voice saying.

Jeanine snapped back to reality, as surreal as it had become, and looked around stupidly. All eyes were on her, as though waiting for some gem of wit from her lips. Mamma was wearing that firm, expectant look that meant Jeanine was supposed to do something. The woman had probably taken it upon herself, as usual, to drag Jeanine forcibly out of herself. *He* was looking at her, too. And she had no idea whatsoever what they had all been talking about.

"Uh…" she said brilliantly.

Ginella, of course, was happy to rescue her. "Jamie, I just adore your accent."

"What accent?" he teased. "You're the one with the accent."

"Hey, as long as we're in Georgia, you're the one with the accent," Daddy put in.

"All right, all right," Jamie conceded good-naturedly. "Although it's funny that you should say that. Whenever I go home to England now, they all say I sound totally American."

"Are you from London?" Ginella asked.

"No, from a town called Warwick, actually. Tourists go there because there's a castle that sort of looms over the town, and because it's near Stratford and Shakespeare's birthplace."

"That's quite a center for theater now, isn't it?" Mamma asked him.

"Yes, it is."

"So you came by your profession naturally, then. You sort of grew up in it."

"No, not really. I acted in *Romeo and Juliet* in Stratford a few years ago, and that was my first experience of the theater there. Richard's the one who lived and breathed all that."

Mamma said, "And how long have you been in America?"

Jamie thought for a moment. "Off and on since I was about twelve. And for the past few years, I'm in L.A. most of the time. But I still have a flat in London and a house in Warwick, as well."

"Wow." Ginella appeared dazed at the thought of so many houses. Then she gasped. "I just had a thought. We should have you read something for us after dinner."

"Like what?"

"Oh, I don't know. It doesn't matter. I just love hearing your voice," Ginella continued.

Jeanine's eyes met Mamma's, and they both gave a discreet shake of their heads, as though secretly asking each other, "What're we going to do with her?" Jeanine felt an uncharacteristic rush of kinship with her mom as she tried to focus on the conversation again.

Jamie was helping himself to more of Mamma's famous garlic mashed potatoes. "I thought perhaps you were asking for an impromptu Shakespeare soliloquy or something."

"No, we're not going to make you work for your supper," Daddy said.

"Oh, I don't mind. Acting is the only thing I can do, so I try to use it to my advantage whenever possible."

"Jamie," Daddy chided, "I've seen you doing any number of things these past two weeks. I believe you could do anything you put your mind to."

"Oh, well, thank you," Jamie said. "Could you tell that to Richard, please?"

"I'm sure your uncle knows how capable you are."

Jamie shook his head. "No, not really. Richard thinks I can act, but aside from that, he's amazed when I manage to tie my own shoelaces. I think Richard looks at me as some sort of idiot savant that he's going to have to take care of for the rest of his life." A slight pause, and then Jamie said rather grimly, "And God knows I've kept him busy at it lately."

The first truly awkward silence fell at the table. He had abruptly reminded them of what they had all been trying so hard to forget—or not think of. But now the questions about all his recent troubles hovered there over them, tantalizing them, daring to be asked. *What really happened that night? What happened to that girl? Are you really as charming and innocent as you seem right now?*

The questions were nudging Jeanine as much as anyone at the table. And yet, she felt a sudden rush of compassion, and such a strong desire to save him from the sudden ugliness that she actually found herself saying, directly to Jamie Newkirk himself, "It must be wonderful to be able to draw millions of people into a world that you created. To take them exactly where you

want them to go and make them feel things that you want them to feel—
what an incredible power that must be!"

Jamie looked at her. The moment of connection was so slight, so brief,
and yet it sent a chill through her. "Do you act?" he asked her.

This was it. The start of the conversation she really wanted to have with
him, rather than all this inane social chatter she was so terrible at. But the
rest of them were all watching closely. So she said gruffly, "No, I don't."

The answer had come out harsher than she had intended, and she could
see that it startled him. Still, he cocked his head and studied her. Suddenly
he straightened, pointing a finger at her. "I know you. You're Eve!"

"Wh-what?"

"In the painting, in Lee's office."

Heat flooded through her. She opened and closed her mouth, unable to
speak, although she wasn't sure why she felt so humiliated.

Ginella naturally decided she had to save the moment. She leaned toward
Jamie and asked, "Do you like living in L.A.? Or do you get homesick?"

Jamie appeared to tear his eyes away from Jeanine with difficulty.
"Oh…well…I'm not exactly certain where home is, so I can't very well get
homesick, can I?"

And then the two of them were off bantering again.

A tremendous weariness and lethargy settled over Jeanine, and she sank
down into her chair and just let them go.

Mamma eventually announced that it was time to serve dessert and
instructed them all to go into the living room to wait for cake and coffee.
Then she said in a sweet voice that meant trouble, "Jeanine, honey, why don't
you help me?"

Jeanine stood up and began to clear dishes with her mother. Neither of
them said a word until they were in the kitchen, and then there was a little
contained explosion from Mamma. "Why do you always do this?" she
demanded.

"Do what?"

"Act like a stone. Sit back with your arms folded and watch your sister
experience life."

Jeanine snorted. "Is that what she's doing now? Experiencing life?"

Mamma took a deep breath. "Okay, Jeanine, I'll admit that I didn't particularly care for either of you to meet this boy at all—"

"Yes, so I noticed." Her body clenched even tighter at the thought that Jamie Newkirk had been so close by, talking and working with her father for days, and Daddy had chosen not to say a word to her. Her head swam a little at the thought of such enormous betrayal.

Mamma chattered on. "But like it or not, he's here. And tomorrow he's going back to L.A. for good—"

"Tomorrow!" Jeanine placed her hand on the back of a chair, steadying herself.

"Yes, that's right."

Jeanine moaned, "This is horrible. One evening! That's all I have? Just this one chance!"

"Jeanine," Mamma said, "get a grip. You're getting to meet a movie star that you always wanted to. Loosen up and talk to him. Make a really nice memory for yourself. Then let it go." Mamma took a knife out of a drawer and said absently, "For once, I'm happy that you and your sister have a sweet tooth and the house is always full of junk food." With that, she started to slice a coconut cake that Ginella had made the evening before.

The after-dinner coffee in the living room was no easier than dinner had been. The more Jeanine told herself that she only had one evening in which to *do something*, the more she felt her brain freezing up. The truly scary part, though, was that Mamma still seemed determined to help her out—which eventually led to the biggest disaster of the evening. Maybe the greatest embarrassment of Jeanine's life to date.

It started when Mamma turned to her and said casually, "Jeanine, why don't you play something for us?"

Jeanine looked at her mother. For a moment the words made absolutely no sense to her. "What?"

"The piano," Mamma said slowly. "Why don't you play *the piano* for us?"

Jeanine felt herself flushing. "Oh, I don't think anybody would be interested—I mean, no, really."

"I'd love to hear you play," Jamie said.

Jeanine looked at him. Could he possibly be serious? "Well…if you're sure."

She stood up on shaky legs, then approached the piano. She had practically grown up at it, had worn out the bench with her bouncing bottom as she learned to beat out jazz and rock and roll. This was her favorite place in the house to be. She would touch the keys and establish a kind of mystical connection with it as music would flow out of her soul and into the piano and back into her body.

Today, however, the piano was not in a good mood. She could feel its hostility as she sat down and tried to think of something wonderful to play. Her mind was a blank.

And then Ginella tried to help. "Jeanine, why don't you play some Beatles tunes?"

Jeanine wanted to hug her. She remembered from fawning teen magazines that Jamie Newkirk was a big Beatles fan. She could start with something poignant like "The Long and Winding Road" or "In My Life," then move to "I Wanna Hold Your Hand," which was catchy and had a great beat but was much easier to play than it sounded—an enthusiastic banging of chords, really.

Unfortunately, Jeanine's fingers were as rebellious as the piano. Trembling with a beat of their own, they felt as stiff as wood as they scraped across the keys and made horrible discordant sounds. Finally, Jeanine did something she had been taught since her first piano recital not to do. She stopped in the middle of the tune and apologized. "I don't know what's wrong with me," she murmured.

Jamie Newkirk said, "Look, if you don't feel like doing this, you don't have to." He shrugged carelessly. "It's not important."

Jeanine felt as though icy water had slammed her in the face. She had been intending to pull herself together and try again. Instead, she got to her feet, every muscle in her back and legs feeling stiff enough to break. "Well then, I don't feel like doing this." She nodded to the room at large. "I have a paper due tomorrow and another one of these job interviews to get ready for. I think I'm going upstairs." She looked at Jamie Newkirk as briefly as possible and said, "It was nice to meet you."

He nodded politely, but she could tell he was bewildered by her whole performance. And she didn't mean the piano.

The excuse about the paper and the job interview was actually true. But for the next two hours Jeanine just lay on the bed in the dark and looked at her ceiling.

God had nudged and teased and worked together thousands of events and circumstances over the years so that she would have this opportunity, so that she and this beautiful boy, who had grown up in the shadow of a castle, would be in the same place at the same time. And what had she done with it? Nothing. It was over. Tomorrow he would disappear back into the void. She curled into a tight ball on the bed and listened to the happy laughter coming from downstairs.

Chapter Eleven

The following Monday, Jeanine drifted out of her first class, carried along by a sea of chattering students. Head down, she stared vacantly at their backs, not noticing anyone in particular until someone took her by the arm.

She jumped, startled, then saw it was Daddy. Her mouth tightened, and she said flatly, "Oh, hey. Did you come to have lunch with Mamma?"

"Well, yes. Something has come up that I need to talk to her about. But I'd really like to run it by you first. Have you got a minute?"

Jeanine cocked her head and studied him. She was still furious at him for his betrayal, but now she was also curious. Finally, she nodded and led him to a bench by the stairs in the Great Hall.

They sat for a moment in silence as Daddy licked his dry lips and cleared his throat. Then he said, "So, what did you think of last night?"

She hugged her chest with her arms. "I think it would have been nice if you had been honest with me all along about what was happening."

"I know, Jeanine, I know, but your mother and I talked it over and we thought it best—"

"You had no right to keep something like this from me. You knew how important it would be to me. And anyway, if I had been a little more prepared, maybe I wouldn't have made such a complete fool of myself."

"I'm sorry to hear that, Jeanine." Daddy sighed. "But for one thing, Jamie asked me to keep it quiet that he was around here. I considered the fact that he was working with the Village a confidence that I shouldn't share. I really thought it would be worse if you knew he was here but you weren't going to get to meet him." Jeanine remained sullenly silent, so he prodded, "But anyway, what did you think of Jamie?"

"I didn't think anything." She searched his face, now burning with curiosity. "Why are you asking me this?"

Daddy took a deep breath. "Okay, I guess I might as well just spit it out. Last night, when Ginella was entertaining our guest before dinner, they apparently took a walk around the property. You know how Ginella is. She probably managed to give him more information than a tour guide at the Alamo. Anyway, she pointed out your grandmother's house, and told him we were thinking of renting it. And for some bizarre reason known only to that boy and God Almighty, Jamie showed up in my office today asking if he could take the house for a couple of months."

Jeanine made herself be still, not move, not let the tiniest ripple of expression cross her face. It took her a long moment to get enough control of her breathing to say calmly, "And what did you tell him?"

"I told him I didn't know. That I would have to talk it over with Marielle. I also told him that you had asked about renting the place yourself after you graduated, but he assured me he would be gone by then."

Jeanine shook her head. "This makes no sense whatsoever. The guy owns three houses already, one in London and one on the beach in Malibu. He could go vacation at any luxury resort in the world. So why on earth would he want to stay in a tiny little cracker box in the middle of nowhere in Georgia?"

"I think the answer may be pretty simple, after all," Daddy said. "At any of those other places, he would be alone." As Jeanine started to shiver, Daddy's eagle eyes noticed at once. "Are you all right?"

"Of course I am. It's just—it's chilly. So…do you think Mamma would ever stand for it? Letting Jamie Newkirk live next door?"

"She's not going to like it. But I think our final answer is going to depend on you."

"What do you mean?" Jeanine demanded.

Daddy's gaze roamed around the hall, as though looking for the right words. "Let me put it this way. If it were only your mother and me involved in this thing, our main concern would be whether the boy was going to have wild parties over there or engage in any illegal activities or otherwise destroy the house, that sort of thing. But I told him this morning that if he rented the place, there were going to be some pretty stiff conditions and that I would have them written into the lease. As for Ginella, she'll find the whole thing exciting for a couple of weeks, and then she'll adjust and probably be bored with him and out looking for new conquests. But you—"

Jeanine raised her eyebrows. "Yes?"

"Well, Jeanine, your mother is just afraid that you've always been a little too emotional about this young man, even when you hadn't met him."

"Oh really?" Jeanine said. "So tell me, what do you think?"

Daddy looked her squarely in the eye. "No. You tell me what's going on. This passion that you've had for Jamie Newkirk over the years…was it just a crush on a good-looking movie star, just pure entertainment and fantasy? Or is it something else?"

Jeanine met his gaze without blinking…at first. Then she faltered. "If I answer that, you're going to think I'm crazy."

"Oh, I don't know about that. My definition of 'crazy' is pretty liberal," Daddy said. "Why don't you try me?"

Jeanine shook her head. "I'm not completely certain I understand it myself. All I can say is that…when we have missionaries speak at church, they'll say they have a burden for China or for the inner city or something. Well, I've always had a burden for Jamie Newkirk." She laughed weakly. "Trust me, I realize that makes me sound like a lunatic, but in my own defense, it would sound a lot crazier if the man weren't about to move into our house."

Daddy rubbed his temples as though they were aching. "Your mother won't find that very comforting."

"Oh, I know." She smiled at him. "Maybe you should stick with the 'harmless crush on a movie star' story. Tell her I didn't even particularly like him after I met him last night. Which is the funny thing. I'm really not sure I do like him." She stood up. "I'm gonna be late. Walk with me to my next class, okay?"

They had only climbed a couple of steps before Jeanine asked earnestly, "What do you think of him, Daddy? You've gotten to know him better than we have. Is he a decent person, or is he involved in a lot of sordid things that would really disappoint me?"

Daddy shrugged. "I think the answer is yes on both counts. I think Jamie is a person who is filled with good intentions but has no idea how to carry them out. And something is eating at the boy's soul, some little demon of guilt or remorse or fear or—who knows? We don't really know who he is, where the truth of all those stories begins and ends. But I also agree with you that he was sent to us for a reason. So how about it? Are you up for it?"

Jeanine stopped at the top of the stairs, rubbed her hand over the polished wood of the railing. "I'm not exactly certain what I'm supposed to do here." She looked up at him. "But sure. How could I turn this down?"

Daddy took her hand and squeezed it. "If we do this Jeanine, I'm trusting you to keep a level head and use good judgment."

Jeanine rolled her eyes. "Yes, Dad, keep stressing that. We all know how reckless I can be."

Daddy laughed. Then, squaring his shoulders, he faced the stairs to the third floor, where Marielle's office was located. "All right then. I'll go talk to your mother."

*　*　*

Jeanine may have had little to say to Jamie Newkirk when he was a dinner guest, but she took charge of getting the house ready for him. A three-year accumulation of dust and grime first had to be scrubbed away. Ginella and Mamma dropped in from time to time to help, but Jeanine did the bulk of the dirty work.

She laundered all the linens that went with the house and made up both beds with fresh, sun-dried sheets that were soft with years of use. After picking out two of her grandmother's hand-made quilts, she folded the one with the log-cabin design across the iron bed that had belonged to Emily, then put a colorful double-wedding-ring quilt on her grandparents' solid pine bed in the larger of the two rooms. At the end of the second busy day, she surveyed her handiwork and decided that it was good. Except…

Flowers and food. She had a vague idea that the British put a high premium on flowers, and as a Southerner, she felt that no one had been properly welcomed without food. So she decided to make a quick trip to the grocery store. She paused for a moment with her hand on the back door and surveyed the inside of the little cottage with a sense of wonder.

"Jamie Newkirk is actually going to stay here," she breathed to herself.

A wave of dizziness washed over her, and she felt as though her feet were about to float up off the floor.

"Grocery store," she told herself firmly. Nothing like the mundane necessities of life to bring a person back down to earth.

Or in this case, crashing back down. As she stood in line at the super-market, her basket full of two bundles of fresh-cut flowers and a few staples like cheese, milk, coffee, tea, bread, and fruit, Jeanine let her eyes wander over the tabloid headlines. The whole Jamie Newkirk scandal had pretty much run out of fuel lately—except for speculation as to where he was hiding out, which she now found extremely amusing—and so she wasn't expecting to see anything relevant.

And then there it was. A terrible photograph of Paula Klein and Jamie Newkirk. Jamie had his arm thrown over the model's shoulders, and they were both smiling broadly with their eyes half-closed, as though half-asleep, or stoned—or just caught by the camera in mid-blink, like a driver's license photo, Jeanine thought charitably. There was a similar candid shot of a beautiful dark-haired woman identified as Teresa Dane. The headline over the pictures was huge and blaring: "Two Deaths in a Malibu Beach House. Is There a Connection?" A smaller heading continued, "Coroner's Findings Suggest There Is."

Jeanine couldn't help herself. She snatched up the paper and hastily flipped the pages until she came to the article:

> Two healthy women in the prime of their lives are found dead in the same Malibu beach house in less than two years—a beach house belonging to one of the most beloved actors of our time, Jamie Newkirk. But that isn't the only connection.
>
> One of the most intriguing notations in the Medical Examiner's report concerned a small triangular pattern of burns found on Paula Klein's body, burns which had probably been inflicted forty-eight hours or more before her death. That in itself is an important finding.
>
> But there is another element to the story that makes it even more significant. Although it was not publicized at the time, the Medical Examiner noted a similar pattern of burns on Teresa Dane's body. The marks on Teresa Dane were believed to have been there for some time, perhaps months or years.
>
> Klein's death was found to be accidental, Dane's was ruled a suicide. But at least one person who is close to the Newkirks has his doubts.

"Jamie's the last one who saw each of them alive," a close friend pointed out. "And besides, what other connection is there between the two of them? They never even met. I've been Jamie's friend, too," he says, "but that doesn't mean that I can keep quiet about this. It's too serious. Teresa and Paula both— they deserve better."

This insider paints a disturbing picture of Jamie Newkirk, far different from the image that has won him the hearts of movie-lovers around the world. He recasts the young actor first as a heavy drug user himself, but one who could keep his own habits under control. But far more serious, he states that Newkirk liked for the women in his life to be dependent on drugs, themselves, as a way of keeping them in line. "He hates women," says this former Newkirk associate. "That's a simple fact. I think it started with his mother. He had a lot of anger toward her. I've been around Jamie when he was drinking pretty heavily, and his tongue would loosen up. And he would start to tell me all these things about her—how she'd used him just to get his money, that she only pretended to want him, things like that.

"The night of Teresa's fortieth birthday party," says our source, "I was there. She was doing great. She was on top of the world, having fun. And then something happened. Teresa and Jamie got in a fight about something, I think, because suddenly she was pale and nervous, and Jamie didn't look any too good, himself. Then everybody left but Jamie. Next day, she was dead."

And then there was Paula Klein. When asked about her, this insider said, "I know exactly when and how Paula got started on the heroin." He tells of a fateful night at a club on Sunset Boulevard when Paula Klein got her first taste of the drug that would eventually kill her—and was bullied into taking that first taste by her companion, Jamie Newkirk.

"I thought she looked like a scared little rabbit, nothing at all like that sexy, confident girl in those ads. And Jamie was in one of his moods. He's a really moody person. You'd never know it from seeing him on the talk shows.

"So then a few of us ended up in a little party in one of the VIP rooms at the club. I had no idea there would be drugs there, but when one of Jamie's other friends showed up with the stuff, Jamie certainly wasn't upset. It was obvious this was something that happened a lot with this little circle, although I don't think Paula had ever been a part of it, either. But she started to leave, and then Jamie got really angry with her. He put a lot of pressure on her. At one point he grabbed her arm and was holding her so tight that he must have left bruises. He said that, frankly, she needed something to loosen her up, and that if she didn't at least try it, they were through. I think Paula would have done just about anything to hang onto Jamie. I remember thinking, she really loves him. But she's scared to death of him, too…"

"Excuse me, Miss?"

Jeanine looked up, startled, and realized that the line ahead of her had emptied, she was next, and the irritated cashier was staring at her with her arms folded.

"Sorry," she murmured, hastily pushing her cart forward and starting to toss the items up onto the conveyor belt. For a moment, she didn't remember that she was clutching the paper in her hands, until the checker finished scanning her other purchases and asked her, "Do you want that, too?"

"Oh," Jeanine said, looking down at the tabloid. She hesitated only a second before tossing it to the cashier. "No, I don't want it. I've seen enough."

CHAPTER TWELVE

JAMIE PACKED UP HIS THINGS AT THE HOTEL IN PREPARATION FOR HIS MOVE TO the country, blissfully ignorant of the latest tabloid storm brewing. He did not, however, remain in that blessed condition long. An hysterical Lindsey and Richard both soon called him, and Lindsey emailed him a copy of the article.

With her usual directness, Lindsey demanded, "How could this be true, Jamie, about these marks on the bodies? How could there be any connection between Teresa and Paula?"

Jamie hesitated for a long moment. "I don't know, Lindsey."

She insisted he get back to L.A. and start taking the situation in hand. But the secret little cottage tucked away in the woods of Georgia suddenly seemed even more attractive, not less, and Jamie had no intention of changing his plans now.

"After all," he murmured to himself, "how much worse can it get? Unless, of course, they arrest and execute me. That would probably be worse."

And then came the greatest shock of all—more than the tabloid article itself. Elliott called.

For a moment, Jamie couldn't speak. Then he stammered, "Wh-what do you want, Elliott?"

"I'm worried about you, Jamie. I'm livid, actually. This article—how dare they drag Teresa into this mess! How dare they!"

Jamie sighed. "Yes, I'm sorry about that, too."

"Who was it—this brave 'anonymous source'?"

For a moment, Jamie considered just ending the call. Then he forced himself to relax and get the conversation over with. "No idea, really. What about you? Any ideas?"

"Well…" Elliott's voice dropped to a low murmur, as though he didn't even want to hear the words himself. "Could it have been Charlie?"

"Charlie!" Jamie dropped into an armchair next to the window. "Why would you—how could you even say something like that? He's my best friend."

"He's also my nephew, and I care about him. But he's not himself lately."

"Yeah." Jamie remembered his shock when Charlie told him he was actually hoping to be sent to Afghanistan.

Elliott was still talking. "And he…his attitude toward you…well, it isn't good."

Jamie wrapped the curtain's pull cord around his hand, twisting it tighter and tighter and watching his throttled fingers turning white. He didn't need Elliott to tell him about Charlie's resentment, either. Still…

"I don't think he would have done anything this low," Jamie said.

A brief silence, and then Elliott said, sounding overly cheerful, "You're probably right. Just forget I even suggested such a thing. I'm just worried about him, that's all. I wouldn't put anything past him, the state he's in." Elliott sighed dramatically. "Sometimes I wish it had never ended. The *Summer* movies, I mean. All of us working together, living together, just one big family. No wonder Charlie's having a hard time adjusting."

Jamie's voice was harsh. "But it did end, Elliott. Hannah Raney's dead. No more books. And you know the deal. No movies unless they're based on the books."

"It must be hard on you, too." Elliott's smooth voice was almost hypnotic as he continued, "Charlie's running off to be a real life hero. Richard can't concentrate on anything but his new wife. Your mother and Paula are gone. You must be feeling pretty alone. And now your career—"

"My career is fine. Or at least it will be. I just have to give it some time." It irked him that Elliott could almost read his mind.

"Maybe. Then again…well, sometimes I hear things. There could be a lot of Bill Vermeers out there, Jamie."

Just hang up on him. Jamie wanted to so badly, and yet he sat there, squeezing the phone in his hand and thinking uncomfortably that Elliott really did know a lot of people, really did hear things.

"Nobody understands like I do, Jamie. We're going through the same thing, aren't we?"

"What?"

"I've lost your mother, my partnership with Richard, and Charlie's deserting me, too, isn't he? So…maybe it's time for us to help each other. Who else do we have? Maybe the time has finally come for us to do that project we've talked about…you know, me producing, you directing. You might have to put up a lot of money yourself the first time, but I know a lot of other people that would want in. Vette Jackson, for instance."

Jamie stared out the window, the phone still pressed to his ear as he remembered a conversation with Richard a long time ago. He had broached the idea with his uncle of producing a picture and letting Jamie direct, and Richard had not only turned him down but had seemed livid at the very idea.

"Look, Jamie," he had said hotly, "there are people who would kill for the ability that you have. Do you know how badly Charlie would love to have your talent, and the opportunities you've had? So why do you want to ruin that, just let it slip through your fingers, and turn your attention to some other ridiculous pursuit that you're bound to fail at!"

And now Elliott's offer…how did Elliott know these things?

Elliott was still rambling on. "I just want to help you, Jamie. I've watched Charlie lose his career, throw his life away. I'm terrified that this Paula business might do the same thing to you."

A stab of fear sliced through Jamie, leaving him feeling shaky and nauseous. He forced himself to breathe, and spoke with more confidence than he felt. "Thanks, Elliott. But that's not going to happen to me."

As Jamie ended the call, his eye fell once again on the tabloid story that Lindsey had sent. He scanned for the tenth time the last line from the "inside source": "In my heart, I know that these two deaths were not accidents. But the police apparently don't have any hard evidence to go on. Who knows? We may never know the real truth."

After picking up the key from Lee's office, Jamie drove directly to the rental house. Lee had told him that none of the DeValerys were home now, and the whole place was still and quiet as he turned off the engine of the Ford.

Feeling a little like an intruder, he pushed open the creaky front door and looked around. The place was frightfully small, even in comparison to the suite at the hotel, but it was bright and welcoming. The windows had been left open and the sheers at the windows were moving slightly. He even found a fresh-baked pecan pie on the kitchen counter with a little note that said, "We're glad you're here. Let us know if you need anything else. Ginella." It must have been the friendly little blonde who had made the place so warm and ready for him, right down to flowers on the table and in the larger bedroom. It should have been a hopeful start for him.

But as he sat down in an armchair in the sitting room and listened to the quiet of the country, he thought rather desperately to himself, *All right, Newkirk. What now?*

CHAPTER THIRTEEN

J<small>EANINE FIDGETED AS SHE LOOKED OUT THE WINDOW AT THE</small> "N<small>EWKIRK HOUSE</small>," as they had all come to call it in the few days that Jamie had occupied it. The unseasonably warm day was perfect for starting on the flower beds. Every year since Mamma Sarah had gotten disabled, Jeanine had kept up the garden that had been the woman's pride and joy. Earlier in the day, she had made a trip to the nursery and bought a few rose bushes for planting, and the older ones were ripe for pruning. Her hands were itching to start digging and mulching. But Jamie Newkirk, blast him, apparently had no intention of going out, even for a couple of hours, so that she could run over and at least get started. It wasn't that she thought he would mind her puttering around out there. He was probably quite accustomed to having servants around taking care of things. But she didn't really care for the idea of working in the yard when he might be watching.

She hadn't even seen the guy since that first disastrous night at dinner. Apparently he had spent another evening at her house, but she had been jamming with Trev's band at the time and had missed it. Ginella was constantly running next door "to check on him," as she put it, but Jeanine didn't have that kind of nerve, especially after their humiliating first meeting. So, precious days had gone by, and every day her mind would wander in class and she would feel a terrible pressure settling on her chest as something inside her screamed, "Do something!"

But what?

Sometimes, she really found it hard to believe that Jamie even existed. She would be up studying at night or playing the piano, and she would look over toward the Newkirk house, and the windows would be as dark and empty as before he moved in. She used to know that Jamie Newkirk was real, before he came here. Now she wondered.

She took a deep breath and squared her shoulders. Well, time to find out. She marched across the yard and tapped on the back door. At first there was no response, so she knocked a little harder, and the Presence himself finally came to the door, looking red-eyed and disheveled. He gave her a nervous, confused look and said uncertainly, "Oh, hello. Jean, right? Or Jeannie?"

"Jeanine."

"Oh yes, of course. Jeanine."

She crossed her arms. "I'm sorry. Did I wake you up?"

"I, ah—" He cleared his throat and tried to smooth his hair. "I think I had fallen asleep, actually. I'm not sleeping all that well at night but I seem to be able to fall asleep in the daytime whenever I stop moving."

"So why don't you just sleep in the daytime?"

It was a genuine question. She had often thought that she would like to do just that, herself, if she could manage to get classes or work at night. But the words had come out sounding pretty snotty. She felt defeated again. "Look, I didn't mean to bother you. I just wondered if you'd mind if I do some gardening in the—in your yard."

"No, absolutely. Of course you can."

So she awkwardly took her pruning shears and started to cut back the rose bushes that surrounded the front porch—with Jamie Newkirk sitting in the porch swing and energetically watching her.

After a few minutes, he said, "I feel awfully guilty just sitting here watching you work. I'd be happy to help you if you tell me what to do."

Jeanine stopped and shoved her hair out of her face, certain that she was smudging on a streak of mud as she did. She leaned back on her heels and looked at him. "I thought the English were enthusiastic gardeners. I would think you could be giving me some pointers."

"Sorry. I grew up in a garage, I'm afraid. When my father wanted to potter, he did it with motor bikes."

Jeanine considered for a moment. "Well, my transmission is making a funny noise."

He smiled at her—a real, genuine smile. "No problem. I'll take a look at it later. You've a great car, by the way. A sixty-six, isn't it?"

"That's right."

"That's my hobby. Classic cars. I wouldn't mind having a Mustang myself. Except you need to put in a firewall. Have you done that?"

"A what?"

"There's precious little between the gas tank and the back seat. You should get your dad to take care of it straightaway. It isn't expensive."

She smiled back at him, "Okay, thanks. In the meantime, you any good at hauling pine straw?"

"Sounds brainless enough for me."

It was almost the moment that she had been waiting for. Jamie hopped down from the porch and was leaning over to hear her instructions when a car pulled up in the yard. An exquisite blonde got out of the driver's seat and started to pull out a couple of grocery bags. She looked at Jamie with mock irritation. "So do you wanna help me with these or what?"

"Oh, sorry." He looked at Jeanine as she struggled to rise up out of the dirt and achieve at least a slightly more dignified height. "This is Debbie. She was a hair stylist on *Right Angle*. I asked her to pick some things up for me."

"Yeah, and your order from the liquor store alone was enough to give me a hernia," Debbie complained.

"I'm just going to help her get these groceries and uh, and things in," Jamie stammered to Jeanine. "I'll be right back."

He wasn't right back. Jeanine started lugging loads of pine straw and spreading them on the flower beds and around the rose bushes herself. After about half an hour she had finished what she thought was most urgent, and frankly she didn't think she could take much more today. She stood up and started to dust the dirt off the seat and legs of her overalls. It was a quite ungraceful action, so naturally Jamie and the Amazonian blonde came out of the door just at that moment.

Jeanine sheepishly dropped her hands to her sides as he looked at her and said, "You've not finished already, surely?"

"For today."

"Everyone's going at once," Jamie fretted.

"Well, sweetie, if I didn't have to get to work, I assure you, I would stick around as long as you wanted me to," Debbie cooed.

"I thought all the film people had gone back to L.A.," Jeanine said.

Debbie tore her eyes off Jamie with obvious effort. "I'm not from L.A. I work for a salon in Atlanta. But sometimes I get film work in the area. I also have a sister here in Middleboro." She looked at Jamie again. "So I get down here from time to time."

"Ah…interesting," Jamie commented vaguely.

"Or I'm sure you'll be wanting to come up to Atlanta," she continued. "Not much to do around here, trust me. Oh, that reminds me. I've got some great connections in Atlanta, if you need me to get anything else for you—if the liquor's not enough."

Jamie flushed and glanced in Jeanine's direction. "No, no, that won't be necessary, I assure you."

"Yeah, well, no problem. I guess you probably do have access to better stuff than I do, anyway. What am I saying?"

By this point, Jamie was red in the face and was practically leading Debbie by the elbow to her car. They muttered a few more words to each other as the girl got inside, and then, mercifully, Debbie was gone. Jeanine was hoping to be out of the Newkirk yard by that time, but before she could get completely away, Jamie jogged to catch up with her.

"Sorry about that," he said. "Look, you can come in for a while if you like. I'm stocked up now, I can probably find something to offer you."

Before Jeanine could think clearly, she blurted out, "Oh, I doubt that I'm interested in anything Debbie brought you. But thanks anyway."

She started walking up the slope to the DeValery house, but Jamie darted around her to block the way. For a moment, she was jolted by how angry he looked. He was breathing hard as he said to her in a low voice, "I really wanted to get along with Lee's whole family, but you're just impossible, aren't you? What a judgmental little—I mean, I'm sure you think you know all about me because of everything you've been hearing and you think that gives you some kind of right to, to—but you don't know me at all. You don't know anything about me."

Jeanine's heart was pounding, but she stood her ground. "Actually, I think I know you very well."

"Oh, really?" he demanded.

She considered him for a long moment. Finally, with the voice of a prophetess, she began to pronounce, "When you were very, very young, just a very small child, you thought that you were eternal. There was no sense of a beginning to you, and no knowledge of an end for you or for anyone around you. You just were. You had always been a child in Warwickshire,

England, and your dad had always been the dad, and it would just go on like that forever—like one of those comic strips where the family just keeps having new adventures week after week and year after year, but no one ever ages or changes or moves away or dies. You were living in a beautiful, innocent garden, and time stood still.

"And partly that sense of timelessness was because every day of your life held a thousand years. By the time you sat down for breakfast, you had visited whole new worlds—incredibly bright, technicolor worlds that you had created and filled with fantastic creatures and heroic people and breath-taking trees and flowers and rivers to cross. Sometimes you felt so powerful, you felt like a god. Everything around you was so alive that it practically vibrated with the energy of it.

"And then, suddenly, when you were somewhere around the age of seven or eight—you can almost look back and put your finger on the day—things speeded up. Not so lovely things started to come into your life. First of all there was a kind of isolation, because one by one, all your friends around you started to lose the gift that you had all shared—the ability to create, the ability to see. It was like watching them all go blind one by one, and you waited for it to happen to you. But it never did. The colors were as bright and as unearthly for you as ever, only you had to keep it to yourself because no one else could see them, and you didn't want anyone to think you were crazy. Sometimes you even wondered if you were insane.

"And other bad things started to happen. Things changed. People came and went out of your life. Every day seemed shorter and less solid than the day before, there was a constant sense of acceleration, of the scenery passing by you in a blur. You learned about accidents and illness, and the really big one—death. And life was very bleak for a long time.

"But then there was another cataclysm, something wondrous and amazing. One day, someone put you on stage, and they told you that the thing that made you different was actually a wonderful gift, not something to be hidden. You were the one with sight that could give some relief to all those others who had gone blind. You could show them the world through your eyes. You were absolutely thrilled to have that feeling again, that feeling of communion with other people, of knowing that you were taking them along with you to some fabulous land. You were powerful again, you had control. You were free! Not stuck in one soul or one situation or one world like the vast majority of humanity, but at least for those times that you were on stage, truly free. For a while, you could make time stand still again."

Jeanine finished her speech—and time did seem to stand still as they regarded one another, motionless and speechless. Jamie looked absolutely flabbergasted, and now that Jeanine was finished speaking, she was startled, herself. Where had all that come from?

The cool, authoritative voice of the prophetess was completely gone as she said shakily, "Well, I'm...I'm going home now."

Jamie nodded wordlessly. She could feel him watching her as she walked the rest of the short distance to her own home.

CHAPTER FOURTEEN

So many pleasant phone calls this week, Jamie thought, looking glumly toward the ceiling of the little cottage as he listened to Richard's voice blasting him all the way from Maui.

"You never cease to amaze me!" Richard declared. "When I talked to you the other day, you didn't tell me that you were going to be more or less living with this fundamentalist preacher. What's the matter with you!"

"Nothing," Jamie said. "I've nothing to do in L.A. and nothing to do in London and nothing to do here. So what does it matter where I choose to stay—to you or anyone else?"

"Now you've put your finger on it," Richard crowed. "You've nothing to do. Precisely. Jamie, you simply must get back to work."

"Well, that would be wonderful, but just what is it you think I should be doing right now? I would have been happy to start on *Conquest*, but unfortunately that's no longer an option. And no one is exactly beating down my door right now with other offers, are they?"

"And whose fault is that—"

"Don't, Richard," Jamie broke in quietly. "I'm just not in the mood, all right?"

"All right, all right, I'm sorry." There was a slight pause. "Do you want me to come home?"

"No, of course not, don't be silly," Jamie said. And then he made himself ask, "So how's the honeymoon going?"

"Fabulous. A few bouts of morning sickness to deal with, but otherwise wonderful."

"Well, I'm sure you'll feel better soon," Jamie quipped.

A few more amenities to wind down the conversation, and this latest encounter with Richard ended. Jamie glanced at his watch and saw with some surprise that it was after midnight. So it was only six in Maui. Richard had rung him just after coming in off the beach, while he and Ruth were dressing for dinner. Soon they would be seated together in candlelight, Jamie imagined, maybe in one of those restaurants that are open on the sides, where the breezes blow in a mingled fragrance of sea air and hibiscus. He pictured Richard and Ruth laughing as they attempted to order the fresh catch of the day—some local fish whose name had at least nine syllables, all of which consisted only of a's and h's and u's—and he felt a stirring of envy.

So go there, he told himself. *You could drive right now to the airport and get a ticket and be on the beach on Kauai tomorrow. Rick and Ruth are on a different island. They would never even know you were there.*

But instead of going to the airport, he went to bed, pulling the curtains back from the already-open window because the tiny room felt close and stifling. He studied the darkness in the direction of the ceiling for a while, then miraculously felt himself starting to relax and drift off toward sleep…

But he never actually arrived there. Instead he got stuck in that dangerous twilight state between sleeping and waking, when the defenses of the body and mind were completely down and absolute truth could flood in. When he was younger and it seemed that every day brought some bizarre new development, in his waking hours, none of it seemed quite real. But in those drifting moments at night, he would suddenly realize with shock, "I'm famous!" Or his mind would whisper to him, "You live in America now. You'll never really go home to England again."

On this night, as he drifted into that twilight country, his unconscious mind immediately started to fire the arrows: *They're really dead, you know. They're rotting in the ground right now.* He drifted past his mother, reclining on her bed and looking peaceful until he got close enough to see the sickly white of her face, the droop of her open mouth.

He jerked and shifted in the bed, relaxing again as the picture changed…Paula at that screening, the first time he'd ever seen her…her eyes sparkling as she plopped down next to him and said, "You just lost your mother, didn't you? I'm so sorry." In his mind, he was kissing her—that first time, her skin smooth and scented like jasmine. But suddenly, his roaming hands felt the sharp angles of skeleton elbows and ribs, and as he pulled back in horror, she collapsed onto the floor in a heap of thin skin and bones, staring vacantly up at him the way she had when he found her that morning, tortured and broken and dead…

Heart pounding, Jamie wrenched himself back to full consciousness. He gulped in lungfuls of air, struggling against the dark and quiet of this blasted place. But after a moment, he had to laugh. *Remember that quiet country living you were so keen to try?*

As he turned on a lamp and scrambled to find his cigarettes, he glanced at his watch in amazement. Only twelve forty-five! Well, fat lot that had accomplished, he sighed, as he went out onto the porch to smoke.

He leaned back wearily in the old cane-bottomed rocker. It required such an act of will to keep the pictures and sound bites out of his mind. Sometimes he was just too tired, like now. Closing his eyes, he allowed his mind to start the mash-up of random memories.

…Seeing his mother for the first time, when she'd recognized him in his first movie and then had come back for him. He'd been playing football in the park, and his security people were all around that day, keeping the starry-eyed pre-adolescent fans at bay. And yet, Teresa managed to penetrate all his defenses and get through to him, as though she were a not-quite-solid mist drifting through the crowd. He walked off the playing field late in the afternoon, the sun low in the sky and practically blinding him, so that he saw her at first just as an indistinct figure moving in the blazing light. She stepped toward him, blocking the sun, and all at once she was clear, distinct, recognizable. He knew her right away from a small picture that he had, and from her obvious resemblance to him. The sight of her nearly knocked the breath out of him. "Hello, Jamie," she said softly. "Do you know who I am?"

…Finding that fabulous flat for Teresa when he was fourteen, loving the way that her eyes shone with excitement and knowing that, even at that young age, he could provide for his mother like a man. The warmth that he had felt as they spent two days hanging pictures and unpacking and talking and laughing. He'd known he was coming home at last, in spite of all the nasty things Richard was saying—that she only wanted his money, that she hadn't cared about him until he was famous. But Rick was wrong, he'd known it, and time would show them all.

…Waking up in that same flat one morning to find Elliott Dane making breakfast in the kitchen with Teresa, the two of them laughing and touching and occasionally even exchanging a kiss. When they spotted Jamie, their smiles didn't dim, and they didn't look the least bit ashamed, even though it was obvious that Elliott had spent the night—and even though Elliott was still married to Charlie's Aunt Phoebe. Jamie had felt a knot forming in his stomach at that moment, a knot that didn't ease for all the weeks that Elliott and Teresa carried on in front of him, while Charlie remained blissfully ignorant. Somehow, Jamie had felt that if he relaxed his clenched muscles the least little bit, everything would fall apart. Charlie would find out about his uncle and Jamie's mother and he would blame Jamie somehow—maybe for not telling him. Maybe the aunt—whom Jamie had only met a couple of times, because it was always Elliott with Charlie when they were filming— would react violently. Maybe she would hurt his mother, or never let Charlie work again. Charlie had said the woman was spiteful. And then…

Nothing like that had happened.

In the rocking chair, Jamie felt himself relaxing, growing sleepy again as he finally came to a good memory. Teresa and Elliott's wedding before a Justice of the Peace, with no guests except him and Charlie, who beamed with delight because he and Jamie were going to be brothers of a sort. And a few days later…the four of them attending the premiere of *Summer Storm* as a family…Teresa the most excited of all with her first Versace gown, her black hair sleek and shiny and her white teeth flashing with laughter as they'd sailed through the night in the limo, then stepped out one by one to a roaring crowd of fans. That had been the best night of his life…

Jamie's mind lifted up, sailed over the red carpet and the fans, out over the hills and toward the beach and the glass house, drifting over his mother lying on the bed, looking peaceful until he got very close.

Again he yanked himself to consciousness. Again he struggled to breathe. As he did, a light popped on in the DeValery house, on the second floor.

He gulped in a deep breath, focusing on the light. That had been one of the most comforting things about stopping here, that the house next door never seemed to shut down. Every night until the wee hours, one light would go off upstairs, another would come on down below. It was comforting, as though someone were keeping watch. Although he suspected that the one who was really responsible, who moved through the house at night trailing darkness and light in her wake, was the dark-haired DeValery girl. The scary one. The little witch who had given him that oracle or prophecy or whatever it was. The piano belonged to her, and he would hear it at all hours, the alternately jazzy or somber strains drifting out of the DeValerys' open windows and carried on the night air like a concert from some ghostly clime.

Sure enough, a light came on downstairs, and the piano started up directly. Scott Joplin selections tonight. *Solace*, he believed it was called. She was quite good, the music almost haunting. Why on earth had she been unable to play for him that first night?

He laid his head back against the wooden rocking chair and felt the tightness in his head—as though there were muscles in his brain that he could clench—starting to relax. After a long while, *Solace* came to an end, and he waited for the next selection, but there was only silence. He raised his head and looked. The lights were still on downstairs in the DeValery house. What was she doing now? If only it were Ginella who kept these odd hours, it would be perfect. He could go over there, tap on the window, call her out for a nice chat, take his mind off things.

He fidgeted for a long moment before standing up and crossing the dark yard. As the old saying went, any port in a storm.

He rapped on the wood beside the DeValery window and was wickedly gratified to see the dark-haired girl jump at the sound. She jerked around toward the window, and then saw him. After the tiniest hesitation, she crossed over to him, unfastening the latch and pushing it up.

"Hello," he said through the screen.

"Hi."

"Umm…could you come outside for a minute, please?"

Another pause. "Okay. I guess." As she moved away from the window, he went to meet her at the porch. She stood up at the top of the steps, and he stood on the ground at the bottom. And there they were.

There were times that Jamie wished he could carry a really good writer around with him who would feed him all his lines. This was one of those times. As the girl studied him coolly with those fathomless dark eyes, he went completely blank. Finally he stammered, "So. What are you doing up so late?"

"Umm…I was reading."

"Oh, yes? Something good?"

"Well, it's a class assignment."

"Oh, right, right."

After another moment, the girl asked, "Are you okay?"

"I'm fine," he said. "Just—I suffer from insomnia on a fairly regular basis, actually, and tonight…well, I was hoping to find someone to hit me over the head with a blunt instrument or something, I think."

Jeanine looked down at the book she was still holding in her hand. "I could read *Moby Dick* to you. I find the experience very much like being hit in the head with a blunt instrument."

Jamie chuckled. "But I thought *Moby Dick* was supposed to be the great American novel."

"If it is, heaven help us. I just finished an entire chapter about ambergris, which is apparently a highly valued substance found in the intestines of sick whales. A whole chapter! This is why I put off taking American Literature until the absolute bitter end. I just had a really bad feeling about it."

"What have you studied that you like?"

At this point, Jeanine apparently saw that this was turning into an actual in-depth conversation, and that it was going to be a while before she could figure out what the devil Jamie was doing on her doorstep at one o'clock in the morning, so she sat down on the top step pulling her sweater tight against the cold. Jamie, in turn, plopped himself down nearer the bottom, then turned so he could look up at Jeanine's face.

"I like English literature, actually," she said.

"What in particular?"

"Oh, lots of writers. Jane Austen, Dickens. But my favorite is *Wuthering Heights*. It's all about love that turns into obsession—beyond all bounds of reason."

"I'll have to read it." Jamie thought for a moment, then said, "I've read quite a lot of Dickens. I have an especial fondness for The Artful Dodger. One of the first characters I played, at least professionally."

Jeanine smiled a little. "I know."

"And then, of course, Danny Summer. He's a lot like the Dodger."

"He's sort of like the Artful Dodger, except…there's also such a sweetness and nobility to Danny's character. His quest to save his mother and sister, the sacrifices he's willing to make along the way. The way that he takes charge of all those other kids and helps them start a new life. Wow. He's a fantastic character. Or I don't know. Maybe it's just the way that you played him."

Jamie grunted. "Well, thank you. But obviously the pathetic bloke that gave him a body has been a major disappointment to you. I'm sure you never expected me to turn out to be a convict in real life."

"Technically, I guess, you never went to jail."

"I did for a few hours while I was waiting for Richard to post bail."

Jeanine wrapped her arms around her knees and drew them up close to her chest. "Yeah, well, I haven't been to jail, but I know what it's like—on a small scale, of course—to live in a fishbowl. I got sick of being the preacher's kid by the time I was six or seven years old and decided to just try to fade into the walls and not draw attention anymore."

She tossed her hair back out of her face in one smooth motion. "Jamie, I am sorry. I truly am. I know I've been rude and just…inexcusable since you've been here. But it's not that I don't like you or don't want you here. Not even that I'm disappointed."

"Then what?" he said, trying to sound casual.

"It's—it's really hard for me to explain," she said slowly.

She fiddled with her hair for a minute, pushing it back behind her ears as she nervously seemed to try to form her next words. In spite of the uncomfortable conversation, Jamie admired the wavy dark mass as she lifted the tendrils and let them fall back into careless disarray. Her hair wasn't as long as Ruth had mentioned, but it swung down past her shoulders as she leaned over her knees again and said in a low voice, "I guess the simplest way to say it is that you make me nervous."

"Me! Make you nervous?"

"Of course you do. Look, I'm not exactly a social butterfly in the first place, and you—well, it would maybe be like you suddenly having the queen move into your house. It cramps your style a little."

Jamie laughed, for some reason feeling relieved.

There was a long silence. Jeanine flipped the pages of her novel, and Jamie wistfully fingered the pack of cigarettes in his pocket. Dragging his hand away from them, he said, "So. Whatever happened to the Great Dane and the pregnant cat?"

Jeanine looked at him in surprise. "What?"

"You know, the pitiful refugees from the pet adoption day that you rescued. I loved that story."

"Daddy told you that!"

"No, Richard's new wife. She was there."

"Oh, I remember now," Jeanine said. "Ruth Christopher. I knew her name sounded familiar when I heard about the wedding. Well, the Great Dane went to live on a farm belonging to one of our church members. We also managed to find good Christian homes for all the kittens. The cat is asleep on my bed at this very minute and is very appropriately named Trouble. I thought my mother was going to kill me when I showed up with them that day."

"It was very heroic of you."

"Yeah, well, I can't resist a helpless stray." She grinned. "Speaking of which, if you can't sleep, do you want to come in for a while? It's freesing out here. We could watch a movie or something."

"Movies depress me," Jamie declared.

Jeanine cocked her head and looked at him. "Did it ever occur to you that maybe you're in the wrong profession?"

"It's a recent development. I find it very difficult to watch other actors who still have careers."

"Oh. Well then, come on in and read *Moby Dick* to me. You'll probably be semi-conscious in minutes and I can actually do something useful like knit while you read." She smiled wickedly at him and, in a perfect imitation of her sister's voice, simpered, "I just love the sound of your voice!"

"All right, all right." Jamie took the teasing with good humor but made one more token protest. "Your parents won't mind me hanging about with you in the middle of the night?"

She shrugged. "Why should they? If they can sleep through my television and piano-playing, a little reading aloud won't bother them."

Jamie raised his eyebrows. "That wasn't exactly what I meant."

As his meaning hit her, Jeanine blushed such a bright red that Jamie could see it even in the dim light from the kitchen window.

"Oh, well," she stammered, "in addition to the fact that the idea of you hiting on me is pretty absurd, I should mention that my father also tends to wander around the house at all hours of the night. So we won't exactly be unchaperoned."

"All right. If you think he won't mind…or beat me up…or shoot me."

Jamie reclined on the DeValerys' worn but comfortable sofa and read aloud for about forty-five minutes. He actually found himself getting caught up in the story. When he paused and mentioned this fact to Jeanine, she just said philosophically, "Oh, well. Maybe it's a guy thing." She laid her knitting aside and stood up from the armchair. "I'm going to go get a Coke. Want something?"

"Yes, thank you, that sounds fine. Jeanine?" She paused near the doorway as he said, "I've been meaning to tell you since we first met in your kitchen. You've got sensational legs."

If possible, her blush went an even deeper crimson. She again turned to leave the room and walked straight into the door jamb. She looked at him rather helplessly, rubbed her injured nose, then managed to get out the door and head to the kitchen. Vastly pleased with himself, Jamie went back to reading *Moby Dick*.

Chapter Fifteen

Jamie opened the back door of the DeValerys' house without bothering to knock and was instantly swept into the rapid current of activity that marked each weekday morning in their kitchen. Bodies swept in and out, hurried instructions for the day were called, toast popped up, coffee brewed, hands grabbed. Trouble rubbed against his leg in a sly bid for scraps. It was lovely.

Marielle was the first to spot him. By now, she seemed to take his appearance at this time of the morning as perfectly natural, and she no longer bothered with the niceties of "good morning" or "how are you." She did, however, study him rather critically and say, "You're starting to look like a pirate."

He touched the fledgling beard on his face. "It was your daughter's suggestion. It's like a disguise."

Marielle rolled her eyes. "Do you want breakfast?"

"Well, I am out of food again, and I don't think I'm sufficiently overgrown to risk a trip to the market yet. Jeanine said I should come have breakfast with her."

Ginella, who was sitting at the kitchen table eating a bowl of cereal, laughed. "Jamie, someone should warn you. When a Southern woman starts worrying about what you're eating and tries to feed you, you should run."

Jamie felt himself flushing as Marielle shot her younger daughter a look.

Then Marielle said to him, "Surely you didn't think Jeanine would be up yet."

Jamie smiled sheepishly. "No, but I was hungry."

Lee came in just then. "Jamie! Just who I wanted to see."

"Oh, really?" Jamie said. "And why would that be?"

Lee stood at the counter and started to pour himself a take-along cup of coffee. "Because I have a little project you can do for me."

"What?" Jamie asked warily.

"Jeanine has full instructions and can tell you all about it." Grinning, Lee managed to balance the cup of hot coffee while picking up a stack of books and papers. Jamie opened the kitchen door for him as he edged out and added, "Don't worry. You'll love it."

Jamie sighed. "Now I'm really worried."

Marielle and Ginella cleared out within minutes. Jamie knew he had truly arrived when Marielle said, "Just help yourself to anything in the kitchen. We're late, okay?"

He poured out coffee for himself and sat sipping alone for a few moments, his eyes repeatedly drawn to the water-color of Jesus above the table. The caption read, "And ye shall know the Truth, and the Truth will make you free." Finally he turned sideways, sat facing the door into the hallway, and thought about the fact that Jeanine was curled up sleeping in a room somewhere above his head. When he couldn't stand it any longer, he bounded out of the kitchen and to the staircase. He climbed a few of the steps and called in a sing-song voice, "Jeannie, get u-up! I'm here for breakfast."

He listened. The lack of response from upstairs was positively deafening. So he shouted, "It's ten o'clock in the morning and you've overslept and you're going to miss your classes and never graduate and ruin your life forever and—"

"All right, all right!" he heard her snap. "I'll be down in a minute, okay?"

She was down in five, which was fairly close. Her face was pink from a recent dousing, and her hair was pulled back in a voluminous pony tail. She was wearing a pair of jeans and an oversized black sweatshirt with the Atlanta skyline painted on it in glittery gold.

After pouring herself a cup of coffee, she plopped down into a chair at the table. "You are a liar and a scoundrel. It's only eight o'clock in the morning, and I don't even have a class until three o'clock this afternoon."

"Oh, really?" Jamie said.

"Why are you so chipper, anyway?" she said grumpily. "You couldn't have gotten much sleep, either. Daddy and I were up talking around two-thirty this morning and we saw that your lights were still on. I was surprised you didn't come over."

Jamie shrugged. "Actually, you should be flattered. I was reading *Next Summer*."

Jeanine set her coffee cup down, splashing some onto the table but not seeming to notice. "My manuscript? Oh, no! What did you think!"

"I'm really amazed. You've a real grasp of the characters—Danny Summer and the other original ones, I mean. The characters you added are intriguing, too, and I could really have seen the series going this way if Hannah had lived to continue it." Jamie drained the last of his coffee. "I must say, though, I'm not quite certain why you did it. Half of a book-length manuscript—you must have put an incredible amount of work into it. But you did know, didn't you, that no matter how well it turned out, someone owns the rights to the characters, even though Hannah Raney is dead? Not really a project with a future."

Jeanine laughed at him, and he raised an eyebrow.

"What?"

"You! You have no grasp of the real world, do you?" she said.

"What do you mean?"

"Jamie, if you come up with an idea for a movie or book, of course people are going to be interested." She shook her head. "It's different for the rest of us. I guess you would technically call this fan fiction, although I never post any of my stuff on the fan sites or anything. I've written a few stories about Danny over the years, but when Hannah Raney died, I couldn't stand it. I didn't expect Danny's story to just end like that. It really depressed me for a while."

Jamie let out a breath. "Yeah, tell me about it."

"The only way I got around it was to realize that Danny didn't die with the author. I figured I could finish the story—at least to my own satisfaction. So that's why I did it. More or less because I had to. Does that make sense?"

He nodded. "Yeah. It does."

"Mmm…Jamie? I was wondering something."

"What?"

"Well…from that first night when I listened to you read *Moby Dick*, I've wondered. Would you read some of my manuscript out loud to me? I mean, hearing your voice—Danny's voice!—actually speaking my thoughts…"

Her eyes were glowing as she finished, and for some reason that Jamie couldn't quite identify, he felt uncomfortable.

But he said lightly, "Doesn't seem too much to ask. Of course I will. Oh! That reminds me. What is it that your father has up his sleeve for me today?"

"Oh, that. There's a woman in our church named Carol Albright. She has three small children, no husband, a low-paying job, and an ancient Chevrolet that's on its last legs. Which apparently needs a horrendously expensive repair. Something about piston rings. A ring job or something?"

Jamie whistled. "That's pretty major, all right."

"Anyway, she called Daddy last night in hysterics after getting an estimate on the job. She doesn't have the money, but she's got to have the car to get back and forth to work, or she's going to have even less money. You get the picture."

"So where do I come in?" Jamie asked. "Does he want me to pay for it?"

"Oh, that would be far too simple for Daddy." Jeanine laughed. "What would that do for your character? As I heard him explain it, the reason it's so expensive is not the parts, it's that it's so labor intensive. So if we could find someone with the expertise and a lot of free time on his hands…"

Jamie stared at her. "You must be joking."

"What's the matter?" Jeanine said. "Isn't it something you can do?"

"In theory."

"Good then." Jeanine got up from the table and opened the refrigerator. "Let's have breakfast, and then I'll take you to Deak's Garage. Deak Rollins said we could use one of the bays there. One of his mechanics is on vacation, anyway."

"We?" Jamie echoed.

"Oh, I wouldn't miss this for the world! I can tell my grandchildren that I saw the great Jamie Newkirk working on cars. So. What do you want to eat?"

"Doesn't matter. Toast is fine."

"No, no, you need more than that. You don't eat enough." She pulled out a frying pan. "I'll make eggs."

Ginella's warning flashed briefly through Jamie's mind, then he mentally shrugged. "Do you have any sausages?"

Jamie wolfed down his food while Jeanine picked at hers and sipped juice. "You are so slow!" he teased.

"If you're bored, you can read to me now."

"I left your manuscript at my place. I haven't finished it yet."

"I wanted you to keep that, anyway, to remember me by. I've still got the original."

And so, shortly afterward, Jamie started to read to her. Within minutes, he found the old familiar voice of Danny Summer starting to flow easily out of him. As always, he became absorbed in the character and the setting, like falling down a well and finding himself in another place and time. But when he occasionally went to turn a page and briefly glanced up, he could see that Jeanine had stopped eating and was completely focused on him, frozen and still and yet, somehow, almost vibrating, as though she were about to float up off the chair.

He stopped and smiled at her.

"What?" she asked him.

"I've got an idea. This next part is mostly dialogue. Let's do a reading, like it's a script. You read Tess."

"No, I just want to listen," she protested.

"Oh, of course you don't," Jamie said.

After a few more token protests on her part, they started. Jeanine was at first distracted and wooden, still concentrating more on watching and listening to Jamie than on doing her part. Finally he rolled up the pages that he was holding and spatted her on the nose. "Are you going to play with me, or do we stop?" he asked.

Flushing, she got down to business. And suddenly, it all started to flow. Jeanine's story started where Hannah Raney's last one had left off, with Danny acquiring through twisted means a Virginia farm for his young charges to work and hopefully keep them out of trouble. But Jeanine had, of course, thought of all sorts of country mischief for them. There was also trouble for Danny, mainly in the form of Tess, the aristocratic daughter of the adjoining plantation.

In the scene they were reading, Danny had engaged Tess's father in a lively poker game the night before and had theoretically won the plantation from him. Danny didn't take this particularly seriously, but then Tess showed up in his kitchen early the next morning, taking it very seriously indeed. So seriously, in fact, that she announced to him, "I love that farm. It's been in our family for generations. It's a part of us, a part of who I am. So I decided last night what I have to do. I'll simply have to marry you."

Danny was less than thrilled. "Are you completely mad? Me! Marry you!"

"Of course," Tess said. "It's the obvious solution."

"I cannot believe you!" Danny continued, dazed. "In the past year, you have personally taken a horse whip to one of my lads—"

"He was trying to look through my window when I was dressing."

"Nearly broken my foot by running over me with your blasted horse—"

"That wasn't intentional."

"And shot at me when I mistakenly took a few steps over your property line. I suppose that was accidental, too."

"Well, no…but I didn't hit you, did I?"

"And now you march in here and tell me that I'm going to marry you, as though I had absolutely no say in the matter. I don't want to marry you!"

An infuriatingly knowing little smile came across her face. "Oh, of course you do."

The scene continued, Jamie and Jeanine giving voice to Danny and Tess as they verbally sparred, the air practically crackling with electricity. And when the moment in the scene came for an abrupt, passionate kiss, Jamie didn't even think. He just leaned forward to Jeanine and pulled her toward him…

And she met him eagerly, her lips those of the confident and aggressive Tess. And then he found his mind slipping, the spirit of Danny leaving him as plain, ordinary Jamie started to wonder just how far she would take this, how far Jeanine would let this fantasy go.

Shakily, he pulled away without finding out. He heard himself saying, "I'm sorry."

"No," she said breathlessly, "no, that was—it was incredible."

He squirmed and looked down at the manuscript, away from her flushed face and shining eyes. A picture of that fan girl outside the Malibu house was flashing through his mind—the one holding the sign that said, "I would die for you."

Shaking off the memory, he cleared his throat. "Well…I suppose we really should—I mean to say, we've got a date at the garage, haven't we?"

The job at the garage actually took Jamie two days, particularly since he was being extra careful. He had never had a family, including small children, depending on his work. Jeanine dropped in and out and handed him tools and provided moral support.

Late on the second day she observed, "Daddy mentioned something in a sermon once. He said that an intimate time to a woman is sitting in candle-light with her man and having a deep conversation about their hopes and fears. But to a man, it's having the woman sit by and hand him tools while he works on his car."

Before Jamie could respond to this, Deak Rollins called over to them, "Jeanine, your daddy's on the phone. I think he wants to know if y'all are about finished. He wants to bring the lady to pick up her car."

"Umm…I think so. Yes, yes, it's all right. Tell him half an hour," Jamie said. Then he glanced over at Jeanine and whispered, "But don't tell him we've been intimate. He'll have a coronary."

In twenty-eight minutes, Jamie closed the hood and stood wiping his hands on a rag. "This car is still not in great shape, and when I drove it a while ago the gearbox—the transmission—sounded wonky. It'll probably go any time. It probably would have been simpler for me to just buy her a new car."

"Don't worry." Jeanine laughed. "When Daddy figures you've put enough work into it, he'll probably let you do just that."

"I'm going to go get cleaned up a bit while you wait for them," Jamie said. "I don't want to be here when they come."

"Too late."

Lee was entering the work bay, followed by a tired-looking woman and three completely non-tired children who were running circles around the two adults and taking an occasional laughing swipe at one another. Jamie felt an urge to run.

"Don't worry," Jeanine murmured. "No one could recognize you through all that grease."

There was some truth in what she said. He felt as though he had bathed in engine oil. What with that, his overgrown hair and beard, and the Braves cap which Jeanine had given him to replace the reviled Dodgers one, he probably looked such a natural part of the garage that the woman wouldn't give him a second thought.

However, Carol Albright studied his face as she thanked him profusely for his help. "You have literally saved our lives," the woman declared. "Well, you and Lee together."

"I didn't do anything," Lee protested. "The congregation contributed the money to the emergency fund that bought the parts, and Jimmy Joe here did the work." Lee grinned widely at Jamie as he said the name, which Ginella had gleefully tagged on him the previous week when they discovered that his middle name was Joseph.

Jamie nodded, patiently putting up with the teasing, and then Carol Albright said thoughtfully, "I've been thinking you look familiar. Have I seen you at the church?"

Jamie was opening his mouth to answer in the negative when the oldest of the little girls, who appeared to be around ten years old, said, "He looks like Jamie Newkirk to me."

Carol looked at Jamie again. "You do look a little bit like Jamie Newkirk."

Jamie smiled sheepishly and looked down at his toes. Then, affecting a Southern drawl, he said, "Yeah, I get that all the time."

"Do you really?" Jeanine said. "I don't see it myself."

Later, when they were in the car and heading back to the DeValery-Newkirk estate, Jeanine punched him in the arm and laughed. "I truly believe you were this close to saying 'Shucks, ma'am.'"

Jamie gave her a look. "I thought my performance was brilliant, personally. It worked, didn't it? And how did you like the accent?"

"Well, it was maybe a little more Tennessee than Georgia, but otherwise, fairly natural." Her voice changed slightly. "You're really incredible, Jamie. I mean—even that garbage that I wrote. You make it so powerful."

"I was just pleased to be given any sort of role again. You're the only one who's made me an offer lately."

"That's not true. I've seen that stack of scripts that your agent sent."

Jamie huffed. "What a load of rubbish! They obviously think I've been moved to the bargain basement." He ran a hand through his now-shaggy hair. "But it has been…difficult. Heroin addicts like Paula, when they're going through withdrawal, sometimes they talk about a horrible feeling, as though things are crawling under their skin. I've seen Paula almost mad trying to make it stop, scratching at her skin until she was bleeding. I know this sounds absurd, but I can almost understand that feeling. The craving for a good part, a role, is almost unbearable at times." He took his eyes off the road and glanced at her. "You know what I mean, don't you? From your writing?"

"Sure, I know," Jeanine said. "Sometimes it's hard for me to sit through an entire class and listen to some idiotic lecture, because my mind just wants to sneak off somewhere else. That's why I've always loved summer.

Everything alive and free again—including me. You finish up your tests and close your books and have all those warm, golden days just to dream and play and create and be whoever you want to be." She said wistfully, "That's why I hate the idea of starting to work a job. Having to sell my thoughts and my brain to someone all day, every day, every season with no end in sight, just seems obscene somehow." She was quiet for a moment. "Somehow this all reminds me. You do know that my first performance with Shady Lane— that's Trev's band—is this weekend, right?"

"I remember. After that, you'll have another addiction."

"No, no, I'm more the writer type who lurks in the background and controls everyone," Jeanine said. "But this should be fun."

Jamie cocked his head and studied her. "I've been thinking you reminded me of someone, and now I think I know. My friend, Charlie."

Jeanine's eyes widened, which made him see the resemblance to Charlie even more in the expression, in the shape and shade of her golden-brown eyes.

"You don't mean Charlie Edenfield, from the *Summer* movies!"

"I do."

Her features relaxing, she laughed. "Funny you should say that. Charlie Edenfield and I have the same birthday."

"Really? Your birthday's July 30, too?"

"Not just that day, but same year and everything. Maybe we were twins separated at birth."

"Uh…what? What do you—how could that be?"

She slapped playfully at his hand. "I'm kidding, silly. Although, who knows? I am adopted, so maybe I have some mysterious past like in all the books and movies."

Now Jamie felt his eyes widening with surprise. "You're adopted? Really?"

"Really."

She spoke matter-of-factly, as though the topic didn't bother her. But she also changed the subject. "So, are you going to be there when I make my debut?"

Jamie was startled. "Jeanine…sweetheart, you know I'm not actually going out in public right now."

Another little silence, and then Jeanine smiled at him. "Yeah, I know that. It's okay. I guess I just got a little carried away by the past few days."

"It's been lovely, Jeannie, and I am sorry—"

"No, no, don't be silly. We're playing a dance at school, not Carnegie Hall. I'm sure it's all pretty small potatoes to you, anyway."

"No, of course it's not," Jamie protested as he pulled the car into the drive shared by both their houses. "Look, would you like to come in for a while?" He switched off the engine. "I can make tea—after I've taken a long, long shower, of course."

"No, thanks," Jeanine said. "I've got class." She slid out of the Taurus, flashed him a quick smile, and disappeared into the DeValery house.

CHAPTER SIXTEEN

JAMIE DIDN'T APPEAR FOR BREAKFAST THE NEXT MORNING. JEANINE FELT A LITTLE pang at his absence, but dressed and went on to class without bothering him. The house next door looked dark and quiet, and she figured that Jamie was sleeping late. But when she got back from the college late in the afternoon, the Taurus was gone.

As that day and the next went by, it became obvious that Jamie had left without a word to any of them. And worst of all, there was no way of knowing when or whether he would be back. At dinner, Jeanine sat silent and pale as the other members of her family tried to figure out what was going on.

"Well, to be absolutely fair, he's not required to tell us where he's going or what he's doing," Daddy remarked, carving the roast beef with gusto. "He's not a house guest, he's renting the place from us. He can certainly come and go without having to explain to us."

"Yes, but I thought Jamie was the type that would be courteous enough to explain, whether he was required to or not," Ginella said between bites of salad.

"Coming here was a whim," Mamma said. "So one morning he got up and another whim took him off somewhere else. He may have even been intending to come back, but he won't. He'll get caught up in this and that and get back to his real life. We won't ever see that young man again, you mark my words."

Jeanine saw Daddy looking at her, deep concern in his eyes. She forced herself to breathe normally, to shrug her shoulders and let her lips tilt up in a rueful little smile; gestures that clearly meant, "Oh well, it was nice while it lasted." His look of relief was her reward for not doing what she really wanted to, which was roll around on the floor and scream in hysterics.

Daddy might have been the hysterical one, however, if he had seen Jeanine creeping out of the house after midnight, armed with the landlord's key to the house next door. She had no excuse for using it. Jamie's car was gone and Jamie was gone and there was no worthy reason for her to be in his house. But she had to look, had to see if there was some clue as to the reason for this sudden, bewildering development. Some indication whether he was gone for good.

She felt some relief as soon as she entered. His books, his laptop, his clothes were still here. He must at least be planning to return. Then her eye fell on the answering machine.

She had thought it was odd when Jamie had a landline phone installed, since he was only planning to be here a few weeks and had an iPhone besides. Jamie explained it was partly so he could get internet service from the phone company, but also because he didn't like giving his cell phone number to a lot of people. Right now, the little digital answering machine was lit up with the number "two," but it wasn't flashing. So there were two messages on it that he had played but not erased. After hesitating a moment, she gave in to temptation and pushed "play."

First she heard a deep male voice. "Mr. Newkirk, this is Lieutenant Regis of the Los Angeles County Sheriff's Department. We've got a situation out here…something I need to discuss with you. If you could call me back as soon as possible. Thanks."

And then a vaguely familiar female voice said cheerily, "Hi, Jamie, it's Debbie. It was good to hear from you, and even better to hear that you're finally coming to Atlanta. In answer to your question, I'll be glad to meet you. I think I've got exactly what you need right now."

Jeanine stood for a moment, listening, but there were no more words, no more messages. She turned off the lights, locked the door of the house, and went back home.

When she got up the next morning, her heart jumped for joy at the sight of the Taurus parked in the dirt driveway next to the little stone cottage. But there was still no sign of life at the house.

You know he got in really late, she told herself, *because he wasn't home at midnight. So maybe he's just sleeping.* She felt slightly nauseous as she thought about who he had probably been with the night before and why he hadn't gotten any sleep, but she tried to put that unpleasant image out of her mind.

When Jamie hadn't appeared or opened the curtains or windows by about four o'clock, she'd had all the wondering and worrying that she could stand and marched next door. She rapped on the back door, then waited. When there was no answer, she pounded. After another long wait, she marched back home, fetched the key and let herself in.

She had never seen the inside of this house so dark and gloomy. There was an immediate feel to it that something was wrong. At the same time, the place was so small that she could hear Jamie's heavy, even breathing coming from the bedroom to her right.

A few weeks ago, she would never have had the nerve to barge into Jamie Newkirk's bedroom uninvited. But now she not only let herself in, she also bent down over him, put her hand lightly on his bare shoulder. "Jamie?" When there was no response, she shook him. "Jamie? Jamie!" Absolutely nothing.

The room felt stifling, as hot as a furnace. She could feel herself starting to sweat, and her head felt as though it were about to explode from the pressure as she tried to decide what to do. What was the matter with him? Was he ill? Had he taken something? If she called an ambulance and there was nothing wrong with him, he would never forgive her for drawing attention to him. The gossips would know where he was, the beasts would be tearing at him again…

But what if he were dying? "Oh, God, please tell me what to do!" she breathed.

She decided to call her father over and get his opinion before actually dialing 911, since Jamie was breathing. She reached for the phone on the nightstand and was just starting to dial when Jamie stirred.

He propped himself up and looked at her groggily, and then, after clearing his throat two or three times, said gruffly, "What the devil are you doing here!"

She hung up the phone and looked at him. "I was worried about you. You didn't answer the door and I—"

"I didn't answer the door because I was trying to sleep," he snapped. He sat up heavily on the side of the bed, started to rub his temples with his hands. "I took a pill to help me sleep, all right?"

"One pill?" Jeanine echoed in disbelief. "Jamie, it's four o'clock in the afternoon!"

He stopped rubbing at his eyes long enough to look at her. "And what business is it of yours if I decide to sleep all day? What are you now, my mother?"

Jeanine felt an ache starting in her chest, her throat. "Jamie, what's the matter? Everything was so nice the last few weeks, I thought we were getting so close. And then you just disappeared without a word. What's wrong? What happened?"

Jamie reached for the pack of cigarettes on the nightstand, lit up, then leaned back against the pillows. "You really want to know what's happened?"

"Yes, I would like that very much."

"What's happened is that I went to sleep in my own home, and I woke up to find an intruder standing over me, that's what's happened."

"Intruder?" Jeanine repeated.

"What would you call it?" Jamie demanded. "I don't recall giving you a key. Look, Jeanine. My privacy is extremely important to me. You can't imagine. I have to be on constant guard, or else I'm overrun with the paparazzi and weirdos and stalkers and—"

"And which category do I fall into?" Jeanine asked sourly.

As Jamie started to stammer some answer, she put her hands up and started for the door. "No, don't worry about it. I won't bother you anymore, I assure you."

She hurried out, trying to get away before she lost her dignity and let this strange new Jamie see the tears that were starting to well up in her eyes; tears of utter bewilderment as well as hurt.

She was sitting in the porch swing with an open copy of *The Scarlet Letter* and staring out at the woods in back of the house when Ginella came and sat down in a chair next to her.

"You okay?" her sister asked softly.

Jeanine opened her mouth to assure her that she was fine. Instead, she heard herself saying, "I don't know. I'm pretty confused, actually."

"So tell me."

And Jeanine did just that, filling her sister in on the details of the past week. How close she and Jamie had become. The sudden change in him, including his unexpected anger at her. The messages on the machine.

Ginella listened intently, and when Jeanine had finished up, she frowned. "I hate to say this, but those stories in the tabloids back in February…well, that supposed friend of his said how moody Jamie is, how he would turn on Paula Klein and his mother—even said that he does drugs. You and I just brushed all that off as lies, but, I don't know. It's beginning to sound like there could be at least a grain of truth in all that, don't you think?"

Jeanine shook her head. "I don't know. Maybe. How do you pick the truth out of all that noise, all those different people yelling their version of what's real? The truth may be in there somewhere, like the spice in a stew— but how do you pick just the pepper out of a bowl of soup?" She slapped her hand down on the seat of the swing. "It isn't supposed to be this way, Ginella. He isn't supposed to go running off to somebody else when he needs help."

"Jeanine, that's a real nice thought, but the truth is, maybe you just aren't the one to give him what he needs. Or thinks he needs."

"And what would that be?"

"Who knows? Sex. Drugs. The point is, maybe you should be glad he went elsewhere. I mean, we really don't know him at all, do we?"

Jeanine wouldn't answer that. She just looked pensively over at the little house next door, its windows dark and lifeless and utterly empty.

CHAPTER SEVENTEEN

JAMIE CREPT INTO THE BALLROOM AT THE COLLEGE STUDENT CENTER AND glanced around at the hordes of partying students. Even though the lights were dim and he was bearded and shaggy-haired, he was certain one of them would notice him eventually. He drifted into a dark corner and was huddling there alone when Jeanine came onstage.

He supposed the rest of the band came on with her, but he never saw them. He only saw Jeanine, as she moved with the fluid motion of a cat to the microphone. Caressing it with her fingertips, she started to sing.

She didn't seem quite real somehow, an exotic creature of light and sound. Her voice was the most solid thing about her—at times, an angry pounding fist and, at times, a gently stroking open hand. He noted her sexy stance, the way she occasionally tossed her hair back over her shoulders. The moves were confident, sensual, totally unlike Jeanine—and yet, vaguely familiar after all.

It came to him in a flash. Tess! It was Jeanine's alter-ego, the same spirit she had put into the land-owner's daughter. And Jamie felt warmed all over, as though he and Jeanine were sharing some secret. Not even Jeanine's band members, cranking out the tunes and trying to keep up with her, understood.

Then Jeanine spotted him in his corner, and he saw the Tess veneer waver. Jamie had a vague memory of an ugly scene the last time he saw Jeanine, and he hoped she could see his apologetic smile. He inclined his head toward the glass door that led out onto the patio, and, hoping she understood to meet him there when she had a break, escaped into the darkness outside.

* * *

Jeanine found him sitting on a bench in a shadowy area where the pools of illumination from the security lights did not reach.

"I can't believe you came," she said.

"I wouldn't have missed it." He patted the seat next to him. "Sit down with me."

"No, I'm okay. I'm too wound up."

He pushed his hair back off his forehead and sighed. "Jeannie, I'm so sorry. I truly am. My behavior these past few days has been abominable, I know. My only excuse is that, well, I had another one of those nasty little jolts I can't seem to avoid lately."

"Oh, really?" she said coolly. "I'm sorry to hear that." *And if you think I'm going to ask you, you're crazy.*

She was wickedly pleased to see him squirming on the bench.

"When you came over," he said, "I was…well, I wasn't myself. I'd been worried and I hadn't slept at all, and finally I was so exhausted by it all…I really needed some sleep…"

His voice trailed off, and there was silence again. Finally, in spite of herself, she asked him, "So what happened? What were you so worried about?"

"Oh, it's stupid, really. But a police detective called me. It seems that Allison Klein, Paula's mother, just won't let this whole thing rest. She's on them constantly, especially since all this started about there being some supposed connection between Paula's and my mother's deaths. Every day it's something different. First she wants my mother's body exhumed, and then she demands that they arrest me. And so on, and so on. Lieutenant Regis was actually quite nice to me. He thinks it's all absurd and that Allison's a pain in the neck, but he thought I should know what was going on. After he called, I just…I couldn't get it out of my head. I finally decided to meet with my attorney."

"Oh, you were in California?" Jeanine said doubtfully, remembering the telephone message from Debbie saying how happy she would be to see him in Atlanta.

"No, Ira flew to Atlanta. I met him there. Why do you sound so surprised? Where did you think I was?"

"I wouldn't know, would I?" she snapped. "So. What did your attorney say? He doesn't think they're going to arrest you again, does he? I mean, what would be the charge?"

"No, Ira thinks I'm in more danger of a civil suit—you know, wrongful death. Ira said that, if Allison finds the same witness the tabloids used, she might at least say I was responsible for Paula's drug habit. Allison's got detectives out, nosing around and trying to see what could be pinned on me. It isn't over, by any means."

"Why didn't you just tell me?" Jeanine asked flatly. "I thought we were friends. I think I deserved better than this."

"You're absolutely right," Jamie agreed. After a long moment, he said, "I didn't want to tell you, and that's the truth of it. I hate there are all these sordid things in my life, and I know you think of them and wonder about them. You must. And I didn't want any of this to come up between us. I just keep hoping it will all go away."

Jeanine shook her head slowly. "I can't tell you how bad that makes me feel, Jamie. I thought we were a lot closer than that, but obviously I was wrong. Look, I should be getting back inside."

"No, don't go yet, Jeannie." He took her hand to restrain her as she started to turn back toward the building. "Please. Look, you're absolutely right. We are closer than that. The last few days have been torture and I realized how much I needed you with me, how much I've come to lean on you. Will you give me another chance? Please?"

Jeanine felt herself weakening. She sat down on the bench next to him. "Well, it was nice of you to be here for me tonight. I know how difficult it was for you."

"I couldn't stay away. And I'm glad I didn't. You were incredible! You have an amazing talent, you know that, don't you?"

She couldn't help but smile at him. "Do you really mean that?"

"Of course I do." He said abruptly, "Jeanine, a few weeks ago, when we first met—when I said you didn't really know me, and then you started to tell me all those things about myself—"

"Oh, yes. That." She felt her face growing warm with embarrassment. "I'm sorry. I've been amazed that you haven't brought that up before now."

"No, but I've thought about it quite a lot. And tonight I realized something. When you told me all those things, you weren't actually talking about me at all, were you? You were talking about yourself."

Jeanine shifted on the bench, looked off into the distance. "It's funny. When I was a little girl, around the time that I first started school, I was popular. No one could think up a good game or story for make-believe like I could. All the other kids were drawn to me. I was their leader.

"But then when I got to be about nine or ten, all the other kids started to be, in my opinion, horrendous bores. Emptied of something vital, somehow. The boys were only interested in sports, and the girls were only interested in boys. I kept waiting for myself to change, to grow up and lose it all. But it never happened, and I more or less found myself alone. The odd thing was, I knew that I was smart enough and good enough at pretending that, if I wanted to, I could pretend to be like them and fit in again."

"But obviously you didn't," Jamie said.

Jeanine turned her head so that she was once again facing him in the semi-darkness. "It was just such a waste of time. I wasn't interested. I could either come home and be happy losing myself in some story that I was writing about Danny Summer, or I could be with somebody boring and mundane and real like the boys in my class, pretending to be somebody I wasn't. No, it was an easy choice." She laughed a little and said, sounding rather sheepish, "As I got older, I kept thinking that if I could ever just meet Jamie Newkirk, he would understand the way I feel. I'll bet he would be just like me." She looked at him. "So was I right? Those things that I said to you— were they true?"

"For the most part, yes," Jamie said slowly. "Eerily so."

"But?"

He didn't answer her. She could feel more than see him studying her face. Normally, this would have would have made her squirm with insecurity. But not tonight. She tossed her hair back over her shoulder, glared back at him boldly, and demanded, "Well?"

She was surprised to hear him laugh at her. He touched her face lightly. "You're still doing it, aren't you? And you don't even know that you are."

"Doing what?"

"Tess! You're absolutely gorgeous tonight, do you know that? Come here."

He pulled her face toward him and started to kiss her. For a minute, she couldn't help herself. It was the dream of a decade; he was warm and solid and real under her touch. She eagerly responded to his kiss, lifted her hands to his shoulders and felt the muscles under his shirt, touched his hair and noted how fine and silky it was against her fingertips…

And then, from out of nowhere, that little voice from the answering machine ran through her head again. "It's Debbie…and yes, I do have what you need."

She pulled away and stood up. "I'm sorry, Jamie. But if this is what you need to cheer you up and help you sleep tonight, you were probably right the first time. I'm not what you need."

Jamie laughed again. He reached up and took her hand. "Jeannie, if you somehow interpreted that little kiss as meaning that I'm trying to get you into bed, then I assure you, you're wrong."

So much for going bold. She slumped and stammered, "Oh, well—of course you're not! That would be—what a stupid idea."

Jamie grinned at her. "There's just no pleasing you, is there?" His voice softened. "Jeanine, I want you very much. I think about it all the time. But I wouldn't do that to you." Making an obvious effort to sound light, he said, "First of all because somewhere in that nine-volume treatise that your father called a lease, I think there was a phrase that said, 'Don't even think about my daughters.' And secondly, I wouldn't do that to you because, because— look, are you sure you want me to share all my sordid little secrets with you?"

"I'd like you to know you can," she said earnestly.

"Well then…" He took a deep breath, then blurted it out. "I think I have AIDS."

Jeanine stared at him, horrified. "You what!"

"Yes, I think so," he continued quietly. "Or the virus that means you're going to have AIDS, or whatever."

Jeanine's voice was shaky. "Why do you—what makes you think that? Have you been tested?"

"No, but, I don't know. I haven't felt truly well in a long time. And just think about it, Jeanine. The things I've been involved in…" His voice drifted away in the darkness again. She heard him take a deep breath before starting again. "In the first place, my girlfriend was an intravenous drug user. That little discovery was enough to scare the wits out of my uncle. And then, well, apparently when I thought I was being so wonderful by trying to keep Paula's drug supply down and was righteously denying her the money for it—when she couldn't get the money from me, she apparently managed to get it from other men in exchange for certain services, if you follow my meaning."

"Oh, Jamie, I—I don't know what to say—"

"Jeanine!"

They both looked up at the sound of her name, and saw that Trev was standing at the doorway of the building. "Break's over, okay! Let's get a move on!"

Jeanine looked back at Jamie, flustered. Jamie squeezed her hand. "Go on. It's all right." He smiled a bit. "If anyone understands that 'the show must go on,' I do."

She stood up like a robot and started to walk back toward Trev. But that mighty, seductive personality of "Tess" had been drained right out of her, body and soul. She hoped she could get it back for the rest of her performance.

CHAPTER EIGHTEEN

JAMIE DIDN'T STAY FOR THE REST OF JEANINE'S SHOW. HE WENT BACK TO HIS little cottage and sat on the front porch, thinking. The azaleas that Jeanine had fussed over had bloomed in March and then faded away. Now he could breathe the heady perfume from the beds of petunias and moonflowers, snapdragons and marigolds, and he could occasionally catch a whiff of wild honeysuckle from the woods. Of course, eventually he lit up a cigarette and ruined the whole perfume thing.

He was sitting and smoking when Trevor brought Jeanine and Ginella home. Jeanine, he was pleased to see, went into her house straight away, but Ginella lingered in the car. Trevor switched off the engine and lights, and Jamie wondered if he should go inside to avoid feeling like a voyeur. Just as he was about to get up, however, the DeValerys' front porch light popped on and Marielle came outside, crossing her arms and looking pointedly at Trev's car. As if by magic, the passenger door popped open and Ginella hopped out, tossing a little wave back in Trevor's direction as she ran lightly up the steps. Marielle also waved as the car cranked and began backing down the drive.

The whole scene filled Jamie with fascination. As Marielle went back inside and turned off the porch light, he thought how strange the scene was to him—a twenty-year-old adult female being monitored by her mother, apparently to make certain there was no moral slippage. And not just being monitored, but accepting the monitoring without argument or resentment—at least as far as he could tell from this distance. How totally bizarre. He couldn't quite figure out whether he was impressed or horrified.

He couldn't help but think of Paula's mother, helping her daughter of that same age move into Jamie's house. And the way Allison Klein had chattered and laughed and carried on—she had seemed happier about the development than Paula.

He tried to remember whether he had ever met a mother like Marielle DeValery. Hmm…Charlie's Aunt Phoebe, maybe? No, she was strict, but not exactly overprotective. Hadn't she always stayed home and let Elliott serve as Charlie's guardian when they were filming? And look how that had worked out.

And then there was his own mother. He tried very hard to picture Teresa worrying about Jamie's moral development. He squirmed in his chair as he tried to picture her being concerned about anyone's morals—including her own. Although…

There was that awful, awful night, when Elliott had brought home that other couple. Where had Charlie been? Off on one of his mandatory visits to Virginia, maybe? Jamie couldn't remember exactly, but he did remember being alone upstairs as he heard the sounds from downstairs and tried not to think about what must be going on, with all four of them together, with his *mum*…

The "guests" had stayed until late the next morning while Jamie cowered in his room and tried to be open-minded and adult about things. If they were enjoying themselves, what was it to him? Only, when he finally went downstairs, Teresa was sitting alone in the kitchen and crying.

"Why did you do it?" he'd asked her. "Why didn't you tell him what he could do with himself?"

"He threatens to leave me. All the time, he threatens."

"You don't need him," Jamie had told her. "I'll take care of you."

"Stupid boy," Teresa had said, drying her eyes with a tea towel. "You're fifteen. What do you know? You think a woman needs nothing but a house and children—" she almost spat the last word—"to make her happy?"

"I've got money. I can get you anything you want."

"Elliott is what I want."

"How can you say that? You're sitting here crying—"

"Because I'm afraid."

As she'd started to cry again, he had shaken his head, bewildered. "Afraid of what?"

"Afraid of losing him. Afraid I can't make him happy, that I'm not enough—"

As she'd dissolved into hysterical sobs again, Jamie had felt a great weight settle on his fifteen-year-old shoulders. Because he had told her he would get her whatever she wanted, and because she wanted Elliott Dane. And because, even at that age, Jamie had known that he could, indeed, give her Elliott. As long as he cooperated. As long as he fulfilled Elliott's needs.

The front door banged at the DeValery house, cutting into Jamie's memories. His heart picked up speed as he saw Jeanine crossing the yard, coming purposely toward him.

She climbed up onto the porch and took a seat nearby in the swing.

"Hi."

"Hello." He tried to sound light. "Are you sure you want to sit out here in the dark with me, after I nearly ravaged you earlier?"

Jeanine waved her hand in dismissal. "Nah, I don't imagine I'm much of a temptation now. I'm just plain old Jeanine again. Kind of like Superman reverting to Clark Kent."

Jamie laughed. "It does feel rather like that, doesn't it? Periods of intense power followed by a crashing return to mediocrity."

Silence fell. Jamie took a deep breath. He knew what was coming, and he dreaded it.

But her words were soft and caressing when she started. "Jamie, honey, just because Paula did those things doesn't mean for certain she gave you AIDS. I mean, you don't know that she was HIV-positive, do you?"

"No."

"Then why don't you just get tested and put this whole thing to rest?" When Jamie didn't answer, her tone grew frustrated. "Sometimes you are really difficult for me to understand."

"In what way?"

"We've talked enough that I know you're scared. You think you're going to die young like your father, and it terrifies you. But at the same time, you seem to almost relish the idea, to want to do all that you can to speed up the process and make sure that it comes true."

Jamie made a little noise of frustration. "If you're still talking about the fact that I took a couple of pills the other day, please! That hardly means that I'm trying to kill myself."

"It's not just that. It's your whole attitude. Like—I know you're scared to death of getting cancer, like your dad and your grandfather did, but you smoke. Where's the logic in that?"

"I don't know, Jeanine. I suppose I—look, do you always understand everything that you do?"

Jeanine thought for a moment. "Pretty much, yes. I don't necessarily understand things that happen to me, but the things I do—yes."

"Well, then, you're very fortunate." He took a long drag off his cigarette—but he didn't enjoy it. "I suppose I just never really thought it mattered. If it's going to happen, it's going to happen. Why fight it? I suppose I've felt the one advantage to having a short future is that I'm more or less free to do whatever I jolly well please."

Jeanine studied him. "Your uncle is pretty healthy, isn't he?"

"So far."

"Does he worry about all this like you do—about getting sick or dying?"

"Sometimes he does. When he's in a bad mood he'll go on about the family curse. But I don't think Rick's got enough imagination to truly scare himself silly the way I do." He smiled at Jeanine. "It's a gift, you know."

"I do know." Jeanine nodded. "For a while, my folks restricted me to only seeing Disney movies because I had nightmares. But then I would hide under my bed after seeing those, too. Witches and dragons and evil villains everywhere! My mother, on the other hand, says that she never has nightmares. She could probably watch slasher movies when she was six and never give them a second thought."

"Yep. You just described Rick."

"You know what amazes me? My mother didn't finish college on her first attempt because she married so young, but back then she was an English literature major, same as me. Literature! She's taking classes again now, and she's majoring in business, which seems a lot more reasonable."

"Perhaps she was different when she was younger," Jamie said. "I find it hard to believe Richard was once an actor. It was his whole life, as a matter of fact."

"Really? When did he quit?"

"Not long after I started. I think he discovered it was more profitable to sell me."

"Jamie!"

"All right. To sell my talents, then. That's how he started producing. First the *Summer* movies, and then other projects in between so I would always be busy. I wasn't always the star of these things, mind you, but he would have me in some meaty little role, and working with legends in the business. The central idea, of course, was that the Newkirks in general would make out like bandits. And the Danes as well—Teresa and Elliott eventually became his partners."

Jeanine looked thoughtful. "Elliott Dane is Charlie Edenfield's uncle, right?"

"Right."

"So if your theory is right about Richard and Elliott and your mother just being in it for the money, why didn't they work Charlie to death, too?"

"Oh, they tried, believe me." Jamie shifted uncomfortably. "I don't want to sound conceited or anything…and Charlie did fine in the *Summer* movies, really. But I don't think he's cut out to be the star they wanted."

"Poor Charlie," Jeanine said softly.

For some reason, Jamie felt a little annoyed, as though her sympathy for Charlie implied criticism of him. "He'll sort it out eventually." Jamie gave a laugh, hoping she didn't notice the sharp edge to the sound. "I told you he reminds me of you, sometimes. He writes amazing stories and poems. Hannah Raney always told him he needed to be a writer, not an actor." Grinding out the cigarette, Jamie spent a silent moment watching the tendrils of white smoke rising against the dark sky. "Jeanine, you asked me tonight if you were right about you and me, about our being alike."

"And?"

"To be honest, I think you've overestimated my abilities, well, quite a lot really. You have a talent and a power I don't have. You know that, don't you?"

She shook her head. "What do you mean?"

"I can take a character someone else invented, and I can give him a body—a voice, movements, expressions. But I could never just create something out of nothing the way you do. I watched you tonight, and I was amazed. You were totally transformed into a whole other creature. And no one had described her to you, or given you her words and her actions to study. You just spoke her into being out of the void. You even wrote some of the songs, didn't you?"

Jeanine nodded.

"And that story you wrote about Danny. I'm amazed! You can do all of these things—I could never do any of that. I toy sometimes with the idea of directing, but Richard says that's absurd, and he's probably right. Your soul is so full, and I'm…" His voice trailed off.

After a moment, Jeanine prompted him gently, "You're what?"

Jamie started to grab at the cigarette package in his pocket, then let his hand fall, empty. "I've never told anyone this."

"What?"

"Jeanine, I know you believe in God and I suppose it follows that you believe He doesn't make mistakes, but do you—don't you think that every now and then, something could sort of, I don't know, fall through the cracks?"

Jeanine looked at him. "What do you mean?"

"I don't know. Something just doesn't come out the way God intended? Someone interferes with someone's actions, or someone doesn't do what God had meant for her to do?"

"Jamie," Jeanine said wryly, "is there a story in all this somewhere?"

"There's a story." Jamie sighed.

Jeanine turned sideways and reclined in the swing, settling in and preparing to listen.

"All right, here goes. Several years ago, I found out that…that when my mother got pregnant with me, she did not view it as a blessed event, to say the least. I found out she actually hated my dad, that she'd only started up with him to spite Richard. It was apparently Rick that she'd wanted all along, but he had snubbed her. And when my mother got something or someone on her mind, it tended to consume her. So when she came up pregnant, first thing she did was go to Richard. She was upset and angry and I think she wanted to make certain he was in that same condition. She started in on him that she hoped he was happy now, and all that. She threw it in his face that my dad was going to have to marry her and, well, Richard wasn't having any of that.

"Richard practically worshipped my father. Dad had been taking care of him since Rick was sixteen and he was eighteen, working in the garage instead of going to university, as he could have done. Richard wasn't about to see him saddled with this woman who didn't want him, and a baby besides. So he made some arrangements in London, threatened her, bribed her, whatever it took—and then took her off to have their nasty little problem taken care of."

Even in the dim light, Jamie could see Jeanine's eyes widen. "Your uncle did that! Oh, Jamie, I find that really hard to believe. Maybe it's not true."

Jamie shrugged. "Oh, it's true enough. Rick and I have talked about it since." Jamie smiled a little. "Poor Rick. He was so dead set against me coming into this world. It must have been a sort of premonition, because he's got stuck with me ever since. He was changing my nappies and babysitting me till he ran off to London to be an actor when I was about four. And Dad dragged me all over England and Scotland meeting long-lost relatives when he knew he was dying, trying to find someone who'd take me in. But it all came down to Richard in the end, and how could he turn Dad down? Still, it hasn't turned out too badly for Rick, all in all. You should see that mansion of his in Benedict Canyon."

"But what happened?" Jeanine asked. "I mean, obviously you are here. Did your mother just change her mind?"

"Hardly. No, Dad showed up. I don't know how he found out, but he came to the hospital or clinic or whatever and begged her not to do it. He promised he would take care of her, or marry her, or take the baby himself, whatever she wanted. Finally she told him that all she wanted was money enough to get out of Warwick for good, and that for enough money and a promise that she would never have to have a thing to do with the baby, she would go ahead with the pregnancy. She knew that my dad had come into a bit of cash from the insurance when my grandmother died, and she asked for every bit of it. And she got it. My dad had been planning to use it to buy the garage that he worked in, but he never got a chance to do that. He got me instead, and he worked at the garage for a wage until the day that he died. And I was five minutes away from not being here at all." Incongruously, he grinned a little. "It must give Rick chills some nights to think of it. That I came that close to being aborted—and that he came that close to losing everything."

"Oh, Jamie," Jeanine breathed. "What a terrible thing to be told! But your father must have wanted you very, very much, and your mother—well, she must have changed her mind. You lived with her for several years, didn't you?"

"Yes. She turned up again when I was thirteen. She begged me to come live with her. I was thrilled at the time to show Rick he was wrong, that she did want me—that someone did. Of course, it didn't have the fairy-tale end-ing I'd expected, but that's not why I brought all this up."

Jeanine watched his face, waiting for him to continue.

"It's hard to explain, but in some way, when I was hearing that story about the abortion, a part of my brain was saying, 'Oh, so that explains it.'"

"Explains what?"

"The vague feeling I've always had that something was wrong with me. Something different. But not the way that you were talking about yourself. You talk about being full, of having music and characters and dreams flow out of you. But I've always thought it's as though, until I take on a character, I'm empty. I give them a body, and they give me a soul. I've always thought that when I act, that's the only time I truly feel alive. And so I thought, maybe that's it. Maybe I don't actually have a soul."

"Oh, Jamie!" Jeanine came once again to an upright position in the swing and dropped her feet to the floor with a resounding thud. "That's the most absurd thing I ever heard."

"No, no, listen to me," Jamie said. "Just suppose…suppose I was never intended to be here. That I wasn't meant to be born. But my dad fouled everything up, and here I am. Do you ever read time travel stories?"

"Uh-huh." Jeanine was still looking at him as though he'd gone mad.

"Well, you know how those stories go. If someone from the future goes into the past, he endangers everything he touches, because he's not sup-posed to be there. If he interacts at all, if he breaks a twig or touches any-thing, everything is thrown into chaos. Well, that's precisely what my life is like. I touch something, and it's like throwing a stone into a pond. These cir-cles of pain and disaster radiate out from it, and they sweep through every-thing I love. My dad, Richard, my mother, Paula—I've done that to all of their lives."

Jamie took a breath. "That's why I don't even bother being tested for…you know, the HIV virus. As long as I don't really know, I can't hurt anyone with it. But if I have to tell Richard that I'm ill, that I'm dying—well, he's been through that once with my dad. I want to avoid that for him as long as possible. Or who knows? By the time anything actually happens to me, perhaps he'll have a home and children and Ruth and be so wrapped up in it all that it won't be as hard for him as I've imagined. And I hope that's true."

"Jamie—oh no!" Jeanine jumped up as a hideous wailing sound suddenly pierced the night. The swing bounced against the back of her legs as her eyes searched the darkness.

Jamie came up from his chair, too, as the screeching was repeated, seemingly coming from numerous tortured throats at once. It sounded like the soundtrack from some cheesy horror movie. "What is that!"

"Trouble!" She jumped from the low porch and ran toward Jamie's Ford.

"Well, obviously," Jamie called as he followed her.

"No…I mean my cat."

The motion-operated porch light popped on, and Jamie had a good view of Jeanine on her hands and knees, peering up under the car. Then she wiggled up underneath, and there was a lot of flailing and thumping and scraping, and then a furry black feline body shot out past Jamie's legs and hightailed it for the woods.

"Stupid Carlsons!" came Jeanine's voice from somewhere under the car. "They need to keep that bully of theirs at home." Her voice changed, and he heard her crooning to Trouble, "C'mere, sweetie. You okay? It's all right now, he's gone."

"Can I help?"

"I think I've got her." Now she wiggled in reverse from underneath the car, dragging a reluctant Trouble along with her. She stood up and cradled the cat in her arms, then pulled one hand away and looked at her fingers. "I think she's bleeding."

"Bring her inside," Jamie said.

Inside, Jeanine examined Trouble and only found a scratch on her ear. There was another bit of excitement when Jeanine tried to clean the wound, and the cat exploded out of Jeanine's arms and shot under the couch. Again Jeanine went down on her belly, this time peering up under the sofa.

Jamie smiled down at the back pockets of her blue jeans. "Jeanine, I've seen a whole new side of you tonight."

"What?"

"Nothing."

Jeanine rolled over and up into a sitting position, leaning against the couch. "She's shivering. Let's just let her calm down." She blew stray hair out of her face and looked at him as he settled on an ottoman across from her. Silence fell. For some reason, Jamie felt as nervous as the poor cat.

He laughed. "You certainly put the fear of God into that big black brute."

"Only for tonight. I guess I should keep Trouble inside, but she was already used to the great outdoors when I took her in."

"She's lucky you found her."

"I don't think it was luck." She pulled her knees up to her chin and wrapped her arms around them. "This may sound crazy to you, but I believe God is in everything. Even the details. Even in leading a stray cat to a good home."

Jamie looked down at his fingernails. "Then why don't they all find good homes?"

"I don't know. But it all comes out right. I believe that." It was her turn to laugh nervously. "I could tell you a pretty incredible story. Something absolutely impossible I prayed about for ten years, and how He answered it in this totally unbelievable way."

"So tell me."

She shifted positions, fidgeted, stretched out her legs and stared at her knees. "Maybe I will someday. Not now."

"Why not?"

"Just—not yet, okay? But Jamie, all that stuff you were saying earlier. God doesn't make mistakes like that." She shrugged. "I have to believe that. My mother gave me up for adoption, so I guess she thought I was a mistake, but I don't think God did. In the Bible God says things to people like, 'Before you were born, I knew you.' I think when God was plotting out the story of the universe, he thought of all of us."

During Jeanine's speech, Jamie had seen Trouble peeping out from under the couch, then creeping out and starting to explore the room. Within moments, she had relaxed enough to jump to the top of the TV, where she reared up on her hind legs to taste a tempting assortment of flowers in a tall vase. But when her front legs touched the lip of the glass, it immediately tipped and went crashing to the floor, along with a small avalanche of DVDs. Trouble immediately followed, ears flat against her head and her body low to the ground as she covered the open floor in two bounds and made once again for the safety of the sofa.

"Whoa there, missy, not so fast!" Jeanine put out an expert hand and caught her. Cradling the calico close, she stood up and declared, "I think we've all had enough excitement for one night. We'd better go."

Jamie straightened up, his arms full of DVDs. "Must you?"

"Yeah, I'm really tired. We'll have to continue the deep philosophical stuff later." She ruffled his hair playfully. "But just remember. Even you, believe it or not, have some purpose."

"Such as?"

"Well, I'm sure Carol Albright's glad you're here, for one." She smiled knowingly and said, "It was the strangest thing. Some anonymous benefactor apparently sent her a brand new SUV this week. I don't suppose you'd know anything about that, would you?"

"I might," Jamie said cagily. "Still, it seems rather a skimpy excuse for an entire life."

"Not if you'd been riding around with those screaming little hooligans of hers, all of you crammed together in a compact car and broken down by the highway," Jeanine declared.

Jamie laughed. "You may be right."

He walked her back outside, and as he watched her glide away, as graceful as a pale cat disappearing into the darkness, he realized with a sudden jolt of pain how desperately he needed her, needed her powerful, steady hand in his life. But he couldn't have her. He wouldn't do that to her. Jeanine was healthy and vital and whole, and he absolutely would not see her sicken and wither under his sort of reverse Midas touch. Just remembering what had happened to Paula and Teresa, just thinking of the events of the past few days—the threats from Allison; his conference with Ira; even that risky and idiotic stop-over with Debbie—it all made him realize how futile it was to think of someone like him with someone like Jeanine.

Still, he wanted to do something for her, wanted to keep her in his life. His mind started to gear up, and he felt almost feverish as the idea suddenly struck him. Find yourself a project, Richard had said. Find yourself a script, put something together for yourself.

The rocker swung wildly back and forth as he jumped up from it, ran into the house and dug Jeanine's manuscript out from beneath a pile of unimportant papers. He looked at it almost reverently, almost as though a divine gift had just been dropped into his lap. Ten minutes ago he had said that he couldn't possibly write a screenplay, but the story, the dialogue, the characters were already here. Danny Summer and his sharp-tongued nemesis, Tess, were already alive in these pages. It was simply a matter of translation on his part.

Jamie started to pace, adrenaline pumping through him. It was perfect! In her lifetime, Hannah Raney had never allowed any movies to be made about Danny Summer unless they were based on her books. But Jamie had once talked about this situation with Walter Raney, Hannah's widower. As her literary executor and sole heir, he had the authority to authorize a writer to continue the book series, and once there was another authorized book, there could be another movie. According to Walter, Hannah had planned her will carefully and had discussed her wishes with him a year or so before she died. She wasn't averse to someone else continuing the story if something happened to her, as long as the right author was found, one who understood her vision. Jeanine's book could be a new beginning for them all.

Jamie jerked up his cell phone and started to dial Walter Raney that very minute. The desire to play Danny Summer again was suddenly so strong that it was like a terrible itch under his skin. Fortunately, just before the call connected he realized it was the same time in Virginia as here. In other words, late. He forced himself to lay the phone down and go lie down, try to get some sleep.

No way he could sleep, of course. But for once, it was excitement keeping him awake. What a glorious opportunity suddenly stretched before him—for himself, and for Jeanine.

CHAPTER NINETEEN

A COUPLE OF WEEKS LATER, AFTER ANOTHER FEVERED NIGHT OF WORKING ON THE screenplay, Jamie headed out onto the porch just before noon with his morning cup of tea and found a note from Jeanine slipped under the front door. He unfolded it and read: "Dear Jamie: Do you think you could manage to pull together a picnic lunch and meet me at school around 1:30? I know a great spot, very secluded. Just some cows nearby and the occasional rabbit or blue jay, none of whom is the least bit interested in celebrities. They're snotty that way. See you at 1:30. Jeanine."

Jamie smiled as he read the P.S.: "I know it's hopeless to assume that you have food. Use the key in the planter outside the back door and see what you can find in our house."

Jamie pulled up in front of the Student Center precisely at 1:30 (they had done this before), Jeanine hopped into the car, and they took off.

"So where is this idyllic, Disneyesque wonderland?" Jamie queried as he left the environs of the campus.

"Well, actually I need to make another stop first, okay?"

She sounded nervous. Jamie glanced over at her. "It won't take long, will it? The food will go off."

"No, not long at all. Turn right there." The tone in her voice changed. "I'm glad you could make time for me. You've been pretty scarce lately. Even Daddy's commented on it." She laughed, but the sound had a sharp edge. "You're not getting tired of us, are you?"

"Of course not. I just have a little project I've been working on, that's all."

"Oh, I see."

Jamie was itching to tell Jeanine the truth, but it wouldn't be fair. He had sent her manuscript to Walter Raney but hadn't got a response. It would be too cruel to raise Jeanine's hopes only to dash them later if Walter didn't agree.

Jeanine said, "Turn left at that traffic light."

Jamie followed her directions and found himself pulling into a doctor's building next to a hospital downtown.

"What's going on?" he asked her.

"It's my gynecologist."

Jamie pulled into a parking space at the back of the building. He switched off the engine and turned to look at her. "Are you all right?"

"Yes, well, I…" She looked at him squarely and said, "Actually, we're here for you."

His eyebrows shot up into his hairline. "What!"

"Come on, Jamie. It's very simple. He draws a little blood, sends it to a lab, and then we can put all this worrying about HIV behind us."

Jamie slammed his hand down on the gearshift. "You told him! You told this man that I—I can't believe this! I shared one of the most private things in my life with you, and you, you've—"

"Wait a minute, wait a minute," Jeanine said. "I have not betrayed your confidence. Dr. MacFarland is a deacon at the church, all right? I've known him all my life. I told him I had a friend who needed a very confidential blood test done and asked would he help. He said of course he would, and that's that. He doesn't know who you are, and if you refuse to come in, I guess he'll never know. But Jamie, come on. Don't do this to yourself or to the people who love you anymore, okay?"

Jamie didn't answer, just let out his breath in frustration. Jeanine touched him lightly on the arm.

"Jamie, even if you are HIV positive, there are medicines today that can delay the onset of AIDS for decades. I did some research. And who knows— maybe by then there would even be a cure. Facing the truth and dealing with it, that's always better than being afraid of monsters under the bed, isn't it?"

Jamie turned on her. "I love the way you and your family are always talking about the truth. How wonderful and lovely it is to face reality. That's very easy for someone like you that's never had to face any harsh realities in her entire life, isn't it?"

Jeanine's eyes flashed, but her voice was controlled. "That's not fair. You don't have a clue what we've been through. The hell that my dad grew up in. Or the extremely unpleasant way that my mother lost most of her family in the space of a few years. I was closer to my grandmother than to my own mother, really. She always seemed to know what I was thinking, or when I was scared or worried, and how to fix it. But by the time I was seventeen, she had Alzheimer's and didn't even know me. When I was eighteen, I was helping change her diapers. Don't talk to me about reality, Jamie."

Jamie threw up his hands. "All right, all right!" But still, he sat sullenly staring out the windshield until he felt Jeanine lightly rubbing him on the arm.

"Jamie, it's going to be okay. I know it is. God's not going to let anything happen to you now."

He turned to look at her. "How can you say that? Bad things happen all the time."

"I know because…" Her eyes blinked with confusion. "It just wouldn't make sense, that's all. Not now."

"Jeanine, you're not making sense. And anyway…suppose you're wrong?"

"Well, if you do have a problem, I want us to find out. I want to get you the medicine I was talking about. And…and I want to take care of you."

He continued to glare at her. She didn't flinch, just continued that earnest look, until he could feel every bit of stubborn, fearful, irrational will being burned away under its confident power. Finally he sighed. "You're sure he can keep it confidential?"

"I'm positive. And he said we could knock on the back door and we wouldn't see anyone but him."

"Oh…all right."

Jeanine squeezed his arm, and they started to unbuckle seat belts and climb out of the car. As they walked toward the unmarked door, however, Jamie couldn't help but grumble, "A gynecologist! Is that really the best you could do?"

"Oh for pete's sake, Jamie. All he's going to do is take blood and send it to a lab. Blood is blood."

"Not if the *National Enquirer* hears about it. I can see the headlines now: 'Jamie Newkirk's Real Gender? Only His Gynecologist Knows For Sure.'"

Jeanine rolled her eyes and tapped on the door.

CHAPTER TWENTY

Jeanine sat on the floor of Jamie's living room, surrounded by stacks of books and index cards. His borrowed notebook computer was in her lap, and she was feverishly clicking away at it. As he started toward the window, his toe caught one of the piles of cards—which covered most of the floor space—and dismantled it. Jeanine let out a little shriek and exclaimed, "*Please* be careful with those! I'll never get them back in order."

"What are they?" Jamie frowned as he closed the window. He hated being shut up with air conditioning, but he was going to have to give in. The heat in May was brutal.

"I told you. This is for my Emily Dickinson paper. I took notes on the cards. Then I sorted them into paragraphs. Now I'm trying to actually string it all together into a decent research paper. This thing counts as a third of my grade."

"And then you've finished, right? With school, I mean."

"I have this paper and two more exams. And then I'm through. Why?"

Jamie snorted. "Because I'm looking forward to it, that's why. You've been entirely too stressed and caught up in all this lately."

Jeanine looked up from the computer, her eyes flashing. "You really don't have a clue, do you?"

"About what?"

"About what's coming. About what's going to happen to us."

"Well, I should hope we'll have more time and you won't be so irritable," Jamie started. Then something on the flickering television screen caught his attention. He reached for the remote and unmuted the sound.

For a moment, he forgot Jeanine was there as he watched a couple of minutes of the awful sitcom. Then he heard her voice, cutting through the laugh-track fog. "That's your friend Charlie, right?"

"Yeah. This show must be a few years old."

"It's an old re-run. It's called *Squeeze Play*, I think."

Jamie laughed weakly. "I told you he was pretty much taking any job he could find for a while. He made guest appearances on loads of rotten TV shows. No wonder he's trying something completely different now. I'd probably be crazy too if I'd had to do this kind of rubbish."

Jeanine frowned at him. "You know, Jamie, some people might think that serving your country is better than acting. Not crazy."

Jamie let out his breath in frustration. "I didn't mean it that way. Of course it's quite noble, if you do it for the right reason." He dropped to the floor, sitting cross-legged across from her. "I think Charlie's just running."

"From what?"

Jamie lifted his shoulders, let them drop. "I don't know. Sometimes I think it's from me."

"But I thought you were like brothers."

"Yeah." Jamie laughed sharply. "Like all those Biblical brothers—you know, Cain and Abel, or Jacob and Esau."

"Seriously?"

He waved his hand. "No, not as bad as all that. But even brothers can have a little rivalry, right?"

He turned away from her concerned eyes, back to the television, but he felt his eyes glazing as he remembered the first time he'd felt that he and Charlie were brothers—the night of the premiere of *Summer Storm*. The week before had felt awkward and weird, as they all moved into that big house in Topanga Canyon together. He'd liked Charlie well enough, but the idea of living with him felt strange. He was still trying to get to know his mum and wasn't sure he was ready to start sharing her. And Elliott Dane—well, the man was just a mystery. Most of time he was full of fun, like a big kid. But Jamie had seen his temper once or twice—usually directed at Charlie.

The night of the premiere, Jamie decided that if Elliott Dane could make his mother so happy, he surely couldn't be all bad, and the four of them fitted so snugly together, laughing and celebrating. Actually, it hadn't felt so much like being out with parents as with a big brother and sister. Late in the evening, when Richard would have been glaring and dragging him home to bed, Elliott was directing the limo driver to one party after another. It was the first time Jamie had stayed up all night—the first time he'd been allowed to taste champagne. He'd laughed when Charlie threw up on some starlet's shoes, but that was all right—Charlie was laughing, too.

By the next afternoon, things had changed. The sound of raised voices cut into Jamie's sleep, and he'd struggled to focus, in spite of the severe ache in his head. He soon realized that Elliott was yelling at Charlie downstairs. "You sit down and read every one of these reviews—"

"I don't want to read any more. I know they're bad."

Oh, Jamie had thought. The Summer Storm *reviews, from the premiere last night.*

Elliott was still fuming. "You're going to read every word. Do you know what I gave up for you? Do you?"

"Yes."

"And this is how you repay me?"

"I'm doing my best—"

"If this is your best, I feel sorry for you." Elliott's next words were lost, the mumbled words running together into a low snarl. The next words to become clear were something like, "—I did to deserve you. Why can't you be more like Jamie?"

Hearing Jeanine clear her throat, Jamie clicked off the TV, suddenly unable to stand the noise of canned laughter. The sad thing was, as he recalled, Charlie's reviews for *Summer Storm* hadn't been that bad. Just not as good as Jamie's.

Jeanine was still studying him, and he heard himself blurting out, "Elliott thinks it was Charlie who sold that story to the tabloid about me."

"What!" Jeanine dropped the pen and notecard she was holding and pulled her knees up to her chest. "That story where somebody supposedly close to you insinuated you were involved in your mother's and Paula's deaths?"

Jamie nodded, feeling miserable even to hear the words.

"But I thought he was your friend. How could he make up lies like that?"

"Ever since Hannah Raney died, he's been different. Distant. Bitter."

Jeanine smiled weakly. "I know a lot of us fans who had trouble not being bitter, when the *Summer* series came to a screeching halt. I can't imagine how it must have hit all of you that were involved in it."

"And Charlie and Hannah had a special relationship. She treated him like a son, encouraged him."

"I knew she was at his house the night she died."

Jamie nodded. "That horrible fire...it scarred him somehow." He sighed. "The trouble is, he seems to take all his resentment out on me."

Jeanine tilted her head and seemed to be thinking. "Because your life—at least your acting life—didn't come to an end that night? The way his did?"

"I don't know. Maybe."

Jeanine fell silent again. When she finally started to speak, her voice had lost its confident tone and she was almost stammering. "Jamie, it—I mean. That story in the tabloids...it was lies, right?"

"Of course it was!" For a long moment, Jamie met her eyes. Then he faltered. "I mean, there was enough truth thrown in to let me know it came from someone who knows me."

"Like what?"

"Like the stuff about my mother and me arguing at the party the night she died. I was angry with her because she was still pining over Elliott, and drowning herself in drugs. I stormed out but then I felt bad about leaving her like that, so I went back, and that's when I found her..." His voice trailed off.

Jeanine cleared her throat. Her voice sounded husky. "So Charlie was there at the party?"

"Yeah, but so were a lot of people. Doesn't necessarily mean anything."

He knew what was coming next and braced himself for it. He could feel the wheels turning in her head. Sure enough, she looked him in the eye and said, "What about the stuff about you and Paula and...the drugs? Was some of that true, too?"

He felt his whole body tighten. "So that's what you think of me, after all these weeks? That I'm some closet dope addict who bullies and beats up women?"

"No, Jamie, I didn't mean that at all."

"Then what did you mean?"

She met his gaze for a long moment, obviously confused and torn. "Jamie," she whispered. "What's the matter with you? What are you so afraid of?"

"What do you mean?"

"I don't know. Sometimes you seem to feel so guilty, so fearful. If I didn't know better, I'd almost think you were being blackmailed, or that you really don't want the truth about all this to come out."

Jamie said quietly, "And what do you think the truth is, Jeanine?"

She started to pick up the index cards. "Well…you've practically lived with us for over three months now, and I know what a good person you are. I think you're kind and sensitive and you think entirely too much for your own good. But having said all that, I couldn't be more confused. There was that other Jamie that I saw a few weeks ago that absolutely bewildered me."

Jamie shrugged. "I tried to explain all that to you. I thought you understood. The main thing is that you haven't let all these stories poison you against me. That you're not afraid of me."

"Of course I'm not!" She looked away from him, out the window and toward the DeValery house. She was silent for a long moment. Then, still not looking at him, she said, "I got a job."

"Oh." He tried to think why she sounded so sad. "Did you really?"

"I really did. No more summers for me. When school is out this time, it's for good."

"But surely you'll be here this summer—I mean—when are you starting?"

"The job is in Atlanta. I'll be moving there a week after graduation."

"You what!" He desperately calculated. "That's less than two weeks!"

"I know."

"But I thought-I thought you wanted to stay in Middleboro. That you wanted to live in this house, as a matter of fact." He thought quickly. "Is that the problem? That I'm living here? Because I can move back to the hotel or something—"

"No, no, it's got nothing to do with that," Jeanine said. "It's just that it's really hard to find a first job with no experience. My mother put in a good word for me with the people in communications at the university's Atlanta campus, and last week, the job came through. It's a writing job—brochures and the alumni magazine and things like that. Nothing too exciting, but it'll be good for me to be out on my own, not still practically living with my parents."

Jamie smiled wanly. "That sounds like your mother talking."

Her lips tilted back at him. "Almost a direct quote."

"But I don't understand. Why would she want you to be all alone?"

"Actually…Trev got a job in Atlanta, too," Jeanine said.

Oh, lovely.

Jeanine turned her face away and started to pack note cards and books into her bag. "Trev's already found an apartment. He's going to tell me if one comes open in the same complex, and maybe we can still keep plodding along with the band. So see? It won't be so bad."

Jamie shook his head, dazed. "Just like that? You've just made your plans to go, and you've not given a single thought to me?"

"Oh come on, Jamie!" She reached for her discarded shoes. "You're not going to be here much longer, either. You've got to promote your movie when it comes out—that one you made in England last fall."

"But that won't be until August," Jamie pointed out.

"Well, I can't just sit around here and wait. I have this opportunity right now." She jerked the laces of her right shoe and tied them with an angry motion. "I have to live in the real world, you know. I have to find a job, go to work. That's what most of us have to do."

Jamie's mind raced, thinking about the proposal he had sent to Walter Raney along with her manuscript. Other than a curt note of thanks and a promise to get back to him soon, Jamie hadn't heard a word from the man. This whole thing could still come to nothing. Telling Jeanine could wait a few days, at least. She wasn't going anywhere yet.

Forcing himself to be calm, Jamie touched her hand. "All right, fine. Tell them you'll take the job. But don't give up, either. I may think of something yet, all right?"

"Sure, Jamie," she said, obviously humoring him. "You do that."

He stretched out on the floor next to her, pensive and quiet. Finally he blurted out, "I hate change!"

"I know," Jeanine agreed with a sigh. "Ginella can't understand why I want to live in this house. But, Jamie, we had such incredible times here! When I was little, we lived in this house first."

"Did you really?"

"Yep. My grandparents built it for us." Jeanine abandoned her attempt to gather up her things. She leaned back against the couch, hands behind her head. "Daddy was just out of seminary and had his first church, one that was too small to supply a house for the pastor, and we were so poor. So we lived here, and my grandparents and Aunt Emily and sometimes my uncle Scott, who was Daddy's best friend, lived in the bigger house. It was like a constant party, especially during the summer. My grandmother cooked these enormous feasts and there were impromptu softball games. And then Uncle Scott married and had kids, and they were always playing here."

She slid down, stretched out on the floor. Now they were both lying on the hard wood, faces turned toward one another and about eight inches apart. Jamie could have sworn there was a slight current in the floor running between them. Jeanine propped her head up on her hand.

"But then it all started to slip away. My grandfather died. Uncle Scott and his family moved to Chicago. Soon it was just my grandmother and Emily in the big house, and we were bursting out at the seams, so we switched. Now they're gone, too. It's just gotten quieter and quieter around here. But at least there are echoes."

"Yeah." After a moment, Jamie said, "You remember I mentioned that I have three houses?"

"Yeah, that's pretty hard to forget."

"I never picked any of them out myself. Never decorated or anything. It's just that I couldn't bear to let them go."

"What do you mean?"

"The one in Warwickshire actually belonged to my friend, Rose Hallifax. Rose is wonderful. The closest thing that I actually had to a mother when I was growing up. In fact, when my dad knew he was dying, he asked Rose to take me, and she agreed. But then her husband had a stroke and became a complete invalid, and she just couldn't handle nursing him and raising me, too. Anyway, I love Rose. When her husband finally died, she had so much debt that the house was going to have to go. So I bought it and I let her live in it, but I like knowing that it's there and it's mine. I had so many great times in it.

"The flat in London was the first place Richard and I bought when I landed the part of the Dodger in *Twist!* and we actually had some money. Rick moved on to a bigger place later, but I couldn't bear to let the flat go. My friend Eric lives in that one while he's at University and looks after it for me. But now, here's the most lunatic thing of all," Jamie said.

Jeanine smiled. "Oh, I can't wait."

"I bought that beach house for my mother a few years ago when she and Elliott split up. She was so depressed, but I was determined I was going to make her happy. I thought it was my job, and that the house would do it. You wouldn't believe what I paid for that house, far more than the two places in

England combined. And when she died and they read her will, she had left it to Elliott Dane."

"Ouch."

"Yeah, well, I can only look back now and think that I must have been having some sort of breakdown. But I bought it back from him."

"You didn't!"

"I did." Jamie started to laugh. "I don't even like the bloody place, and I've bought it twice!"

Jeanine started laughing, too, and for some reason that neither of them could have exactly put into words, it was all suddenly the funniest thing they had ever heard. They lay there companionably on the floor, literally writhing with laughter and gasping for breath. With tears streaming down her face, Jeanine finally managed to say, "Okay, Jamie! You win! You're crazier than I am!"

"Thank you!" he gasped.

As the hilarity died down and the giggles turned to quiet smiles, Jamie was left feeling cleansed and peaceful and warm. Judging by Jeanine's flushed face, she felt the same way. He reached across the eight-inch gulf and took her hand. When she squeezed his in return, he moved over her and touched her lips softly with his. He felt her reach up and lightly touch his hair, the back of his neck.

He pulled away from her a little and smiled down at her. "Wow. A whole kiss. You must feel pretty safe, knowing that I haven't got those test results back yet."

She tried to smile but faltered. "I'm never going to see you again, am I?"

"What do you mean?"

"I'm going to move to Atlanta. You'll go off to promote your movie, and maybe you'll even intend to keep in touch with me. But then you'll get a job and you'll fly off to Africa or somewhere to shoot it. You'll meet somebody new. And I'll never hear from you again."

He shook his head. "No. No, it's not going to be like that."

"Of course it is," she said. "But it's okay. I wouldn't have missed this for the world, Jamie. I love you."

Jamie was stunned. "What did—what did you say?"

"I love you. You're everything good about my life, all wrapped up in one package. You're my childhood."

Jamie touched her face, and she closed her eyes tightly. Her eyelashes suddenly looked moist, and he felt as though someone were tearing his heart out of his chest.

"Jeannie," he whispered desperately. "Jeannie, I never want to leave you. I would marry you if I could, I swear it." He breathed in deeply, then said all in a rush, "In fact, Jeanine, if that test comes back negative, if I'm okay and I can start all over again, would you marry me, then?"

Her body started to shake, and he was alarmed, thinking she was sobbing. But then she shoved him away and sat up, and he saw with irritation that she was laughing again.

"What is so blasted funny?" he demanded.

"You are," she declared. "Boy, you must be pretty confident that you're dying, huh?"

"I was serious, Jeanine!"

"Oh, Jamie," she chided, "you need to be a little less impulsive. Any day now, you're going to get that test result back, and it's going to be negative, and you're going to have a whole new life ahead of you. And you're going to think to yourself, 'Uh-oh, what have I done! Didn't I say something awfully rash to that DeValery girl? What's her name? Jane? Jean? Something like that.'"

"Very funny. Just you wait. I was serious, you know."

"Okay, I believe you," she said, maddeningly calm. "But right now I've got a Literature paper to finish, and I obviously can't concentrate here. I've got to go home."

"Oh, must you?"

"I simply must," Jeanine said, playfully aping his accent.

"Don't make fun of me." He grinned.

"I'm not making fun." She got to her feet and grabbed her bag. "I love the way you talk. Very staccato and crisp and BBC."

"Whereas you sort of hang onto the words and caress them in your mouth like a fine wine," Jamie observed.

Jeanine looked at him suspiciously. "Is that good?"

"Very sexy."

Jeanine considered. "All right, then. I'll accept that." She started for the door, hesitated, and grabbed his laptop. "I'm taking this too."

He waved his hand, giving her permission. And she was gone.

Jamie walked to the mailbox the next day as soon as the white post office truck had pulled away. It had become a habit, ever since the blood test. But he had pulled open the box in anticipation only to be disappointed—or relieved—day after day, so he was shocked to find the envelope from the lab actually lying there, real and solid and undeniable. He took it out with a shaky hand and walked back to the porch and sat down on the steps.

He stared at it for a long moment. *If you don't open it, it's not true,* he told himself. *You could just chuck it away, tell Jeanine it never came.*

But finally, hating himself for the fear and the hiding, he ripped into the envelope almost viciously. He stared at the brief words from the lab, concise and emotionless words, and he could feel his heart almost choking him with its pounding. He crumpled the paper in his hand as he stood up, automatically starting to move toward the DeValery house as though drawn there by its light. But that wouldn't do. She wasn't home. Jeanine wasn't home. She was at the university.

He considered for only a moment, then grabbed the car keys. He had to find Jeanine.

Fortunately, he remembered that Jeanine spent time between classes in the library. He crept along the tall rows of books and avoided most curious eyes until he spotted Jeanine at a table by a sunny window on the third floor. Although there was a book open in front of her, she was slumped over it asleep, her arm tucked up under her head as she soaked in the warm rays from the window like a cat.

He touched her lightly on the shoulder and she jumped, startled. Her eyes widened when she recognized him. "What's the matter!"

"I'm sorry, but I couldn't wait." He shoved the paper with the test results—which by now was damp from his sweaty palms—toward her. "I believe we had an arrangement based on the results of this test."

She glanced down at the lab report and then let out a little scream, which bounced around off the high ceiling and the stone walls and seemed to go on forever. Jamie looked around nervously, expecting to see startled, disapproving heads peering round at them. When none appeared, however, Jamie got back to the matter at hand. He knelt down by her chair at the battered wooden table and said, "So how about it, Jeannie? Will you marry me? Will you?"

Chapter Twenty-One

When Jeanine told her mother that Jamie was taking her to dinner at Richard and Ruth's new house in Atlanta, the woman's mouth fell open in amazement. "Jeanine! He's actually taking you home to meet his family!"

"No, no, don't make a big deal of it. They're celebrating his birthday, that's all. I'm sure they told him to invite his friends. And I'm right here handy."

Mamma gave her a shrewd look. "Did he invite Ginella?"

"Umm…not that I know of."

"Didn't invite us, either."

"Oh, Mamma, please." Jeanine rolled her eyes and tried to act nonchalant about the whole thing, even as she touched her fingers to the collar of her shirt and felt the new diamond ring lying underneath it, dangling from a gold chain against her skin.

He'd given her the ring a couple of days after that bizarre scene in the library but had asked her to keep it their secret for a while, at least until he told Richard. Which was fine with her. She needed a little time to adjust, like trying to find her legs after getting off a wild ride at the fair.

Besides, she had liked having a little time to enjoy the dream, before reality and people put a damper on things. She wasn't looking forward to telling her folks about this, and Jamie seemed even more nervous about telling his uncle. But she had known for half her life that Jamie was meant for her. The power of God was on her side, so she prepared for the dinner at Richard and Ruth's with hope, if not confidence.

When Jamie came to pick her up, her heart nearly stopped at the sight of him. He had shaved the pirate beard and his freshly-cut hair reflected mahogany highlights in the porch lamp. When they got into the car, he rested his hand on her knee, and she laid her hand on top of his. As she leaned back against the seat, she basked in their casual acceptance of each other. *Everything has changed*, she thought. *We're a couple.*

When they pulled through the gates of Richard and Ruth's new house in Atlanta—a huge Tudor in Midtown—a sudden pang of insecurity bubbled out of her in a laugh. "Wow. I guess they intend on spending a lot of time in Atlanta, huh?"

"I don't know what Richard's planning anymore." Jamie sounded grumpy. He put the car into park with a jerk of his hand. He came around to open her door for her, and as she got out, he said, "Let's just play this thing by ear tonight, all right? Telling them the news, I mean. I need to gauge his mood."

"Whatever you say."

As Jamie clutched her hand tightly enough to cut off the circulation, it was his mood she wondered about. But when Richard and Ruth greeted them at the door, he continued to hold her hand. And he sounded calm as he introduced her. "This is Jeanine DeValery, Lee's daughter."

Apparently, Jamie hadn't told them she was coming, because Richard's eyes narrowed to slits and he momentarily seemed speechless. Ruth, however, looked back and forth between her and Jamie with great speculation in her eyes as she babbled a welcome. "I'm so glad you could come, Jeanine. What a nice surprise! We've met before, you know."

"I remember," Jeanine said. "The animal shelter, right?"

"That's right."

Richard remained quiet throughout the dinner but gradually started to thaw. There was even one lovely moment when he put his hands on Ruth's swollen belly to feel the baby kicking, and when he saw Jeanine watching intently said, "Would you like to feel it? If it's all right with Ruth, that is."

"Of course it's all right." Ruth waved her over, and as she felt the little life moving under her fingers, Jeanine felt herself relaxing in amazement as the baby went from a vague idea in her head to solid reality under her fingers. Its kick ran through her like a shock. When she glanced up, everyone was smiling at her, and for a second, she felt a flood of happiness and belonging and was certain that everything was going to work out—with Jamie and his family.

That nice feeling didn't last long. She knew Jamie was just trying to make small talk and had no idea he was starting a controversy when he asked, "So, Rick, how's it going with *Right Angle*? All set to premiere?"

"It's not due out until Christmas," Richard answered. "And we still have to do some fine tuning. There's a fairly brutal murder scene that we're either going to have to edit or else the ratings board won't let us get by with an 'R.' Rather a shame, really. It was the most powerful scene of the film."

Jeanine frowned a little. "What's this movie about? I've only heard that it's a suspense film."

"I suppose you could call it that," Richard said. "It's about a, um, mentally deranged man who becomes convinced that God is speaking to him, telling him which of his fellow citizens are actually demon-possessed and should therefore be dispatched, to free their souls and for the good of all. So this killer terrorizes the town, then centers in on the heroine of the film and starts to stalk her."

"I see," Jeanine said. A little voice inside her told her to just smile and nod and change the subject, but she couldn't do it. Trying to keep her tone neutral, she said, "And it would be my guess that this killer always quotes Scripture before a killing, and maybe even invites the victims to pray with him. I would guess that he's shown praying often."

"Why would you say that?" Richard asked, sounding defensive.

"Oh, well, any time that I hear a character quoting Scripture or praying in a movie, I know that he's a psychotic killer. So, was I right?"

"To some degree. The character has to do those things so the audience understands his motivation," Richard said. "But what are you trying to tell me, Jeanine? That we shouldn't be allowed to make a movie like this?"

"No, I'm not saying that at all." Shifting her chair, she glanced at Jamie to see if she was embarrassing him or if he appeared angry with her, but he just looked interested. Encouraged, she continued. "I just wish sometimes that you people in Hollywood would send us more things to uplift our souls instead of send us into despair. And I personally would like to be able to go to movies the way they did in the old days, without feeling such a hatred spewing out of them for everything I believe in."

Richard threw his napkin down on the table. "I don't know how to break this to you, but my job is not to turn out propaganda films supporting your beliefs or anyone else's. First and foremost, I run a business, and I aim to turn a profit."

"Is that really true?" Jeanine asked. "Because if money's your main motivation, I would think that you would want to steer clear of these violent movies. I mean, Jamie told me that a G- or PG-rated film is five times as likely to place in the top movies as an R-rated one. Isn't that right, Jamie?"

"I do seem to recall telling you that, yes," Jamie said easily.

But then things took an uglier turn. Richard said quietly, "Then maybe you are right that I'm not entirely mercenary. Because I frankly couldn't hold my head up among my peers if I did nothing but turn out little pieces of feel-good fluff that don't reflect life or truth at all."

Jeanine shook her head in amazement. "So you're trying to tell me that you don't want to do any more films like the *Summer* movies, that were about redemption and sacrificing yourself for others—and that were a huge commercial success to boot? You're telling me that you'd rather repeat what you did with *Milk and Honey*, that was dark and depressing and a financial flop besides? I know it was a critical success but…you'd rather do something like that, even knowing how it affected Jamie just acting in it?"

This time, she saw Jamie wince. But she just couldn't seem to stop herself. "Jamie and I have talked a lot about his career. I know he doesn't want to do things like that anymore. God has far better things in mind for him than that."

Richard toyed with a spoon, tapping it against the side of his glass. He said softly, "Tell me, Jeanine, how would you know what God has in mind for Jamie? Does he talk to you? Does he tell you?"

Jeanine's lips tilted wryly. "Who? Jamie or God?"

Richard smiled sourly back at her. "Either, actually. I'm just wondering where all this divine direction is coming from—never having experienced it myself, you understand."

Jamie guffawed. "Oh come on, Richard! How can you say that? You can't look at our lives and see some kind of divine intervention? If we'd been left to ourselves, you'd be driving a taxicab right now and I'd probably be working in a garage. But look at us."

"He's right, Richard," Jeanine said earnestly. "It is a miracle, all of it. You have to see that, that God picked you out of the masses and blessed you, and that there's a reason for it. He has some great purpose for you."

"Well then, I wish he'd let me in on it. I haven't heard a word myself." Richard jabbed a finger in Jamie's direction. "I'll tell you another thing. All this talk of miracles, of God just reaching down and handing us all this fame and fortune. Well, I'm sorry, but it felt like bloody hard work to me. Every day for years, I woke up without a clue, sweating it out, trying to figure out what to do next, where to find you a job, what to do for your career—for mine. So excuse me if I find it just a bit annoying to have it all attributed to some sort of cosmic magic now that it's all done."

"Just because things are hard, or a struggle, doesn't mean that God's not in them," Jeanine said slowly. "But I have to believe in miracles, Richard. You just can't imagine. I mean, I've never even told Jamie all of this..." She looked at their expectant faces, then finally said hesitantly, "When I first saw Jamie in *Summer and the Sea*, I knew it right then."

"Knew what?" Richard demanded.

"That I would meet him one day. That God intended him to be part of my life."

"He? Danny Summer, you mean?" Richard said sharply.

Jeanine felt her cheeks burning, but continued. "No. Jamie."

Complete silence fell at the table. Ruth looked perplexed. Jamie seemed intent on rubbing a minute speck out of the tablecloth. Richard frowned deeply, and the tapping of his spoon sounded like someone beating out Morse code.

Finally Richard asked her, "And why do you suppose God would go to all that trouble, Jeanine? Are you planning to live happily ever after with Prince Charming here?"

She hesitated a moment, hoping Jamie would speak up—they were engaged, after all. But he didn't, so she said, "I just always thought we would be friends." She turned to Jamie, wishing he would look at her. "We are at least friends, aren't we?"

To her relief, he looked up. He heaved a deep breath, but then he smiled. "Of course we are."

Dropping the spoon, Richard folded his arms and studied her. "Oh surely there has to be more to it than that, if God himself went to the trouble of speaking to you."

Why oh why had she blurted this out now? In this situation? Trying to keep her voice level, she said, "What do you mean?"

"Oh, I don't know. In relation to what you were saying earlier, perhaps. Maybe you're supposed to help Jamie make better pictures, films that help 'uplift the soul,' wasn't that how you phrased it? Or help spread your faith?" His voice mocked a Southern drawl as he finished up breezily, "Take Hollywood for Jesus!"

"Bravo, Richard, bravo!"

Jeanine whirled toward the doorway of the dining room at the sound of this new voice. A vaguely familiar-looking man with salt and pepper hair was clapping his hands and smiling broadly. A long, thin, red-haired woman stood next to him, a frown creasing her otherwise smooth, white skin. The man was so attractive and the girl so exotic, Jeanine was sure they were some of the Newkirks' Hollywood friends.

"That was quite a speech, Richard," the man continued as he breezed into the room. "I always did say you should have stuck with your acting."

"Elliott…" Jeanine heard Jamie breathe next to her. "I—I didn't know you were coming."

The man smiled broadly. "I wouldn't have missed your birthday for the world, my boy!"

"Me either," said the redhead, staring at Jamie with her huge green eyes. Jeanine was reminded of Trouble's dilated eyes when she was stalking a butterfly and about to pounce.

"Elliott…and you brought Vette, too." Jamie sounded dazed. "I can't believe this."

"Oh, the biggest surprise is yet to come," Elliott said.

"There's more?" Jamie said. He sounded strangled.

The man made a grand, sweeping gesture toward the doorway, like a game show model unveiling a new car. Instead of a car, a familiar-looking boy appeared. Even with his usual thick mane of hair cropped brutally short, Jeanine recognized him and gasped. "Charlie Edenfield!"

Jamie's hand, which had been resting lightly on her shoulder, tightened convulsively.

CHAPTER TWENTY-TWO

Ow!" JEANINE PULLED AT JAMIE'S FINGERS, WHICH WERE DIGGING INTO HER shoulder.

"Sorry," he said, releasing her.

"No problem." As she rubbed her offended shoulder, she glanced at Richard and saw that he looked almost as astonished—and unhappy—as Jamie.

Ruth must have been shocked, too, but her Southern hospitality kicked in. As she pushed back from the table, she smiled brightly. "What a nice surprise! Let me just speak to Mae about setting more plates."

"Oh no, no, we wouldn't dream of imposing," Elliott said. "We decided at the last minute to give Jamie a little birthday surprise but we thought we'd be coming late enough to avoid crashing your lovely dinner."

Richard jumped to his feet and pulled out a chair. "Vette, won't you sit down?"

Vette Jackson! Jeanine thought in amazement. That's who the woman was. What a bizarre evening.

Jamie was standing and crossing to Charlie, extending his hand to shake, and when he spoke he sounded breathless. "How—I mean, how—you're supposed to be in the Army!"

Charlie's face lit up as he laughed. "It's not prison, Jamie. I'm through with boot camp so every now and then they let me out of their sight."

Charlie's soft accent reminded Jeanine that he was from Virginia, the same as Hannah Raney had been—and like the character of Newt. It had helped him get the part in *Summer and the Shore*, the one where Danny and company land in the eighteenth-century colony. She vaguely wondered where Elliott was from. His speech was so polished it almost seemed accent free.

Elliott leaned back in his chair and laid a casual hand on the table. "Charlie and I were talking and he mentioned wanting to come for your birthday, but he didn't think he could manage it—"

"I could only get a twenty-four-hour pass," Charlie said.

"I remembered that Vette has her own plane—"

Vette broke in, speaking for the first time. "Jamie's used it before."

Jamie appeared startled. "No I haven't! When?"

Richard cleared his throat. "That little Gulfstream, when you came to Georgia."

Jamie's eyes were wide. "That was Vette's? You didn't tell me that."

"Didn't I?" Richard picked up his spoon and started to tap it against the side of his glass again.

Charlie Edenfield made a choking noise, sort of like the sound Daddy made whenever he tried to cover a laugh with a cough. Jeanine caught his eye and he smiled at her. She smiled back, thinking how it lit up his face, thinking how utterly unlike the raucous character of Newt Fairchild he appeared to be. As he lingered in the doorway, he stood straight and poised, his hands clasped behind his back in a pose the Army had probably just taught him. And the close-cropped military haircut made his face look more angular, his jaw more pronounced. She was almost surprised she knew who he was, since her main experience of him was the *Summer* movies, when he played the almost-hyper Newt.

"You can use the plane any time you like, Jamie," Vette Jackson was gushing.

"Anyway," Elliott continued. "It turned out that Vette was not only willing to provide the plane so we could make a really fast trip out here, but she wanted to come, too."

"Oh, yes." She nodded vigorously, causing the unnaturally-red curls to bounce around her head.

"So we made a stop in Texas to pick up Charlie, and here we are."

Jamie gave his head a little shake, as though trying to clear it. "If you wanted to surprise me, you certainly did." Looking at Charlie, he said, "I really appreciate this. Especially all the effort it took. Especially…" His voice trailed off, but Jeanine saw him glance toward Vette, then back at Charlie. Then both of them tightened their lips, as though trying not to laugh. And suddenly Jeanine could feel how close they were, could feel the years of inside jokes and shared friendships and stories and experiences. And for one lonely moment, she felt very much the outsider.

"Well, even if you won't have dinner with us, you have to have dessert," Ruth said. "Why don't we all go in the living room and get comfortable?"

As they stood, Elliott looked at Jeanine. "Is anyone going to introduce us to your guest?"

Jamie and Ruth started to babble apologies. "We were too shocked to remember our manners," Jamie said. And then he introduced Jeanine, explaining her as his "new friend" and "my landlord's daughter."

To her surprise, Charlie stared at her with deep interest. "So you're Jeanine DeValery?"

"Uh…yes." She shot Jamie a questioning glance, but he looked just as puzzled.

"How have you heard of Jeanine?" Jamie asked him.

For a moment, they all froze and looked at Charlie, but after a quick glance around, he said to Jamie, "I'll tell you later. There's cake and presents waiting."

As they all started to troop into the living room, Jeanine whispered to Jamie, "So you haven't mentioned me to him?"

"No. I've had very little communication with him lately. I didn't even know he was stationed in Texas now."

"Then what's going on?"

"No idea."

Jeanine wanted to pursue the matter, but just about then, Vette Jackson hooked her arm through Jamie's and purred, "I brought you something very special."

"Oh…wow." As the singer led him away, he glanced back over his shoulder at Jeanine, as though asking for help.

But Elliott Dane had sidled up next to her. "So you've only known Jamie a few months?"

"That's right."

"You appear to be pretty close."

"Uh…maybe. He's needed someone to talk to, I guess."

"I heard the end of that little, uh, discussion you were having with Richard when we arrived."

"Oh." Jeanine felt herself growing warm again and knew she was probably beet red. "I get carried away sometimes."

"No, no, don't apologize. I meet so many shallow people, it's nice to hear someone passionate about what they believe. I mean, I assume you do believe what you were saying."

"Well…yes, I do." She grimaced. "Although if I had it to do over, I probably wouldn't make a public declaration of it at the dinner table."

Elliott chuckled. "Don't be embarrassed at all, Jeanine. No wonder Jamie's so fascinated by you."

"Oh, I wouldn't say that…" She sighed, staring into the living room, to where Vette and Jamie were now huddled alone in the corner. Jamie's face was creased with concern as he talked to the young woman. What in the world could they be so intense about? Jeanine wondered.

Elliott followed her line of vision to the pair across the room. "Jeanine, please don't worry about Vette. She has quite the crush on Jamie—and I had to bring her along since we were using her plane. But she doesn't stand a chance. She's not at all his type."

Jeanine felt her mouth twisting. "Who is his type? Paula?" Because she had little in common with Jamie's former girlfriend, either.

The man turned to study her. "I can't say. I didn't really know Paula. After Jamie's mother and I divorced, he kept his distance from me for quite a while, and that was the time he was involved with Paula." He smiled tightly. "But after his experience with her, I'd imagine he's looking for something different, wouldn't you?"

Jeanine didn't answer. She wasn't sure what to say, plus she was still distracted as Vette, her face animated and bright, looked up at Jamie and babbled on about something. Mae brought her and Elliott a cup of coffee as Ruth handed out slices of a rich white cake with intricate flowers.

Elliott set his cup down as Vette leaned her body into Jamie's, clutching his arm. "I'll just go and pull Vette off him, shall I?" he said.

Even after Elliott's intervention, Vette ended up sitting on one side of Jamie as they brought him his presents. Jeanine was on his other side, while Charlie Edenfield sat to her left. *I'm sitting between Danny Summer and Newt Fairchild,* she thought. If she had ever seriously believed she would be in this position, she wouldn't have expected it to feel like this. Sort of tense and weird and…ordinary. She felt annoyed that she was experiencing something amazing and couldn't seem to grasp it. Like trying to picture the ecstasy of Heaven and only coming up with bland gray clouds.

Vette shoved a small package in Jamie's face, causing him to flinch back into his chair. "Open mine first."

As he gingerly peeled the paper away, Jeanine saw a photo of Vette revealed. And "revealed" was a good word, since in the picture, the singer was sprawled across the hood of a limo and was wearing nothing but a see-through teddy and high heels.

"It's my latest CD," Vette said. "An advance copy. It doesn't officially come out until Monday."

"Wow, I'm…really flattered. Thank you."

Vette leaned across the arm of her overstuffed chair, laid her hand on Jamie's and murmured to him—just loudly enough to enable Jeanine to hear it, of course—"I gave you that CD because I wanted you to hear track five, *Night Sky*."

Jamie thrust the CD towards her. "Why don't you go play it for us, then?"

Rising to her feet, Vette raised her arms above her head and stretched— the long, luxurious movement of a cat. "I'll do better than playing the CD," she purred. "I'll sing for you."

"Great! Why don't you play it, too? Ruth, can Vette use your piano?"

Jeanine shot him a look. As Ruth led Vette across the room, he muttered, "I'm sorry, but I was desperate. I was afraid she was going to sit in my lap to sing."

A low chortling sound came from Charlie. Jamie didn't seem to notice, but Jeanine caught his eye, and they exchanged a smile.

Vette started to play, and at first Jeanine found herself wincing at the banging of the chords and the singer's rough voice. But as she adjusted to the sound, she heard the poetry in the lyrics about the night sky, the longing in the girl's soul for…something. As the sound and the piano and the naked yearning filled the room, the singer herself seemed to grow smaller and smaller, more fragile-looking. There was something oddly familiar about her. And then Jeanine realized with a jolt. Paula. What was it that Trev had said about Paula's appeal, all those weeks ago? The frailty, the vulnerability, the need for protection. Passion and addiction. Funny that Elliott had said

Vette wasn't Jamie's type. If past choices were any guide, she was exactly his type.

A heavy, cold feeling of lethargy started to weigh down on Jeanine, to push her down into the cushions of Richard's leather armchair. What in the world was she doing here with all these people—with *Jamie*? Whatever had she been thinking? She hadn't experienced such a feeling of futility since that first disastrous evening Jamie spent in her house. This was her dream, wasn't it? Why didn't it feel better?

Vette crashed into a loud crescendo of chords, and Jeanine felt Jamie's muscles jerk at the noise. He squeezed her fingers with his left hand as he hid his face in his right. She could feel him shaking, and for a moment she was worried, until he peeked up at her between his fingers, and she could tell that he was trying desperately to keep from laughing out loud. He took a deep breath and sat back up, his face remarkably composed. From the side of his mouth, he murmured to Jeanine, "I'd love to tell you that this is an unusual evening for me, but unfortunately it isn't."

Vette came thundering to an end, then shot one brief, spiteful look of triumph Jeanine's way before settling her gaze on Jamie once again. The applause was enthusiastic—as it should have been, Jeanine admitted grudgingly to herself. Although she couldn't bring herself to clap as loudly as everyone else.

Elliott bounced to the piano, squeezed Vette's shoulders and gave her a little peck on the cheek. "You see, my dear, that's why Richard and I are so anxious to put you and your music in a film—to capture that passion of yours for all time."

"True," Richard said, his voice sour. "It would be a gold mine for Elliott and me."

Elliott shot him a look that could have killed. The others were looking at Richard, too, but they mostly looked puzzled. All except Vette, who simply wiggled out of Elliott's grasp like a child avoiding a hug from her grandpa. "You promised we wouldn't talk about that tonight," she whined.

Vette went to Jamie and dropped to her knees in front of him. "What did you think of my song?"

"Oh. Brilliant."

She laid her hand on his knee. "I'm so glad you liked it. I wrote it for you."

"Really? Jeanine writes songs, too. And plays the piano." He whipped around to her, his eyes pleading. "You two probably have a lot to talk about." Sliding out from under Vette's hand, he managed to get to his feet. "I'll be right back...uh...bathroom."

After Jamie had fled the room, Vette turned to Jeanine. Her eyes didn't look nearly as dreamy and unfocused now, and her voice was mocking when she spoke. "So, you play piano, do you?"

Jeanine licked her lips. "A little."

"Really?" She made a sweeping gesture toward the piano. "Then by all means, why don't you show us?"

And now they were all looking at Jeanine. Vette's eyes looked like a hungry cat's but the rest of them only looked polite—almost bored.

Except Charlie. He focused on her with genuine interest. "I'd love to hear you, Jeanine. I'd especially love to hear something you've written."

"Oh, yes," Vette agreed, with sarcasm dripping from her voice. "I'm sure we'd love to hear one of your little songs."

Anger surged through Jeanine, white-hot. All their eyes were on her, either blatantly flaunting or politely hiding their thoughts of her, but she knew they were all thinking the same thing. *Prude. Hick. Hillbilly.*

Almost without realizing what she was doing, she jumped to her feet and practically ran to the piano. It briefly occurred to her that the last two times someone had asked her to show off her musical abilities like this, nerves had choked her and she hadn't done very well. But this time felt different. The very opposite of paralyzed, she was practically vibrating with rage. In fact, she made herself take a deep, calming breath before touching the keys. Remembering the effect her original Civil War ballad had at Trev's party, she started to move her hands and conjure the opening scales.

The rage subsided. The room opened, receded, disappeared. There was nothing but the timeless time of the song, so that when she once again played the eerie scale that brought the story to its close, she felt vaguely disoriented, as though she could have been playing for hours.

Unlike for Vette's song, there was no immediate applause, and she felt a twinge of doubt. In the second of silence before they started to clap, their faces appeared puzzled. But then they started to babble, gushing the same questions as the college kids at Trev's apartment.

"So was he a ghost?" Ruth asked her.

"If she told you that, it would take all the fun out of it."

That had come from Jamie. She pivoted on the stool to find him loung-ing in the doorway with a huge smile on his face. Part of her wanted to smile back while the other part wanted to kick him. She could feel them all staring at her, and he had put her in this position. Although it probably had done her good, with most of them, anyway. A quick glance in Vette's direction told her that this might not be a good moment for extended eye contact with the woman, sort of like provoking a wild animal. But really, who cared? She got up from the piano and went back to her chair, basking in the glow of approval coming from Jamie and, oddly enough, Charlie.

When she caught Charlie's eye, he nodded slowly and said, "That song was really powerful. I knew it would be. You're a born storyteller. I could tell from reading your *Summer* manuscript."

Jeanine gasped. "You've read my manuscript?"

He nodded, and she whirled on Jamie. "Who said you could send him my story? I mean, why—"

"Whoa, whoa!" Jamie held up his hands as though fending her off. "I did not send your manuscript to Charlie. I'm as confused as you are."

Now everyone's eyes were on Charlie, which didn't appear to bother him. "It's not that strange—well, actually, if you don't know the whole story, maybe it is."

"So tell us." Jeanine could hear a definite edge in Jamie's voice.

Charlie shrugged. "You sent the manuscript to Walter Raney, and he—without mentioning it to you, apparently—sent it to me."

Jeanine and Jamie exploded at the same moment. At the same time that she turned on Jamie and demanded, "Why in the world did you send my manuscript to…someone?" Jamie was asking more or less the same question of Charlie.

Charlie held up his hands. "I'm sorry, Jamie. I had no idea it was a secret or anything. Especially from Jeanine." He pursed his lips. "How could you send a manuscript anywhere without the writer's permission?"

"Thank you!" Jeanine said, nodding vigorously. She turned to Jamie. "How could you?"

Jamie cleared his throat. "Uh, maybe we could talk about this some-where else. I doubt anyone else is interested."

"On the contrary," Richard said with a grin. "We're fascinated."

"I'm not," Vette said. She plopped back down on the piano bench and started plinking some tuneless, jarring noise at the keys.

"If someone doesn't tell me what's going on, I'm going to scream," Jeanine said.

"You first," Charlie said to Jamie.

"Okay. Well…" He glanced around the room and started to speak in a calm, low voice—although he had to raise it after only a few words to be heard over Vette's piano, which got louder and louder every time he mentioned Jeanine. "A few weeks ago, Jeanine let me read a partial manuscript she had written—her idea for the next chapter in the *Summer* series."

"Which I only did for my amusement," Jeanine said. "I mean, if I had felt like sharing, I could have posted it on a fan fiction site online."

"I know, I know how private you are about it, but I had a crazy thought while I was reading it. It felt so…authentic. So much like something Hannah Raney might have written."

Charlie was nodding. "That's true. I felt that, too."

"I knew that Walter Raney, Hannah's widower, has the right to authorize someone to continue the series. He's just very protective of those characters, of her memory. But I wondered, if I showed him what you had written, if he might not be willing to authorize you—"

Jeanine gasped—and the gasp sounded so loud to her that it startled her. But as she glanced around the room, embarrassed, she realized the sound had been amplified because she wasn't the only one who had reacted in surprise. Elliott and Richard's eyes were as wide as hers must be, and she assumed it was because the very idea of the hick preacher's daughter as a follow-up to Hannah Raney was so preposterous.

A moment later, she realized she may have been on the wrong track. Elliott's lips twitched into a knowing smile, and he said, "It wasn't just the book you had in mind, was it, Jamie?"

"What?" Jeanine said. "What do you mean?"

Richard's voice was quiet. "No more books, no more movies. That's the way our contract with Hannah worked. So the movie series came to an end when she died, too. But if there were more books authorized by her estate—"

Elliott clapped his hands together. "Then we would be back in business. Don't tie up all those loose ends on Headwind Productions yet, Richard! It may not have gasped its last breath, after all."

The surprised expression on Richard's face was morphing into something different—something unpleasant. "Wait a minute, wait a minute. Talk about getting ahead of ourselves. No one has said that Walter Raney approved of any of this."

"Uh, yeah." Charlie looked sheepish. "That's kind of where I come into this."

"Oh, right," Jamie said. "That's why we started this conversation in the first place, isn't it? So how did you end up with the manuscript?"

"The thing is…" Charlie's voice trailed off, and he licked his lips nervously as he looked around at them. "The thing is, Hannah actually chose me to write the next *Summer* novels."

CHAPTER TWENTY-THREE

AGAIN, THERE CAME A COLLECTIVE INTAKE OF BREATH, SEEMINGLY FROM EVERYONE in the room.

"Chose you?" Richard demanded. "Chose you when? How?"

"You mentioned awhile ago that Walter Raney is the one who can authorize another author to continue the series—if he ever chooses to do it. He doesn't have to. But apparently, he and Hannah talked in a kind of theoretical way a few months before she died. She told him—just like she told me a few times—that she was convinced I was more of a writer than an actor, and that no one understood the *Summer* world and characters the way I did. She told him she didn't want to put it in writing or even tell me, because I was too young. Hannah planned to talk to me about it and make it a formal part of her will when I was mature enough, in her judgment, but she told Walter that if anything happened to her before that time, he could discuss it with me and ask me to continue the series." Charlie took a deep breath. "As a matter of fact, she pretty much told Walter that if I didn't choose to continue the series, she didn't want anyone to."

Jeanine felt an odd sinking feeling in the pit of her stomach, and realized she was disappointed. She mentally told herself to snap out of it. She hadn't even known there was a possibility of her being the next *Summer* writer until a few minutes ago. The important thing was, the *Summer* series might be revived, and that was a good thing, whether she was involved or not. Another little thrill went through her as she realized that she was involved, after all. This time around, she would personally know the producers and actors. Now she was shaking her head in amazement.

"But of course, if Hannah didn't put all this in writing, it's not really binding, is it?" Elliott was saying.

Jeanine snapped herself out of her daze to look at Charlie's uncle, wondering why he would have said that. Maybe he was worried about Charlie being cheated.

Jamie snorted. "As though Walter Raney would ever go against Hannah's wishes."

"That's true." Charlie was licking his lips again, which Jeanine was beginning to recognize as a nervous habit. "So, the whole question of whether the *Summer* series continues—books and movies—rests squarely on my shoulders. Can you imagine if the fans knew about that? I'd probably be getting death threats."

"But why?" Jeanine asked him. "Trust me, I'm one of the biggest fans out there, and the idea that someone is going to continue the series—no, not just anybody. Someone who loves the series and the characters is going to continue it." She felt herself breaking into a grin. "It's amazing! I'm excited already!"

A troubled look flickered across Charlie's face. "That's just the thing. I can't do it."

"What do you mean?" Richard asked.

"Of course you can do it." Jamie's words were supportive, but they had a sharp edge to them.

"No, I really can't." Charlie sounded matter-of-fact. "It's not as though I haven't tried."

"Obviously you haven't tried hard enough." Elliott sounded even harsher than Jamie.

Charlie laughed, but he didn't sound amused. "Wow. If y'all are reacting this way, can you imagine how the fans will be?"

Richard leaned toward Charlie, and surprisingly, he sounded understanding. "Is that why Walter sent you Jeanine's manuscript? To sort of help you get started?"

Vette's tinkling at the piano, which had grown softer as the conversation turned to Hannah Raney and Charlie, suddenly grew louder as Vette banged on the keys.

Jamie shot her a look of irritation, which she obviously didn't see, then turned back to Charlie. "I sincerely hope Walter didn't intend for you to steal

Jeanine's work. I realize he technically owns the characters, but still."

"You know Walter better than that," Charlie said. "And I certainly hope you think better of me." Charlie's eyes flashed.

"You're right, you're right. I'm just confused, frankly."

"Walter sent it to me for a couple of reasons. First, because it was kind of weird."

"What was?" Jeanine had to ask.

"Hannah didn't leave detailed outlines of the next books. If she had, maybe I would have stood a better chance of going on with them. But she did leave a couple of guides—a brief overview of the rest of the series, plus a two-page synopsis of what would happen in the next book. And your manuscript was pretty darn close." He shook his head in wonder. "You even guessed the secret about Danny's origins—the one people have been arguing and speculating about for years."

Jeanine realized her mouth had fallen open in surprise and made herself close it.

"That was one reason Walter forwarded the manuscript. It sort of astounded him. And then, of course, it came from Jamie, so Walter didn't want to just dismiss it out of hand. He asked me to look at it and see what I thought." Charlie frowned at Jamie. "And yes, he mentioned that if I liked it or thought it had potential, maybe we might either pay Jeanine a fee—like for a ghost writer—or ask her to collaborate with me. Stealing was never mentioned."

Jeanine's stomach made another wild lurch, and there went her fantasies again, taking flight like a phoenix from the ashes of her dead dreams. If these people kept toying with her, with all these rapid-pace ups and downs, she was going to end up vomiting on Ruth's lovely Oriental rug.

"Oh." Jamie sounded appeased. "So…you came because you're considering it?"

"Well, no. Not really. I came mostly for your birthday," Charlie said. "And also…" He looked at Jeanine. "I was hoping to meet the girl who writes like Hannah Raney."

The girl who writes like Hannah Raney. Jeanine started to laugh like an idiot, pure joy washing through her. They were all staring at her, speechless. Which was just as well, since Vette was now crashing down on the keys so violently that no one could have heard each other, anyway.

CHAPTER TWENTY-FOUR

JEANINE WASN'T ENTIRELY CLEAR AS TO WHAT HAPPENED OVER THE NEXT HOUR OR so. She floated through in a happy fog, drifting in and out of the random small talk that Ruth diplomatically steered them into. Only twice was she jolted out of her happy daze—first, when Richard abruptly stood up and said to Jamie, "Do you mind stepping into the study with me for a minute? There's something I'd like to talk to you about."

Judging by Jamie's face, he was taken aback, too, but he got up and followed Richard into the hallway. Of course, the talk could be about anything—including the possibility of another *Summer* movie—but Jeanine couldn't help assuming it had something to do with her. And she didn't think it was good.

The next shock came right after they left, when Elliott focused on her with a smile. "So Jeanine, tell us. Just how close are you and Jamie?"

The piano fell silent, and Vette swiveled on the stool to glare at her. Ruth and Charlie were looking at her with interest, too.

"Oh, ah…we're uh…good friends, I think." Her hand went to the chain around her neck, and she pretended to adjust it, making sure the ring was still hidden under her blouse. She felt so warm with embarrassment she expected to burst into flames at any moment.

Ruth smiled as if she knew all about their relationship—and Jeanine wished she was that certain, herself. She had a ring from the guy, but couldn't let anyone see it. And all night, Jamie had just called them friends. What was going on in his mind, exactly?

184

Elliott's voice was teasing. "Just friends, huh? So you're fair game for anyone else who's interested, then." He glanced at Charlie, who turned as red as Jeanine probably was. She wondered if it was possible to die of humiliation.

A few minutes later, Ruth made her apologies and said she wasn't feeling very well. "Probably a combination of pregnancy and three slices of cake," she said. "But I think I need to go lie down for just a bit. Just make yourselves at home and call Mae if you need anything."

As Ruth left, Vette jumped to her feet so quickly the piano bench overturned. Ignoring it, she headed for the door. "Elliott, I'm not feeling too well, myself. I need some air. Show me where the patio is."

With a deep sigh, Elliott started after her. But he paused in the doorway. "Jeanine, we have to get Charlie back to Texas tomorrow afternoon, but maybe we could all have a late breakfast at the airport. Get to know one another better."

For the first time in her life, she was happy to have an exam scheduled the next day. Before she could make her excuses, however, Charlie snorted and said, "I'm not sure she'd live through another get-together with Vette."

"Hmm, you may be right. Well, Charlie, maybe just you and Jeanine, then, while I try to keep Ms. Jackson happy. Which could probably only be done by bringing Jamie along with us, unfortunately."

"Oh, I'm sorry. I have a test tomorrow. But thank you for, um, suggesting it." She refused to look at Charlie, afraid he would look disappointed. Or relieved. For some reason, either one would upset her.

"Elliott, I'm waiting!" Vette called, her voice shrill and totally devoid of the dreamy quality it had possessed early in the evening.

"See what I mean?" With a sigh, Elliott turned on his heel and left the room.

With Elliott's departure, she found herself alone with Charlie. After a long moment of silence, Jeanine cleared her throat. "So. Do you think I made everyone sick? Or was it you?"

Charlie chuckled but didn't say anything. She had an uncomfortable feeling they both suspected that people were trying to leave them alone together.

"It's been a really weird evening," Jeanine said.

"Yeah, well, if you keep associating with this crowd, you'll have a lot of those."

"Is that why you joined the Army? To get away from this weirdness?" Jeanine clamped her hand to her mouth, horrified that the words had popped out.

She was relieved to see Charlie's eyes twinkling.

"Can you blame me?" Then he grew more serious. "No, really, everybody seems to think I'm nuts. But I think I have pretty good reasons for what I'm doing."

Jeanine felt herself relaxing, and leaned back in the armchair. "If you still think so after basic training, you must have good reasons."

"I actually kind of enjoyed it."

"You're kidding!"

"I know. I guess it was the attitude I went in with. I was wanting something tough, to prove myself, I guess. My Aunt Phoebe always said I had a banty rooster complex." He cocked his head. "You probably don't have a clue what that means, do you?"

"Sure I do. Bantam roosters are small, but they're tough and…well, mean, right? I'm a country girl too, you know."

"Too? Oh, that's right. You said you were a fan, so I guess you know where I'm from."

"Yeah. It was a great relief to hear someone else say 'y'all' a little while ago."

Charlie was still on the "fan" track. "I bet it was Jamie you were always interested in, though. Right?"

"Well, I—"

"It's okay," he assured her. "I have no illusions on that score. Getting back to the banty rooster thing, you're being a lot nicer than Aunt Phoebe. She always said it was somebody smaller than everyone else who constantly picked fights so he could prove he was just as strong and mean as anyone else."

Jeanine tilted her head, skeptical. "You seem pretty calm to me."

"I've worked on the temper tantrums over the years, but maybe I do still want to prove myself." He laughed. "It's not easy growing up with virtual Greek gods like Jamie and Eric Thomas and Camilla and all those great actors we worked with."

Jeanine grimaced. "I had a hard enough time just growing up with a perky blonde sister."

He chuckled again and reached up as though to push back his hair, and ended up rubbing his practically shaved head. Jeanine figured it must still feel weird to him.

"So did the other soldiers give you a hard time, you being famous and all? I can't imagine what that must have been like on either side. For you, trying to adjust to a totally different lifestyle. And for everyone else, finding themselves going through basic with a celebrity."

Charlie shrugged. "First couple of weeks, I got a little bit of everything. Some who didn't have a clue who I was, had never even seen one of the *Summer* movies. A few guys who were excited because they were fans—had been reading the books and going to the movies since they were kids. And of course, a few who had some kind of complex, themselves, and wanted to pick fights or put me in my place."

"That doesn't sound very pleasant."

"I told you, I've been known to pick a few fights myself." He leaned in toward her. "If Jamie wasn't so darn nice, I could beat the crap out of him frankly, even if he is bigger than me."

Jeanine found herself laughing in spite of herself. "He really is nice, isn't he?"

"Yeah, it's disgusting." Charlie sighed. "But I digress. Actually I digressed a lot. Weren't you asking me why I joined up in the first place?"

"Right."

"Reason number one was purely practical. I finally made myself face the fact that I'm going to be one of those child stars that's just not gonna have a career as an adult."

"Oh, but I think—"

"No, no, it's okay." He put his hand up to silence her. "There are more important things in the world than acting." He studied Jeanine, as though trying to make up his mind how much to say. "Are you a big enough fan to know the story of how Hannah Raney died?"

"Oh, uh…well, I know she died in a fire."

"At my house."

"Yeah. I did know that." For some reason, Jeanine felt herself flushing.

He looked off into the distance, as though seeing something other than Jeanine. "The night that she died…well, of course it was horrible. But it was also a turning point for me. I was fine but Aunt Phoebe and Hannah both got hurt and both needed help getting out." Charlie's voice was starting to shake. "I was totally useless."

Jeanine shook her head. "No. That's not what I heard. You…" She stopped. What did she know, except what she had heard through the media? Filtered through publicists like Jamie's, maybe? "I'm sorry," she said. "You must think I'm an idiot, pretending to know anything about your life."

"No, I appreciate your support, trust me." The corners of his mouth lifted. "And I did try to save them, but…anyway." He took a deep breath. "I hated myself for ages after that fire. In all those movies, we're so heroic— Danny and Newt and all the rest. But when it came to real life, I couldn't do anything."

"Danny and Newt struggle, too."

"I know, I know, I'm just saying…I decided I wanted to do something real for a change. I've always sort of lived inside my head, in a fantasy world. I wondered what it would be like to tackle something heroic in real life, for a change. Or at least to see if such a thing is possible."

Jeanine nodded slowly. "That makes sense. Jamie said you were going into the medical corp."

"Yep. I started training in Texas last week. Eventually I hope I can be deployed somewhere that I can be of use."

"That's pretty amazing," Jeanine said. "And interesting."

"How do you mean?"

"Well, you usually hear of people trying to escape reality. You're the first one I ever heard of trying to escape fantasy."

Charlie grinned. "You have quite a way with words, Ms. DeValery." His eyes grew wistful. "I sort of wish this stuff about the book and the movie had come up before I joined the Army, but it's something I have to do right now. You understand, don't you?"

"Sure." Amazed at her own boldness, Jeanine touched his hand. "I think it's pretty great what you're doing. Although, as a fan, I can tell you I want that next *Summer* book. And movie."

He shrugged. "Maybe someday. Just not right now."

Before Jeanine could answer, Elliott's voice came from the doorway. "Charlie, sorry to break up the party, but I think Vette is ready to go."

He had his arm around her and appeared to be supporting her. Her eyes looked sort of vacant and glassy now.

Vette reached up and rubbed at her forehead. "I want to go now," she said dreamily.

"All right, all right." Elliott gave Charlie an exasperated look. "Will you thank Richard for us and say good-bye to Jamie?"

"Okay." As Elliott and Vette disappeared toward the front door, Charlie got to his feet and stretched. "Sorry to cut it short, but they're my ride. Walk with me, okay?"

Jeanine did as he suggested, amazed at how quickly she felt comfortable with him. They chatted easily as they walked down the hallway toward Richard's study, but Jeanine hung back before they reached the door and motioned for Charlie to go on.

Charlie tapped once on the door and swung it open, and before he could get inside, Jeanine heard Richard's voice. "You need to think it over, Jamie. I'm serious. After what I saw tonight, I can promise you she won't fit into your life out there."

And then the door swung shut behind Charlie, and Jeanine didn't hear anything else.

Chapter Twenty-Five

The first fifteen minutes of the drive back to Middleboro passed in complete silence. Jeanine tried to scrape up the courage to ask Jamie about his little talk with Richard, but every time she opened her mouth to start she would catch a glimpse of his lips set in a tight line and couldn't manage it.

When she absolutely couldn't take the quiet any more, she tried to sound cheerful. "So, did you enjoy your birthday? It must have been a nice surprise to have your friend Charlie there, at least."

He slowly turned his head and gave her an odd look, then faced the front again. "I need to apologize to you, obviously. For sharing your manuscript without your permission."

"Oh." With everything that had happened, she had almost forgotten her anger of a couple of hours ago. "No, it's okay. I think all that got explained pretty well, and if it had worked out…wow."

"Yeah. Obviously, I had no idea what the situation was."

"I know." She hesitated. "Do you think he'll ever write it?"

Again came the odd look from Jamie, which was beginning to annoy her. "Who knows? So. What did you think of him?"

"Charlie? Seemed nice enough."

"And Elliott?"

"Okay, I guess." She decided to go for it, blurting the words fast, before she could chicken out. "So what did Richard want to talk to you about?"

"Oh…business stuff, mostly."

Business. Yeah. She waited for him to say more, but when he didn't, she prompted him, figuring she could ease him around to what she heard at the end. "Did he want to talk about Charlie's announcement?"

"We talked about it for a minute. Mostly he wanted to warn me not to get my hopes up. He doesn't think Charlie can do the job."

"Poor Charlie."

"Poor Charlie?" he echoed. She didn't particularly care for the tone of his voice.

"Well, yeah. He doesn't seem to have a very high opinion of himself," she said.

"What exactly did I miss while Richard had me trapped in his study?"

He still sounded snarky, but she tried to ignore it. "Not much. Small talk."

Jamie snorted. "With that crowd, it had to be more interesting than that. So tell me."

"I really don't remember anything very interesting. Vette threw a little tantrum after you left and practically dragged everyone out. And Elliott tried to get me to come back up to Atlanta tomorrow morning—well, I guess he wanted both of us to, actually. He wanted us to have breakfast together before they had to take Charlie back to his base."

"What!"

"He said he wanted us all to get to know each other better."

"Oh, did he really?"

"Yes, really."

After that one little outburst, Jamie fell silent again. Just before Jeanine's own irritation turned into an explosion, he distracted her again by taking an exit ramp. They must need gas, she figured. No point in starting an argument if he had a good excuse to get out of the car and slam the door while she was talking. So she waited.

But he didn't turn into any of the gas stations. Instead, he pulled into the parking lot of a motel, put the car in park, and cut the engine. Okay, so he must want to talk, after all. They were getting pretty close to Middleboro so time was running out.

She folded her arms and waited for him to say what was on his mind. It was a long wait. She could see his Adam's apple working as he swallowed hard, and he wasn't looking at her.

Slapping the seat in frustration, she said, "Okay, I've had just about enough. If you have something unpleasant to say, just go ahead and—"

In a sudden move, he leaned across the seat, cutting off her words by pressing his lips against hers. Caught off guard, she slid back against the car door before she quite realized what was happening. Placing her hands on his shoulders to steady herself, she returned the kiss, glad that he was kissing her instead of breaking up with her. At least she supposed she was glad. Everything felt so different—the hard pressure of his hand on the back of her neck, gripping her as though desperate to hold on. That was it. Desperation.

She pulled away and tried to catch her breath. "Jamie, are you okay?"

"Yeah, I just..." He leaned his forehead against hers, still holding tight. "I love you, Jeannie."

"I love you, too." She took a deep breath. "You're upset because of Richard, right?"

"What do you mean?"

"Well, I...I didn't exactly make a great impression on him, I know. And I know he's important to you."

He massaged the back of her neck and whispered, "Let's just try very hard to forget about my whole crazy family for a little while, okay?"

She had to laugh. "Fine with me."

"Good. I...I really need you right now, Jeanine. You can't believe how much."

She smiled and stroked his cheek. "Feel free to tell me."

"I want to show you."

"Yeah?"

"Very much. I want to be with you. Is that so terrible?"

It took her a split second to realize what he meant, and then she could feel herself blushing, not so much at his suggestion as with embarrassment that it had taken her that long to understand. Richard was right, she was a backwards hick. The guy had pulled the car into a motel parking lot—no, not just the parking lot. They were practically in front of the door marked "Registration," and what he was obviously thinking had never even occurred to her.

"I know this isn't exactly what we had planned..." he was saying. And then he said some other stuff, but her mind was spinning and working so fast that it ran right past his words, zipping off in all directions and running back again, like a dog playing fetch. Off it would go, *oh dear Lord, where is this coming from, after we talked all this over and decided to take it slow and wait and now…is it a test? To see if I'm some crazy fundamentalist like Richard told him I am? So if I say no is he gone?* Back to Jamie, trying to focus on him explaining how much he needed her and asking if it would really be so terrible and her feeling herself shaking her head. And then off again. *My first time. With Jamie Newkirk. Jamie Newkirk. Isn't that exactly what I always dreamed of? Then why is it just so nauseatingly awful?*

A beat-up SUV pulled up next to them and disgorged an entire family with bright shirts and shorts and brighter sun-burned skin. Probably returning north from Disneyworld. She watched the two boys jump up on an iron railing, yelling at the top of their lungs, and could see the inside of the motel lobby as they shoved open the doorway and ran inside. Without even going in, she knew the place. She could smell the slightly musty smell of the air conditioning units and feel the rough carpeting under her feet, because she had been in these interstate motels on family trips her whole life. It was the stuff of nostalgia, but not the stuff of romantic dreams.

It was a test. She was sure of it. And she had to pass the test, right?

She felt herself nodding at whatever Jamie was saying. "Yes," she said. "All right."

And then she sat there waiting—waiting for him to go arrange for the room, because that's what the man did, right? Even her father did that, on a family trip to Disney. But Jamie just sat there, looking sheepish.

"I know this is awful," he said. "But if I go in there, someone will recognize me, and I'll have to get the room in my name, and—"

"Oh."

"Yeah. So, I'm really sorry, but could you go in and get the room?"

She must have looked as shocked as she felt, because Jamie hurriedly reached for his wallet. "I don't expect you to pay for it, of course." He pulled out a wad of cash, and held it out to her.

She felt the laughter bubbling up, bubbling over, and there it came, shaking her body and taking her breath. She doubled over, practically screaming with it. It would have been like the fit of giggles she'd had on the floor of Jamie's living room, except that she felt more hysterical than amused this time. And this time, Jamie wasn't laughing with her. His eyes were wide and somewhat horrified.

He dropped the money onto the console and cranked the car. "I'm sorry, Jeannie. I'm really sorry."

She struggled to catch her breath and stop laughing as he babbled. "I don't know what I was thinking, Jeanine. That was absolutely unforgiveable of me. I mean...I just...I just wanted to be with you so badly tonight, and I knew it would never happen if we got back home right under your parents' noses. But still. It was horrible of me, even asking something like that of a girl like you."

A girl like you. The laughter died as abruptly as though someone had punched her. They drove the last miles back home in silence. When he pulled up next to her house, she turned her face toward him just enough to let him give her a quick brush of his lips on hers, and then she ran into the house, calling an excuse to Mamma, who had no doubt been waiting up to hear all the enchanting details, as she fled up the stairs to her room. As she collapsed on her bed in the dark, the certainty hit her.

She had failed the test.

After a sleepless night of tossing around in the bed and changing positions and trying everything she could think of to calm her racing mind, she finally got out of bed around five and went down to the kitchen to study for her exam. Naturally, with a textbook and a job in front of her, all she wanted to do was sleep, although the way her mind was still bouncing around in all directions, she probably couldn't have managed it if she had tried. As she was trying to focus on the mystery of the narrator in "A Rose for Emily," a sudden thought snapped her mind back to full alertness. What if the test hadn't been from Jamie, but from God?

The idea gave her a sick feeling. Not once in the sleazy motel parking lot had she thought about what God wanted her to do—even after all her lofty declarations of principle to Richard. All she had thought about was what she needed to do to have the desire of her heart...which was Jamie, right? Sure, she had made it home unsullied, but only because of a fit of hysteria.

More to distract herself than anything, she got up for another cup of coffee and was pouring it with a shaky hand when she glimpsed a shadowy figure through the curtain at the kitchen door. Startled, she jumped, splashing the hot stuff on her hand—which made her jerk and splash it again, which made her yelp in pain.

"Jeannie, are you all right?" came Jamie's voice through the door. He rattled the knob. "Let me in, okay?"

She did, even though she didn't feel like it. She didn't have the energy yet to talk about last night, especially not with her fingers throbbing and no caffeine in her system.

She was just about to tell him that when he blurted, "I have to go to Atlanta."

"Wh-what?" She sucked on her burned fingers, which he didn't even seem to notice.

"I've got an emergency, and I didn't want to leave without telling you, like last time."

"Oh no. Is it Ruth? Is the baby okay?"

"It's not Ruth." Looking miserable, Jamie shoved his disheveled hair out of his face. "It's Charlie. He's in hospital."

CHAPTER TWENTY-SIX

"CHARLIE! HE SEEMED FINE WHEN WE LEFT. WAS THERE AN ACCIDENT?"

Jamie avoided her eyes. "We talked on the phone last night, and he was in the hotel lounge having a drink with Vette. At some point after that he apparently lost consciousness and they called an ambulance." He took a deep breath, then slowly let it out. "It'll be a while before they get the results of the tests, but they suspect drugs. Specifically, some kind of opioid like OxyContin."

"Drugs!" Jeanine heard herself spit out the word like a profanity. "More drugs!"

Jamie's eyes flashed for a second, then he slumped and just looked miserable. "Yeah, Jeanine. More drugs."

She felt groggy and disoriented, from lack of sleep and from too much to think about. She headed back to the coffee pot, shaking her head as she went. "I don't know what to say. This just doesn't seem like something Charlie would do."

Jamie gave a harsh laugh. "Got to know him really well, did you?"

She turned to face him. "No, but I thought it was fairly reasonable to assume that a guy who loved the physical challenge of boot camp and was excited about his medical training and serving people wouldn't do something this stupid a few hours later."

"I've told you before, Jeanine. People don't always make that much sense."

"The ones in your life certainly don't." The brief burst of energy left her, and she slumped against the counter, feeling sad and defeated. "So I take it he's done things like this before?"

Jamie hesitated. "Well…no, not like this. I mean…I can't say Charlie is perfect. But he's not a user, and I have to admit you're right. This is weird. I almost wonder…" His voice trailed off.

"Wonder what?"

"Oh, never mind." He gave a dismissive wave of his hand. "There's no point speculating. I'm going up there and hopefully I'll find out more."

Jeanine nodded. "Do they think he's going to be okay?"

"I think they got him in time. He went into respiratory arrest, so he's lucky to be alive."

"Thank God," Jeanine said. She almost asked him if she should go visit Charlie, too. Preachers' daughters were raised to visit the sick. But she didn't think Jamie would like the suggestion. So she just said, "Tell him he's in my prayers."

"Yeah, okay."

"Do you have any idea when you might get back?"

Jamie's shoulders sagged, and Jeanine didn't like the look of misery that came into his face.

"What else is wrong?" she asked quietly. Although she had a feeling she knew what was coming. With a shaking hand, she carefully set her untouched coffee down on the counter, afraid of sloshing the hot stuff on her hand a second time.

"Jeannie, I think…I don't think I'm going to be coming back."

She struggled to take a breath, but reflexively set her features into a blank mask. "Oh, really? And what exactly does that mean?"

Jamie gestured toward the kitchen table. "Let's sit down, okay?"

She shook her head. "No, just go ahead and say whatever you need to say." She liked the feel of the solid countertop she was leaning against. She was afraid to leave its support. As wobbly as her legs felt, she might not make it to the table.

Jamie didn't sit down either. He stood in front of her, arms tightly crossed as he started to talk. "Jeannie, I've just been thinking…how fast we've been going…" His arms came uncrossed as he started to gesture with his hands. "I mean, really, I do love you, but…I reckon getting engaged so soon was really—"

"Stupid," Jeanine said flatly.

"No! Just...fast."

"Funny thing. It didn't seem too fast for you until we spent an evening with your family."

"Jeannie, I—"

"Until certain relatives of yours pointed out to you my lack of sophistication, and how terrible I am for you."

"Jeanine, no one said that."

"Oh, please. I know what Richard thought of me."

"I don't care what Richard thinks. And this has nothing to do with any of that."

"Oh, so you're saying that you breaking up with me has nothing to do with your family?"

Reaching behind him, Jamie groped for one of the kitchen chairs and sank down into it, as though suddenly out of energy. "This has everything to do with my family, just not the way you think."

"Oh, come on, Jamie. I understand perfectly." She felt hot tears forming in her eyes and clenched her jaw until she could blink them back and speak calmly. "I failed your test."

"What?" Jamie appeared perplexed. "What test?"

"At the motel. I was supposed to show you that Richard was wrong— that I'm all worldly and sophisticated and could handle that situation you threw me into. Instead, I basically became hysterical." She couldn't keep the quaver out of her voice as she finished up. "I failed."

Jamie moaned and leaned his head in his hands, then snapped back up to face her. "Yes, that stupid thing last night is part of it. But not like you think."

"Then explain it to me."

"First, listen. I don't want to break up. I just want to slow down a bit. Let's just...take a breather. I imagine after all this, you need some time to think, as well."

"Think about what?"

Jamie snorted. "I can't even believe you're asking that." His eyes locked on hers, and they looked almost pleading. "Jeannie, do you really want to be involved with my crazy family? You're right. Last night was a fiasco. You didn't fit in." He shook his head slowly. "And I don't want you to."

"Oh come on, Jamie," she said quietly. "Do you think I'm an idiot? I'm supposed to believe you're leaving me because I'm too good for you? Yeah, right!" Feeling the ache in her throat that signaled tears, she breathed deeply and calmed herself again. "But I guess the reason really doesn't matter." Her hand went to her throat, feeling for the chain but not finding it. "Oh, the ring is still upstairs. I'll go get it for you."

"Don't be ridiculous, Jeanine. I don't want the ring back."

"I don't want your ring, Jamie. Not while you're 'thinking things over.' I'll be right back."

She ran up the stairs, hoping to get through this whole scene before she came apart. Plus, she could hear her parents stirring and wanted Jamie gone before they came down. She nabbed the ring from her room and, without taking time to remove it from the chain, ran back down to the kitchen.

But Jamie was already gone.

CHAPTER TWENTY-SEVEN

JAMIE MANAGED TO MAKE IT TO CHARLIE'S HOSPITAL ROOM WITHOUT RUNNING into any paparazzi or reporters. So far, Charlie's overdose hadn't seemed to hit the news, but it was bound to soon. Sighing in resignation, he tapped on the door that the nurses had directed him to and pushed it open.

Charlie was alone, either asleep or resting with his eyes closed, but he opened them and looked toward the doorway as Jamie came in.

"Hey," he said, unsmiling.

"Hey. How are you feeling?"

Charlie snorted. "Just peachy." He closed his eyes again.

Jamie dragged a chair up next to the bed and settled into it, then waited for Charlie to open his eyes. When he finally did, Jamie said softly, "So what happened?"

Charlie's shoulders jerked, which Jamie took as a shrug. "I don't know. I guess somebody slipped me something in my drink."

"Huh."

Now Charlie's eyes were wide, accusing. "You think I did this to myself?"

Jamie shook his head. "No, I don't, Charlie. I really don't."

Charlie studied him for a moment, then his face relaxed. "Well, thanks. That's more than I can say for my commanding officers."

"What do you mean?"

"I'm out of the Army."

"What!"

"Yep. Didn't take them long to make that decision, did it?"

"But this is not your fault."

"It's called Entry Level Separation. They can chuck you out pretty easily in the early days. And they don't like drugs."

"Surely you can appeal it."

"I don't know. Maybe."

"But you're not going to."

"I don't know, Jamie." Charlie squeezed his eyes shut again. "It's all happening so fast."

"Yeah, you can say that again." Jamie thought of that weird dinner party, and all that had happened with Jeanine since. "I feel like I've lived about two lifetimes since yesterday."

"Yeah, well, my life is certainly different than it was yesterday morning." Charlie stared at the ceiling. "Sometimes I feel like someone is actively trying to screw up my life. Every time I decide what I want to do, something like this happens."

In the silent moment that followed, Jamie knew they were both thinking of the fire that killed Hannah. But Jamie went on a different track. "Do you think someone was specifically targeting you last night?"

"Honestly…I think it was Vette."

"You think Vette put something in your drink?" Jamie leaned forward in his chair.

"No, no, of course not." Charlie laughed. "I mean, I think someone was trying to dope her. It got pretty crazy in that bar last night. A bunch of fans spotted her, and she just ate it up, of course. She loves being the center of attention. And for a while, people were coming and going to our table, and she was working the room and even went to the piano—"

"And you left the table to call me, didn't you?"

"Yeah. There was no way I could have heard you in that racket, so I went outside."

"Could it have happened then?"

"Yeah, sure. And the way everybody was moving around, playing musical chairs, somebody could have thought they were spiking Vette's drink. Maybe a guy that had plans for her."

"Yeah," Jamie said, trying to sound convinced. "Well, anyway, the important thing is you're going to be okay. You are going to be okay, right?"

"Yeah, sure. Unemployed with no direction, but otherwise just dandy."

Charlie's mouth twisted in a rueful smile. "I bet I know what you're thinking."

"That's a neat trick. I'm not even sure what I'm thinking."

"Of course you are. Like we said, a lot has changed since last night. So you're probably thinking, why don't you just pop out that *Summer* book now, ole boy? You got nothing else to do."

Jamie's stomach gave a lurch, and he suddenly felt queasy. Charlie was right. It really was as though someone were arranging things, herding them in a certain direction. Shaking his head, Jamie said, "No, Charlie. I wasn't thinking that at all."

Charlie raised his eyebrows. "No? Why not? You were all hot to continue the series, weren't you? You're the one that contacted Walter about it."

"Yeah, but…like you said, a lot has changed."

"Oh, I see."

"What?"

"You just wanted your girlfriend to write it. You're not interested if I'm going to do it." As Jamie started to protest, Charlie raised his hand to stop him, then weakly dropped it back to the bed. "It's okay. Her writing really was good. Better than mine. It makes sense." His smile looked wistful. "You want to work with her. I understand, believe me."

Jamie took a deep breath and blew it out slowly, trying to calm himself. "Charlie, you're right. I didn't know about Hannah's wishes for you and the book when I sent that manuscript to Walter, or I wouldn't have done it. I assure you, I regret doing it. It's your job to do or not do. You don't have to decide right now, although…"

"Although what?"

"Just…I don't know. Nothing." And then he heard himself blurting the words. "Elliott wasn't with you in the lounge last night?"

Charlie looked startled. "No. Why do you ask?"

"I just…like you said, sometimes it does seem as though someone's working things behind the scenes, doesn't it?"

"What's that got to do with Elliott?"

"Haven't you ever noticed? Things usually seem to work out in his favor."

Charlie's face was flushing. "I'm not sure what you're getting at, but Elliott Dane is the one person who has stood by me and supported me over the years."

"Oh, really? Awhile back, he insinuated you might be the one who sold that story about me to the tabloid—the one about me getting Paula started on drugs, and about the night my mother died."

"What!" Charlie's face went as white as the sheets he was lying on. "That's not true!"

"What's not true? You didn't give the story to the tabloid, or you don't believe Elliott said that about you?"

"Neither...either. Why would Elliott...I mean...how could you ever even think such a thing about me?"

"I didn't believe it...not really. I only ever had it in my mind because of Elliott. But I shouldn't have said anything about it." He grunted. "It was probably Elliott who sold the story in the first place, if they paid enough."

Charlie struggled to sit up. "Elliott barely even knew Paula. He only met her once or twice."

Jamie noticed that the readings on the electronic gizmos measuring Charlie's vitals were rising fast, so he put up his hands and said, "Okay, okay, calm down."

Jamie stood up. "Look, I didn't mean to upset you. I'm going now."

"Jamie, wait."

With his hand on the door handle, Jamie turned back to him. Charlie had collapsed against his pillows again and was frowning—probably in the grips of the "oh crap" phase. He said, "You are coming back, right?"

"Well, of course I'll see you again soon. But you're probably not going to be in hospital long, are you?"

"Probably not."

"So maybe I'll see you in L.A."

Charlie looked puzzled. "I thought you were going to be in Georgia indefinitely."

"No, I'm heading back to L.A. today. I have some business to take care of. Is that where you're going when you're discharged?"

Charlie shook his head slowly. "No idea, Jamie. No idea at all."

As Jamie closed the door of Charlie's room behind him, he almost collided with a woman in the hallway. As he stepped back and apologized, he immediately recognized the lady with honey-colored hair so much like Charlie's. "Phoebe!"

"Hello, Jamie," she said, in a lilting tone that also reminded Jamie of Charlie. She steadied herself and straightened her jacket. Phoebe was always straightening something.

An awkward silence fell.

Phoebe cleared her throat. "So…how is he?"

Jamie shrugged. "Confused. Upset. Who wouldn't be?"

"If he's all right physically, maybe this is all for the best. I wasn't entirely happy with this Army business, even though he's certainly got to find something to do with his life."

"So you know he's out of the Army?"

"I spoke to him on the phone awhile ago, yes."

Jamie was a little surprised that Charlie hadn't mentioned that. "Well…go easy on him, okay? He's in pretty bad shape."

Phoebe tilted her head and drilled a hole in him with her eyes. "What exactly do you mean by that?"

"Just…you know." Jamie felt himself wilting under that laser gaze.

"No, I don't." Phoebe shifted her weight from one foot to the other and straightened the handbag hanging from her shoulder.

"I just mean…this wasn't his fault. Someone probably slipped him the drugs in his drink."

Her mouth twisted, and her face took on an expression he couldn't quite read.

"Mmmm…yes," she said.

Before he could stop himself, he blurted out, "Do you think Elliott could have done it?"

"Elliott!" Her eyes narrowed. "Why would you think that?"

Briefly he told her about the dinner party, the latest development with the *Summer* series and Charlie.

Her eyes narrowed as she spoke. "Charlie hadn't told me any of that."

"It was a surprise to all of us," Jamie said hurriedly. "But anyway, as usual, things seem to be working out pretty well for Elliott."

"Things don't always work out well for Elliott," she mused.

"What do you mean?"

"The fire that killed Hannah. That stopped him living off the *Summer* gravy train, didn't it? I imagine that was pretty unexpected for him."

Jamie nodded. "Yeah…That fire. So weird. I know a lot of the bad stuff with Charlie—you know, depression, and crazy stuff like joining the Army-I know a lot of it's come on gradually…" For a moment, he broke off, distracted by the sound of Elliott in his memory, snarling at Charlie, "Why can't you be more like Jamie? You disgust me." He took a deep breath and continued. "But the fire made everything worse. Somehow Charlie saw that as the end of his acting career, I guess."

"Yes, but…it's more than that." Phoebe's face took on a far-away look. "Charlie's always been a dreamer, but not about acting and careers. He dreamed of stories and heroes. He dreamed of being a hero. That fire…" The woman heaved a deep breath. "I've never told anyone this…and it's just a suspicion, mind you…but…the night of the fire, I was trapped in my room for several minutes. Critical minutes. The fire was blazing in the hallway, and I needed to go out the window but couldn't get it open. I started calling for help…I…" Swallowing hard, she seemed to force herself to continue. "I heard Hannah calling for help, too. I eventually managed to break my window and crawl out. Thankfully, I was on the ground floor. By the time I got outside, Charlie was dragging Hannah out. It was too late, of course, but still…I've always wondered…"

Her voice trailed away. Almost not wanting to hear, Jamie forced himself to say, "Wondered what?"

Lifting her head, she met his gaze, her eyes sharp and steady again. "I've wondered if Charlie didn't hear us both crying for help and decide to go to Hannah first."

"Oh, Phoebe, no—I'm sure he loves you and he didn't—"

"No, no, that's not why I'm bringing it up now." She waved her hand, seeming to dismiss the issue of Charlie's love as unimportant. "I have no illusions about my relationship with Charlie. But you see the point is…he's always dreamed of being a fantasy hero, someone larger than life. But in the first place, he didn't manage to save anyone from that fire. And in the second place…well, if he did choose the woman who represented his career over his own flesh-and-blood, I would imagine he's struggling with that a bit, wouldn't you?"

Jamie nodded glumly. "Yeah, I would."

She jerked the sliding handbag strap up onto her shoulder again. "Look, Charlie is still laboring under the delusion that Elliott loves him." She laughed sharply. "That Elliott is capable of loving anyone other than himself.

Now is not the time to shatter that dream for him, too, all right?" She smiled sourly. "In my experience, Elliott is mainly a danger to unfortunate women who fall in love with him."

"Okay, whatever," Jamie mumbled.

"Good. Well. It was very nice to see you again. I'm going in to see Charlie now." The strong emotion of a moment before was gone from her face as she turned away from him.

"Phoebe, wait," Jamie said hurriedly. "I know I shouldn't ask this, but…"

She gave him an icy look. "Yes?"

"My mother and Paula…they both had a mark…like a cigarette burn…I was just wondering if you…" His voice trailed off as he completely lost his nerve.

Her face had gone a brilliant red, and her eyes were like daggers. "How dare you even think of asking me a question like that!"

He put up his hands. "I'm sorry, okay? Really."

"I should hope so." She nodded a curt good-bye and turned on her high heel, stomping to the door of Charlie's room. But as she pulled the door handle with her right hand, Jamie could see her fingering the neckline of her blouse with her left—near the area a burn scar like Teresa's would have been.

CHAPTER TWENTY-EIGHT

JEANINE STARED AT THE BLACK BAR OF THE CURSOR, RHYTHMICALLY BLINKING against the white computer screen, until she was in a drowsy stupor. The blank screen was, of course, supposed to be filled with a flow of black words, inspiring words which would incite the university's alumni to jump up with their checkbooks and rush to mail in their annual fund gifts. She had pretty much figured out that that was going to be the point of almost everything she wrote for this job. These alumni evidently had a short attention span. She yawned deeply, stretched in her chair, and forced herself to put her hands on the keyboard. But then there was a "ding" from the computer's speaker, and the email-box's flag started to wave in excitement. She had new mail!

"Don't be an idiot," she told herself harshly as her heart picked up speed. She'd sent Jamie that message a full week ago, giving him her new address, phone numbers for home and work, and her new office email address. And every time she'd gotten a new piece of mail since then, her body had reacted with heart-pounding, giddy joy, as though she'd just received word of a million-dollar inheritance, only to find that it was a junk e-message concerning some sorority's charity car wash or a new assignment from her boss.

But this time, there it was. JamieN@newmail.com Re: New Address. Her hand shook so hard that the mouse pointer jumped all around and she could barely click on the message. Finally she hit the target and the full text appeared: *Thanks for the info. I'll keep it handy. Hope the job's going well and you're settling in nicely. Jamie.*

She read it over three times, but it didn't get any better. She sat dead still in her swivel chair, the glow of the computer screen burning her eyes and causing her to blink back tears.

The phone buzzed, and her entire body jerked at the noise. It sounded off again before she could manage to pick it up. It was Anne, her boss.

"Have you got a draft of that annual report letter?"

"Almost." She bit her bottom lip and winced as she switched back to word processing and found the screen as blank as ever.

"Good. I want to see it first thing in the morning."

"No problem," Jeanine said, her voice a perfect, perky imitation of her female co-workers.

She sighed as she hung up the phone and resolutely placed her hands on the keyboard. It was going to be another late night.

The June days were long, but twilight was nevertheless setting in when Jeanine decided she had a passable draft. Her brain was like a puppy frightened by a clap of thunder, hiding and shaking under the bed. She had dragged it out, scolded it and tried to make it get down to business. But every now and then her wounded mind would start to slink away again, cowering and shaking and wondering what in the world she had done to deserve that snotty little brush-off: *Thanks for the info. I'll keep it handy...*

She exited the red brick Crane building and started the stroll across campus to her car. Normally, she would have enjoyed the walk across the springy grass and through the grounds, with the harsh heat and the bustle of the day winding down into the cool evening, handfuls of students lounging about and talking. She turned onto the sidewalk, vaguely noticing a single white pickup truck driving slowly past her.

Richard Newkirk. That was what had gone wrong. She had met the man who pulled the strings, and she had exposed far more of herself than she ever should have—even to Jamie, actually. What had possessed her at that dinner party to babble on as she had done, spilling out secrets that she had carefully guarded for a decade, as though she were a carefully aged, vintage bottle of champagne that had suddenly blown its cork and spewed randomly all over the room. She felt her cheeks flush with shame at the thought of it. She had behaved like a lunatic, and Richard had naturally proceeded as though she were one. He had pulled Jamie off into that room and...what? Threatened? Blackmailed? Cajoled?

Maybe he hadn't found it necessary to threaten or blackmail Jamie.

Maybe Jamie had decided she was a lunatic, too. Who knows, maybe she was.

She stepped off the curb, then paused before crossing as a vehicle popped around the corner. It picked up speed as it went by her and turned at the stop sign without even slowing down. A white pickup truck, she noted absently. Funny. There were so few vehicles around tonight and two white pickup trucks. Or the same one twice. They'd both had unusually dark-tinted windows, she noted absently. Oh well, it was easy to get lost on this campus. She was still proving that every day.

The moment she was inside her apartment, she threw herself face-down across the bed, closing her eyes and longing for the obliteration of sleep, for an end to the whirling in her brain. Trouble was, if she allowed herself to come home and go straight to sleep, she'd be right back at work again in no time, with nothing in between except unconsciousness. What kind of existence was that?

So she forced herself to get up and make herself a strong cup of tea, just the way that Jamie had shown her, with some of the boiling water sloshed around in the pot to warm it up before the leaves were added so as not to "shock" the tea, and just the right, precise amount of steeping. She took a cautious sip while it was still scalding, nodding in satisfaction. "Perfect." At least her time with Jamie hadn't been a complete waste.

The tea did the trick, reviving her enough to sit down on the piano bench and run her fingers up and down the keys. In times like these, she used to daydream…about Danny Summer's latest adventure, about meeting Jamie. The pictures in her mind, the longings in her heart would creep along her nerve endings until the piano was electrified and somehow it was all translated into music, into sound.

Now, however, she felt flat. Empty. The only thought in her head was that stupid report she had probably bungled. There weren't any pictures in her head at all.

She wasn't sure how long she had been staring out the window, seeing nothing, before she became aware of the vehicle sitting way too long at the stop sign across the road, with no traffic in sight and no reason to linger, its lights trained on her apartment building. It wasn't there long enough to cause her any alarm, only mild interest, then slowly made a right turn and drove away. She caught a flash of white, but couldn't really tell what kind of vehicle it was and wasn't interested enough to look very hard. Twenty minutes or so later, however, a vehicle again pulled up to the stop sign, pausing there just that bit too long, again drawing her attention. This time, it made a left turn, cruising slowly past the driveway of her building. The vehicle was clearly visible under the street light. It was a white pickup truck.

She jumped up from the piano bench so quickly that she turned it over, briefly tangling her feet up in its legs. By the time she dialed the phone, she was out of breath. "Trev!" she gasped, when he finally answered. "Can you come over here? Now?"

"What's wrong?"

"I'll tell you when you get here."

CHAPTER TWENTY-NINE

Just as Jamie had pictured, Lieutenant Regis's eyebrows shot up into his hairline when he looked up from his desk and saw who was standing in his office door. But he recovered from his shock quickly. By the time Jamie said, "Do you have a minute? I need to talk to you," the man's eyebrows had returned to their normal position.

"By all means." He motioned to the chair in front of his desk. "Have a seat."

Jamie sat. Lieutenant Regis rocked back in his chair, folded his hands into a steeple and waited. Finally, Jamie took a deep breath and plunged in. "I didn't tell you everything…that night."

The cop's smile was sour. "In other words, you were lying. Just like I said."

"Not exactly…okay, I suppose I was lying."

"But now you're ready to tell me." It was a statement, not a question.

"Yes."

"Okay."

The chair creaked as the man rocked and waited.

How to start? "Well…I wasn't the only one at the house with Paula that night."

"Oh?" This information only prompted a slight raising of the brows. "Who else was there?"

"My stepfather. Elliott Dane."

"I see. And why didn't you tell me this?"

"Several reasons. For one, this whole thing is pretty…" Jamie drew a deep breath. "Repulsive. Humiliating. And secondly, Elliott didn't want me to tell." Jamie spat out a laugh. "He's always pretended he barely knew Paula. I found out the truth—I'll tell you more about that later—but…well, he can get pretty ugly when he's crossed."

"Ugly how? Like beating you up, or—"

"No, no, more subtle than that. I don't know. Honestly, I'm not sure Elliott's ever done anything horrible to me directly, but he…he arranges things. He manipulates. And he…he knows some things about me that I'd rather not go into. Not anything criminal," Jamie said quickly, seeing the man's eyes widen with interest. "But, I don't know. You somehow get the impression with Elliott that it's better to let sleeping dogs lie, if you can. And at first I didn't think it mattered. I thought Paula's overdose was an accident and it didn't matter that Elliott was there."

"But now you think differently?"

Jamie nodded slowly. "I do." The firmness of the words almost surprised him. Was he really that certain? He started to backpedal. "Or at least, I've been wondering—"

"Why don't you just tell me what happened? Let me see what I think."

"Okay." Jamie drew a bracing breath. "Well, first I have to give you a little background. I met Paula at a screening, not long after my mother died. I was having a hard time and I didn't feel well, and I went outside before the picture ended to get some air. Paula came out, and everything she said was just right. Exactly what I needed to hear. Like an idiot, I thought I had found my soul mate—that she had been 'sent' to me." Jamie made air quotation marks around the word "sent," then laughed. "She'd been sent, all right. By Elliott. He'd sent her to the screening for the sole purpose of meeting me. He told her everything to say and how to act."

"And why did he do that?" The detective's voice was flat, but his eyes showed interest.

"Over the years since the first *Summer* movie was made, Elliott had made a lot of money, basically without exerting any effort whatsoever. First he made money off of Charlie, and then after I became his stepson, Richard took him in as a partner and he made a killing off of my pictures that Richard made. But then everything started going wrong for Elliott. The *Summer* movies came to an end, and so did Charlie's career. After Elliott and my mother had that nasty break-up, I didn't want to work with him any-more, and so Richard decided to dissolve their partnership. So all of a sudden, Elliott was faced with the prospect of having to make a living all on his own. And he didn't like that.

"Meanwhile, he had met Paula and her mother somewhere. Paula's mother is just about as grasping and manipulative as Elliott himself is, and she trained up Paula to be that way, too—although to be honest, I don't think she knew just what she was getting herself into. Anyway, Paula originally had a fling with Elliott—"

"With Elliott Dane!"

"Yeah. She thought she had found herself a powerful movie producer that would get her career started. I don't know at what point she realized what a sham Elliott was, and how little he could do for her directly. But they worked it out that he would help her get in with me. Elliott studies people, he knows what they want, knows how to push their buttons. He told Paula exactly how to get to me, and it worked for a while. I thought I was head over heels in love."

Lieutenant Regis tilted his head, looking perplexed. "What exactly did that do for Elliott?"

"Paula was supposed to be a sort of middle man. After I was so enamored I would do anything for her, she was going to persuade me to do a picture with her, so she could break into acting. And then it would just happen to be a picture produced by Elliott Dane—at least in name. I'm sure he would have found someone else to do most of the work. With his silver tongue, he could no doubt have managed that if he could say I'd be starring in it." Jamie smiled apologetically. "I know how conceited that sounds, but for some reason my name seems to be worth a lot of money."

Lieutenant Regis waved his hand. "Yeah, yeah, I know how all that works. Go on."

Jamie shrugged. "I would have even invested in the picture myself. We had started talking about the project. I was a little surprised to find out Paula knew Elliott, and I have to admit I started to sour on the relationship a little at that point, but still, I kept going full steam ahead. Until…"

"Until she got on the drugs."

"Yeah. Everything changed then." Jamie leaned forward, rubbing his sweaty hands on the knees of his jeans. "Things between us got ugly. She and

Elliott kept talking about doing the film but I started backing out. I told Paula she was in no shape to do a picture if she was strung out all the time and I wouldn't work with her in that condition. I think she honestly tried to get off it, but she just couldn't. Once she tried the heroin, it owned her, body and soul. I tried to keep her away from the stuff, and she'd get furious and scream at me. In one of those fits, she told me everything about what she and Elliott had schemed from the very beginning. How she had never been interested in me except as a meal ticket. Things like that." Jamie's face and eyes burned with the memory of that horrible, horrible row.

"Was that when you broke it off with her and went to England?"

"No, actually…" Jamie ran his hand through his hair. "I stayed with her for quite a while after that."

"Why in the world would you have done that? *How* could you have done that?"

"I didn't stay with her romantically, but…I didn't want to desert her…the drugs and all."

The detective's mouth twisted in a sardonic smile. "How selfless of you."

Jamie glared at him. "No, it wasn't. I felt responsible…guilty…I don't know."

"Why would you feel guilty?"

Jamie laughed. "I feel guilty for everything. I feel guilty if it rains. I'm like that."

"I see."

Again, the cop rocked back in his chair and studied Jamie, who had a terrible feeling that the man did, indeed, see.

"I wanted to get her off the drugs. Then I felt I could leave her and be done with it. Only it just wouldn't work, because of Elliott. When I would try to cut her off, she would run to him and he would give her what she needed."

"Elliott was giving her drugs?"

"Yes, he was."

"But why would he do that? It seems to me that would be working against his own best interests. Maybe if he could get her off the drugs he could get his plan back on track."

"That's how a normal person would think. You don't get Elliott."

"So enlighten me."

"First of all, he already knew Paula had blown it. The picture was dead from the time Paula confessed their scheme to me. Do you know what Elliott once said to me, when he knew I was trying to get her off drugs? He said I was stupid, that I had missed a golden opportunity. That it was a wonderful thing to have a woman with a weakness for something—drugs, love, sex, whatever—because then you knew exactly how to control her. Give her just enough and withhold it when you need to."

"Wow."

"Yeah."

"So what about the night she died? What happened then?"

Filled with a surge of energy, Jamie felt a sudden desire to run. Or at least stand and pace around the room. Instead, he squirmed around in the chair. "What I told you was true. How I hadn't seen Paula until she showed up that night, begging for help, dying for a fix. The part I didn't tell you was that I called Elliott and told him to come over, that she was his problem. And then…I was exhausted from the flight, and disgusted, and I didn't want to deal with her or Elliott anymore. So I went up to my room and shut the door and went to bed."

"You never saw Elliott?"

"No."

"But you're sure he was there?"

"Yeah. I heard her let someone in, heard her talking to someone. And anyway, he's admitted being there. He says he brought her what she wanted—"

"Hang on. Is Elliott a user? A dealer? What?"

"He's a controller. It's like I told you. He knows what you want, what you think you need. When he was with my mother he kept a supply of her drugs of choice, from OxyContin to cocaine. So I'm sure he had a supply of heroin that he kept to dangle in front of Paula's nose. To keep her in line." Jamie rubbed his forehead, which was beginning to ache. "Anyway, he says he gave her the fix she wanted and she was happy and he left. But I don't believe that."

"What do you think?"

"I think she was a nuisance. An irritation. She had failed at the task he gave her and so, to him, she had no reason to exist anymore. So I think he gave her an overdose to get rid of her, the same way he would have swatted a fly that was annoying him."

Feeling drained now that he had said it, Jamie slumped back in the chair while the detective scrutinized him. Finally, Regis said, "What I'm curious about is—why now? Why come forward with this now?"

Jamie sighed. "I've come to hate Elliott over the years and I knew he was controlling and manipulative, but I didn't think he would actually hurt anyone. Actually *kill* someone. But I've had a lot of time out in the country to think, and it really started to nag at me…Paula's injuries, that cigarette burn—which my mother also had." He almost mentioned Phoebe at this point, and the way she fingered the spot under the neck of her blouse. But he dismissed the idea and went on. "I thought about all the people Elliott's used, and how—after he's used them all up—they just seem to go away. Like my mother, for example."

There went the eyebrows again. "Your mother killed herself, as I recall. She left a suicide note."

"Yeah, I know that's how it appeared. It's what I believed at the time. But again…I had finally convinced her to leave Elliott—which meant I was finally free to break with him, too. He had been trying for months to patch things up, but the night she died he had come over—supposedly to bring her a birthday gift—and had more or less told her that women didn't leave him. That she would either come back to him or her future didn't look very bright."

"You heard him threaten her?"

"No, but she told me. That's what our famous fight was about, the one that got reported in the tabloid. He had her so upset and scared, she told me she was going to go back to him and be done with it. I got really angry and forbid her to do it." Jamie swallowed hard against the sudden ache in his throat. "I told her he was bluffing, that he was too much of a coward to do anything other than make threats. That I would keep her safe. I handed her my cell phone and had her call him and tell him she was through with him. And a few hours later, she was dead."

Regis frowned and stroked his chin. "Look, I agree with you the guy's a jerk. And you did the right thing coming clean with this—even if it's a little late. But I'm thinking you're making quite a leap, deciding he somehow caused their deaths."

Jamie huffed in frustration. "Brilliant! See, this is why I didn't say anything to begin with. I knew this is what everyone would say." He leaned toward the detective, jabbing his finger at him as he spoke. "But I can't just let this go now. He's got to be stopped." Thinking of Jeanine, he swallowed hard. "Before he hurts someone else. So what can we do?"

The detective let out a sigh, creasing his forehead in thought. "I suppose we could try another autopsy."

"On who? Paula or my mother?"

Regis shook his head. "I just don't know that they could find much of anything else on Paula. Or that we would get permission to exhume the body. But your mother…well, they might have thought a suicidal overdose was so obvious that they weren't looking very hard at other possibilities."

Jamie nodded, trying to push the picture out of his head, of what they were thinking of doing. But he'd been expecting this. "Am I the one who can give permission?"

"Did your mother actually divorce Elliott Dane?"

"She did. It was final just before she died."

"Then yes, it would be you."

"Then let's do it."

As Jamie walked to his car, he pulled his phone out and checked for messages out of habit. His stomach clenched when he saw he had an email from Jeanine. For a moment he stood still in the middle of the carpark, trying to think how to respond. Eventually, he pushed the delete button with a sharp jab of his thumb, jammed the phone back into his pocket, and moved on.

CHAPTER THIRTY

As busy as Jeanine was, the afternoon seemed to drag. She spent the last two hours of the day in a meeting on the dedication of the new Student Union building. Approximately ten minutes of it applied to her, when they assigned her a couple of press releases and an article for the university publications. The rest of the time she squirmed in agony, wondering when Jamie might get her latest email, whether he would respond, what he would think. When she made it back to her desk a little before five and saw her email flag waving, she felt a cold wave of fear go through her stomach, a presentiment that it had to do with Jamie, and that it wouldn't be good.

She read the message in total bewilderment: "Message undeliverable as addressed." An entire page of computer gibberish followed, describing all the places the message had bounced. She pulled the hard copy of Jamie's earlier message and compared the two addresses. They were exactly the same. So sometime in the last week, Jamie had dropped this account, or changed his screen name, whatever. The bottom line was, she no longer had his address.

On a sudden dark hunch, she pulled out her cell phone and dialed his number. And sure enough, she heard that horrible three-note tone that meant trouble, followed by the recorded message: "The number you have dialed has been disconnected…"

She dropped the cell phone onto her desk from limp fingers. This time, she didn't even stare at the computer screen, but off into the space of the room, focusing on nothing, her eyes blurry and her body feeling weak and exhausted.

She was still sitting that way when there was a sharp rap on her door. It was Martha, the elegant, thirty-something receptionist.

"Jeanine, are you okay? I've been standing here for ages."

She pushed her hair back from her face and sat up straight. "I'm sorry. Just one of those days."

Martha smiled knowingly. "Well, I'll bet you're about to perk up considerably."

"What do you mean?"

"You've got a visitor. A gorgeous one." Martha leaned in toward Jeanine and lowered her voice. "Why didn't you tell us you knew a good-looking celebrity?"

Jeanine's heart had been sinking ever since she dialed Jamie's number. Now it leapt back up toward her throat so quickly that she nearly choked. Struggling for breath, she jumped up from her chair and pushed past Martha, trying not to run toward the reception area. The email and the phone didn't matter at all. He'd had some reason to change them, maybe some creepy fan had broken the code or something. It didn't matter; it had nothing to do with her. He was here, in person, he was back! He was...

Not here at all. The celebrity awaiting her in the lobby was none other than the famous movie producer, Elliott Dane.

Elliott waited around in the reception area until Jeanine got off work an hour or so later, apparently enjoying all the attention he was getting from most of the women in the office. As they walked out to his car, she faltered for the briefest second, but Elliott noticed.

"Anything wrong?"

"Oh, no, nothing. I was just looking at your car. Really nice." And it was. A nice, *white* BMW. Since the incident with the white pick-up truck, she had noticed a number of white vehicles that seemed to be creeping along behind her, or sitting too long in front of her apartment. Mentally calling herself paranoid, she laughed to cover her discomfort. "I expected you to be driving something a little flashier, that's all."

"It's a rental. As a general rule, they're bland and colorless." He laughed. "Cars owned by rental agencies, the government, and private eyes."

"Hmm...interesting." Oh well. It wasn't as though she'd seen anything as fancy as a BMW following her around, so she shook off the thought as she slid into the passenger seat. Pulling down the visor mirror and checking her face and hair, she asked him, "You sure this is a good idea?"

Elliott glanced at her. "I know it's good for us—for Charlie and me. Hopefully it will be good for you, too."

"I had no idea he was still in Atlanta."

"He doesn't know what to do or where to go so he just hasn't done anything."

"Does he live in L.A. or Virginia?"

"That's a good question. I'm sure he still considers Virginia home but he doesn't spend much time there. I think his Aunt Phoebe tried to convince him to go back with her, but...I think they argued before she left and that didn't work out." He huffed and said, "Nothing surprising about that. I always found it impossible to avoid arguing with Phoebe, myself. Anyway, he was renting a place in L.A. but he let it go when he went into the Army."

"So he's just been hanging out here in a hotel since he got out of the hospital?"

"I'm afraid so." Elliott sighed. "I think he's recovered physically, but he's depressed. I don't seem to be much good at cheering him up." He flashed a smile her way. "That's why I'm hoping you can help."

"It's really good of you to stay with him like this."

"For all practical purposes, he's my son," Elliott said. "Phoebe and I took him in when he was less than a year old. I always wanted to adopt him, but for some reason, Phoebe disagreed."

"It's funny how much he and Jamie have in common. It seems to be just Jamie and his uncle, and Charlie only has you."

Elliott's voice took on a chill. "I don't think I'm anything at all like Richard Newkirk."

Jeanine started to backpedal. "Oh no, no, I only meant—" She broke off with a nervous laugh. "Trust me, if I thought you were anything like Richard Newkirk, I wouldn't have gotten into the car with you."

Elliott was pulling into the drive of a high-rise hotel downtown. "Here we are."

Jeanine climbed out as Elliott tossed the keys to the eager valet. From the way the guy beamed and hustled, Elliott must have already established himself as a generous tipper. Her stomach started to flutter with nerves again as they crossed the luxurious lobby. She couldn't believe she was doing this.

How much must it cost to stay in this place for one night? More than she could afford, no doubt. And she was supposed to have some positive effect on a guy who could afford to move in here and hang out night after night, simply because he was depressed?

As Elliott inserted the key card into the door of their suite, she had to force herself not to run away in a panic. It's just another visit to comfort the sick, she told herself as they stepped inside. Just like Daddy does all the time.

They stepped into a dark, gloomy room. By the flickering light from the TV, she could tell they were in the suite's sitting room, and that there was a figure sprawled motionless on the couch in front of it. Elliott threw his keys down on a table near the door. They made a loud clanking noise, but the figure didn't even move.

Elliott cleared his throat loudly. "Charlie. I brought a surprise for you."

"Oh, yeah?" He didn't move or look away from the car chase on the screen.

Elliott looked at her as though asking for help, so she forced herself to speak. "I hope it's a good surprise."

At the sound of her voice, Charlie snapped up into a sitting position. "Oh, wow…Jeanine, right? From the other night?"

"That's right."

He winced and held his hand up to shield his eyes as Elliott opened the drapes, letting in the bright sunlight of the early summer evening. Now she could see how Charlie had deteriorated in a short period of time. The several days' growth of beard was probably due to his bad mood, but she had no idea whether the puffiness around his eyes and the slight tremble in his hand were from the recent illness or depression.

"What are you doing here?" he asked, sounding cross.

Frankly, she had no answer for that. She felt ridiculous, and the idea of her cheering up a movie star—especially one she had only met once—was downright humiliating. "I'm not entirely sure," she mumbled.

Elliott didn't appear discouraged as he opened an ice bucket and started plunking cubes into glasses. "Oh come on. I figured you could use some cheering up, and you two seemed to have a good bit in common the other night."

Charlie frowned, looking suspicious. "Oh, yeah? Like the book we both want to write—but neither of us can?" He smirked a little and, sounding totally different from the friendly, relaxed guy from a couple of weeks ago, said, "You because of all the legal crap and me because…well, because I write like crap."

For some reason, that struck Jeanine as funny. Fortunately, she didn't reach hysteria level the way she had in the car with Jamie a couple of weeks ago, but she laughed. "You definitely have a way of putting things, don't you? I seriously doubt you write like crap."

To her surprise, Charlie's face relaxed into a grin. "Hey, I can prove it."

She nodded. "I'll take you up on that. I love reading crap."

Elliott handed her a glass. She took it, but shot him a questioning look. He smiled and answered before she asked. "Diet Coke." He handed one to Charlie and said, "Same for you."

Charlie promptly set his down on a side table, and she wondered if he had been drinking something else while he was holed up in this room. Maybe that was another reason Elliott was trying to distract him.

Charlie leaned toward Jeanine, hands on his knees. "So. Was this Elliott's idea, or Jamie's?"

Jeanine almost choked on her Coke. "Jamie?" she sputtered.

"Uh…yeah? I got the impression you two were pretty close."

"Were, indeed."

Charlie raised his eyebrows. "Oh, really?"

"You know Jamie changed all his contact information after he left Georgia," Elliott said. "Apparently, he didn't share any of that with Jeanine."

Charlie shook his head. "Wow."

"Yeah."

A little silence fell. Then Charlie said, "Wait a minute…you don't live in Atlanta, do you? Surely you didn't drive up here just to see me?"

"I live here as of two weeks ago," Jeanine said. "I just graduated college and started my first real job."

"Oh. That's good."

"That's what everybody tells me."

"Oh. Not so good, then?"

She shrugged. "I'm grateful to have a job, but…I don't know. You spend all these years in school having your head filled with lofty ideas and goals, and then you face…"

"Reality," said Charlie.

"Yeah." She chuckled. "This is the most interesting conversation I've had since starting my job. I had a fifteen-minute conversation in the break room the other day about the way I make tuna salad." She proceeded to describe the scene, embellishing her colleagues' horror at the fact that she had thrown things like apples and nuts into her tuna instead of the traditional eggs and pickle relish until Charlie was laughing and shaking his head.

"It's funny," he said. "You're supposedly telling me about something boring and mundane, but you make it sound like a scene from a Roald Dahl book. You're going to be a great writer, I'll bet." He cocked his head and looked at her. "So…would you like to see the synopsis Hannah Raney left me?" Jeanine nodded, feeling a tremor go through her body at the very thought. Her voice came out in a hoarse little croak. "Yes, I would like that very much."

* * *

As soon as the clock on Jeanine's computer flashed five o'clock, she shot up from her desk and was outta there. She swung her purse in time to the song she was singing as she headed for the car, she felt so light. Having another meeting scheduled with Charlie had actually made the work day harder, in a way, because the ideas for *Summer and the Rainbow's End*—the name Hannah Raney had intended for the next installment—were flashing through her head like a DVD on fast search. But now that she was free for the evening, the distraction felt very, very good.

When Elliott had taken her to meet Charlie the other night, she had ended up staying for hours. Once he had handed her the magic paper, the paper on which Hannah Raney had inscribed her secrets in her own fevered handwriting, it was as though she had fallen down a rabbit hole into another land. The document was short, but the words and ideas rich and powerful. And Charlie was right. Many of those same ideas had been showing up in her little fan fic, including the secret behind Danny's quest. Without formalizing anything or making it into a boring business deal, she and Charlie had somehow just started doing it—fleshing out the story based on Hannah's synopsis and using parts of Jeanine's story. They were both so excited they were babbling, words and ideas tumbling over each other. Charlie had grabbed his laptop and started writing it all down, and amazingly that momentum had continued, day after fevered day.

Jeanine's mind was in a dreamy orchard centuries away when Elliott opened the door, so it took her a second to register that something was wrong. The worried expression on his face hit her the same time as the sound of raised voices from inside.

She heard Charlie first. "I'm telling you, I can't do it without her. I've never been able to have one coherent idea for this thing without her."

Instead of letting her in, Elliott started edging out into the hallway with her, trying to pull the door shut on the noise. "Uh, Jeanine...maybe it would be best if you came back in a little while."

She started to protest, but even with the door just barely cracked, she could hear his voice, *the* voice. Jamie. She pushed past Elliott and shoved the door open, and heard him in midstream, his voice raised. "—absolutely absurd. She got you inspired, got you going. Fine. But we don't need her anymore. You can do this book—this movie—without her. And furthermore, if she is involved, I'm not. Just see how far you all get with a *Summer* movie without me playing Danny."

She must have made some kind of noise. Did she gasp, or moan, or—whatever. They looked up and saw her standing there, and both their faces went from angry red to white in a flash. She understood. She felt the same way. As a matter of fact, she was fairly certain that she was about to throw up.

She turned on her heel and ran for the door, slamming it behind her and barreling toward the elevator. She heard the door open again almost immediately, heard Jamie calling her, but she only ran faster. A couple was just exiting the elevator, and she almost knocked them down trying to get past them, trying to hit the button to get the door closed. She could hear him still, calling, "Jeannie, wait! I need to talk to you." Just before the door closed, she saw his face, eyes wide, mouth open and panting as he reached for the door and tried to insert his hand, tried to keep it from closing—

But it slid shut.

After only a second, she hit the button for floor number six, even though she needed to go down to the parking deck. But Jamie might be running down the stairs or taking the next elevator after her, and he would check the lobby level and the parking deck. So she walked out onto this random floor, collapsed into a chair set in a nearby alcove, and prepared to wait.

* * *

Jamie searched the lobby, the parking deck, everywhere he could think of, but he couldn't find Jeanine. White-hot anger directed him back to Charlie and Elliott's suite, where he balled up his fist and pounded on the door until Elliott opened it a few seconds later. The man's face looked so calm and unconcerned that Jamie wanted to pound him.

"All right, all right." Elliott stepped aside to let him in. "You don't have to break the door down."

Jamie stepped into the room. "You'll be very lucky if it's only a door I break."

Elliott appeared mildly surprised. "What, exactly, are you blaming me for this time?"

"Are you kidding me? You're responsible for this mess."

"What mess exactly?" Charlie didn't bother to get up from the sofa where he was sprawling. Jamie tried to remember when he had ever seen those golden eyes of Charlie's looking so unfriendly. "Everything was going quite well around here until you showed up and freaked out."

"I had every right to freak out." Jamie turned to confront Elliott. "You and your arranging, your manipulating. You're starting the whole thing all over again, aren't you?"

Elliott's expression was blank, but his voice took on an edge. "What whole thing, exactly?"

"You know what I mean," Jamie said. "You've always got one of these games going, haven't you? My mother. Paula." He gestured toward Charlie. "Your Aunt Phoebe."

Now Charlie sprang up, his body rigid. "What the devil are you talking about?"

Jamie looked from one to the other of them. They were both staring at him, ice on one side and fire on the other. Did he really want to do this now, this way? It was going to take a lot of convincing to ever get through to Charlie, and trying to talk to him in front of Elliott was pointless.

He put up his hands in surrender. "Look, never mind about that. The point is…I'm serious about what I said. If you continue to involve Jeanine DeValery in this project, I won't touch it. I'll kill it."

Charlie drew himself up straight, and his mouth tightened into a grim line. "Then I guess it's already dead, because I won't—I can't—do it without her."

Jamie nodded slowly. "Well, that's unfortunate. But I suppose it's dead."

* * *

Jeanine went a little nuts after the to-do at the hotel. After hiding out on the sixth floor for a long time, she crept down to her car like a fugitive and raced away from the place. She felt weird, not just hurt and bewildered by what she'd overheard from Jamie, but also panicky and paranoid. Even though Jamie had seemed to be making it clear to Charlie that he didn't want anything else to do with her, he had run after her to the elevator, and she had a creeping feeling on the back of her neck that he was still pursuing her. Why, she wasn't exactly clear, but she was afraid he wanted to tell her to her face to leave him alone, or how little he thought of her. And she didn't think she could take it. She could let him go—she had been doing that for weeks now—but she couldn't stand in front of him and let him shatter her, her entire world of dreams and beauty, like throwing a brick through a delicate stained glass window. She still needed Danny, even if she couldn't have Jamie.

Reacting to that instinct of being followed, watched, she circled the parking lot of her apartment building from the road before pulling in, and sure enough, she saw the car she was expecting. Not a white one that she couldn't identify this time, but the little blue Taurus that Jamie was apparently still renting. As quickly as she could, hoping he hadn't spotted her also, she turned around and drove away from the apartment. Not able to think of anywhere else to go, she drove to the college campus and parked near her office building, where she spent the entire night first sitting, then lying in the back seat, hunched up into an uncomfortable ball.

As the sun rose, she tried to figure out her next step. Soon it would be time for her to report to work. She tried to picture sitting in that office all day—no, it would be worse than that. She had meetings all morning, to discuss the new fund-raising brochures. She was supposed to interview some Very Important Alumnus who was going to be chairman of the capital campaign. Well, she couldn't do it in these clothes. First of all, she was rumpled and dirty and entirely unpresentable. Plus her co-workers would tease her for showing up in the same clothes. Jeanine had to smile and shake her head as she thought about the conclusion they would draw. How wrong could you possibly be?

So, she should probably get moving. Go home and change. Make a pot of very strong coffee and drink the whole thing. Try to pull herself together.

But she couldn't picture doing that either.

So she sat, moment after moment, hour after hour. It was now past eight o'clock and employees were starting to pull into the parking lot near her. One of her co-workers threw up a hand and waved, and Jeanine thought she had a curious look on her face. Jeanine managed to raise a hand and wave weakly back, but once the woman had disappeared into the building, Jeanine cranked the car and drove away.

CHAPTER THIRTY-ONE

FROM THE MOMENT RICHARD ANSWERED THE PHONE, JAMIE COULD TELL something was wrong. Obviously trying to sound casual—and failing—Rick asked him, "So, where, uh…where are you?"

"I'm in Atlanta, actually," Jamie said.

"Atlanta! Who…I mean…why are you here, of all places?"

"Mostly to see Charlie."

"Mostly?"

"Yeah…well…Charlie and you, I suppose." It suddenly hit him that Richard might be freaked out because the baby was coming. "Any sign of the newest Newkirk?"

"Doctor says any time now." There was a pause, and then Rick changed the subject. "So…how is Charlie?"

"Pig-headed and infuriating."

"Ah. Won't write the *Summer* book for you, eh?"

"I don't care about that stupid book or the film, or…or any of it, all right? It's everyone else, you and Elliott and Charlie—"

"Hang on now. What did I tell you when we talked in my study that night, the night of that crazy dinner party?"

Jamie heaved a sigh and, as though he were reciting for class, said, "You told me you were tired of producing and directing. You said this whole business of reviving the *Summer* series frankly made you nauseous, but if it was important to me, you would do it." Jamie's voice took on an accusing note. "And what did I tell you?"

"You said you weren't interested any longer, but I find that hard to believe."

"Why?"

"Why?" Richard barked a short laugh. "Because you're the one who started the whole thing with that girl's manuscript, weren't you?"

"And I can't tell you how sorry I am about that. Look, I was trying to impress a girl, okay? It was stupid, and it's over."

"Oh, really?" Again, that fake-casual tone came into Richard's voice. "So you're not seeing the girl anymore?"

"No, I'm not."

"You haven't heard from her at all…well, you wouldn't have, would you, since you changed your phone number? But you haven't got in touch with her?"

"No. Why do you ask?"

"Oh, just wondered."

"Oh come on, Richard. What the devil is going on?"

He heaved a deep sigh. "All right. There's something I need to tell you."

"Yeah?" Jamie's stomach started to flutter.

"Jeanine DeValery is apparently missing."

"Missing! What do you mean, missing?"

"Calm down. It's not that big a deal, she just didn't show up for work yesterday morning. Actually, that's not entirely true. A co-worker saw her in the parking lot outside her office building yesterday morning, but she never came inside. And her family hasn't been able to get in touch with her."

"And you don't think that's a big deal!" The flutter in Jamie's stomach was exploding into a wild churning.

"Not really. I don't know anyone that age who hasn't got their knickers in a twist over something and dropped out of communication for a bit, including you. And Lee said—"

"Lee?"

"Yes, he came to see me a while ago. Anyway, she's been down lately, apparently the stress of her new job."

"Her job. Yeah, right." Jamie was starting to feel sick. Jeanine might not be crazy about her new job, but that wouldn't be why she was depressed.

"Her car is gone, too, so she drove herself away from the place. Probably just having a nice sulk and will turn up any time now."

Jamie ignored that for the moment. "Why did Lee come to see you? Why didn't he call me?"

"How? You changed your number and email address and all that, didn't you?"

Jamie moaned. "Yeah, I certainly did."

"I do think you should call Lee now, though, and show some concern."

"*Show some concern!*" Jamie jumped to his feet and started to pace. "Do you know how much you sound like Lindsey? Like it doesn't matter what's happened to anyone else, as long as I put on a show and make myself look good!"

"Jamie, that's not what I meant, but—well, you do need to look out for yourself right now, actually."

"What do you mean?"

"Lee DeValery went to the police about Jeanine, but they weren't impressed. They told him Jeanine is an adult and if she wants to stay out of work one day, that's her choice. I never would have believed Lee DeValery would be so shrewd, but it occurred to the good Reverend that the police might be a lot more interested if they knew of his daughter's association with you."

"Yes, brilliant!" Jamie nodded vigorously, as though Rick could see him. "Maybe that will get them moving."

"Are you completely mad! Jamie, the last thing we need is for the media to believe that yet another woman in your life has come to harm."

"Do you honestly think I care about that right now?"

"Well, you should, because there is nothing wrong with Jeanine DeValery. Look, Jamie, I said a few more things in my study that night, didn't I—some things about Jeanine DeValery."

Jamie spoke through gritted teeth. "Yeah, you certainly did."

"All that religious talk—she sounded delusional. I'm extremely relieved you've broken with her, and made it hard for her to contact you—but at the same time, I'm sure it was a blow to someone as obsessed with you as that girl obviously was. She's off somewhere having a good cry and—"

"You're wrong, Richard!"

"Wrong—wh-what?" Richard's rant spluttered to a halt. "What do you mean?"

"I didn't break up with Jeanine because she's crazy," Jamie hissed. "I broke up with her because we're crazy, and I didn't want her to get hurt."

"What are you talking—"

"I love her, Rick."

"Love her! Jamie, you can't possibly mean that."

Jamie didn't wait to hear any more. He punched his phone to end the conversation and headed for his car.

CHAPTER THIRTY-TWO

PRETENDING IT WAS ELLIOTT'S FACE, JAMIE HAMMERED ON THE DOOR OF THE hotel suite, not letting up until someone jerked it open. The momentum took him forward a step, and he kept his fist balled up and was ready to swing.

But it was Charlie standing there, not Elliott. "We really need to get a doorbell," he sighed, as Jamie blew past him, into the suite.

"Where is he?" Jamie moved from one doorway to the next, with Charlie trailing along behind him.

"Elliott? He went out."

"When? When did he go out?"

"Hey, calm down, okay?" Charlie put a light hand on Jamie's arm, but Jamie threw him off.

"Don't tell me to calm down," Jamie said. "You have no idea what's happening."

Charlie's eyes flashed. "Oh, I think I do, after the visit by the nice policemen."

Jamie blinked. "The police were here?

"Yeah. So did they come to see you, too?"

"Uh…not yet." He thought back to his call to Lieutenant Regis in L.A., telling him about Jeanine, and that she was missing, and that he suspected Elliott of being involved once more. He had told the detective that the Atlanta police didn't seem interested, but honestly, Jamie hadn't thought Regis sounded impressed, either. The man had said he would call some contacts in Atlanta and "make some inquiries," but Jamie had thought that was a nice way of putting him off. In fact, even though Regis had ordered him not to do anything himself, as the hours went by with no word, Jamie had to do something before he exploded with anger and anxiety.

"So how did you know she was missing?" Charlie's eyes narrowed. "I assume that's what you're here about."

"Yeah. Umm…her father went to see Richard and told him. I've been driving around looking for her. I couldn't just do…nothing."

Charlie nodded, his expression hard to read.

"So what happened?" Jamie asked. "What did the police say?"

"They just asked us a few questions."

"Both of you?"

"Yeah." Charlie gave him an appraising look. "Why not both of us?"

"I don't know, just…what did they ask you?"

"How well did we know her, when was the last time we saw her, what we were doing in Atlanta, that sort of thing." Charlie frowned. "They knew, of course, about my recent to-do with the drugs, so they were giving me very suspicious looks the whole time. I think it ticked Elliott off."

"You!" The word came out like an explosion. "They were suspicious of you?"

Charlie laughed humorlessly. "Yeah, Elliott was surprised at that, too. He couldn't believe they weren't going after you. 'Another one of Jamie's spurned girlfriends,' I think that's how he put it."

"He said that!" Jamie clapped his hands to his head, stunned. In another moment, he might literally be tearing his hair out.

Charlie, on the other hand, suddenly slumped into a chair. "You didn't do something to her, did you, Jamie?"

"What the devil are you talking about?"

Charlie appeared to be on the verge of tears. "I don't know, I just…I saw how mad you were at her the other night, and she ran off, and you went after her. And I'm not sure anyone has seen her since. Honestly, I'll be surprised if the police don't come knocking on your door soon, and I just don't want to see you go through this again." He leaned his head in his hands. "I don't want to go through this again."

Jamie stood for a moment, trying to decide whether to put his hand on his infuriating friend's shoulder and comfort him—or throttle him.

He sank down onto the loveseat near Charlie. "You don't really think I did something to Jeanine, do you? That I did any of those things—to Paula or my mother or—or any of it."

Charlie looked up, studying him for a long moment. Then he shook his head. "No, Jamie. I don't believe you did, but..." He shook his head. "Why are all these things happening to us? What in the world is going on?"

Jamie took a deep breath. "Come on, Charlie. You know the answer to that, deep down inside. Don't you?"

Abruptly, Charlie got to his feet. "You want something to drink?"

"No. I want to talk about this for once."

Ignoring him, Charlie headed to the fridge and pulled out a couple of beers. On reflex, Jamie put up his hand to catch the one that Charlie tossed him, then figured he might as well open it once he had it. As Charlie took a deep swig, however, Jamie stood watching him, listening to the hiss from the open bottle. "Charlie?" he said softly. "Come on."

Charlie held the cold bottle against his temple, as though his head ached. "You mean Elliott. Again." He laughed sharply. "I remember your last accusation against Elliott—back in my hospital room. You said maybe he sold that story to the tabloid. Well, I knew that was crazy, so I checked it out."

"You did?"

"Yeah, I did. That tabloid story wasn't completely fabricated, you know. Parts of it were true—about what happened that night, at the club. You know what I mean, Jamie?"

"Yes, Charlie, I know what you mean." Jamie felt himself growing hot.

"I thought to myself...now how would Elliott have known what went on at the club that night?" Charlie continued. "I didn't tell him, did you?"

"Of course not."

"I didn't think so. So I did what was sensible, and thought about who *was* there. Called up a couple of them. Didn't take me long to identify the sleazeball."

"Oh yeah? Who?"

"George Brevard."

A light seemed to dawn in Jamie's mind. "Oh...right."

Charlie was nodding, his mouth set in a smug line. "Yeah. A pretty boy actor-slash-dealer who sold to most of the people we know. How obvious can you get!" Charlie's face took on a wistful look. "I just really wish I could have chatted with him about it in person, instead of over the phone." He clenched and unclenched the hand that wasn't holding his beer, as though his fist were itching to punch George Brevard on the nose.

Jamie waved his hand in dismissal. "Okay, so Elliott didn't sell the story. That's one small point. Let's get back to the major one—how things, as usual, seem to be working out as though Elliott had planned everything for his benefit."

Charlie slammed the beer down on the counter so hard that some of it sloshed over the top. "For the life of me, I can't see how a missing preacher's daughter from middle Georgia is going to benefit him."

"Oh, please."

"I'm serious."

Jamie took a deep breath and carefully set his bottle down, not a drop spilled or drunk. "You know very well that Elliott wants the *Summer* series to continue. He was maneuvering you and Jeanine together, figuring— rightly, it would appear—that Jeanine would get you going and help you write it. But then I come along the other night and we have a big blow-up. The whole project comes to a standstill because of Jeanine's involvement. But Elliott figures that's really okay. Jeanine has done her part and frankly, she's expendable now. Not only that, she's in the way, because I don't want to work with her.

"I can just see the wheels turning in Elliott's head," Jamie continued, pacing and waving his hands. "Jeanine has got you started, he thinks, and you've already written enough that you can surely finish on your own. If something magically happened to remove Jeanine from the picture, things would settle down and you and I would go back to being friends."

"Wait a minute," Charlie said, "now you think Elliott's trying to manip- ulate us into being friends again? A few weeks ago you said he was trying to turn you against me, telling you I might have sold that story to the tabloid."

Jamie nodded. "I'm sorry to be so crass, but back then, you had nothing he wanted. Or so he thought. He wanted me to think he was the only one on my side, that it was Elliott and me against the world, so I'd be tempted to work with him. But now, you have everything he wants. He figures he has you on track to finish the book. After the book would come the movie—the begin- ning of a whole new series of *Summer* books and movies, probably. Elliott would be set for life. If only that blasted DeValery girl were out of the way."

Silence fell. Charlie stared down at the floor, refusing to look at him.

"Charlie?" Jamie prompted. "Say something."

"Why? You know how I feel when you talk about Elliott like this."

"And I usually back off. But I can't right now. Jeanine is missing and—" He swallowed hard. "I love her, Charlie. I was planning to marry her."

Charlie's head jerked up. His eyes were wide, and for one sickening moment Jamie was afraid of what Charlie was feeling, of what might have been developing between him and Jeanine in the past few weeks. Then he decided he didn't care, it didn't matter now. He shrugged. "Maybe you're falling in love with her, too. Right now I don't even care who she ends up with. I'd step out of the way gladly, if we could just get her back alive and well."

Charlie clenched and unclenched his fists, looking miserable. "What do you want from me?"

Jamie threw up his hands. "Help me. Back me up. Give me some ammunition I can take to the police. Something. I swear I've got to get them moving on this, Charlie, or I'll…"

"Or you'll what?"

Jamie was surprised how calmly the statement came out. "Or I'll make him tell me where she is, myself. I'll make him, or I'll die in the process…well, one of us will, anyway."

Charlie appeared stunned. Before he could recover enough to respond, they heard the door of the suite opening. Jamie reflexively took a step toward it, but Charlie pulled him back. "Give me a chance, okay?" he murmured. "Play along." As the door swung open and Elliott's loathsome figure appeared, Charlie whispered, "I have an idea."

CHAPTER THIRTY-THREE

JEANINE DOZED FITFULLY, A THROBBING IN HER KNEE GRADUALLY CUTTING INTO her sleep. She tried to shift and get more comfortable so she could go on dozing, but after squirming around for a moment, she realized her left leg wouldn't move. Groaning, she jerked at it, but was rewarded with a sharp pain slicing through her side. She gasped and opened her eyes.

Nothing made sense. Her brain scrambled, trying to fit her surroundings into her room in Middleboro, or her new apartment, then gave up and settled down. She rolled her head back and forth, not being able to move much else, trying to make sense of where she was.

She could hear a high-pitched hum from cicadas and felt a light breeze against her damp skin. So she wasn't buried or trapped in a building collapse or anything...well, not entirely, anyway. Her eyes fluttered shut again, feeling as though they weighed about fifty pounds each, and she felt herself relaxing again, not caring so much about the mystery of where she was, just wanting to sleep...

The pain cut at her again, waking her, making her try to squirm into a more comfortable position—again without success. She forced herself to open her eyes, to lift her head again. And this time she saw it. Tangled and hanging at a weird angle by the side of her face was the beaded cross that usually hung from the rear view mirror of the Mustang.

The realization washed through her, throbbed through her like the pulsing pain in her leg. She was trapped, wadded up in the twisted remains of her Mustang. But where? And why?

Groaning, she let her head fall back again and struggled to remember. What in the world had happened? Something—probably the caved-in driver's door—pushed against her ribcage and made each gasp for breath a torment. Panic bubbled up in her, so that she gasped even harder and wondered if she was suffocating, if she was going to run out of air and die from lack of oxygen.

Calm down, calm down. She took a tentative breath. *It's okay.* Still painful, and she couldn't quite inflate her lungs all the way, but better. Again, she felt the cool breeze and took inventory. No major pain, other than her ribs, which were maybe cracked. Her leg seemed to be stuck between the dash and the seat and her foot was asleep, which scared her. Was her leg crushed? Losing circulation? Dying, so that even if someone did find her and rescue her, it would be too late for her leg…

Stop it!

God, help me, she breathed. She tried to think of a more coherent prayer, but all she could do was scream in her mind. *Help me, please. Help me.*

With that loop still playing in her mind, she tried again to remember something. Anything. Okay. She had moved to Atlanta, she remembered that. And Charlie Edenfield…a warm feeling came over her as she remembered the time she had been spending with him, working on the *Summer* story, her imagination and her hope for the future sparked and glowing again.

And then she remembered Jamie. That horrible fight with him, and running out of the suite, racing away from the hotel. Had that been when it happened? Had she crashed the Mustang trying to escape that horrible scene with Jamie? But if she had, wouldn't she be hearing traffic and sirens and people, not cicadas and flies and behind that…nothing.

Cicadas and flies. A smell of damp earth and rotting vegetation. Her whole body clenched as it hit her. The sounds and the smells meant she was far away from the city, and if there were insects, there were probably other things. Like snakes. And possums and raccoons and…what else? That depended on where the devil she was precisely.

She continued to try to remember, but she didn't relax again. By now her head was hurting and her left eye burning. She felt her sticky-wet hair matted against her temple and eyelid, and in trying to push it away, she succeeded in rubbing what was probably blood into her eye and making it burn

more. But she breathed a prayer of thanks that she didn't seem to be seriously injured. Twisting her sore neck to the right, she saw a patch of blue sky
above her, through the broken remains of the passenger side window,
through a gap in the tangle of vines and limbs. Through the driver's side
windshield, she couldn't see much of anything, just dirt and more vines. The
car must have been lying on the driver's side, maybe wedged down into the
dirt by the impact. To get out, she would somehow have to free her leg, get
out from under the steering wheel, and climb up to the broken passenger
window and out.

Okay. So do it.

Over and over, as the patch of blue sky became a fiery hot glare from the
sun, until she was drenched with sweat and frying in the metal and glass, she
tried. After each small burst of activity, of squirming upward and pulling her
leg, and trying to slide out from under the steering wheel, she would collapse, thoroughly exhausted and dizzy. Each movement caused stabs of pain
in her rib cage, and by the time the sun had peaked over her, then started to
move down the sky again, she wasn't sure that she had made any progress.

But she had to rest. Just for a little while, maybe until the sun went lower
and the breeze might come again to cool her off. She closed her eyes and let
her head fall against the ruined door. Just for a little while.

CHAPTER THIRTY-FOUR

CHARLIE'S EYES WERE PLEADING. JAMIE COULD HEAR ELLIOTT WHISTLING A cheerful tune as he entered the suite, and the sound set his blood boiling. But since Jamie really didn't have a plan and Charlie apparently did, he nodded reluctantly and forced his face, his body, to relax.

Elliott appeared only mildly surprised on seeing Jamie. "To what do we owe the pleasure?" he asked lightly.

Before Jamie could say anything, Charlie answered. "He got a visit from the police, too."

Elliott's eyebrows rose. "About the girl?"

Jamie forced himself to nod.

Elliott shook his head and pursed his lips, as though deeply troubled. "I hope this isn't going to get you into another media disaster."

"That's not what I'm really worried about right now," Jamie said, trying to sound calm.

"Oh, I know, but you must admit, the girl was a flake."

"Was?" Jamie's heart lurched at the word.

Elliott shrugged. "That's the way she seemed when I was around her. I seriously doubt anything has happened now except a childish fit of temper. Mark my words, she's run away from home because you snubbed her the other night."

Jamie opened his mouth, preparing to lash out, to curse Elliott and tell him he wasn't fooling anyone.

Before he could, Charlie cut in. "You're probably right, Elliott. And I

240

hope you are. Because Jamie and I talked and we got the whole mess worked out."

"What do you mean?"

Jamie felt like echoing him, "Yeah, what do you mean?" But remembering Charlie's prompt, he stayed quiet and tried to look as though he knew what Charlie was talking about.

Charlie shook his head, giving Jamie a look of good-natured disgust. "Turns out Jamie was just throwing a fit himself the other night—of jealousy."

Elliott's gaze darted from one of them to another, as Jamie forced himself to give a little nod. Focusing on Jamie, Elliott said, "So you thought there was something going on between Charlie and Jeanine? Other than writing, I mean?"

Jamie tried to look sheepish. "Well, what was I to think? I go out of town for a while and find her hanging about at his hotel when I get back. Plus, I…" Jamie was surprised to feel a sudden lump in this throat. "I definitely thought there was a spark between them at the dinner party that night."

Elliott laughed. "That dinner party was such a fiasco, it was hard to tell what was going on."

Charlie chuckled along with him. "Yeah. Enough intrigue for a soap opera."

Elliott's face grew more serious. "But you say you've worked it out now?"

"Oh, yeah. We talked it out, and Jamie realizes what a blithering idiot he was." Charlie sounded remarkably genuine as he said this. "And he also realizes now what a perfect situation it would be, don't you?"

"Oh…yeah," Jamie mumbled.

"He knows now that I have to have Jeanine. We'd made a great start, but I can't finish that book without her."

Elliott furrowed his brow as he looked at Jamie. "And you would be all right with it now? The two of them working together?"

Dimly, Jamie thought he was beginning to catch on to Charlie's plan. He shrugged. "I can't say I'm a hundred percent thrilled with the two of them being so cozy together, but yeah, I trust Charlie. He says they have a professional relationship, so I can live with that." Again, he felt that lump forming. Swallowing hard, he said, "I can't imagine anything I'd like more right now than having Jeanine show up, and all three of us working together on *Summer*." With a sick feeling in the pit of his stomach, Jamie realized he was telling the truth. Why hadn't he just let things go forward in that direction? He had manipulated and schemed, trying so hard to keep Jeanine away from his family and their dark plots. He had decided to keep her safe, even if it meant giving her up for the time being. But his plan had backfired. Maybe he should have just taken the direct route and taken Elliott out with his own two hands, if he couldn't get the police to do it. Maybe he should still do that now.

He took a step toward Elliott. Charlie must have read Jamie's intent in his expression, because he stepped between his friend and his uncle. Sounding almost pleading, Charlie said, "But you believe she's just hiding out somewhere and trying to think things out, right, Elliott?"

Elliott appeared to be considering. "I...I do believe that, yes. But Charlie, I hate this attitude of yours that you can't do anything worthwhile on your own. You can do it without her."

Charlie shook his head. "You're wrong."

"But you did so much together already on the book, surely you can finish—"

"No, Elliott. I absolutely can't."

A moment of silence fell again, during which Jamie watched Elliott's face, trying to read his expression. But as Jamie had noticed on other occasions, the man's eyes were curiously flat and devoid of emotion, even when he frowned and talked as though he were troubled. Even when, like now, he smiled and tried to appear cheerful and encouraging. The man clapped a hand on Charlie's shoulder, and looked from one of them to the other. "Just try not to worry, either of you. She'll turn up when she's gotten over sulking—and figured she's made you all suffer enough for being mean to her. Meantime, I have a poker game to get to."

Charlie and Jamie stood in complete silence while Elliott, whistling, went to retrieve his wallet. They remained that way until Elliott had waved good-bye, admonished them once again not to worry, and shut the door behind him.

The moment the door closed, Charlie exploded, pointing a shaky finger toward the door. "He was whistling, Jamie. Whistling and going to his poker game. Does that look like a guilty man to you?"

"A normal man, no. Elliott? Yes."

Charlie threw up his hands. "You're determined to blame him for everything. I don't know what else to do or say." Looking disgusted, he heaved a deep sigh. "I don't believe for a minute that he knows where Jeanine is. But you do. So I've just planted the idea in his head that all will be well if she comes back, but he'll lose out if she doesn't. So if you're right—if he paid her off to leave or coerced her into going away or something—then he's going right now to fetch her."

"Yeah, Charlie. I caught what you were doing, and it's brilliant. Except for one thing."

"What's that?"

"What if he didn't hide her away somewhere? What if..." Jamie stumbled, not able to say to Charlie what he was thinking—that Elliott might have killed her. Not able to say, *what if she's already dead?*

CHAPTER THIRTY-FIVE

THE THIRST WAS AGONY, WORSE THAN THE THROBBING OF HER HEAD AND LEG, worse than the pain that sliced through her side with every movement. Her whole body seemed to ache for water. Her tongue stuck to the roof of her mouth so she had to tear it away to swallow. Only there wasn't much of anything to swallow and the effort made her choke and cough.

For hours, she had alternated attempts to free herself from the wrecked car with descents into exhaustion, sometimes sleeping fitfully and sometimes just losing track of large chunks of time. She knew time was passing because the sun had climbed higher and higher into the sky. The breeze was long gone and the blaring sun was frying her in her glass and metal trap. Little by little, she had managed to wiggle and pull and free her foot, and with a large chunk of glass she had managed to slice through the seatbelt. So theoretically, she should be able to get up to the window, even though her attempts so far had left her dizzy and retching.

But she had to keep trying. She still wasn't sure exactly where she was or how she had gotten here, but she was starting to doubt that anyone was going to find her in time. Occasionally, about a hundred feet above her, she heard a car whoosh past and once or twice saw a quick flash of color as a vehicle zoomed by, so she knew the roadway was up there. She had wasted precious energy on those occasions trying to yell for help. But no one could hear her, and no one would see her from up there unless they were specifically searching for her. Was anyone searching, especially in this area? She had no idea, but she couldn't count on it. She had to depend on God and herself.

Trying to rouse herself from another of her exhausted trances, she once again grabbed the back of the passenger seat and started trying to haul herself up, up toward the broken window and the patch of white-hot sky. Then she froze at a sudden sound. Her heart thumped hard as she listened, because the crashing sounded way too loud to have been caused by a rabbit or squirrel or anything so small. She was trying very hard not to even think about bears when she heard voices—laughing children's voices.

Laughing with relief herself, she started yelling. "Hey! Somebody help me!" She stopped and listened. The laughter and joyful whooping continued without interruption, and she wanted to scream in frustration. Why couldn't they hear her when she could hear them so clearly, so tantalizingly close? "Help me! Please! I'm hurt! Can't you hear me?"

A twig snapped, only a few feet away. And then a boy was peering down at her, through the broken window above her. She could only see part of his face, but his solemn black eyes, the dark hair falling across his forehead, seemed so familiar.

He spoke to her in a whisper, but she could hear him perfectly plain. "What're you doing down there?"

She huffed in frustration. "Well, obviously I had an accident. I can't get out."

He pushed back his hair with a familiar gesture and frowned as he studied her intently, and she could see now that he was only eleven or twelve years old. And yet, she could feel herself relaxing at his presence. It meant…something. Something she couldn't quite grasp, that danced around the edges of her memory, just like the story of how she landed here.

"Why can't you get out?" the boy asked.

She rolled her eyes. "I'm stuck, and it's too hard for me."

"No, it isn't. Come on. I'll help you."

He stuck his hand into the car and she snorted, knowing it was too far above her, knowing that this small boy couldn't pull her up from the wreckage. But a moment later, she was slipping up toward the open window, gliding with no more weight than a balloon, and then she found herself sitting on the side of the car.

The boy laughed, and now his serious eyes twinkled. "See, I told you."

He held out his hand and she took it, allowing him to help her to her feet. She still expected pain when she put her weight on the leg, but none came.

"Come on," he said.

Taking her hand lightly, he started to lead her deeper into the ravine, into the woods and undergrowth. She took a couple of steps, then hesitated as she realized he was leading her away from the hill that climbed up to the road. He stopped too and looked at her, a question in those deep black eyes, and after another moment, she took a step toward him, and they continued on toward the woods.

At first it struck her as odd that she wasn't taller than the little boy. If anything, he seemed to be towering over her, as though she were younger or smaller. The other odd thing was that her feet were bare, but maybe she had lost her shoes in the accident. Her naked soles glided across the rough ground, tickled by the grass. Even though the ground was scattered with pebbles and sticks, she was perfectly comfortable.

The undergrowth thinned again, and now the trees were different— tall and gnarled and set out in rows, with wide grassy spaces underneath. It looked like a pecan grove, actually, and there were children everywhere. Some were industriously collecting pecans from the ground while others shrieked and ran and played. Oddest of all, a few were climbing ladders and picking fruit from the trees' limbs. Fruits of all kinds—apples and juicy plums and some lovely round blue things she couldn't even identify. All of these things hung from the various trees, even though they all looked like pecan trees. She thought it was a little strange at first, but then she felt a bubble of laughter rising in her chest as she realized it wasn't odd at all.

For a long while, she stood at the edge of the grove, content simply to watch. But a sense of longing started to fill her, expanding in her chest like a balloon until she felt it would either explode with the pressure or suffocate her. She was suddenly aware of a deep thirst, and she jealously watched a few of the children biting into the luscious fruits, her throat aching at the sight of the bright red and blue juices running down their faces. She took a tentative step into the grove, then stopped. No one had noticed her yet, but she had a feeling she shouldn't be here. She looked around for the boy to ask him, but he had vanished.

She took another step or two. The children moved so quickly she had a hard time focusing on faces, but they all looked familiar. She realized that some of them were from the *Summer* stories, which explained the linen smocks and breeches and caps. But others wore jeans and tennis shoes and she could have sworn she went to school with them, years ago.

One more step closer…and they all stopped what they were doing and turned to stare at her. Now she could see their faces full-on and she gasped, because they were all contorted with rage.

"Go back!" one of them yelled.

"You can't be here!" called another. "You'll ruin it for everyone."

"But why? Why would I ruin it?" she pleaded, even as she took a step back from the angry mob.

"Because you're dirty."

"You're wearing the wrong clothes."

Even as she looked down to examine her clothing, which truly was covered with blood and grime, two or three surly boys started to lob pieces of fruit at her. One hit her on the cheek before falling to the ground, and although it was so soft it didn't really hurt, it stung her feelings and brought tears to her eyes. At the same time, she was so thirsty that she ran her tongue around her lips to snatch at the drops of juice. And then, ashamed of herself but unable to resist, she snatched up the fruit that had fallen on the ground.

It was a deep purple plum, and she stuck it to her mouth and tried to suck out more juice, then gagged because all she had managed was a mouthful of mud. The children were still jeering at her and a couple threw more juicy plums that splattered against her, but all she could do was stand in place, doubled over and retching because of the mud. The muddy juice splattered against her face and eyes in great drops, so that she squeezed them shut…

And when she opened her eyes, everything had changed. Or rather, everything was the same as before the dream. She was still lying in the wreckage, only now, rain was pelting her from the broken window, which was as far away as ever. Lifting her face toward it, she laughed at the relief of the cool moisture on her face. She opened her mouth wide, she licked raindrops from her hands. She found a wadded drive-through napkin and held it up until it was heavy with water, then squeezed it into her mouth, laughing at the faint taste of mustard and the thought of how disgusting she would have found this a couple of days ago.

All too quickly, however, the rain became too much of a good thing. The upper half of her body was soaked and miserable. Water pooled under her and crept down the legs of her jeans. As the sky grew darker and darker, she first started to feel chilly, then downright cold. Before long, her teeth were chattering and her body shivering so violently that it hurt her ribs and sore muscles. She couldn't help but think of the irony, if she managed to die of hypothermia in Georgia in July.

CHAPTER THIRTY-SIX

WHAT IF SHE'S ALREADY DEAD?

Even though Jamie wasn't able to speak the question, Charlie apparently got it, because he threw up his hands in frustration. "If she doesn't turn up soon, I'll tell Elliott that I think I could write the blasted book if only I had closure about Jeanine one way or another. That way, when he doesn't lead us to her dead body—"

Jamie winced.

"—maybe you can finally admit that Elliott hasn't done anything to her. In the meantime, don't you think you'd better get moving?"

"Moving…oh, right!" Jamie had been sluggish at following Charlie's plan, but now it hit him. If Elliott did know anything about Jeanine's whereabouts and if he thought she was still alive, and if he had taken Charlie's bait, well. It was a lot of "ifs," but Jamie needed to make sure not to lose sight of the man, just in case.

He almost screamed with impatience when, just as he made it to the door of the suite, Charlie called him. "What?" Jamie demanded, pulling the door open at the same time.

Charlie's voice was quiet. "I may have a hard time forgiving you. After you find out how wrong you are about Elliott."

Jamie couldn't think of anything to say. At least, nothing he could say quickly enough. So he just left.

* * *

Wasn't that just the way of things on this Earth? If Jeanine hadn't been so terrified, it would have been almost amusing. A spiritual high, a moment when she was so close to eternity and wonder that she thought nothing physical would ever bother her again. The lovely raindrops bringing hope to her soul and refreshment to her tongue and energy to her body—for about ten minutes, before she was miserable and worrying about hypothermia. Yep, that was life in a nutshell.

She had to get out of this car. No more excuses. And apparently the water had energized her, because this time when she grasped the seat back and heaved, she made actual progress. Further revived, she pulled again and again until she managed to poke her head and shoulders through the broken car window above her. Wiggling out without ripping herself on the jagged remains was tricky, but at least the rain had almost stopped. When she first started, she'd had water shooting up her nose every time she looked up toward the window. And then, finally, with one gargantuan effort, she was out!

She had to rest for a while, lying on the side of the car and trying to get her breath. But she forced herself to sit up and push on as quickly as possible. The sun was going to set soon, and she had to get moving before nightfall. Not just because she was still cold, but she also wanted to try to get up to the roadway before dark.

She tried to put her weight on her leg. The pain nearly shattered her as her leg immediately buckled. Rolling to her side, she lay gasping for breath, waiting for the throbbing to subside. She wanted to cry, wanted to give up. Climbing that hill wouldn't be that difficult for someone with a working set of legs, but how was she supposed to manage it in her shape? Maybe she should just forget the whole thing. She had managed to get out of the water, and the rain seemed to be subsiding. She could just lie down right here, rest for a while, maybe for the whole night…

No. She shook her head, trying to wake herself up. She had to try something else. Crawling? No, that wouldn't work, either. She couldn't take the pain on her knee. After a moment of assessing her body, she decided to try going at it backwards. Sitting with her back toward the hill, she planted her hands on the ground, stretched out her bad leg so it would be doing as little work as possible, and shoved off with her good foot. When she was rewarded with a sort of undignified scoot totaling a few inches up the hill, she near-

ly laughed in delight. A couple more scoots, a few more inches. She was getting tired, but the exhilaration of actually accomplishing something seemed
to be renewing her energy. True, when she swiveled her neck and looked up
toward the road, it still seemed dauntingly far away, but she was no longer
trapped, and no longer at the absolute bottom of the hill, either.

And then a pain shot through her hand, and when she jerked it up, she
saw blood dripping from the palm. Twisting around as she pressed her palm
against her filthy shirt to staunch the flow, she realized she'd been lucky not
to have cut herself sooner. Great shards of glass and bits of metal lay scattered down the hillside. She shuddered as she realized how the car must have
crashed into the ground and flipped over and over in its trip down the hill.
She was glad she couldn't remember it.

She kicked her good foot in frustration. She'd finally come up with a
working plan and now this. After looking around a moment, she saw something familiar, lying a few feet down the hill. Her shoulder bag, which had
apparently been thrown from the Mustang on its trip down to the bottom of
the ravine. Just thinking of sliding back down the hill, losing even a few inches of the painful progress she had made, nearly brought her to tears. But her
choices were to do that or shred her hands—and probably her bottom and
legs, too—scooting up the hill on shards of glass and metal.

So she reversed her course, pushing herself down the hill this time
instead of up, and watching out for sharp things as she went. Descending was
actually harder than going up. Her bad leg kept trying to fold under her, and
throbbed so badly she had to stop for a while. But when she finally reached
her shoulder bag and drug it over, she felt a shock of delight. First, she found
half a bottle of water and a package of crackers inside it, both of which took
her about twenty seconds to put away. The crackers had been reduced to
crumbs, but they tasted better than anything she'd ever eaten as she held up
the package and poured them into her mouth. Feeling better about having
to come down the hill, she rummaged in her bag looking for her cell phone.
It might be dead after all this time, but who knew? She was fervently praying
for a tiny bit of a charge on the battery and enough of a signal to make a call
when she realized the phone wasn't there.

Her eyes roamed the hillside, the bottom of the ravine as it disappeared
into the thick tangle of trees and bushes, the flash of red of her Mustang. She
supposed the phone must have been thrown out of her bag in the crash,

although everything else seemed to be there. Some of the purse's contents like the crackers hadn't survived too well, but they were there.

Maybe her phone was still somewhere inside the car. Had she been making a call, maybe, when the crash occurred? She grimaced at the thought. Maybe that's what had caused the accident, if she'd been careless enough to be using her phone while driving.

But then something else occurred to her, out of the blue—an image in her mind of Elliott at her apartment, asking if he could use her phone. He had apparently left his in the car or at the hotel or something, he said. She had been preoccupied, throwing some clothes into a bag while struggling to think clearly through a sleep-deprived haze. The memory came to her in that one sharp image, then like fireworks dispersed and faded. Try as she might, she couldn't grasp it. Couldn't remember why Elliott would have been at her apartment, or what had happened before or after.

Once again, she started the long, backwards process of pushing herself up the embankment. Only this time, she sat on her shoulder bag like a tiny sled, using it to shield her from the glass. In her hands, she held two large rocks and pushed off with those instead of putting her skin against the ground. She winced a little every time she pushed her cut palm against the rock, but compared to her leg, it was nothing.

After a while, she would have sworn she had been doing this for days. That she had pushed and inched up the hill for hours, and that the roadway was just as far above her as ever. Her brain went into a kind of tired fog, barely registering her surroundings or forming any coherent thought, just forcing her arms and legs to keep pumping, pushing, sliding, pumping.

At some point she quit. When she came to herself, she realized she had been sitting staring into space, in a sort of daze, for who knew how long? The shadows seemed much longer, and she knew there was a very real possibility she was about to spend the night out here. But when she managed to turn her head, which felt as though it had grown to the size and weight of a boulder, she nearly cried with relief at the sight of the asphalt roadway only six inches or so above her. A couple more mighty heaves, and she was collapsing on the shoulder of the road, gasping for breath and trembling all over, but happy.

A minute or so later, a truck blew past her, so close she could feel a hot blast of air from it. Wouldn't that be just peachy, if she went through all this just to get mowed down by a truck? She wiggled as close as she could to the side of the ravine without falling off again, weighing her options. How could she best position herself to be seen without putting herself too close to oncoming vehicles? Especially if she was still out here when it got dark. She couldn't stand up, that was for sure. She was rooting around in her shoulder bag and trying to think of something to use for a flag, or something to help draw attention, when she heard the sound of voices.

Two men had appeared out of the woods on the other side of the road. They hadn't noticed Jeanine yet, and her first reflex was to shrink back and hope they didn't. But even as the hair stood up on the back of her neck, she saw with a rush of relief their hiking boots and loaded backpacks, and a marker for the Appalachian Trail. One of the men unfolded a map while the other pulled out a bottle of water. So she pushed herself forward and started to yell. "Hey! Over here! Can you help me?"

If they had startled her, it was nothing compared to what she did to them. One jerked so badly that water shot from the top of his silver bottle, and the other dropped the map. Then they spotted her, and after a split second taking in her appearance, they rushed over.

It took very little to make them understand what had happened. From a car speeding down this road you might not be aware of the wreck. But once she pointed it out to them, it was obvious, from the black skid marks on the asphalt, to the torn-up chunks of dirt and scattered debris, to the splash of red metal just visible among the broken bushes and limbs at the bottom. She felt a lump forming in her throat at the thought of her old Mustang crumpled down there, but she quickly swallowed it. She was alive, and she was safe, and not a moment too soon. She had no energy left, and that feeling that her head was too heavy and big for her shoulders was just getting worse. She gratefully let the younger of the two men—who was really a teenage boy, possibly the other guy's son—position her to lean against a big rock, while the other one pulled out a cell phone and tried to call for help. Best of all, the boy handed her his water bottle, and she shamelessly guzzled every last drop of it.

After a minute, the man shook his head. "I'm not getting a signal."

"I'll try to flag somebody down," the boy said.

She felt herself drifting away from it all, letting them handle it. She couldn't hold her head up anymore. And anyway, she had made it. The nightmare was over. One way or another, they would get help for her.

She heard the boy jabbering, whistling through his teeth. She cracked an eye open and saw him waving a t-shirt or towel or something above his head, and it was working. A big gray car was slowing, pulling over to the side. It was over. It was over.

She cracked her eyes again at the sound of a car door slamming, and felt only mildly surprised to see someone she knew. Elliott was getting out of the car.

Chapter Thirty-Seven

Frustrated and unable to think where to go, Jamie whipped the Ford back into the drive of Charlie and Elliott's hotel. Not only was there no progress on finding Jeanine, but they had also somehow let Elliott slip through their fingers. Jamie had wasted too much time with Charlie before heading after Elliott. Now, even with the help of the private detectives he had previously used for keeping an eye on Jeanine, and even with tips from Charlie about the poker games and strip clubs the man frequented, they were still coming up empty. Jamie could feel the minutes, the hours passing by. Even though he had no idea what had happened to Jeanine or where she might be, he couldn't shake the feeling they were counting down her life.

As Jamie handed his keys to the valet, a familiar figure caught his eye. Charlie was jumping into a car a few lengths ahead, and he tore out of the hotel's drive so fast he nearly sideswiped a hotel van.

Jamie pulled the keys back from the valet, hesitating. Where was Charlie going in such a hurry? Did he know something? Jamie was just about to jump back into the car and follow when another idea struck him. After a panicky moment of indecision, he handed over the keys and hurried inside, planning to look for a maid and try to charm her into letting him into Charlie's suite. He was always a little disgusted with himself when he played the film-star card, but this was no time for such scruples.

He pulled up short in the lobby when someone called his name. Turning impatiently, he saw a female security guard smiling and waving at him. He remembered her from a couple of days before, when she had waylaid him with a camera and an assortment of items to autograph. He'd barely gotten away then, he certainly didn't have time to deal with her now. So he threw her a quick wave and headed for the elevator...and was almost inside before he realized what an idiot he was being.

Hurrying back across the lobby, he smiled his most charming movie-star smile. "Sharon, wasn't it?" he said as he approached.

She beamed at him, obviously delighted he remembered her name. "That's right. Is there anything I can do for you, Mr. Newkirk?"

"Actually there is, Sharon. There is, indeed."

* * *

Jeanine slid in and out of sleep. Every time she managed to pull her eyelids open, the scene seemed to have skipped forward a few frames. First she heard the older hiker and Elliott talking about not being able to get a cell phone signal, and then Elliott was reassuring him that he would get her to a hospital and alert the police. Next thing she knew, she was being helped into the passenger seat of Elliott's car, and then another brief skip, and the scenery was flashing by her, and they were motoring along, and Elliott was talking. She tried to focus, but it was hard to make sense of what he was saying. He seemed to want her to wake up. As they rolled to a stop, he handed her an open bottle of cold water.

She took a few sips, not quite as anxious for the stuff now, and started to drift off again, but Elliott gave her arm a little shake. "Jeanine, listen to me. Can you hear me?"

She pushed her eyes open, and saw they were sitting at a stop sign. Elliott was gripping her arm, looking intently into her eyes, and as she met his gaze, a flood of memory came rushing back. She remembered Elliott showing up at her apartment, when she was so depressed she thought she was dying; Elliott telling her that Charlie wanted her to join him for the weekend at a cabin he had rented in the mountains. He said Jamie was jealous of her relationship with Charlie but they could work in secret on the book while they worked on Jamie's attitude.

She remembered how she had felt in that moment, so hopeful that she could have it all again, including the thrilling work on the book. And Jamie was jealous! So maybe he would come around and at least be her friend again, even if he didn't love her or want to marry her. She had grabbed at

Elliott's offer the way she had grabbed for water when she was dying of thirst, even though the hairs on the back of her neck were prickling with warnings. Her mind was prodding her, wondering why he wanted her to keep the trip a secret even from her family, even from Trev. But she shut down her mind and listened to her heart. Isn't that what all the great stories told you to do— follow your heart?

So she had obediently climbed into her Mustang to follow Elliott, supposedly to a rendezvous with Charlie at the mountain cabin. But her blasted brain just wouldn't stay shut down. Alone in the car, she couldn't help but think—especially after they were out of the city, winding around the hairpin curves with the exposed rock wall of the mountains on one side and the sheer drops into lush green depths on her right, focusing on Elliott's license plate in front of her to keep from veering out of her lane. Somewhere in the course of her frenzied thinking, wondering if she was doing the right thing, something hit her.

When Elliott had been trying to convince her to make this trip, he had said something about Paula. "You've got a future in the business, Jeanine. And I can help you get there. I did it for Paula, you know."

"Paula?" she had echoed, confused.

"That's right. I recognized her modeling potential and got her started in that business, with my connections. I would have had her in movies, too, if...well, things hadn't gone wrong."

At the time, like an idiot, only certain words had jumped out at her. *Future. Help you. Connections. Movies.* But later, as she wound around the curves behind Elliott, climbing the mountain toward her future, she had replayed the whole conversation in her head, and that's when it had struck her.

Elliott wasn't supposed to know Paula. She had come into Jamie's life after he and Elliott were more or less estranged, and she had heard both Charlie and Elliott say that the man had only met her once or twice, for a few minutes at a time. Now he was talking as though he had practically been her manager, had been extremely close to her.

For a moment she kept driving, following Elliott, turning this realization over and over in her head. Did it even matter? What difference did it make how well he knew Paula? Only...

It couldn't be just a simple mistake. How can you forget knowing someone if you were close enough to them to help guide their career? And if everything was perfectly innocent, why would Elliott lie about knowing her? At the very least, this showed that the man had something to hide, that he was less than truthful—and here she was ditching her job to follow him out into the wilderness?

She couldn't ignore the alarms going off in her head any longer. First, she had reached into her purse for her phone, not sure exactly who she was planning to call, but wanting someone to know where she was, to help her decide what to do. But her phone was missing, and when she remembered that Elliott had made an excuse to borrow her phone back at the apartment, and had never given it back, she went cold with fear. For a few horrible minutes, she continued to weave behind his car, trying desperately to figure out how to turn her car around, stuck between the rock wall and the drop-off into the gorge.

Finally, she spotted a pull-out where drivers could pause and admire the breathtaking view across the valley to the blue-tinged range of mountains in the distance. Waiting until the last moment, until she saw Elliott disappearing around the curve in front of her, she whipped into the pull-out and turned around as fast as she could, her movements jerky and panicked. She expected at any moment to see Elliott reappear when he noticed she wasn't behind him anymore, although she hoped he would have trouble turning around, too.

Sure enough, she'd barely gotten a mile when she saw the familiar silver hood popping into view in her rear view mirror. Simultaneously, her heart leapt and her foot stomped down on the accelerator, but Elliott kept pace with her. Within moments, she was terrified not just of Elliott, of whatever he was planning for her when he got her alone at some secluded cabin, but of this crazy drive around the hairpin curves. She was going way too fast, and Elliott was staying so close to her bumper that she was terrified to brake for the curves in fear that he would slam into her. In fact, he was so close that when she glanced in the mirror, she could see his face, could actually see his livid expression and his mouth working as he no doubt yelled at her. He was gesturing wildly, motioning for her to pull over—although just where she would have done that, she wasn't sure. And then he started hitting the horn, over and over, so that if the wild ride hadn't frayed her nerves, the blaring noise was enough to rip them to shreds.

This seemed to have gone on forever, as she prayed to reach the highway and civilization and help. And then suddenly it happened. Her body slammed forward, caught hard in the seatbelt as Elliott's car hit her from behind, and she reflexively hit the brake, trying to stop the car as it swerved toward the edge. At first she thought it had been an accident, that Elliott had been following so closely he was bound to make contact. But then Elliott whipped around beside her, and for what seemed like a long moment she could see the look on his face—the anger drained away, replaced by an almost passionless look of determination as he jerked the steering wheel toward her, and the Mustang leapt toward the edge, and then over it, and down into the ravine.

Now, sitting in Elliott's car, all of this flashed through her mind in a couple of seconds. Even before the memory was complete, as she was remembering the long, sickening drop over the edge, she was grabbing for the door handle of Elliott's car, throwing it open and leaning out. Before she had time to wonder what she was going to do next, considering the state of her bum leg, Elliott had pulled her back.

"Jeanine," he said, while tightening the grip on her arm, "be still. You're going to hurt yourself more."

She laughed harshly. "I'm sure you're worried about that."

He frowned, and appeared so confused that for a moment, her faith in the memory wavered.

"I'm very worried, yes. Shut the door, will you? We need to get you to the hospital."

She shook her head. "You're lying. You're not taking me to the hospital."

In a soft voice, he said, "Jeanine, you're hurt. You've bumped your head. I don't know what's going on in your mind right now, but you're confused. I'm just trying to help you."

The truth was, she did feel confused and sluggish. She tried to think of something to say. "You knew where to find me. And that's because you're the one who put me there."

"What!" His eyes grew wide. "Jeanine, dear, you wrecked your car. A simple accident. And I knew to come look for you up here because you were supposed to meet Charlie at his cabin. When you didn't show up, he got worried and called me, and we—well, more than the two of us actually. Jamie, too. We've all been searching the whole route from Atlanta, trying to find some sign of you."

"Jamie?" she said weakly. This wasn't making any sense. Nothing made sense, and her head hurt so badly.

Elliott nodded. "That's right." Still holding her arm, he leaned in close, so that the smell of his cologne heightened the queasy feeling in the pit of her stomach. "As soon as we can pick up a signal, I'll call Jamie and Charlie and they can meet us at the hospital. Your parents, too, of course. Your dad has been very worried."

"Daddy…"

"That's right. Jeanine, look at me."

She turned and gazed into his eyes. They were round and innocent, and it was hard for her to imagine those expressions from her memory—first of rage, then of calm determination to finish her off—on this concerned face.

He was still talking. "Jeanine, everything is fine now. Do you understand me? Charlie and Jamie had a long talk, and Jamie's gotten over his jealous snit. Both of them want to work on *Summer,* and they both want you involved." Again he leaned in, and again the sickly-sweet reek filled her nose. "Everything you ever dreamed of is yours…if you don't ruin it by babbling about fantasies you have due to a knock on the head. Do you understand?"

She struggled to process what he was saying. "I…don't…"

"They're my boys, Jeanine. They're both practically my sons, and I've always arranged things for them. For us. I assure you, they will not take the side of an outsider like you. So it's going to be your choice, how you come out of all this. With a brilliant new future, or losing everything. It's all up to you, what you do or what you say. Do you understand?"

He kept saying that. *Do you understand?* And in spite of the haze in her mind, she thought she was beginning to. Still, she couldn't think what to say, what to do.

Before either of them could say anything else, another car pulled up behind them at the stop sign. Jeanine started to twist around toward the door again, and even though Elliott held onto her arm and she knew she couldn't stand up or run away, she leaned as far out as she could and yelled toward the car stopped behind them. "Help me, please!"

The door opened. The driver got out, started to walk toward her.

It was Charlie.

CHAPTER THIRTY-EIGHT

"Turn right."

Jamie obeyed the tinny voice from the GPS, turning so sharply onto the road leading up the mountain that he fought to regain control of the wheel for a second or two afterward.

"Slow down, take it easy," he coached himself. "You can't help her if you crash the car."

Still, he beat on the steering wheel in frustration. He was so far behind. All that time he had taken bumbling around in Atlanta, searching the hotel. Elliott had such a head start.

And Charlie. Jamie shook his head, denying the thought trying to form. He would not believe that Charlie was involved in whatever Elliott was doing. Not yet. Still, he wished he could talk to Charlie and find out just where he had rushed off to. Was he on his way to join Elliott? And was Elliott going to be up here, or was Jamie on a wild goose chase, wasting more precious time?

Charming the security guard into letting him into the hotel suite had been painfully easy. And almost immediately he had found the laptop in Elliott's room, sleeping but not shut down, so that when he touched it, there it was right on the screen. A confirmation email for his rental of a cabin in North Georgia. Elliott had rented the place shortly after Jamie's fight with Charlie and Jeanine at the suite. So Jamie had jumped in the car and headed north.

He had notified everyone he could think of along the way—Lieutenant

262 ‎ R O B I N ‎ J O H N S ‎ G R A N T

Regis, the private detectives. And all the way up here, he had dialed Charlie, then Elliott, over and over. Neither of them answered, or returned his calls.

As the Taurus hurtled around a curve, he had to brake to keep from running up on a knot of police cars and people standing at the side of the road, looking down into the ravine. Before he could form a coherent thought, his body knew, shooting a sickening rush of adrenaline through him. It was Jeanine.

He was out of the car the moment it came to a stop, running for the nearest policeman even as he tried to peer down the embankment, to see what everyone was pointing at as they murmured. He stopped dead still as he saw it. A splash of red metal among the green leaves.

A cop approached him, pulling him back from the railing. "Sir, I'm going to have to ask you to—"

"That's my—that's Jeanine." His words were coming out in gasps. He stared wildly at the policeman. "Is she…is she…"

"The woman in the car? She's already out."

"She's alive!" Jamie felt his knees going weak. A grungy-looking man with about a three-day growth of beard was approaching, but Jamie ignored him. "Where is she? Has she been taken to hospital?"

It was the grungy man who answered. "My son and I found her. We were trying to call for help but couldn't get a signal. But some other man stopped right after and said he would take her, so—"

"A man? What man?"

It only took a few more words from the man for Jamie to realize. Jeanine had been driven away from the scene by Elliott Dane.

Jamie ran through the hospital, not really expecting to find Jeanine or Elliott there, even though the policeman had sworn they had arrived at Emergency some time before. But there they were, Elliott and Charlie, sitting in the waiting room for all the world like they were her concerned family members. As Jamie stood in the doorway, fists clenched and body stiff, they rose to their feet.

Charlie's face was ashen. "Jamie! I was just about to call you, but…" He licked his lips and glanced at Elliott. "He said we should wait until we had some definite news."

Elliott nodded gravely. "We didn't want to scare you."

Jamie felt himself choking. "You didn't…excuse me? You didn't want to scare me!" His voice was getting higher and louder, but he didn't care. "Like I haven't been scared out of my bleedin' mind all day!"

Charlie put up his hands in a soothing gesture. "You're right. You're absolutely right, but I was about to call you, I swear. She's going to be fine."

"She's okay?" Jamie felt himself go so weak with relief, he had to put a hand against the wall to steady himself.

As Charlie nodded, Elliott said, "A concussion and a fractured leg. And some cuts and a couple of cracked ribs. But those seem to be the worst of it. She's incredibly lucky."

Charlie sounded slightly out of breath. "She was down in that ravine for two days, trapped in the car. Two days!"

Jamie turned on Elliott. "How did this happen?" Somehow, he was across the room, with the front of Elliott's shirt clutched in his fist. "Tell me what you did."

Jamie felt Charlie pulling at him. "Stop it, Jamie! Elliott brought her to the hospital."

Forcing himself to let go of the shirt, Jamie stepped back and ran his hand through his hair. "Of course he brought her here. That was the plan, wasn't it?"

Elliott's eyes narrowed as he smoothed the front of his shirt. "Plan? What plan?"

Jamie pointed at Charlie, who flushed and remained silent. "I told him you knew where she was, that you had done something to her. Frankly, I was afraid she was dead, but the most I could convince Charlie of was that you had—I don't know. Paid her to go away, or lured her off somehow. So he thought if we fed you that line about all of us coming together and holding hands to finish the *Summer* series—but only along with Jeanine—you'd lead us to her." He shook his head, amazed. "And apparently, he was right."

Elliott shot Charlie a look. "Is that true?"

Charlie spread his hands. "I was trying to get Jamie off my back."

Elliott drew himself up and said with great dignity, "So…I spent these last hours trying to help you, trying to find the girl you were so worried about. I thought you two were doing the same thing, and all the while you were plotting against me."

Charlie dropped his face, staring down at his shoes, while Jamie just stared from one to the other of them. An odd sense of déjà vu washed over him. How many times had he been through this? His body, his mind, his soul primed to confront this man—this devil!—once and for all. Only to see those flat blue eyes meet his with total confidence as he shimmied and slithered and talked his way completely out of the whole mess. And usually there was some-one standing with him, taking his side. Teresa. Paula. Charlie. How many times had it been Charlie? Elliott made them suffer and then they stood there next to him, backing him up, until eventually Jamie backed down.

But not this time.

He went after Charlie. "Look at me," Jamie said gruffly.

Charlie seemed to lift his head with difficulty, and Jamie again noted how pale he was. He looked as bad as he had in the hospital after the over-dose.

But Jamie squared his shoulders and plowed ahead. "I don't know what he's told you. I can't even imagine. But you know the truth, don't you? Jeanine disappears, spends two days trapped down in a ravine. No one knows where she is. But miraculously, when we want her back, he goes right to her."

Charlie was in agony, Jamie could see it in his face. But Elliott said quite calmly, "Actually, that's not the way it happened at all. You don't know the whole story."

Jamie put his hands over his eyes, feeling a dull throbbing starting there and wanting to moan in frustration. "There's always a story, isn't there, Elliott?"

Elliott ignored that comment. "I'm surprised Charlie didn't tell you this earlier. I guess he didn't want you to know."

Jamie removed his hands from his eyes to look at Charlie, who had returned to staring at the toe of his shoe.

Elliott was continuing, "When you had that blow-up with Jeanine and said she couldn't work on *Summer*, well…Charlie and I knew you would come around. And they had such momentum going on the story. So we—and I mean all three of us, Jeanine included—decided to rent a cabin up here so Charlie and Jeanine could work in secret without upsetting you while you were in the process of coming around. Isn't that right, Charlie?"

Charlie licked his lips, shifted his weight from one foot to another. Still not looking up, he gave a little nod and muttered, "That's right."

Jamie snorted. "And you just happened to forget she might be up here while we were desperately looking for her, Charlie?"

Charlie glanced up, his face burning red, but Elliott cut in smoothly. "She wasn't supposed to be up here yet. We were going to start next weekend. But we finally decided to come check, and apparently it's a good thing we did. Jeanine must have been so upset she needed to get away and thought we'd provided the perfect place for her to be alone and think things over."

Jamie felt a familiar fog coming into his brain, as he tried to navigate another of Elliott's murky stories. They were always just so very possible. "So when I go into Jeanine's room, this is what she's going to tell me, too?" he demanded, rubbing his aching head.

"Of course."

"Well…" Charlie glanced from one of them to the other. "You've got to admit, she was pretty confused in the car, Elliott."

"True enough. But we were all on good terms by the time we got here, weren't we, Charlie?"

He shrugged and nodded.

"Could that have happened if she really believed we had tried to hurt her?" Elliott said.

Jamie noted that Charlie's head jerked up at Elliott's use of "we," and that Charlie was now staring at his uncle.

"Jeanine's leg was hurting and she feels terrible physically, but she was in a good mood when we got here. We told her that you and Charlie had patched things up, so she was pretty happy. And why shouldn't she be? She has her friendship with you," Elliott nodded toward Jamie, "and about to begin a new career in film. All her dreams are coming true. Unless…"

"Unless what?" Jamie asked.

"Unless you ruin everything by bringing up these childish fantasies of yours."

"And that's what you want too, Charlie?" Jamie asked him. "All of us one big happy with Elliott?"

Before Charlie could answer, the waiting room door popped open, and a woman in blue scrubs stuck her head in. "DeValery family?"

"That's us," Elliott said, bounding forward.

"Uh, he's not actually her family," Jamie said, grabbing the man's arm.

"Oh. Ms. DeValery was asking for her parents."

"They're on their way," Elliott said.

"They've been called?" Jamie asked Charlie. "You're sure?"

"I did it myself."

"We're friends of the patient," Elliott said. "May we see her?"

"I think that would be fine," said the nurse.

As Elliott started to follow the nurse from the room, Jamie actually made a move to grab him. He wanted to throw him against the far wall, to use him like a punching bag while demanding what could possibly make him think he had the right to stroll down the hall to visit Jeanine? Instead, he restrained himself, let the door swing shut behind the slimy git, and turned to Charlie instead. "You wait right there just a minute, while I make sure the nurse isn't going to leave Elliott alone with Jeanine," he said urgently. "Then, I need to show you something."

* * *

Even with the drugs pumping into her through the i.v., Jeanine couldn't sleep. But when she heard Elliott's voice in the hallway right outside the door, she squeezed her eyes shut and pretended. A moment later, he was in the room, murmuring softly with one of her nurses. They were trying not to wake her, so only a few words jumped out, like "concussion" and "confusion." For some reason, the words set her blood to pulsing with anger. Her eyes flew open as she tried to raise herself up in the bed.

"Ah, you're awake." Elliott beamed at her. "How are you feeling?"

"Just great." She winced and shifted in the bed. "Has anyone called my parents?"

"They're on their way." He crossed to the bed and touched her arm. "Everything's going to be just fine."

"You're right, it is. When my folks get here, they can take me home and I can get on with my life. In the meantime, I really wish you would get out of my room. I don't want anything to do with any of you anymore."

"Surely you don't mean that," Elliott started, obnoxiously cheerful, as though nothing had happened. "We have big plans, all of us. All your dreams are about to come true." A slight edge entered his voice. "You don't want to throw all that away, do you, Jeanine? Remember what we talked about in the car? Or are you still confused?"

She heard the trace of mockery in his last question, so subtle the nurse probably missed it. But she didn't. "No, I'm not confused at all," she said quietly.

"Good. Then you should also remember our discussion about Jamie." He glanced toward the nurse, hovering at the door. "Could you give us just a moment of privacy?"

"Umm…I believe it might be best if I stay."

"If you've got something to say, Elliott, just say it," Jeanine said.

"I tell you what," said the nurse. "I'll just step right here in the hallway and leave the door open. That way you can talk more privately."

When she had stepped outside, Elliott sat in a chair next to Jeanine's bed. In a low voice, he said, "I'm sure the police will be here soon, Jeanine, wanting to know how you wrecked your car. This is a turning point in your life, do you understand me?"

She met his gaze. "Yes, I do, actually."

"Good. On the one hand, you can tell the police the simple truth. You were upset and needed to get away, so you decided to leave town early and come to the cabin Charlie and I told you about. You lost control of your car and went into that ravine. Charlie and I decided to come check, just in case you had decided to drive up here early. And I found you. End of story. They'll fill out a police report and we can get started on *Summer*. You can have everything you ever dreamed of. Not only that, you can make everyone happy—including Charlie. Including *Jamie*." He leaned in disgustingly close. "On the other hand, you can tell this idiotic story you dreamed up after a knock on the head, and all hell will break loose."

"For you."

Elliott shrugged. "Nothing I can't handle. You and Jamie on the other hand—well. He's the real meat of any story, isn't he? The media will tear him to pieces. Awfully coincidental, isn't it? Another of his women falling victim to foul play—"

"I am not his—"

"I wonder how your poor family will feel, after the tabloids and the talk shows and the blogs get through dissecting your relationship, wondering, speculating—"

"Stop it!"

Elliott suddenly straightened up and looked toward the doorway. Jamie was entering, closely followed by two men she didn't know. It wasn't hard to figure out who they were, though, since one of them was in uniform.

As one of them shut the door, making the little room feel close and claustrophobic, Jamie crossed to her bedside. His eyes were red and watery. In fact, he looked thoroughly exhausted and miserable. There was a sort of pleading in his eyes as he gazed down at her, and he seemed to be trying to communicate something to her. But all he said was, "Jeannie…are you okay?"

"I will be," she said gruffly, looking away.

One of the strangers stepped forward. "Ms. DeValery, I'm Deputy Sheriff Anderson. Do you feel up to telling us what you can remember about how you wrecked your car?"

This was it. The room went silent, and everyone stared at her. All four men were poker-faced, but she could feel waves of silent communication radiating from Elliott and Jamie, like deep silent screams.

Elliott was right. It would be so easy to say she just wrecked her car. Daddy was on his way up here to get her, and he would take her home and they would fuss over her. Life would be quiet, and maybe Jamie would smile at her again. Maybe there really would even be a *Summer* story to work on. Her dreams were dangling in front of her, shiny and juicy, almost in her grasp. The thought made her think of her dream. The beautiful fruit turned ugly with rot. The sudden memory of her mouth full of mud and slime almost made her gag. She glanced up at Jamie's pleading eyes, then away again. She couldn't let herself be pulled down into those fathomless black eyes of his.

Still looking straight ahead, she said, "On Friday morning, Elliott Dane told me he had rented a cabin, and that Charlie Edenfield wanted us to work on a writing project together. He said he would lead me up here. But as we got closer, I started to feel uneasy about the whole thing. So I tried to turn around and when I did, he chased me in his car and rammed me from the back, then pulled up next to me and basically ran me off the road. Then he drove away." She could hear her own heart monitor bleating, picking up speed as she thought about what this man had done to her. She looked him in the eye. "He drove away and left me lying there for…well, I don't even know how long. Forever."

"Two days," Jamie murmured.

Elliott's voice was as calm as though they were discussing the weather.

"That's not true. I came up here to look for her, but I did not come up here with her on Friday." His eyes flooded with sympathy. "It's understandable she would be confused, isn't it?"

"She isn't confused," Jamie said.

Jeanine glanced over at him, his firm support causing her to feel a little lighter.

Elliott ignored him. "Anyway, you'll find we can get this straightened out pretty easily. My nephew Charlie will back me up on everything—how we rented the cabin and told Ms. DeValery about it, and that I was with him in Atlanta last Friday. All of it."

To Jeanine's surprise, Jamie smiled broadly. "Actually, Elliott, you're in for a bit of a nasty shock there."

Elliott's eyebrows came together in such a sudden frown, Jeanine was comically reminded of Mr. Spock's V-shaped brows and fought the urge to scream with laughter. Wouldn't do for them to decide she was hysterical, after all.

"What do you mean?" Elliott was demanding.

Jamie had stopped smiling, but his eyes gleamed with triumph. "As of about five minutes ago, Charlie has finally come to understand the truth about you. I don't think he'll be lying for you, or—what did you call it? 'Backing you up?' He's not going to be doing that anymore."

For the first time, a flicker of doubt came into Elliott's eyes as he considered Jamie. "I can't imagine what you're talking about."

"You don't have to imagine," Jamie said, pulling out his cell phone. "I can show you just what I showed Charlie a few minutes ago. And I imagine these two officers might be interested in it, as well."

Jamie stuck the phone in Elliott's face, and the two officers moved around behind him so they, too, could see the phone's tiny screen. Then Jamie said, "I'm sure Elliott will know exactly what this video is showing, even as small as it is. Charlie did. But maybe I should give a little background for the rest of you. A few weeks ago, my friend Charlie—who is Elliott's nephew—was kicked out of the Army for supposedly taking illegal drugs. Charlie claimed all along that someone had spiked his drink in the hotel bar that night, but no one looked into it much. But then I got friendly with a security officer at the hotel, and asked her if she could look at security footage from that evening. Which she did. And she emailed this clip to me."

For a moment they all stood silent, staring at the screen. Jeanine felt a stirring of curiosity, although judging by the nasty shade of red flooding Elliott's face, she suspected what they must be seeing.

When the short clip ended, the officers looked at Elliott. Jamie looked at her. "Want to see?"

"It was Elliott, slipping the drugs into Charlie's drink, wasn't it?"

Jamie nodded, but Elliott gave a derisive snort. "If you can get that out of that blurry little mess, your eyesight must be better than Superman's. Anyway, what does that have to do with Jeanine's car accident?"

"Other than the fact that Charlie's left the hospital and won't be around to 'back you up' anymore, maybe not much," Jamie said. "But if you'd like something a little more direct, Detective White may have something for you."

Elliott lifted his head and looked down his nose at the squat, plain-clothes detective. "And just who exactly are you?"

"I'm from the Atlanta Police Department. And I really have the private investigators that Mr. Newkirk hired to keep an eye on Ms. DeValery to thank for this—"

"The what! Ow!" Jeanine sat up straighter, so fast that her leg shot a quick reminder of its condition to her.

"Tell you later," Jamie said.

"Before our department was truly involved in this investigation—"

Jeanine saw Jamie's mouth turn down at that, and guessed there was a story about the police involvement, too.

"—these private investigators were trying to figure out what Mr. Dane here was up to. One curious thing they noticed was that on Friday afternoon he turned his rental car in and got a different one. So they went to the rental agency to see if they could figure out why. Along the way, they got a chance to examine the car he'd turned in, the one he'd been driving Friday morning, and do you know what they found?" The detective looked over at Jeanine and gave her a wink. "A little tiny splotch of red paint on Mr. Dane's car. So small the rental folks hadn't even noticed it yet, but the p.i.'s called us, and we went and collected a nice sample of it to compare to the paint on Ms. DeValery's Mustang."

Jeanine hadn't realized she was holding her breath until she started to let it out in a kind of satisfied sigh. Again, she had to fight a crazy urge to laugh, but as she met Jamie's eye, she saw his eyes shining as though he wanted to let out a whoop of triumph, himself.

"Well, this is all interesting, but quite ridiculous," Elliott said. Still with that haughty tilt to his head, he started to move toward the doorway. "I have better things to do than stand here and listen to all of you make these idiotic accusations."

Both policemen stepped smoothly between Elliott and the doorway. His face flushed an ugly shade of purple as he came to a halt.

"I'm sorry, but whatever those things are you were planning to do, well…you're going to have to cancel them, I'm afraid." Detective White smiled tightly. "There are so many cops in so many jurisdictions who want to talk to you that our main problem is going to be figuring out where to start."

"What the devil do you mean?"

"Well, we haven't even talked about a certain Lieutenant Regis in L.A., for example." The cop nodded toward Jamie. "He's just gotten results from a new autopsy on this boy's mother—"

"What!"

"And it seems Jamie was right. They did miss something the first time around. There wasn't anything noticeable on the outside, but on the back of her head, underneath her scalp, they found a skull fracture. Now why do you suppose a woman who apparently took enough drugs to kill herself and was found lying peacefully on her bed would have a skull fracture, Mr. Dane?"

"I'm sure I don't know."

"And that's not all. They found an injection site between her toes. No reason they would have looked for such a thing before."

Elliott gestured toward Jamie. "As I understand it, he was the one who found her. The one who fought with her that night. The one who found her supposed suicide note, too. He knows more about all of it."

"That's not true."

Jeanine, along with everyone else, turned her head toward the doorway at the sound of the new voice. Apparently none of them had noticed Charlie slipping in. Even now, he looked gray and somehow insubstantial, standing just barely over the threshold of the room, as though he might flit back out of the room at any moment. But his mouth was set in a determined line as he stared at his uncle, and Jeanine thought randomly of the ghost in Hamlet, come back just long enough to make his accusation.

Elliott started to move toward him, but Detective White held up his hand to stop him. "Go ahead, son. What were you about to say?"

He glanced around the room, and he and Jamie exchanged a long look. "I told Jamie this a little while ago. I should have told him before, but...I always wondered about Teresa's suicide note. A couple of days before she died, Elliott was raging about a letter he'd gotten from her. He was furious that she had dared to leave him—and that she had that fancy house in Malibu and a new Jaguar and all kinds of goodies, courtesy of Jamie. It was like she was flaunting it that she was better off without him."

"He was trying to get her to come back," Jamie said.

"I know, and just before she died, she wrote him a letter in response. Elliott showed it to me—he was so mad, he was dying to show it to somebody. It was two pages long, and the first of it was her saying she would never come back to him, and how much Jamie was doing for her. Then she talked about how horrible Elliott had been to her. I remember the letter really well because I thought it was odd that she started out talking about what all Jamie had done for her and bought her and how she was better off without Elliott, sort of like someone had told her what to write to really get under Elliott's skin."

Jamie was nodding. "Yeah. I kind of made her write the letter. But I never saw the whole thing."

"At the end of the letter she suddenly switched and talked about how depressed she was, and how she couldn't sleep and couldn't face life and hated herself. Totally different—like maybe when Jamie stopped looking over her shoulder, she was telling how she really felt."

Elliott nodded in triumph. "You see? The woman was suicidal. There's no mystery here."

Charlie gave him a withering look. "I always remembered that letter, and sometime after that, when Jamie was talking to me about what Teresa's suicide note said, I remember thinking it sounded just like the second page of that letter she wrote Elliott."

"Not surprising," Elliott snorted. "The woman was like a song with only one note, played over and over to the point of nausea."

Charlie seemed to be making a point of not looking at Jamie. "I tried to shrug it off. Tried to think like Elliott—that it probably wasn't weird that the woman would describe her feelings the same way in another letter. So I just didn't think about it. Until..." He took a deep breath. "Until Paula."

"Paula!" The word popped out of Jeanine's mouth in spite of herself. "He was involved with Paula, too?" She looked back and forth, from Charlie to Jamie. "That's what made me turn around and not follow him all the way to the cabin. It suddenly hit me that he had mentioned getting Paula her start in modeling and was bragging about what he had done for her, and I remembered that he supposedly didn't know her. So I got suspicious and decided I shouldn't go anywhere with him until I found out what was going on."

Jamie finally spoke. "You have very good instincts."

Charlie nodded a little. "Elliott knew her a long time. She was over at his house a lot, even before she met Jamie. And eventually, he…" Charlie's pale face took on a flush of color. "Well, Elliott wasn't treating her very well toward the end."

"He specifically went to the rehab hospital and coaxed her out of there," Jamie said. "He couldn't stand that he might be losing control over another one."

Charlie shrugged—a tight, jagged jerk of his shoulders. "I didn't know any of that at the time. But it started to strike me as strange, the things that were happening to all these women in Elliott's life." His mouth twitched at the corners. "Unlike most of the world, I knew it couldn't have been Jamie hurting them. Anyway, not long after Paula died, I went through Elliott's desk, looking for the letter from Teresa. I found it…but only the first page, not the part that sounded so much like her suicide note."

Jeanine sucked in her breath and looked at Jamie.

Charlie went on. "I tried to forget about it, tried not to think what I was starting to think. But at the same time…" He reached into his pocket. "I kept that one page, just in case."

The Atlanta detective reached greedily for the paper Charlie was unfolding. His eyes gleaming, the cop looked at Jamie. "I don't know what that suicide note looked like, but I would imagine you remember it pretty well. Do you think you could tell whether there might be some connection?"

"Oh, we can do you one better than that," Jamie said quietly. He looked at Charlie. "Or at least, I think we can." He looked at Charlie. "Did you get it?"

He nodded. Radiating misery, he pulled out another paper. This one appeared to be plain white printer paper. Without looking at it, he handed it to Detective White. "I told Jamie this story a while ago. He made a phone call and had a copy of the suicide note faxed here. Obviously, I don't know for sure, but—"

"But they fit together like peas in a pod," said the detective. He held the pages side by side. "There's even a nice flow from one page to the next. The first page ends with, 'You know, Elliott that,' and the second starts with 'I have always struggled with depression. With doubts. With knowing how I fail.'"

Jeanine looked at Elliott, and nearly cried out in surprise. His eyes were still flat and untroubled. He even managed a little smile. "I'm afraid you're going to end up very embarrassed if you try to build a case out of that."

The detective heaved a deep sigh. "I can't say how this will come out either, Mr. Dane, but I can tell you we have some wonderful forensics people who are going to be delighted to compare these two original pages. I also think maybe I should advise you of your rights, just in case."

The other cop cleared his throat. "Um, excuse me, but we are in my jurisdiction. And there's a little matter of this car crash."

"All right, all right." The detective made a grand, sweeping gesture. "Be my guest."

When the policemen and Elliott had gone, Charlie looked Jeanine in the eye for the first time. "I'm sorry. I really am."

She opened her mouth to tell him that it wasn't his fault, that she didn't blame him. But before she could get anything out, he had melted from the room, letting the door swing shut behind him.

She turned to Jamie, the only one left in the room with her. "Will he be all right?"

"I hope so," he said.

"You should go after him."

"I will directly. I'm more worried about you at the moment."

She grimaced. "I don't think I can get in much trouble just lying here in this bed."

Now that all the bodies standing between Jamie and herself had vacated the room, he started to move closer, and she felt her palms getting sweatier with every step he took. Partly to head off anything he might be planning to say, she said, "So, this little scene with the cops. Was it another test? Was I supposed to keep my mouth shut about what Elliott did and not make trouble? But no, maybe that wasn't what you wanted. Maybe you wanted me to show high principals and moral purity and not show any interest in fame and fortune. It's so hard to tell what I'm supposed to do to pass."

Jamie plopped down into a chair next to the bed and rubbed his eyes. "I've never given you any tests, Jeanine. And certainly not this time."

"Oh, really?" She stared down at the huge lump under the covers that was her bandaged leg.

"Really. Before you said anything, I showed Charlie that security video and talked him out of lying for Elliott. I asked him to get the other page of that note faxed. Does that sound like I was testing you?"

"Well, no."

He dropped his hands from his eyes. "But this is all my fault."

"It was mostly the man's who pushed me over a cliff, but yeah, I would say part of this is your fault." She looked up from her legs, and found him studying her with such misery that she felt her anger cooling in spite of herself. "Why couldn't you be honest with me? I could take it, whatever it was."

"I know, and I did realize I had to tell you everything—eventually. I ran after you, when you got so upset at the hotel the other night. I knew I needed to tell you things, for your own protection. But I couldn't find you. I went to your apartment."

"I know. I saw you in the car outside. But I didn't want to talk to you." She heard her voice catch, and cleared her throat firmly. "I didn't think I could bear to hear anything else from you that night."

"I can't say I blame you. But I wanted to warn you about Elliott. I'd been trying to protect you, I swear. I had private investigators watching you for a while after you came to Atlanta, to make sure he hadn't set his sights on you."

"Really?" For a moment she was flabbergasted at the thought of someone watching her, but then she remembered the creepy white vehicles. "They scared the devil out of me."

"You weren't supposed to see them." He frowned. "I may have to have a talk with their boss. But anyway, they told me everything seemed fine, so I let them go." He spat out a laugh. "Elliott was too slippery for me, as usual."

Jeanine shook her head. "I just don't understand all this. I mean…I heard enough to know that Elliott was apparently involved in your mother's death, and maybe Paula's, too. And he slipped drugs into Charlie's drink. But I don't understand why."

"I know. It is hard to understand. That's why it took us so long—Charlie and me—to begin to accept the truth. I suppose you could say…it's all about control for Elliott. Power and control." And then he started from the beginning, telling her how Elliott had come into his life when he and Charlie had been making the first *Summer* movie together, had charmed his way into his and Teresa's lives like a cobra, and then gradually took over.

"I knew from the night of the dinner party that you might be in danger," Jamie said. "I would never have taken you there that night if I had realized Elliott was going to be there. Especially if I had known about Charlie and the book rights." He shook his head. "I started this whole mess by sending your manuscript to Walter Raney. I'm the one who put you at risk, just like I…"

As his voice trailed off, he was left staring at her, his eyes filled with that same pleading look of misery she had seen earlier.

"Just like you what?" she asked softly.

"Just like I did to Paula." He breathed in, then exhaled slowly, so that when he spoke again, he sounded quite calm. "I killed her, Jeanine. All those people were right, when they talked about me, when they hated me. Allison Klein is right. I killed Paula."

Jeanine stared at him, wide-eyed. "Jamie, what are you saying? I thought…I thought Elliott…"

"I handed him the weapon, same as I did with you. Well, no, that's not true. It was worse with Paula. I was at least trying to do something good for you, but Paula…" Another deep breath, and then he blurted out, "I'm the one who got her started on the heroin."

She shook her head, so furiously it made her dizzy. "No. I've known you all these months. If you were shooting heroin, if there were something that had that kind of control over you, I would know it…wouldn't I?"

"No, no, it isn't like that, either." He got up and started to pace back and forth. "I try things, Jeanine. All kinds of things. I keep thinking that I'll actually discover some magic pill that takes the pain away, that makes everything better."

"But?"

"But I haven't. Only my acting has ever made much of a difference, really." He stopped at the window, staring out into the darkness. "The first time I tried heroin was at one of Teresa's parties. She had been doing cocaine for months, but that night, Elliott brought out some heroin and really pitched it to her. Told her that heroin was the choice of the young. And that's what Teresa wanted, to be young. Especially in Elliott's eyes."

Jeanine struggled to grasp what he had said. "So you all just sat down at a party and started sticking needles into your veins?"

"No, no, of course not. You don't have to do that anymore. Heroin's purer—and stronger—these days. Most people smoke it or snort it. Something like that. Of course, that also makes it more volatile, more unpredictable, it's so much more potent now."

"But you said that Paula had needle marks and—"

"Well, Paula used it so much that she had to go that route to get a hit. It wasn't working for her anymore. Anyway…at that party of my mother's, I'd already been drinking a lot, and so I…well, I hardly gave it any thought at the time. I just did it. And I won't lie to you, Jeanine. It was a pretty incredible feeling. But not so incredible to make me want to keep doing it. I was too terrified the next day when I realized that I'd actually messed about with that stuff."

"But you did try it again?"

"Only once or twice, and months apart. I know now, Jeanine, how fortunate I am that I don't have some horrible addiction, that I haven't got myself into that kind of bondage. I deserve to be. But I've tried things now and again, then gone on. Got myself an acting job and totally lost myself in being someone else and didn't even think of needing drugs or any of that, at least not for a time. So I took it for granted that everyone could come and go through that door as they pleased." Shaking his head slowly, he turned to face her. "But not Paula. She opened that door one time, and there were demons behind it, reaching out for her, dragging her down to hell. And I shoved her in—threw her to them—and slammed the door after her. She never got out again."

A moment of silence passed. Then Jeanine asked him, "How did it happen?"

He settled himself in the chair next to her bed again. "We went to a club on Sunset one night, and we ran into some friends."

Something tickled at Jeanine's memory. "That tabloid story…it talked about this."

"Yeah. It was pretty accurate, actually—although I hope I wasn't quite as brutal as it made me sound."

"So…was it Charlie who gave them the story?"

"Charlie was there, but no…it was one of the other guests." Jamie grimaced. "Anyway, that night, we ended up in one of the VIP rooms, and somebody brought out some heroin. Paula was sort of interested, but she genuinely did have a thing against drugs. She'd seen too much with her parents and their friends when she was young, and she didn't want anything to do with their lifestyle. But I was impatient with her—so sick of her mood swings! Wild, childlike joy one moment, and absolute despair the next. Frankly, it was too much like my mother, and I'd had enough of unstable people to last me a lifetime. Paula had spent most of that day harping on me about one thing or another, and flying into hysterical tears. And I resented the time I ended up spending with Elliott because of her friendship with him.

"So that night, I told her, 'Oh come on, Paula, I've done it myself. It won't kill you. And frankly, one way or another, we need some relief.' I turned my back on her, and I think she got the point that I was reaching my limit with her, that she was close to losing me. So she did it. We both got high, and she really seemed to feel better, to like it.

"When we were going home, she was still flying. I gave her a very stern lecture and warned her that this stuff was serious. That it wasn't something she could mess about with, or do often. But I've never seen anything like it. From that moment, she was obsessed. Paula loved heroin the way my mother loved Elliott Dane. It made her happy, it made her mad, she sold herself to it utterly. And eventually, when there was nothing left but the madness and the horror of it, she hated me. She said it was my fault. And, of course, it was."

Jeanine squeezed his hand, not knowing what else to do, but he barely seemed to notice it. He looked at her. "You understand now, don't you? Why I couldn't plead 'not guilty' when they arrested me last December? Why I couldn't stand the thought of going on the television and denouncing all those accusations as lies? Saying how much I loved poor Paula and how good I always was to her, how shocked and appalled I was when I found out about her drugs?"

"I think so." She studied him, searching his deep black eyes. "But I still don't understand why you left me, kept me in the dark, pushed me away. Why didn't you just tell me? I mean, I thought we…I thought we…" Her voice faded away to nothing.

Now it was Jamie giving her hand a gentle squeeze. "We did…we still do,

I hope." He was silent for a second, and seemed to be waiting for something. When she didn't speak, he sighed and went on. "I was a coward. I wanted to protect you, but I wanted to find a way to do it without having to tell you all this, frankly. Without you knowing the ugly truth about me. I thought if I just distanced myself from you and if Elliott thought there wasn't going to be another *Summer* project, it would give me time to try to get some evidence on him and maybe get him out of our lives for good."

"Great plan," Jeanine said, wincing as she tried to shift her leg.

"Yeah. I told you I need a writer in real life, too."

"Yeah."

A long silence fell. Jeanine pulled her hand away from Jamie and sat staring at the doorway. Finally, Jamie cleared his throat and said hesitantly, "So. What are you thinking?"

"I'm thinking about a weird dream I had, actually. While I was trapped in the car and sort of delirious, I guess." She proceeded to tell him the hauntingly vivid dream about following the boy—Danny Summer, of course—into the pecan grove, and the beauty and the longing that had filled her as she approached it. "I can't even begin to express the feeling I had at that moment. Like nothing I've experienced before, waking or dreaming. It was as though…every worry was gone. I was filled with such a peace, such a knowledge that everything in the place was innocent, and lovely, and that it would last forever. It wouldn't change or die."

"And then what happened?"

She laughed harshly. "It changed. It died. It turned ugly, the way everything does in this life."

Jamie's mouth twisted into a rueful smile. "You mean like your real-life dream about meeting me?"

She was trying to think how to answer him, whether she wanted to blast him and end this whole thing right now, or comfort him, or let him down easy, when the door of her room popped open again, and Mamma and Daddy rushed in like a cleansing breeze, and she gave herself up to their clucking and fussing and praising the Lord for saving her.

At some point—she wasn't exactly sure when—Jamie slipped out of the room and disappeared.

CHAPTER THIRTY-NINE

JAMIE CHECKED INTO A NEARBY MOTEL AND SPENT THE NIGHT LYING AWAKE AND wondering what he should do next. Stay away from Jeanine and let her get on with her life? That was probably what she wanted—what she needed. Then again, he was responsible for the state she was in. How could he just desert her?

By six a.m., he had decided he had to go check on her and give her the opportunity to tell him to get out of her life once and for all. She deserved that satisfaction. He was dawdling in the hospital hallway, dreading the ugly scene he was expecting, when the door of her room swung open—and Richard popped out.

"What the devil are you doing here!" Jamie felt his muscles tightening even more. "You haven't been harassing Jeanine, have you? That's all she needs."

Richard put his hands up. "Of course not. When I went in, I thought you would be in there. But honestly, I wanted to visit her, too." Before Jamie could ask why, Richard nodded toward the waiting area. "Can we talk for a moment before you go in?"

Jamie nodded and wordlessly followed his uncle, wondering if Richard had the job of telling him Jeanine wanted no more visits from Newkirks.

They sat down across from one another in the hard plastic chairs.

"How is she this morning?" Jamie asked.

"Her leg was hurting a bit. Otherwise fine." After more silent fidgeting, Richard said, "She's a very strong young woman."

Jamie nodded. "Yeah."

Rick leaned forward and looked earnestly into Jamie's eyes. "Why didn't you tell me all this before? About Elliott, about…all of it?"

Jamie shook his head. "It's hard to explain. Until recently, I didn't trust my judgment about him. I thought I must be crazy—not Elliott." He glared at Richard. "Do you see now how wrong you were? Jeanine needed protecting from our weirdness—certainly not the other way round."

Rick shifted in his chair. "I resent being lumped into that 'our.' I'm also still not comfortable with the fact she believes God spoke to her and promised to deliver you over to her. Then again, Charlie tells me she's a great writer, and what artist isn't a little mad?" Richard fell silent, tapping his finger against his lip and obviously thinking. Jamie was dying to know what Rick and Jeanine had discussed just now, but before he could ask, the man said, "Jamie, I told you in my study that night that a girl like that could never be happy in your world—the celebrity, the movie business, all of it."

Jamie sighed. "I know."

"But it's occurred to me that maybe that's not the right question. Maybe the real question is…can you be happy in that world, either?"

"What!"

"As much as I disliked that girl when I first met her, I had to admit to myself that you looked healthier and happier that evening than I can remember. And that was in the middle of this Paula mess. I, um…I haven't really told you about my new business venture in Atlanta, have I?"

Jamie shook his head, feeling dizzy trying to follow Richard's winding train of thought. "You've been pretty reluctant to tell me any specifics."

Richard shrugged. "I suppose I was embarrassed, but—" He took a deep breath, reached into his coat pocket, and threw a thick envelope down on the table. "Take a look at those."

Jamie opened the envelope and drew out a stack of photographs. The first showed the outside of a gothic-looking gray stone building. The next were interior shots—rows of cushioned theater-style seats, many of them torn or broken; a large stage with a grotty-looking curtain hanging down from one side.

"It's a theatre…and?" Jamie prompted.

"Not just a theater," Richard said. "My theater. In Atlanta."

Jamie's eyes widened. "You bought a theater! Whatever for?"

Richard smiled. "You know, it's rather odd. I'm forty-three years old and you're twenty-five, but we both seem to be reaching our mid-life crises at the same time."

"Yes, well, when you start your career at the age of eight, you arrive sooner," Jamie pointed out.

"Marrying Ruth and having this child—I just got thinking about my life. I loved acting. Passionately. It suddenly occurred to me that I've got enough money to last several lifetimes. I should be able to do whatever I jolly well please. I was never as good an actor as you, but I think I'm good enough for a small, regional theater."

"So you just went out and bought one?" Jamie said in amazement. "Just like that?"

"Just like that."

"I am really impressed!"

"I had this grand dream," Richard continued, going almost starry-eyed. "I'd choose the plays, choose great roles for myself, things I've always fancied doing."

"So has something gone wrong?"

"It's about to." Richard snorted. "I can't believe I'm doing this, but I'm about to offer you a partnership."

A slow smile spread over Jamie's face. "You're not serious!"

"I suppose I must be. I've been carrying those pictures around with me for days, trying to talk myself out of it. The thought of being upstaged by you again—and in my own theater, at that!—is rather revolting. But I've done a lot of thinking recently, and I suddenly remembered how you always wanted to be a stage actor, how you begged me not to make you do any more movies."

Jamie was amazed to see the man's throat working, as though fighting back emotion. "Oh, Rick, it's okay. Obviously it turned out well."

"Did it really? Well, anyway…we both have all the money we need. Why should I get to live my dream now, and not you?" Richard smiled broadly. "You are my nephew, after all, and I suppose I'll never really be rid of you. So. Are you interested?"

Jamie started to stammer, trying to think. "But—but Richard, what about the *Summer* movies? Are we really going to just abandon all that?"

Richard cocked his head and studied him. "Are you worried about *Summer* for yourself—or for Jeanine?"

Jamie didn't answer. He couldn't think what to say.

"You know," Richard said, "I think you're the one who thinks the girl is delusional."

"What do you mean!"

"You don't think she's interested in you. You think she wants Danny Summer."

Jamie nodded slowly. "Maybe you're right."

"But what I'm asking you right now is, what do you want?" Richard asked. "What does the great Jamie Newkirk want?"

After a long moment of thought, Jamie laughed. "Everything. I want it all."

CHAPTER FORTY

"I'M PROUD OF YOU FOR GOING, DADDY." FROM THE BACK SEAT, JEANINE CAUGHT her father's eye in the rear view mirror for just a second before he had to glance back at the road.

He shook his head and grumbled. "It wasn't easy. A good Baptist preacher having to sit through an infant baptism."

Mamma pulled the visor down and started fussing with her hair in the mirror. "Well, at least they're going to church now."

"Very true," said Jeanine. "And I guess Episcopalian is pretty close to Church of England."

She tensed as they approached Richard and Ruth's house. She should have expected it, but a crowd of people with cameras and microphones milled around, as well as a couple of uniformed policemen who were hopefully keeping the paparazzi under control. The whole media situation had exploded again, of course, with Elliott's arrest. And it wasn't going to die down any time soon, because prosecuting Elliott was going to be a long, drawn-out affair. So far, he was charged in her hit-and-run, but every day there was something new to be dragged out and speculated about. The day the forensics report was released concluding that Teresa's suicide note was in fact the second page of the letter to Elliott was a huge day. And Allison Klein was making the rounds of talk shows, supposedly agonizing over whether to let poor dear Paula's body be exhumed for a more in-depth autopsy. No one seemed to doubt there were more charges coming for Elliott Dane, but Jeanine had been forced to accept that it could drag on for years. As the mysterious new girl in Jamie's life who had caused all this to break, Jeanine had gotten a bitter taste of the hunted, trapped feeling Jamie had been experiencing when he first came into her life, and she was enjoying it just about as much as he had. She sighed as the police drew near their car and waved them into the gate. There was nothing to be done about it. She would just have to get used to it.

A couple of minutes later, Daddy was shaking his head again as a valet rushed up to park the car for them. And apparently the Newkirks had hired several valets for the christening party. Ginella and Trev, in the car behind them, were already being attended by another white-clad young man.

"Unbelievable," Daddy said, as he handed over the keys.

Their valet bounced on his feet and fidgeted as they dealt with getting Jeanine out of the car. Her leg was mending nicely, but she still had a cumbersome cast and crutch to deal with and her ribs still hurt with sudden movements. Daddy was leaning in, helping her slide out, when Jeanine heard a familiar, deep voice behind him. "Allow me."

As always, her heart gave a little flutter at the sound, and it doubled in speed when Daddy stepped aside and she saw Jamie clearly. Her body's automatic reactions annoyed her, but she mentally shrugged and decided to just give in to the pleasant shivers today, when everything was so beautiful.

As Jamie slipped his arm around her and supported her while she got her crutch into place, Ginella laughed. "Wow. Just like Bella and Edward at the end of *Twilight*. Bum leg and all."

Jeanine felt an urge to kick her sister, if she had only had two good legs, but Jamie was frowning good-naturedly. "You actually read that stuff?"

"Oh, please." Ginella waved her hand, dismissing him. "As if you don't. I'll bet you tried out for the part."

Jamie guffawed and pointed to his deeply tanned face. "Do I look like I could play a vampire?"

"Mmm, true." Ginella cocked her head and studied him. "I suppose they could have dusted you with sparkly white powder, but there's probably not enough in the world."

By this time, they were all laughing, even Daddy and Jeanine. It felt good, so good. As she hobbled up the steps and into the house, surrounded by all the ones she loved most, everyone laughing and happy for this one moment, she was reminded of her beautiful dream of the orchard—at least, the part before it turned on her.

Their little group dispersed once they were in the house—greeting Richard and Ruth, taking gifts to the appropriate table, checking out the food. Jeanine found herself alone with Jamie, his arm still under hers for support, even though she had her crutch.

An awkward moment fell, with neither of them speaking. Trying to fill the silence, Jeanine blurted, "Is Charlie here?"

The happy twinkle in Jamie's eyes dimmed. "Yes, he's here somewhere."

Now she wanted to kick herself. "I'm sorry, Jamie. I just wondered if he's okay."

"Yeah, I think so. Come on, let's find you a place to sit down."

After helping her to a loveseat in the living room, Jamie fetched them cups of punch and sat back down with her. "Yeah, Charlie's here somewhere, although I think he's hiding out right now. He doesn't like crowds. This has been hard for him, but good."

"Like amputating a bad limb," Jeanine mused.

"Yeah…" Jamie sipped his punch in silence for a moment, not looking at her. She sensed he was preparing to say something, maybe something difficult, so she just waited. "Jeanine, we never needed Elliott to do the *Summer* project. That was just him trying to manipulate everything and make sure he was in the picture. But we can still do it. I mean…" His mouth tightened, and he sounded as though he were forcing out the next words through clenched teeth. "Charlie still says he'll do the book if you work with him. And Richard's willing to produce another movie."

"Even though that was not in his plans." Richard came to join them, standing over them with the newest Newkirk in his arms.

"Oh, he's so beautiful," Jeanine gushed, holding out her arms. "Can I hold him?"

As Richard passed little Robert James Newkirk to her—still decked out in his lacey white christening gown, but now with a terrycloth bib over it—Jamie huffed in disgust. "You just have to steal the scene, don't you? How can I compete with that?" He pointed at the baby, lying sleeping in Jeanine's arms.

"Get one of your own, I suppose." Richard appeared mortified. "But not any time soon, all right?"

Jeanine looked away, embarrassed, as Jamie laughed.

Richard pulled over a parson's chair and settled in front of them. "As I was saying, I'm willing to jump back into the fray and do more *Summer* movies, if that's what we decide we want. But there is another option." He looked at Jamie. "Did you tell her?"

"No, not yet."

Jeanine looked back and forth at them. "Tell me what?"

Richard pulled out a packet of photos and handed them to her, taking the baby back so she could look at them. As she thumbed through the pictures of the beautiful old building obviously under renovation, Jamie told her about the theater that Richard had bought. Then Richard jumped in and explained how he was tired of the craziness of producing, and how he was ready to realize his dream of acting, even on a small scale like this.

Jamie cleared his throat, but still sounded husky. "He thought I might want the same thing. He knows I want—no, I need to act. But I hate all this other stuff. The media, the craziness. The way they tear at your every move."

She focused on Jamie now. "And what did you tell him?"

"He hasn't given me an answer yet," Richard said.

Jamie plowed on ahead, "Richard thought you would love staying here, being involved in the theater."

Jeanine looked at Richard doubtfully. "Is that true? I thought you hated me."

Richard shrugged. "You're obviously good for Jamie." He grinned. "And you're growing on me."

"Sort of like a fungus?" Jeanine said, laughing with relief.

"Something like that, yes." He got to his feet, patting the baby on the back and trying to hush his fussing. "I don't expect an answer right now, but think about it, will you?"

And then she and Jamie were alone again. Well, they were surrounded by people, actually—by mingling couples and groups, chatting and sipping and eating. But for all intents and purposes, it was just her and Jamie.

He reached for her hand almost shyly, then looked into her eyes. "So, what do you think?"

"What do you want to do?" she asked earnestly.

"Are you…" He cleared his throat again, still looking shy and boyish. "Would you consider doing either with us? The theater or the *Summer* project?"

"This is unbelievable. Either one…it's what I've dreamed of, since I was a little girl. But…do you remember that dream I told you about?"

"The one you had while you were trapped in the car, about the orchard?" Jamie looked a bit confused by the apparent change of subject, but he nodded. "Yes. It was beautiful but then it turned ugly…oh." His face fell. "You're saying it's turned ugly. Your dream of writing and performing, and…" He almost whispered the last word. "Me."

She shook her head. "It's that, and it's not that. It's hard to explain." They sat in silence for a moment. Jamie watched her while she tried to organize her thoughts. "Yes, I have learned that there is no happily ever after on this earth. But…there can be one eventually. In that dream or vision or whatever it was, just standing on the edge and looking at that orchard filled me with such joy. And such energy. I had almost given up, but after that, I was able to get myself up that hill. Oh, I know I had water and maybe it was just that, but—"

"But 'man does not live by bread alone.'" Jamie smiled. "Or water either, I suppose."

She looked at him in surprise. "Exactly." She took a deep breath, feeling frustrated. "I'm not expressing this very well, but even though everything in this life is temporary, I think the glimpses that we get of something that's beautiful and eternal and beyond…they're so important. They keep us trudging along. And those glimpses can come from so many places. Our dreams and our stories, to name a couple." She felt her eyes growing hot with tears. "That's what I was trying to express to Richard that night at the dinner table, when we argued. I just did it badly."

Jamie smiled a little. "I think he got it. Or he'll get it eventually. But, Jeanine, I'm still not sure what this has to do with our—with your—plans."

"I'm not sure, either. But I do know that even though doing any of this stuff—the book or the theater or whatever—won't be exactly like I dreamed of when I was a little girl, it's still important. Maybe it will give me those glimpses. More important, maybe we can give other people those glimpses."

Jamie's eyes brightened. "We?"

She felt herself starting to laugh, even as she wiped away a tear. "Yes, idiot. We."

Now Jamie was laughing with her, and he even leaned in and kissed her, until a couple of whistles and catcalls from the other party-goers brought them back to their surroundings and caused them to pull apart. Jamie helped her get to her feet, and waving lightly at the laughing guests, got her out onto the back deck where they were truly alone—and she quickly realized why, as the heat and humidity had her linen dress sticking to her within moments. At the same time, the sky was so blue, and the trees so thick with fluttering birds that she was reminded of the orchard, and she didn't really mind the heat.

Jamie started talking, sounding forlorn. "I can't bear to think what a disappointment I must be to you." He smiled ruefully and said, "You were looking for Danny Summer, and look what you got instead. If I'd tried to bring those kids to America, I would've somehow managed to sink the ship and drown them all."

Jeanine laughed, and he couldn't help smiling back at her. She took his hand. "Jamie, don't you know what I really hoped for when I met you?"

He shook his head in the negative, and she started slowly, "I looked at you on that screen and I thought—no, I felt—there's someone who would be able to see the things that I see, who could truly be one with me in all my stories and songs and dreams. Like that day we did the reading from my manuscript, and it got so intense. I haven't felt anything like that since I was six years old on the playground and made a witch so real to one of the little boys that he was hysterical for an hour. I created that witch, and she was *there*. He saw her. I've been so alone, Jamie, since I left childhood, and you changed that. I could never call it a disappointment."

"Jeannie," he answered her shakily, "as bad as this year has been for me, it was nothing compared to last fall. When I finally made the break with Paula and we put her into rehab, it was as though all of the guilt of the past decade just came crashing down on me. Some days I wanted to kill myself. If I hadn't been making *Message to Marilyn*, I probably would have done. I was trying so hard not to turn back to drugs or booze. I didn't want to foul up the movie, for one thing. But one night, I hit rock bottom, and I remember practically screaming inside my head that if God were really there, now would be a good time to show me, maybe send a little help my way. It was a nasty, sarcastic prayer, really...but who knows? Because here you are, Jeannie."

He smiled and looked at her intently, serious and joyful all at the same time. "I think He sent you, Jeanine. You're my glimpse."

ACKNOWLEDGEMENTS

It's rather terrifying to start naming names and thanking people. I've been on this writing journey for so long and have needed so many people to keep me from throwing in the towel that I know I'll forget someone! But here goes.

My brilliant niece, Kristi Israel, wrote Jeanine's song "The Dying Hill" specifically for this book—and of course, gave me permission to use the lyrics. Sandra Mayo and Elizabeth Drinnon loaned me their professional proof-reading skills. (And this might be a good place to acknowledge that Bible verses in the book are from the King James Version.) Author's photo is by Ken Hill, and the beautiful cover design is by David Angsten.

I want to thank the other authors who encouraged me and kept me going—particularly Nancy Grace, Elizabeth Musser, and Terri Blackstock. Each of them came along at just the right time and were willing to read my work, mentor me, and offer advice and referrals, and I will be forever grateful!

Thanks to Ken Atchity and Dawn Gray at The Writer's Lifeline for helping me edit and rewrite and make *Summer's Winter* the story I wanted it to be. And I also want to thank Janet Benrey, my first agent and the first professional to believe in me enough to actually have me sign on the dotted line.

I couldn't do without my "inner circle" of friends and family—the first to hear good or bad news, read my frequent rewrites, and offer encouragement and advice: Dave Grant, Frankie Israel, Kristi Israel, and Laura Wilson. Really, I have so many faithful friends and family who helped with reading, rewriting, or cheerleading: Susan and Brittany Jordan, Sandra Mayo, Felicia Haywood, Robin Perling, Melanie Dickerson, Sally Bradley, Christina

Tarabochia, Sherrie Ashcraft, Rose McCauley, Elizabeth Drinnon, Kathleen Morphy, Rebecca Grabill—and my parents, Arthur and Ewell Johns. My daddy always believed in me even on days that I didn't believe in myself, and it saddens me that I never published and placed a book of mine in his hands while he was living. He never stopped expecting it.

And saving the best for last, I have to thank God. A couple of years ago, in the midst of a very discouraging search for publication, I was rewriting and rewriting and trying to follow the whims of ever-changing publishing house guidelines. One day, I finally asked Him to be my editor, my agent, my publisher, everything—and things started to fall into place. I truly can "do all things through Christ who strengthens me."

AUTHOR'S BIO

ROBIN JOHNS GRANT has been writing for most of her life. In fact, she's been following her publishing dream so long that she crowned herself The Queen of Perseverance on her blog, where she encourages other weary dreamers. While waiting for her writing to pay off, she wrote and edited university publications; managed an office for a firm of private investigators; and worked as a university financial aid counsellor. She now lives in Georgia with her wonderful husband Dave and formerly feral feline, Mini Pearl. And she has her best day job ever as a college librarian, which keeps her young by allowing her to hang out with students.

CPSIA information can be obtained at www.ICGtesting.com
Printed in the USA
LVOW12s0740151014

408733LV00003B/3/P